UNTAMED TEMPTRESS

Daniel imprisoned both of Addie's arms as he yanked her close, holding her against him with one powerful arm.

"You've become a wildcat, my love," he appreciatively observed, "a beautiful, gloriously untamed wildcat."

"Let go of me, damn you!" she wrathfully commanded, twisting futilely.

His head relentlessly lowered and she gasped softly, a scream of protest welling up deep in her throat as his lips triumphantly captured hers.

His kiss, at first hard and bruising, gradually became warm and persuasive, and Addie felt herself overcome by the bewildering sensations which she had long since forgotten. She was shocked at her body's traitorous response as she stilled within Daniel's forceful embrace, all her resistance rapidly melting away with the force of his seductive assault.

For four years she had staunchly quelled such deep yearnings, such disturbingly sensual impulses. How could she do this now? After all, though they were still legally married, she was no longer Daniel's true wife.

"No!" she exclaimed when she found the strength to protest, frantically clutching at the edges of her bodice.

But as he gazed into her eyes and reached out once again to caress her pale, enticingly rounded flesh, she knew that although this man was her enemy, he was also the man she would always love. . . .

TEXAS TORMENT
CATHERINE CREEL

ZEBRA BOOKS
KENSINGTON PUBLISHING CORP.

ZEBRA BOOKS

are published by

Kensington Publishing Corp.
475 Park Avenue South
New York, NY 10016

First printing: September 1985

Printed in the United States of America

To some real "Texas belles":

My little sister, Carol
My mother, Shirley
My grandmothers, Ida and Mayna

One

"It's the truth, Miss Addie. We heard he showed up here in town only yesterday. He's the one, all right."

"Have any of you seen him yet?"

"No, but we heard tell he's a fair-sized man, as well as being a far sight younger than any of us thought he'd turn out to be."

Adelaide Caton's lips curved downward into an expressive frown, her hazel eyes glowing with visible displeasure. Damnation! she swore inwardly, impatiently tucking a wayward strand of sun-streaked chestnut hair behind her ear. Her shining, waist-length tresses were twisted into a severe chignon at the nape of her graceful neck, and her beautiful features reflected a deepening irritation at the news she had just received.

So, she mused with another frown, the enemy has finally gathered enough courage to take possession of his new property! The talk and speculation of the past several months had frequently centered around the

7

Yankee who had bought the Ferguson place, the very ranch which bordered Addie's.

"Does anyone recall hearing his name?" she asked quietly, climbing into the buckboard and firmly grasping the reins. The three men standing on the dust-caked boardwalk in front of Turner's Mercantile shook their heads in near-perfect unison. They were all a great deal older than the independent young woman staring down at them, each of them rather fatherly, yet respectful, in their behavior toward Addie.

"No," Ike Henry finally replied, "but his name doesn't matter. The only thing I can think about is the fact that his kind helped put my boy in the ground."

Ike's lined, bearded face tightened into a look of such hatred that Addie hastened to say, "That kind of thinking won't help any, Ike. I don't want him here any more than you do, but we don't know for certain if he even fought in the war." She glanced overhead at the gathering clouds in the late afternoon sky, thinking that there would more than likely be a storm before nightfall. They had yet to be cursed with any snow, and Christmas was only two weeks away. Addie told herself that it was about time for the onset of the harsh winter that had been predicted, and she sighed inwardly at the thought of the effect such weather would have upon her ranch. Things were certainly bad enough without her having to be bothered with a new, most definitely unwanted neighbor!

"There're several of us who are planning a little 'reception' for this fellow," John Hayward remarked, chuckling softly with bitter humor. He was tall and heavyset, his clean-shaven features darkened by many years spent beneath the blazing Texas sun. Ordinarily a

8

generous, easygoing man, there now appeared a certain malevolent light in his brown eyes.

"Yeah, and we aim to find out right away whether or not he means to act like all the other damned carpetbaggers we've had shoved down our throats!" asserted Thomas Bowman, the shortest of the three. He was the one Addie liked the least, though he had proven to be a good neighbor to her and her father. His thin, gray hair was plastered against his head, and his fierce gaze flashed up at Addie.

"I don't think you should do it," she replied, her expression growing even more solemn. "You'll only be causing more trouble, and that's the last thing we need right now. We've all got more than enough to worry about without stirring up another hornet's nest!"

"We thought you'd throw in with us on this, Miss Addie," Ike told her, his eyes boring deep into hers. "After all, it concerns each and every one of us, doesn't it? We're not planning to cause any real trouble. But, hell, if we don't let it be known that we don't aim to just take everything lying down, we'll not have anything left to us. Nothing."

Addie opened her mouth to speak, but she suddenly appeared to be at an uncharacteristic loss for words. Her expression grew thoughtful, and her hands tightened on the reins as the horse moved restlessly against the harness. Before she could think of a suitable reply, another acquaintance hurried along the boardwalk to confront the small group. It was a boy of about thirteen, a towheaded, fresh-faced youngster who was obviously excited about the news he was bringing them.

"I seen him! He was in my pa's place just now!"

"Who was?" questioned Addie, smiling faintly at the boy.

"The Yankee that bought the Ferguson ranch! He was in the livery stable, asking my pa about buying a mount. Those eyes of his are the coldest damn eyes I ever saw! Why, I'd say he's just about the coolest son of a bitch—"

"Kyle," Addie broke in to admonish sternly, though an indulgent grin tugged at the corners of her mouth.

"Did your pa sell him anything?" Ike demanded, as if the very act of doing business with the man would be considered traitorous.

"I don't rightly know. I left before they'd finished talking," Kyle Townsend admitted rather sheepishly. His face suddenly brightened again as he raised his head, his blue eyes sparkling with visible interest as he exclaimed, "There he is! That's the one—right over there!" He rudely pointed at the man who had just appeared on the boardwalk less than a hundred yards away.

His height was the first thing they all noticed, for he was well over six feet tall. He carried himself proudly, assuredly, his broad shoulders and well-proportioned body accentuated by the fitted, double-breasted cotton shirt and tailored woolen trousers he wore. His boots were of gleaming black leather, and in one large hand he carried a felt hat and a heavy canvas overcoat. His entire demeanor bespoke a seemingly arrogant confidence in himself and a virile masculinity that was hard to deny.

Addie gazed curiously at the mysterious intruder, though she still had not been afforded a glimpse of his face. He turned then, placing the hat atop his thick, wheat-colored hair that was cut short in the military fashion. His tanned, ruggedly handsome features were viewed by the hostile group as he began striding toward the spot where they were so avidly watching him.

Adelaide Caton's heart leapt within her breast as she glimpsed his face. Her breath caught upon an audible gasp, but none of her companions noticed it as they began murmuring amongst themselves once more. They were oblivious to the fact that she was absolutely paralyzed with shock, her eyes widening with alarmed recognition as the man approached.

Dear Lord, it couldn't be! Not here; not now! she told herself. It wasn't possible. It must be a mistake. He couldn't be there on the boardwalk before her; he couldn't be moving toward her at that very moment!

But it was most definitely him, more devastatingly attractive than ever, more treacherously captivating than she had remembered. She was too numb to think, to move, to do anything other than sit as if rooted to the spot, her gaze never wavering from the handsome, never-forgotten face. It was different, and yet the same.

He was moving closer and closer. He would see her in a matter of seconds, would see the mingled pain and fear mirrored in her eyes. Dear God, Addie prayed in silent anguish, what am I going to do when he sees me? Please, please, what do I do?

She was nearly frantic when he finally recognized her. For only a fraction of an instant, his steely gray eyes narrowed imperceptibly as he momentarily halted a few feet away. Their gazes met and locked, and an involuntary shiver ran the length of Addie's spine. Then, as if he had looked clear through her, his steps resumed and he continued on his way, past Addie and the men beside her, leaving her to stare numbly at his retreating back.

"Acts like he owns the whole blasted town, doesn't he?" Thomas growled.

"I can see right now that we'll have to go ahead with plans for that 'reception'!" mumbled John, glaring belligerently after the tall man.

"Didn't I tell you?" Kyle interjected excitedly. "Didn't I tell you those eyes of his are the coldest you've ever seen?" He appeared to be quite proud of himself as he spun about on his heel and scurried away, his exuberant steps leading him back down the boardwalk to his father's livery stable.

"If that don't beat all," Ike muttered, watching the tall stranger until he had disappeared inside another building a short distance away. "He had the gall to act as if we didn't even exist. Hell, you could tell just by looking at him that he won't prove to be any different from the other damned scalawags who've been pouring in here!"

"What did you think of him, Miss Addie?" Thomas now queried. He and the others turned their gazes upon her, finally noting her silence.

Addie stared unseeingly at the reins still clutched in her hands, hands that were faintly trembling. Her cheeks were slightly flushed, her eyes filled with perplexing tears. It took her several more seconds to regain some small semblance of her former composure, and she was painfully aware of the way the three men watched her, waiting with deferential patience for her to speak.

"I . . . I think I'd best be getting on back to the ranch," she murmured stiffly, with no outward evidence of the turmoil within. As she lightly slapped the reins above the horse's back, Ike unexpectedly put out a hand to detain her.

"You'll be coming with us tonight, won't you, Miss Addie?" His searching gaze lingered on her impassive face, and Addie swiftly averted her eyes, not knowing exactly how to answer him. "We're just going to have ourselves a talk with him. That's all," he quietly assured her.

"What good do you think that's going to do?" she demanded in a voice that was barely audible. She glanced down at her hands again, vaguely surprised to see the way she was fidgeting with the reins. Get hold of yourself, Addie, her mind silently commanded. Don't let them see what's going on. Don't let them guess.

"We just want to get a few things straight," Ike added. They were all gazing at her expectantly again, and she heaved a defeated sigh as she finally acquiesced.

"All right. You can all meet at the Rolling L tonight." She didn't wait for a reply before snapping the reins quite firmly and guiding the buckboard away from the boardwalk toward the other wagons and horses traveling along the main, dusty street of the town. She was oblivious to the sights and sounds around her as the buckboard rolled past the unfinished stone courthouse in the center of the town square then past the deserted officers' quarters still standing on the northeast side. Most of the businesses surrounding the square were still empty and locked, for the town was only now beginning to come back to life after the devastating blow the war had dealt it.

Addie, however, didn't notice the unoccupied

buildings and houses. She didn't notice the crowd at the blacksmith shop or the flour mill nearby. Her turbulent thoughts were centered around the man she had just seen again after what seemed like an eternity. Four long years suddenly melted away as she recalled the first time she had ever set eyes upon Daniel Jordan . . .

It was a pleasantly cool evening in March of 1861. Strains of a popular Virginia reel filled the air as Addie and her closest friend, Carrie Jordan, made their entrances at the dance being held in the gaily decorated ballroom. They were seventeen, each of them beautiful and full of youthful vitality, eager to meet life's challenges.

"Did you see that dreadful gown Miss Kent is wearing tonight?" Carrie impishly whispered, her red curls bouncing riotously as she nodded her head in the direction of the older woman surrounded by a giggling crowd of her pupils, her buxom figure encased in an unattractive creation of mauve velvet.

"Why did I ever allow you to talk me into this?" Addie demanded a bit crossly, ignoring her friend's remark concerning their headmistress. Never mind that each and every one of the other girls at Miss Kent's Academy for Young Ladies was ecstatic over the prospect of attending such an affair. She, Adelaide Caton, was certainly the exception!

"You needn't snap my head off!" Carrie countered good-naturedly, her lovely, freckled countenance displaying her usual broad smile. "After all, it's the first dance Miss Kent has allowed in several months. The

14

last time was only about a week before you came. Aren't you the least bit glad that you decided to attend?"

"Why should I be glad? We've only just arrived, and I already feel like leaving!"

"You'll change your tune as soon as you meet that big brother of mine. I wonder if he's here yet," the petite redhead murmured, her eyes hastily scanning the crowded room. She was quite a bit shorter than Addie, and the two of them made a striking pair. While Carrie was attired in a gown of pale yellow satin, Addie had chosen to wear a new, simple white moiré trimmed in turquoise blue velvet. It had been a gift from her cousin, Martha Jane Hamilton, a much older woman who lived in St. Louis and had been charged by Addie's father with keeping an eye on his beautiful, tomboyish daughter while she attended Miss Kent's Academy there.

Though Addie had argued and pleaded and stormed, Will Caton had had his way eventually, insisting that it was high time his only child learned a few of the feminine graces. She had absolutely despised the school at first, stubbornly telling herself that she'd already learned everything she wanted to know. She could ride, shoot, hunt, and herd cattle as well as any boy back home! Adjusting to an infinitely more cultured, refined lifestyle had been extremely difficult for her, but Carrie had helped to make things easier once the two of them became friends.

"There he is!" Carrie announced in a voice brimming with undisguised excitement. "Oh, and he's brought Alan Rogers with him!" she squealed, her young face coloring rosily. Addie immediately glanced up to see

15

two tall young men in blue uniforms making their way through the doorway and across the room, their faces partially obscured as they stopped to greet their hostess. That solemn-faced woman detained them for several long moments, and then they moved away, past the crowded dance floor and toward the spot where Carrie and Addie stood on the opposite side of the large, brightly lit room.

"You didn't tell me he was in the Cavalry," Addie said with a slight frown, turning to confront her friend.

"I didn't tell you much about him at all!" replied Carrie with a mischievous laugh. "Since I wasn't at all certain he would come, I didn't want to arouse too much of your interest!" she teased with another giggle. Carrie was totally unperturbed by the quelling look Addie flashed her, and the two of them turned their attention back to the young officers who were now stepping up to speak to them.

Addie raised her eyes as Carrie greeted her brother and the other man, noting that both of them were undeniably handsome in their dark blue dress uniforms. Their jackets were short and trimmed with yellow shoulder patches, a matching yellow stripe running down the side of each trouser leg. Their black leather belts and boots were gleaming and polished to perfection, and the jaunty gloves with gauntlet cuffs tucked into the belts at their waists lent even more dash to their impressive military attire.

But it was not the uniform which drew Addie's attention to one of the tall young officers. It was his eyes, dark gray eyes that were like weathered steel, eyes that met her irrevocably drawn gaze and flashed with an answering fascination.

Adelaide Caton suddenly found her breathing strangely affected. She was unaware of Carrie's introductions, unaware of the other young man, unaware of anything or anyone but the ruggedly handsome man before her, the most thoroughly masculine and powerfully attractive man she had encountered in the course of her young life. Never having particularly cared one way or the other about the opposite sex, she now found herself totally swept away with vivid feelings, and raw emotion flared deep within her very being.

Daniel Jordan stood equally transfixed, a slow, utterly entrancing smile curving his well-formed lips as he stared down into the chestnut-haired beauty's sparkling hazel eyes. His gaze traveled leisurely, caressingly, up and down the length of her breathless form, noting every detail, every delectable curve. The ball dress, with its short, puffed sleeves and neckline edged with silk flowers, displayed a seductive expanse of her full young bosom and graceful shoulders, and he suddenly found himself wondering what she would look like with her splendid mass of hair loosened from the confining pins to cascade unrestrainedly about her perfectly rounded softness.

"Addie!" murmured Carrie in growing puzzlement, nudging her friend sharply in the side. "Addie, are you listening to me? I said I should like to present Lieutenant Alan Rogers."

With a great exertion of will, Addie tore her gaze from the tall young Adonis with the thick, wheat-colored hair, at long last transferring her attention to the man's companion.

"How do you do, Lieutenant Rogers?" She managed

17

to respond cordially though she remained acutely aware of the other man's steely gaze which never wavered from her faintly blushing features. She smiled briefly as Lieutenant Rogers gallantly raised her hand to his lips.

"And this is my brother, Lieutenant Daniel Jordan. Daniel, this is my dearest friend in all the world, Miss Adelaide Caton." Her duties finally performed, Carrie happily accepted Alan's request for a dance, and the two of them moved toward the dance floor. Addie was left alone to face the tall, gray-eyed man who possessed the bewildering and quite startling power to render her entirely speechless.

"If I'd only known what charming company awaited me here tonight, I'd never have resisted my sister's persistent efforts to persuade me to attend," Daniel remarked with a merry twinkle in his mesmerizing gaze.

His voice was deep and resonant, and Addie decided that it fit him perfectly. Everything about him appeared to be perfect, she reflected dreamily.

Stop this! the voice of reason at the back of her mind tersely ordered. You're behaving like an absolute jackass, Addie Caton! And just what in thunder do you think you're doing, going all mush brained like you are? He's only a man. You've seen plenty of men before, haven't you?

Taking a deep breath, she blinked as if to clear her head, then said, "Your . . . your sister can be very persuasive, Lieutenant Jordan." Where was the Addie Caton she knew? What had happened to the girl who had grown up as wild as any boy on the Texas prairie, who had spent countless hours roaming the countryside in her bare feet? And where was the defiant young woman who had declared that no man would ever tame her?

"Would you grant me the honor of this next dance, Miss Caton?" Daniel quietly requested, taking hold of her gloved hand and drawing it through his arm before she could answer him.

"I'd be delighted, Lieutenant Jordan," Addie boldly asserted, smiling warmly up at him. Her hooped and ruffled skirts swaying gently against his long legs as they moved to the dance floor, Addie still felt as if she were in some sort of daze . . .

Love at first sight, she remarked to herself with bitter sarcasm, slapping the reins again as she urged the horse homeward through the chilling afternoon wind. The two-storied frame ranch house beckoned in the near distance, promising a welcome shelter from the plunging temperature as the storm clouds thickened overhead.

Addie sighed heavily as she pulled up before the large stock barn, unhappily realizing that the house would offer no refuge from the storm in her heart. The pain and bitterness, the memories she had believed long ago buried, now came back to haunt her forcefully once more.

"Looks like we're in for snow, don't it, Miss Addie?" Trent Evans observed, peering up at the darkening sky as he hurried out of the barn to unhitch the horse and lead it inside.

"Just what we need," Addie muttered irritably, climbing down from the buckboard and snatching up the two bundles she had earlier tossed onto the seat beside her. "I'd appreciate it if you'd give Smokey a little extra hay tonight, Trent. I'm afraid I drove him a little hard on the way home just now." She spared only a passing glance for the black-haired man of medium height, then she turned and hurried across the yard to the back steps of the house, clutching the bundles against her bosom as she stepped inside the warm, spacious kitchen that was always filled with pleasant aromas.

"Me and Silas was beginnin' to get a mite worried about you, honey," declared a tall, plump black woman of indeterminate age. She was stirring a pot of red beans at the huge iron cookstove, and her kindly face took on an expression of maternal concern as she caught sight of Addie.

"No need to worry, Esther. I . . . I simply remained in town a bit longer than I planned." She placed the bundles on the round oak table near the doorway then drew off her woolen gloves and buckskin jacket with unhurried movements. There was a definite air of preoccupation about her as she headed for the steep, narrow staircase leading to the sanctuary of her room. Esther Fremont did not fail to notice the younger woman's pale features or her unusually tense expression, and she frowned to herself as she placed the heavy lid atop the steaming pot of beans.

Addie, meanwhile, softly closed the door behind her as she entered her upstairs room, a room that was cheerfully decorated in various shades of blue and cream, the same room that had been hers since shortly before her mother died, twelve years ago. She had always loved the delicate, floral wallpaper her mother had chosen and the elegant pieces of furniture that had been so carefully selected by Lilah Caton. But she took no notice of the things which normally gave her pleasure as she sank down upon the softness of the quilt-covered bed.

She remained quiet and still for the space of several minutes before abruptly rising to her feet and moving quickly to the large cheval glass in one corner of the dimly lit room. Turning up the lamp which burned atop the dressing table beside the mirror, she gazed with narrowing, critical eyes at her reflection.

Her skin had been tanned to a golden, tawny hue by the sun, and there was a light sprinkling of freckles across the bridge of her slightly upturned nose. The loose-fitting linen blouse and the plain gathered skirt she wore were durable, though hardly flattering. They only served to conceal her slender curves, as if hiding her femininity from the eyes of others. The fabric was drab and lifeless, and Addie reflected that the young woman facing her now was worlds apart from the naïve girl who had accompanied Carrie Jordan to that fateful dance all those years ago.

Frowning darkly, she reached upward and began yanking the restrictive pins from her hair with a vengeance, vigorously shaking her head so that the magnificent chestnut tresses fanned about her in glorious disarray. The waist-length brown curls were streaked with lighter strands, also the result of years spent out-of-doors without benefit of a protective kerchief or bonnet.

Her hair had always been her crowning glory. She

knew that she was still considered pretty, even with her hair arranged as it had been, in its usual, serviceable style. A sigh escaped her lips as she stared deep into the multicolored depths of the revealing reflections of her own eyes. The image of the lighthearted schoolgirl of four years ago had been vastly altered.

Why in heaven's name am I doing this? she scornfully asked herself, her eyes flashing at their reflected counterparts. My appearance doesn't matter. The way I look has absolutely no significance in this . . . this situation!

By what must certainly be viewed as some unexplainable quirk of fate, Addie reasoned, Daniel Jordan had surfaced in her life once again. After more than four years of total, heartbreaking silence, years containing miserable times when she couldn't keep herself from wondering if he were alive or dead, he had appeared in the very state, the very town where she lived. Why had he come? And why had he behaved as if he didn't even know her?

Turning away from the mirror, she approached the bed again, cursing herself for her weakness as hot tears burned against her eyelids. She was powerless to prevent them from multiplying and spilling over her dark lashes, and she choked back a sob as she flung herself facedown upon the quilt. It was the first time she had wept so uncontrollably since the death of her father two years earlier. She felt as if a dam had burst, and her sobs grew in intensity as she finally allowed herself the luxury of such a dramatically emotional release.

Much later, as she lay in a drained, semiconscious state upon the bed, her thoughts were relentlessly drawn to the past once again. It was her wedding night, a clear, moonlit evening in late March of 1861 . . .

"And I still believe we should make the facts of our marriage known," argued Daniel, cradling his young bride against his lean, muscular hardness.

"Secrecy is what an elopement is all about!" Addie laughingly reminded him, seductively pressing her soft, naked curves against his hard flesh. "If you hadn't swept me off my feet, Daniel Jordan, we wouldn't be in this predicament, would we?"

"You make it sound as if I am solely responsible for our whirlwind courtship, my love," he replied with a low chuckle, his gentle fingers following the tempting path up and down his new wife's smooth, silken back. He smiled to himself, inhaling deeply her feminine, lavender scent, then releasing his breath upon a contented sigh. "You'll have to accept a good deal of the blame. I was powerless to resist you from the first moment I set eyes on you!"

"It did happen with astonishing speed for us, didn't it? It's difficult to believe that night was only two weeks ago." She raised herself up on one elbow, facing him with a sudden, faint frown. The small interior of the hotel room was bathed in the pale golden light given off by a single lamp burning on a table beside the large, four-poster bed. "Daniel, you do understand why we can't tell anyone just yet, don't you?"

"Not entirely, no," he honestly admitted, his steely gaze catching her slightly troubled one.

"But I've explained it all to you. And, aside from my reasons, there's still the problem of your receiving

23

permission from your new commanding officer to bring a wife to the post, remember?"

"To tell the truth, I started moving through the proper channels regarding that particular matter a few days ago. I foresee no trouble whatsoever. Which brings us back to your reasons."

"It would break my father's heart if he heard about it from anyone other than me!" Addie feelingly asserted, pushing herself up to a sitting position and drawing the sheet up modestly to cover her bare breasts. "Please, Daniel, please do as I ask in this. It will only be for a few weeks. Your furlough ends within a fortnight, doesn't it? I promise you that I'll think of some way to break the news to him before then." Addie's eyes were soft and shining, her beautiful young face flushed with the afterglow of their passion. Her glorious chestnut tresses swirled about her like a curtain as her eyes silently pleaded with him to understand.

"Very well." He finally capitulated, favoring her with a mock scowl. "I'll humor you for now. I'm so much in love with you that I can't deny you anything that's in my power to grant, you little vixen!"

"You'll not regret your decision, my darling," Addie declared gratefully, snuggling against him. "It will be so exciting, meeting like this, won't it? A secret rendezvous whenever I can sneak away!" she said with a delighted little laugh.

"You just better make sure you manage to sneak away with great regularity," Daniel murmured, his deep voice growing husky with renewed desire. "I'll never get enough of you, Adelaide Caton Jordan. I want to hold you like this. I want to make love to you every night." He pulled her into his warm, powerful

24

embrace, his strong, sun-bronzed arms crushing her willing softness against him.

"I give you my word that I shall do my absolute best to grant you your wish!" she breathlessly responded, moaning softly as his lips claimed hers in a searing kiss, his hands roaming masterfully across her trembling curves. There was none of the frenzied swiftness of their first union as Daniel kissed her now, his lips moving sensuously, provocatively, upon hers. Her mouth parted beneath his, and their quickened breaths mingled as the flames of passion were kindled once more.

Soon his lips roamed across her face, traveling to the sensitive flesh of her ear, lower to the graceful curve of her neck, then lingering at the base of her throat where her pulse was beating with rapidly increasing speed. She gasped softly as he leisurely drew the sheet from her quivering body and his lips forged a fiery trail downward to the full young breasts which strained upward for his caress.

Daniel's mouth fastened tenderly about one of the rose-tipped peaks, and his warm fingers parted her thighs as his tongue teased evocatively at the nipple of her breast. The thoroughly erotic sensations he was creating within her caused Addie to feel faint, her senses reeling as she surrendered herself completely to her youthful passion, a passion that met Daniel's on an equally rapturous level.

It wasn't long before Daniel was easing within her velvety warmth, his movements initially slow and gentle then escalating to an urgency that served to heighten Addie's newly awakened desire. When their joyful, mutual fulfillment came, it was a shattering climax to the ultimate union they shared.

The world was sweet, the future bright, as the young lovers clung to one another in the secret privacy of their own special world . . .

There was a quiet yet insistent knock at the door. Addie's eyelids fluttered open as she came crashing back to reality, and she hurriedly dashed away the tears which still sparkled on her lashes.

"Miss Addie? Honey, can you hear me?" Esther called out, her voice low.

"Yes, Esther. What is it?"

"I've brought up a tray. Thought you might be gettin' hungry by now," explained the black woman who was more a family member than a servant. She eased the door open and stepped inside, another worried frown on her plump countenance. "Are you feelin' poorly, honey?" She stared down speculatively at the young woman on the bed noting the telltale circles beneath Addie's reddened eyes.

"I . . . I'm fine," Addie lied, her voice not quite steady as she hastily averted her gaze. "I'm sorry you went to all that trouble, Esther. I'm not hungry." She abruptly bounced off the bed and wandered over to stand at the calico-curtained window. It had started to snow, just as she had believed it would, though she took no notice of the gleaming white flakes as they filled the air and coated the waiting ground.

Esther opened her mouth to speak again but apparently changed her mind. She placed the tray on the uncluttered surface of the dressing table, threw Addie one last long, solicitous glance, then left. She

26

knew better than anyone else that it was best to leave the headstrong young woman alone when something was troubling her. No matter how much anyone wanted to help, Esther repeated to herself as she descended the staircase and returned to her work in the kitchen, it was best to leave Miss Addie to her thinking.

"Daniel," Addie whispered aloud, staring out aimlessly toward the frigid, whitening landscape. "Why have you come?"

Two

Daniel Jordan touched the rounded tips of his cavalry spurs to the horse's flanks in a gentle but firm command, his fingers holding the reins with a light, sure grip as he expertly guided the animal along the snow-covered wagon road. Drawing the heavy canvas coat more closely about his body, he was relieved to glimpse the large cabin situated in the midst of tall, leafless cottonwoods. Soon he was able to make out the other buildings on his new property, and he smiled faintly to himself as he urged his mount onward toward shelter from the chilling white flakes which fell to glisten upon his hat and shoulders as he rode.

The ranch appeared anything but prosperous, but he was well aware of the fact that he had invested in a less than profitable venture. No matter, he told himself. He was determined to bring it to life once more . . . just as he was determined to bring something else to life again as well, he mused.

The cabin looked well built and sturdy, and the barn and other buildings appeared equally solid, he mentally concluded, drawing the horse to a halt. He led the snow-coated animal inside the gray, weathered barn, satisfied to discover that there was still a good deal of hay stacked in the loft. It was dark and musty inside the deserted structure, but such details mattered little to the cold, weary horse as Daniel unsaddled him and rubbed him down with a handful of the aromatic hay.

Less than ten minutes later the ranch's new owner was stepping across the threshold into the log cabin. He moved to light a lamp that had been left on a rough-hewn, lopsided table near the open doorway. The flame flickered and burned with increasing brightness as Daniel held the lamp in one hand, his steely gaze sweeping about the damp, dusty room in which he stood. There were a few pieces of unimpressive furniture remaining, and a pair of homespun curtains at one of the windows.

Deciding to inspect the rest of the cabin at another time, Daniel returned the lamp to the table and stepped over to the huge stone fireplace. He smiled to himself as he caught sight of the few sticks of pine kindling stacked on the floor, and he turned to go in search of the woodpile—if such a thing still existed, he thought wryly to himself. He returned moments later, his strong arms laden with the damp logs he had found near the rear of the cabin.

Following several unsuccessful attempts, he was gratified to see he had the fire lit and sputtering to life. He waited until it displayed the satisfactory evidence of a true blaze, and only then did he take a seat on one of the small wooden benches nearby, his gray eyes gazing deep into the dancing flames.

Addie. His mind repeated her name over and over again, his heart aching almost unbearably. She was even more lovely than he remembered. These past four years had only increased her proud, spirited beauty, he reflected, his features visibly tightening as a tiny muscle twitched in his sun-bronzed cheek.

Had it really been more than four years since the night they had quarreled so bitterly, the last time they had seen each other? Was it truly possible that two people so passionately in love could have been so philosophically different?

That night had haunted him throughout four long years. Now it became a painfully vivid image in his mind once more . . .

"You . . . you cannot be serious!" Addie gasped in shock, her beautiful hazel eyes wide with disbelief. She was trembling faintly, still dazed by the news she had heard earlier that day.

"Perfectly serious," replied Daniel, a deepening frown on his handsome features. "Surely you realized that this might happen. There's been talk of a war for quite some time now." He and his bride of less than a month faced one another like two combatants, all alone in the confines of the hotel room where they had previously shared so much joy and laughter.

"I'm well aware of the trouble that's been brewing!" she snapped, her eyes blazing up at him, her thick, dark hair threatening to escape the confining pins. She was clad in a demure gown of pale yellow and looked very much like the schoolgirl she was. Daniel, however, was quite familiar with the fire and passion which lay just beneath this schoolgirl's deceptively innocent appearance.

"Addie, surely you must see that I have no choice in the matter. I'm in the Cavalry. It's my duty to serve my country. I have no choice," he firmly repeated, reaching out to draw her against his uniformed chest.

"You have a choice! You can choose not to fight against your own countrymen!" She resisted his embrace and, instead, angrily jerked away and stalked to the single, shaded window, her hooped skirts flaring outward as she turned.

"Very well. Perhaps I do have a choice. If so, then I choose to fight to preserve the unity of my country," he quietly responded, his gray eyes glowing dully.

"But you . . . you will be fighting against your own wife's people!" Addie pointed out as she whirled to face him once more.

Daniel stood in silence now, the look of outraged betrayal his young bride sent him twisting like a knife in his heart. What seemed to hurt him more than anything was the fact that Addie apparently refused to try to see his viewpoint in the matter. He would have to reason with her, would have to make her realize that he was following the only course of action open to him.

"Addie"—he spoke in a low, soothing tone of voice, stepping forward to place his hands gently upon her shoulders—"I love you. You know I do. And I know you love me. We can't allow this to tear us apart. I knew something like this was inevitable, but I didn't think it would be able to drive a wedge between us if we loved each other enough. Won't you at least try to see—"

"Try to see what?" she interrupted, tears swimming

in her wounded gaze as she looked up at him. "Try to see that you're going to fight against everything I hold dear?"

"I believed I had been given the impression that you held me dear."

"I did! I loved you desperately, Daniel Jordan! I thought you loved me in the same way!"

"I did, and I do. And if you love me still, you'll understand that I can do only what my sense of honor demands."

"Sense of honor? What honor is there in killing other men?" Addie furiously countered, abruptly moving away from him again. She dashed impatiently at the tears which coursed down her flushed cheeks, certain that her heart was breaking. "Don't do it, Daniel. Please, don't do it," she now pleaded, her tremulous voice barely audible. She was facing the door with her back turned to her husband, and she was unable to view the shadow of pain which crossed his face.

"I must follow my conscience. And you, as my wife, will have to follow my decision."

"If you fight against the South, you fight against me."

"No, Addie," he quietly disagreed, a faint sigh escaping his lips.

"Yes. For I am a part of my homeland." When she turned slowly back to face him this time, there was a set look to her beautiful countenance, a determined light in her eyes. "All right then, Lieutenant Jordan, do what you must. But don't expect me to accept your actions!"

"And what is that supposed to mean?" he tersely demanded, striding forward to stand towering above her, his narrowed gaze boring into hers.

"I loved you. You are destroying that love," Addie stated evenly, squarely facing him with her head held proudly.

"What you are saying is that if I do my duty as I see fit—if I follow the orders I have been given—you will no longer love me?" Daniel queried bitterly, his features visibly tightening.

"I am saying that I cannot remain married to the enemy."

He did not speak for the space of several long moments, his handsome features becoming impassive. Finally, after Addie could not refrain from averting her eyes from his scrutinizing stare, he said, "Have it your own way then. If I mean so little to you—" he began, only to break off. When he continued, it was as he was brushing past her and turning the doorknob. "If you should come to your senses, Mrs. Jordan," he remarked, placing a special emphasis on her married name, "you may reach me at my brother's house until morning. Carrie will be only too happy to furnish you with the address. I will be traveling to Washington tomorrow."

He hesitated in the doorway for an instant, his lips compressing into a thin line of anger when he received no response from Addie. Then he was gone, leaving Addie alone in the silence of the room and leaving a shattered part of himself behind as well . . .

Four years had passed—years of unspeakable horrors, of constant death and dying, of a certain, terrible numbness deep within. He had been wounded twice, the first time at Fredericksburg in the winter of '62, the

34

second at Petersburg in the last days of the conflict. Eventually promoted to the rank of captain, then major, then colonel, he had rarely traveled outside the state of Virginia throughout the entire course of the war, though he had been fortunate enough to make it home to St. Louis once. And even then, he reflected with a heavy sigh as he stared unblinkingly at the crackling fire, he had been viewed as both enemy and defender.

And Adelaide Caton Jordan had never been far from the front of his mind. The worst times had been when he was wounded. Lying there half out of his head with pain and fever, Addie had appeared to comfort him, to help him past the horrible, debilitating weakness that took hold of him and wouldn't let go. Thoughts of Addie had been both a blessing and a curse, for once he had recovered, a dull, never-ending ache had remained in his heart.

Had she ever truly loved him? he asked himself again. That one particular question had plagued him, tormented him, for four years. Now, he silently vowed, he would have the answer.

Rising to his feet, Daniel winced slightly at the sharp twinge of pain in his leg, a stubborn reminder of his last injury. It had healed almost completely, though he had been warned that twinges such as the one he had just experienced would more than likely continue to occur for quite some time yet.

He suddenly frowned to himself as his ears detected an unexpected noise, a noise much like the sound of muffled hoofbeats. Puzzled at who would be approaching his newly acquired ranch on such a day, he instinctively retrieved the Colt he had placed on the oak mantle above the roaring fire, checked to make sure the gun was loaded, then slipped it into the belt at his waist. After pausing briefly to don his hat, he flung open the cabin door and peered outside.

There were more than a dozen of them, but Daniel's rapidly scanning gaze was irrevocably drawn to the only woman in the group. He displayed no outward evidence of how seeing her again affected him, his ruggedly handsome countenance inscrutable as his eyes traveled to the other members of the mounted group. He stood framed in the doorway of the cabin, a faint, mocking smile curving his lips.

"Good evening, gentlemen. And lady. I take it you have a specific purpose in paying this call on such a fine day?" He knew why they had come, had anticipated encountering more than a little difficulty with his new neighbors.

"We sure as hell didn't come to welcome you!" gruffly proclaimed a large, bearded man. Daniel recognized him as one of the men Addie had been talking with in town a few hours earlier.

"We all figured you might as well know from the start that we don't want your kind around here, mister. We've already got more than our share of damned bluebellies!" another man ground out, his ruddy, clean-shaven features barely visible beneath his hat.

"The war is over," Daniel countered evenly, his eyes flitting back to light upon a silent, grim-faced Addie. She was bundled against the cold in a man's caped overcoat, her lustrous curls tucked up into the broad-brimmed hat she had pulled down low on her head. She sat staring ahead stonily, refusing to meet his disturbing, steely gaze.

36

"Not here it ain't!" a young fellow of perhaps twenty venomously exclaimed. "It ain't never gonna be over as long as your kind keeps on takin' what ain't yours!"

"I have a deed to this property. Mr. Ferguson apparently had no objections to selling me his ranch," Daniel responded with another faint smile.

"He didn't have any choice!" the first speaker interjected. "The war broke him, just like it damn near broke everyone in these parts. But we didn't come here to talk about Ferguson. We came to get a few things straight. You'll not be able to say you weren't warned."

"All right then. Let's hear your warning," instructed Daniel, his deep voice dropping even lower. Again, his eyes moved to linger upon Addie's beautiful face, though she continued to avert her own gaze.

Daniel was completely unaware of the turbulent emotions warring deep within her breast, of the overwhelming impulse she felt to rein her horse about and escape his unsettling presence. Dear God, Addie silently pleaded in increasing desperation, don't let me go to pieces now!

"You already know you're not wanted here. We don't aim to use violence to make our point, but we will if the need arises. We don't want to have anything to do with your kind, so you'd best keep out of our way. And you're to make certain that your stock doesn't mingle with ours, understand?"

"I thought this was free range country."

"Not to you. This land belongs to those of us who put blood and sweat into the soil, those of us who stayed during the darkest times and hung on. This land will never be yours." The bearded man paused a moment, then scowled fiercely as he said, "And there's one more

37

thing. Something we'd all like to hear from your own lips." He paused again before demanding in a low, hoarse voice, "Did you fight in the war? Did you kill our boys, Jordan?"

"Ike, what difference does that make?" Addie intervened at this point, surprising even herself by actually seeming to rush to Daniel's defense. Her eyes flew to his face then, and she suffered a sharp intake of breath as she found herself looking into his unfathomable gaze. Did she merely imagine it, or did those gray eyes of his take on an answering glow?

"It makes a difference," Ike Henry quietly asserted. "It makes a difference to me." He shifted in his saddle, glaring down at the tall Yankee as he awaited the fateful response. He noted absently that the snow had lightened some, though the cloud-thickened sky promised more.

"I'll answer your question," Daniel unhesitatingly replied, acknowledging Ike's glare with a slight narrowing of his own eyes. "Yes, I served—for the entire four years. There was no one more grateful than myself when the war ended. And it *has* ended." His words were met with charged silence. Several long moments passed before the men began muttering amongst themselves, their expressions rapidly growing more ugly and menacing.

Daniel looked toward Addie again, his handsome face appearing proud and unafraid, though he was inwardly wondering if perhaps this would be the last time he saw her. How ironic, he mused, the ghost of a smile touching his mouth, to wait four long years to see her again, only to die that very day!

But he had no intention of allowing himself to be

killed. Perhaps, if he kept his wits about him, he wouldn't find it necessary to use the gun still tucked into his belt.

"My son was killed at Gettysburg. And nearly every family in these parts lost a son or brother as well," Ike tersely declared, battling the temptation to draw his own weapon. "Keep out of my way, Jordan. I promise you that it won't take much to prompt me to put a bullet through your damned, murdering heart!" He reined his horse about and swiftly rode away. The others remained for only an instant, their own expressions silently threatening, before following after their apparent leader. Finally, only Addie sat astride her horse before him.

"You should have lied about the war, Daniel," she softly murmured.

"Addie, we've got to talk," he stated quietly, facing her across several feet of white-blanketed ground. The sound of her name upon his lips brought the hot tears stinging against her eyelids once more. She threw him one last, dispassionate glance, then took off after the other riders, her heels spurring the animal into a gallop across the frozen landscape.

Daniel stared after her, oblivious to the biting cold as he stood in the doorway and watched until she was out of sight. There was a deep frown creasing his brow when he finally turned and stepped inside the cabin again, slowly pushing the door to with one hand. The warmth of the fire welcomed him back as he reassumed his seat upon the bench.

The animosity of the men who had just left was pushed far to the back of his mind as he thought of Addie. She would come. She would have to come eventually, if for no other reason than to demand that he leave. Beautiful, proud, spirited Addie . . . he mused.

If only he had been able to come to Texas sooner. Perhaps that would have helped, at least a little. But there were all those weeks in the hospital, then those endless months until he was mustered out. It had been anything but easy to arrange his purchase of the ranch bordering hers, but he had been quite determined. And he was still convinced that patience and determination would reward him with the one thing he wanted more than anything else in the world—Addie.

He was so lost in his silent reverie that he was at first unaware of the door being slowly edged open, of the rush of cold air filling the room. When the chill touched his face, he jerked about and rose to his feet, his hand reflexively moving to the gun at his waist.

His hand dropped to his side once more as he viewed the lone figure crossing the threshold, and he smiled faintly as he said, "Come in, neighbor."

Three

Addie shot him a distrustful look as she moved inside the dusty, wood-smoke-scented cabin. She closed the door behind her with stiff movements, her entire demeanor bespeaking an obvious reluctance at her own actions.

"I only came back to ask you something—to get a few things straight," she warily explained, remaining by the door.

"To get a few things straight," echoed Daniel, schooling his features to conceal the wild stirrings of his blood at seeing her alone again in such intimate surroundings. "Like your friends?" he mockingly queried. Then, murmuring half to himself, he added, "Seems like everyone is anxious to 'get a few things straight' today." His tall, undeniably masculine form was outlined by the fire's golden light, and Addie swallowed a sudden lump in her throat.

"Why, Daniel? Why are you here?" she impatiently demanded, the questions bursting forth. "Why did you buy this ranch?"

"Because I wanted it," he maddeningly replied, his eyes moving boldly, hungrily up and down her coat-covered body. She had as yet to move any farther inside the room, and Daniel suppressed a smile as he viewed the flash of haughty defiance reflected in her magnificent hazel eyes.

"That's no answer, and well you know it!"

"It's my answer."

"Answer me, damn you, Daniel Jordan! Why did you come here? You could have bought a ranch anywhere. Why this one? Why Texas?" Her beautiful countenance became increasingly stormy as he waited several long moments before responding again.

"My purchase of the property was arranged through a friend. It was an attractive bargain. Do you perhaps flatter yourself that I came here because of you?" he sardonically remarked.

"Don't be an idiot!" she snapped, reaching upward to snatch the broad-brimmed hat from her head as she faced him with a militant light in her eyes. The glorious chestnut tresses tumbled freely about her face and shoulders, falling in splendid disarray to her slender waist. "I suppose it doesn't really matter why you came. What's important to me is that you make plans to leave again!"

"I have no plans to leave. I intend to make this ranch my home for a good long time," Daniel calmly pronounced. He moved away from the fireplace, leisurely crossing the room to stand towering above a very wide-eyed Addie, the top of her head barely reaching his shoulder. She held her breath as she gazed up at him expectantly, feeling the panic welling up deep within her. She wasn't accustomed to experiencing such fear, and she staunchly told herself that she was an utter fool to allow Daniel Jordan to make her feel so frightened.

"You heard what those men said. You're not wanted here!" He made her feel so small, so unsure of herself, something no man had ever done, save her loving but domineering father. She stared proudly up at him, meeting his steely gaze with unflinching fortitude, determined to quell the despicable weakness his close proximity caused.

"I'll remind you just as I reminded them, Addie—the war is over. I'm free to live where I choose. Neither you nor your friends can prevent me from doing as I wish." She looked so desirable, so vulnerable, with her hair down, he thought, summoning an admirable strength of will to restrain himself from reaching out and fingering the shining curls that had always seemed to beg for his touch.

"They'll make you leave if you give them reason enough," she warned, frowning slightly as she brushed past him and hurried over to the warmth of the fire.

"You might as well take off that coat and sit down. I think we're both aware of the fact that there are still a few things to be settled between us." He followed after her, resting a hand against the smooth edge of the fireplace mantle as he stared down at her again, his eyes drinking in the sight of the beloved profile presented to him as she stood gazing intently into the flames.

"Only one," she amended in a voice barely above a whisper. "There's one thing I have to know." She turned to face him, her cheeks becomingly flushed by the comforting heat. "Are you planning to make it known that we were . . . that we were once husband

43

and wife?" She raised her chin slightly in an unconscious gesture of pride, bewildered and unaccountably flustered at the way Daniel suddenly smiled down at her.

"I thought the little matter of that particular legality would surface in the conversation sooner or later," he wryly commented. Then he grew serious. "No one here knows?"

"No," she answered, averting her eyes again. "I've never told anyone."

"Not even your father?"

"No. Not even him. It would have broken his heart."

"I see," murmured Daniel, his features visibly tightening. "Would his broken heart have been caused by the news that his daughter had eloped with a virtual stranger, or because she had married a 'damned Yankee'?"

"Both!" Addie vehemently supplied, her eyes flashing. "But the issue of what would have caused my father great pain is not what we are discussing!" she angrily pointed out. "Do you or do you not intend to make the facts of our marriage known?"

"I see no reason at this point to reveal the true nature of our relationship," he replied evasively. "What's past is past. But there is something that puzzles me."

"What?" she coldly demanded.

"Why didn't you ever file for a divorce, Addie?" he softly questioned. He could hear the way her breath caught upon a gasp, could see the startled, anxious look in her eyes. Once again she glanced away.

"I . . . I did not know if you were alive or dead. And I thought it best to simply try to forget anything had ever happened between us. If I had made inquiries into such a procedure, if I had remained in St. Louis long enough to take such action . . ." her voice trailed away, then strengthened again. "I came home without delay. I suppose I should have filed, but I did not."

"You thought that if you simply pretended I had never come into your life you could effectively obliterate all evidence, is that it?" he bitterly demanded.

"I did not know what to do!" Addie furiously cried, whirling away from him and sweeping back across the room to the window near the doorway. "When I heard nothing from you, nothing to indicate—"

"What are you talking about?" he demanded, his own long strides leading him to her side once more. "I wrote you—twice. I instructed you to send a reply to me in care of my sister in St. Louis."

"I received no letters from you!" she countered in obvious disbelief, rounding on him with narrowed, blazing eyes. "You never wrote to me, did you, Daniel?"

"Whatever else you may feel about me, Addie, you know in your heart that I'd never lie to you," he told her, his voice low and even.

"I know nothing of the sort!" she irrationally exclaimed, shaking her head and causing the curtain of thick hair to swirl about her beautiful, angry features. "I know nothing about you at all, Daniel Jordan! I never did. It was a terrible mistake to marry you. It was a terrible mistake for you to come here!"

"Mistake or not," he ground out, the pain of her words slicing through him, "what's done is done!"

"Much to my everlasting shame and regret!"

The two of them stood nearly quaking with the force

of their respective, bitter anger, their furious gazes locked in silent combat. Daniel sighed inwardly as he forcefully regained his composure. He hadn't meant for them to exchange such heated words, hadn't meant to lose his temper. Such violent confrontations would avail them nothing.

"I'm sorry, Addie," he murmured, his handsome face wearing a rather tired look. "We shouldn't be doing this. The past should be buried. Four years should have erased the painful memories, not added fuel to our sense of wrongdoing. We were both much younger then. Isn't it about time we got on with our lives?"

Addie didn't immediately reply. Her senses were reeling, and she felt as if her world had been turned upside down in a single day. Why did he have to come? she asked herself for at least the hundredth time.

"The past should indeed be buried," she finally agreed, glancing downward for a brief instant. When she raised her eyes to his face again, there was the unmistakable evidence of moistness glistening in their hazel depths. "I still don't know what your reasons are for coming here, but they don't matter. Now that you're here . . . well, I think it's finally time for one of us to set about dissolving that brief, unfortunate marriage that should never have been."

"Addie, I—" Daniel began, only to break off abruptly. She gazed up at him with a questioning look in her expressive eyes, suddenly experiencing a deep and heavy sadness. They had been so young, she thought, so foolishly enamored of one another, so innocently certain that their love could weather all obstacles which lay ahead . . . But there was no use in dwelling upon what might have been. There was too

46

much pain in thinking about the past, Addie reflected with an inward sigh.

"I'll be going now," she quietly announced, donning her hat and leaving her long hair flowing loose about her body. She was feeling strangely empty inside after what had just occurred, and at that moment she desired nothing more than to escape those gray, searching eyes of Daniel's. She turned and placed a hand upon the doorknob, startled when his larger hand moved atop hers. "Daniel, what are you—" she gasped, perplexed by the strange light in his intense gaze, the inscrutable expression on his face.

Before she quite knew what was happening, he had pulled her hard against him, his powerful arms encircling her slender, womanly form as he captured her lips with his own. Addie was so shocked by his unexpected assault that she could at first do little more than stand soft and pliant against him, embarrassingly aware of his mastery over her. His warm, skillful lips demanded a response, and, for just one fleeting moment, she did respond. She returned his kiss with a passion she believed long dead, moaning softly as his arms tightened about her curved softness.

Then reason returned. The purring kitten became an outraged tigress as she raised her clenched fists to push him away. He held fast, however, and she struggled almost wildly in his grasp, her breautiful face flushed with rage.

"Take your hands off me, damn you!" Addie imperiously commanded, emphasizing her words with ineffective blows upon Daniel's broad, muscular chest. "I hate you, Daniel Jordan! I'll always hate you!" she dramatically asserted, her hair now streaming about

47

her face in a tangled mass. She gasped aloud when he abruptly released her, and she took an unsteady step backward as she raised wrathfully indignant eyes to Daniel's impassive visage.

Neither of them spoke for what seemed like an eternity, the silence hanging heavy between them. Addie sought to control her ragged breathing while still glaring murderously at a seemingly unaffected Daniel.

"Is this what you came for, Daniel? Did you expect me to fall headlong into your waiting arms?" she demanded with biting sarcasm. "It will be a cold day in hell when I let you touch me again!" Her rage only increased when he did not reply. There was an unfathomable glow in those gray eyes now, an almost imperceptible tightening of his damnably handsome face.

Finally Addie pushed past him furiously and flung open the door, pausing in the doorway to offer a parting shot.

"You ruined my life four years ago. I'll not allow you to ruin it again!" With that, she was gone.

She and her mount had become nothing more than a tiny speck on the darkening horizon when Daniel closed the door again. Resuming his seat in front of the dwindling fire, he smiled softly to himself.

No matter what Addie had said, no matter how loudly she had protested, there had been a responsive spark when he had kissed her. And, although their turbulent encounter had shown him that his goal would be even more difficult to achieve than he had at first anticipated, it had also shown him that he could, with the right amount of skill and perseverance, succeed in his pursuit of the wife who had never been

48

able to bring herself to divorce him.

Addie, meanwhile, was left pale and shaken by their emotional confrontation. She retired to the privacy of her room as soon as she reached her home once more, which was less than a mile from Daniel's cabin. But in her preoccupation she failed to realize that her uncharacteristic behavior had caused Esther's concern to deepen.

Daniel's kiss still burned upon her lips, and she rubbed the back of her hand across her mouth as if to erase his disturbing caress. Muttering a silent curse, she reflected that things had gone even worse than she had believed possible!

Why in heaven's name had she gone with Ike and the others? Why had she placed herself in such an uncomfortable position?

This Daniel was so different from the one she had once known. He had been a young, dashing, relatively carefree man of twenty-three when they had eloped all those years ago. Now he had been transformed into a veritable stranger, a man obviously matured and hardened by the war. But then, she grimly reasoned with herself as she took a seat upon her bed and began drawing off her worn leather boots, who hadn't been matured and hardened by the war?

Times had certainly been hard for the few families remaining in and around Fort Worth, she recalled, her thoughts leaving Daniel for a moment. The city's population had dwindled to a mere two hundred and fifty by the war's end. A terrible depression had settled upon the strong-willed people who had struggled through four long years of war to keep the once-prosperous settlement going. She and her father had certainly done their part.

"Oh, Papa," Addie murmured with a desperate little sigh. Rising to her feet again, she unbuttoned the drab linen blouse and drew it off. Then she removed the divided skirt of soft calfskin that had been a present from her father shortly before he died. Though she had always ridden astride, her skirts had been a constant nuisance. Her father, however, had refused to allow his daughter to wear men's trousers, so he had compromised with the divided skirt. Such attire was still considered quite scandalous by the ladies of the town, but Addie didn't care. She hadn't cared much about anything since the death of her father, except the ranch.

The ranch had become her whole life, and the exhausting work something in which to bury herself. There had been little else to do but work during the past four years, she bitterly mused, wandering aimlessly to the window of her room.

It had been snowing for more than two hours, and yet there was little more than an inch of accumulation evident on the ground, she vaguely noted, turning away from the window again and heaving yet another audible sigh.

Had Daniel Jordan actually come to Texas with the intention of claiming his rights as her husband? she asked herself, sinking down upon the bed again, her face appearing quite pensive. Her fingers moved to the ribbons of her soft cotton chemise, which she soon drew off, then to her plain, untrimmed pantalettes, easing them down over her rounded hips.

Shivering in the cool air of the room, she hurried across to the huge oak chest in the opposite corner, opening a drawer and quickly snatching out a

50

nightgown. It was still early in the evening, much earlier than when she usually retired for the night, but she was feeling extremely weary all of a sudden. As she turned to shake out the folds of the white cotton garment, she caught sight of herself in the tall mirror nearby.

Although normally not given to standing naked before a mirror, she found herself drawn to her beckoning reflection. The nightgown slipped from her grasp to fall unnoticed on the bare wooden floor as her eyes widened in something akin to amazement.

Was that totally feminine, perfectly curved image staring back at her truly herself? The skin was smooth and silken, flawless, and tanned to a light golden hue. The breasts were high and firm and full, the waist slender and just the correct size in proportion to the well-rounded hips that flared down into slim thighs and long, shapely legs. The shining darkness of her long reddish brown tresses were in striking contrast to the paler beauty of her soft, womanly flesh, and Addie stared dazedly at the revealing sight.

What would Daniel Jordan think if he saw you now? an impish voice at the back of her mind challenged. Would he still think you beautiful? Would he still desire you as he had desired the Addie of four years ago?

"Miss Addie? I know you said you wasn't hungry, but—" Esther was defensively explaining as she suddenly opened the door and bustled into the room without warning. She took one look at her young mistress, still standing completely unclothed before the mirror, and remarked in loud tones of obvious disapproval, "The Lord have mercy! What in the name

51

of heaven are you standin' there naked as a jaybird for? Why, it's plumb near to freezin' in here!"

Addie, who had started guiltily when she first perceived the older woman hastening through the doorway, could feel the hot color rising to her face. Humiliation washed over her at having been discovered in such a shocking state.

"Damnation!" she muttered, bending down to retrieve the nightgown then pulling it over her head with a vengeance. Now her reflection showed a frowning young woman clad in a prim, high-necked, long-sleeved, decidedly unfrivolous creation that effectively concealed the feminine charms of its wearer. "I . . . I was preparing to go to bed!" she almost defiantly offered, averting her face from the perceptive gaze of the woman who had been with Addie's family since long before the birth of Will and Lilah Caton's only child.

"That may be, but you were sure enough just beggin' to catch your death of cold by standin' there in your birthday suit!" Esther chided with the maternal severity she frequently affected, crossing her arms against her amply cushioned chest.

"What did you come up here for, Esther?" Addie quietly demanded, taking up her hairbrush from the dressing table and beginning to methodically stroke the tangled chestnut curls. Her cheeks still burned with embarrassment, though the humiliation she experienced was more for her thoughts than for her actions.

"You ain't had anythin' to eat since noon. You know as well as anybody that you can't keep goin' without somethin' in your belly. Why don't you come on downstairs with me and let me fix you—"

"Thank you, but I'm still not hungry," Addie interrupted, continuing to brush the tangles from her hair. She'd had a perfectly healthy appetite until today! she angrily reflected.

"Why are you goin' to bed so early?" Esther then probed, fully realizing that she was going against her earlier conviction that she should leave the younger woman alone. Miss Addie just hadn't been herself since coming back from town, she thought with a shake of her head.

"Because I happen to be tired," Addie answered simply, returning the hairbrush to the dressing table and finally raising her eyes to meet Esther's. "It's been a long day. While I appreciate your concern, dearest Esther, I desire nothing more at this particular moment than to seek my rest!"

"Come mornin', if you're not feelin' a whole sight better, I'm gonna take it upon myself to send for Doc Bennett!" announced Esther as she frowned but finally took her leave.

Addie released a long sigh a moment after the door closed. Stepping back to the four-poster bed, she blew out the lamp and climbed beneath the several layers of covers, feeling thoroughly disgusted with herself. She punched almost viciously at the unresisting softness of her pillow, then turned swiftly upon her side and stared toward the dwindling gray light streaming in through the window.

Daniel's face swam before her eyes. She could still see him staring down at her in that infuriating manner, could still see the light that had come into his eyes just before he had kissed her. Why had she hesitated before beginning to struggle? Why?

She had told him that she hated him, that he had ruined her life. Did she truly feel that way about him? Did she perhaps wish that he had been killed in the war, that Daniel Jordan no longer existed?

No, she immediately answered herself. She would certainly never wish him dead. But now she did just as certainly wish him far away again!

She silently cursed his disturbing reappearance in her life as she rolled to her back and resolutely closed her eyes. Though she desperately yearned for blissful unconsciousness, sleep eluded her for quite some time.

Four

When Addie descended the stairs for breakfast the following morning, the ill effects of a restless night spent tossing and turning in her bed were displayed in the telltale circles beneath her eyes and the faint pallor of her normally glowing features. Esther and her husband, Silas, were waiting in the kitchen, the two of them speaking together in rather hushed tones. Their talk abruptly ceased when Addie stepped through the open doorway, prompting her to favor them with a narrowed look that conveyed her suspicions that she had been the subject of their conversation.

"Good morning, Silas, Esther," she murmured, her head proudly erect as she moved across to the iron cookstove. Her greeting was initially met with silence, which only served to confirm her suspicions. That, and the furtive glance the married couple exchanged.

"Now honey, you just set yourself down and let me get your breakfast," Esther declared finally, rising to her feet and hurriedly ambling over to stand beside Addie. She reached out to take the coffeepot from the younger woman's hands. Addie was at first reluctant to relinquish her grip upon the blackened pot's handle, preferring to pour her own cup of the fragrant brew, but she did not feel inclined to argue over such an inconsequential matter, so she finally let go and moved to take a seat opposite Silas at the small, round table.

"You look a mite peaked this mornin', Miss Addie," remarked the tall, lean black man, his deep, rumbling voice echoing pleasantly about the warm kitchen. He was nearly sixty years of age, and his frizzled black hair was generously peppered with gray. Like Esther, his features were kindly, and, as was usually the case, Addie felt compelled to confide in the man who had always been like a second father to her.

But she staunchly battled the powerful urge to tell him about Daniel, suppressing it just as she had done for the past four years. It had been extremely difficult at times, she reflected, staring downward at the gingham-covered surface of the table, but she had been determined that no one would ever learn of her disastrous, heartbreaking mistake.

"I'm fine," she easily lied, then hastened to change the subject. "How much snow did we get last night, Silas?" She smiled briefly up at Esther as the older woman brought her a plate piled high with scrambled eggs and sourdough biscuits. "Esther, why in heaven's name do you persist in placing so much food before me? You know good and well I can't eat even half of this!" she chided good-naturedly. It was the same thing every morning, she told herself in fond amusement, her troubles momentarily forgotten.

"You ain't had nothin' to eat since noon yesterday, remember?" Esther pointed out, bringing the coffeepot and a cup as well. She settled herself in a chair between Addie and Silas, her meaningful stare making it clear that she wanted her young mistress to finish off the entire breakfast.

"Looks like we got nigh onto six inches," Silas finally answered, raising his own cup of the steaming black liquid to his lips. "My, my, if this coffee don't taste like pure heaven!" he remarked with an appreciative grin.

"Anything would taste better than what we've had to drink around here for the past few years!" Addie declared, wrinkling her nose in remembered distaste and laughing softly. A little coffee had been smuggled in from Mexico for a few months after the beginning of the war, but supplies had swiftly been depleted, and the greatest majority of the people had been forced to substitute a hot liquid concoction of parched barley and wheat. It had been better than nothing, Addie recalled, but just barely. "Do you think we'll get any more snow?" she asked Silas, returning to the subject at hand as she forced herself to lift a forkful of the eggs to her mouth.

"Too soon to tell. The clouds are still churnin' somethin' fierce. Could be we're in for a mighty bad spell."

"That's what I've been afraid of," murmured Addie, a worried frown on her face now.

"We might ride out and see how many head we can find," Silas suggested quietly, his gaze catching Addie's.

"That's what I planned for us to do today. Go on out and tell the men. I'll meet you over at the bunkhouse in a few minutes."

"All right, Miss Addie," he responded with characteristic deference, easing the chair back and rising to his feet.

"You take care out there in the cold, old man, you hear?" Esther lovingly admonished, returning the broad smile he flashed her before he turned and exited through the back door.

Addie had eaten less than half of the food on her plate, just as she had earlier predicted, when she stood and moved to the hooks hanging on the wall near the back door and began lifting down her gloves and coat. She had dressed in a simple, unadorned woolen blouse and skirt, pulling on denim knickers beneath the fullness of her gathered skirts so that her legs would be protected as she rode astride. Underneath the outer layer of clothing, she had first drawn on a pair of warm, flannel long johns. Her leather boots completed the rather odd, but nevertheless adequately insulating costume, and she now tucked her thick hair, which she had decided to wear in braids, under her hat. Wrapping a woolen scarf about her neck, she turned back to Esther.

"Don't you stay out there too long, honey," cautioned the older woman.

"We'll stay as long as the job demands." She was looking forward to the day's grueling work. Perhaps it would serve to keep her mind too occupied to think of— No, she sternly commanded herself, don't even think of his name! "Oh, and Esther, would you please pack us—" she suddenly remembered to ask.

"Some food?" the older woman finished. "It's already done. Got it right here." She handed Addie the small, woven hamper she had just produced from its place beside the stove, adding, "That old coffeepot of your pa's is in there, too."

"Thank you. I've no idea when we'll return, so don't worry," said Addie as she opened the door and disappeared outside. The cold hit her like a slap in the face, and she shivered in spite of the way she had bundled herself against it. Her hurried strides led her in the direction of the small wooden building located a short distance away from the stock barn, as her boots crunched noisily upon the frozen ground. The snow had apparently melted slightly before freezing again, leaving it hard and icy and treacherous for walking.

"Mornin', Miss Addie," said Trent Evans as Addie entered the smoke-filled bunkhouse. The smoke came from the lamps burning tallow, and additional, distinctive aromas emanated from old work boots, the licorice in the ranchhands' chewing tobacco plugs, and the unwashed bodies of the men themselves.

"Good morning, Trent," Addie politely responded, nodding briefly in his direction. "Clay, Billy," she murmured, punctuating their names with a nod as well. The two younger men shyly acknowledged her greeting with tentative smiles.

"Mornin', ma'am," they each replied in turn. Clay Miller was a dark-haired boy of perhaps eighteen years of age, while blond Billy Kendrick appeared to be about a year older. As young as the two of them were, however, they had both served in the Conferate Army throughout the last desperate months of the war. Addie liked the slender young men well enough, for they seemed to be good, basically hardworking fellows, at least as far as she had been able to discern after these first few weeks of their being in her employ. But Trent— She told herself that she still didn't quite know what to make of him.

He had been at the Rolling L for nearly eight months now, having appeared in town shortly after Lee's surrender to Grant at Appomattox. Addie had first encountered Trent Evans at the blacksmith shop, where he and the blacksmith, a burly man by the name of Josh Wilkes, were both sourly complaining about the new "government," a force of one officer and twenty black soldiers who carried orders to round up the county voters for a roll call. Martial law was in effect, though it was the carpetbaggers and scalawags who moved in to rule the town with their own brand of justice.

Addie had listened to the two men grumbling about the hated authority, their talk interspersed with blistering curses leveled in general at the victors of the recently ended conflict. Josh had introduced Addie to the new man in this nearly deserted town, and Trent had then proceeded to startle Addie by asking her for a job.

Although she had made it clear from the outset that she had no money with which to pay his wages, Trent had eagerly insisted that he'd be willing to work for room and board alone until the ranch became prosperous again. He had ridden home with her that same day. She had been shocked at her own impulsiveness, but she was in desperate need of a good ranch hand, and the man had seemed honest enough.

Silas and Esther had disliked him from the very beginning. Though they had warned their young mistress not to take him on, she had nevertheless gone against their advice. He had proven to be a hard worker and surprisingly knowledgeable about ranching. Even

60

Silas had begrudgingly accepted the man's worth, though he still made no secret of the fact that his initial feelings toward Trent had not undergone a complete transformation.

Trent was a mysterious man, a quiet loner who kept to himself, Addie reflected as she watched the hands slipping on their bulky coats and broad-brimmed hats. She had never heard him talk to anyone as freely as he had to Josh Wilkes that day. Though he had been in her employ all these months, she still knew very little about him. He took his meals with the other hands in the bunkhouse but had eaten alone before Clay and Billy had been hired. She had often wondered where he came from, and if he had served during the war, but she had never intruded upon his privacy.

Silas and the two younger men filed out of the bunkhouse now, leaving Addie momentarily alone with Trent. She felt a bit discomfited all of a sudden, and she turned to follow the others out into the cold.

"Wait a minute, please, Miss Addie," Trent requested in a low voice. He wasn't a particularly attractive man, but, Addie told herself, she supposed some women would find his dark, hawkish features appealing. The unbidden image of a tall, ruggedly handsome man with gray eyes and hair the color of ripened wheat rose in her mind, but she staunchly ignored it.

"Yes, Trent? What is it?" she asked in puzzlement.

"I don't mean to sound too bold, ma'am, but you look like something's troubling you. Thought I might be able to help." The concern reflected in his brown eyes appeared to be sincere, but Addie grew uneasy at his offer and she faltered.

"I . . . I thank you, Trent. But there's nothing troubling me." Once again, the lie came easily to her lips. The last thing she wanted to do was to confide in one of the hired help, she silently reasoned. Her father had always cautioned her to hold herself just a little bit aloof from the hands, warning that becoming too friendly with them would result in disaster when it came to her position of authority.

"Well, I just wanted you to know you can count on me if you should ever need my help," murmured Trent, his gaze flitting downward before returning to Addie's face.

"I appreciate the offer," she replied cordially, moving through the open doorway and toward the barn. It was a bit odd, the way Trent had just spoken to her, she reflected as she marched across the coated ground. But she dismissed him from her thoughts as she and the men began saddling their mounts.

It wasn't long before they were riding away from the ranch buildings and out toward the open range. Will Caton had acquired more than twenty-five hundred acres since the time he had come to the area just west of Fort Worth back in 1850. The land had been only scarcely populated back then, still wild and untamed and brimming with Indians, both friendly and hostile.

"How many head you reckon we'll find today, Miss Addie?" Clay queried conversationally as he maneuvered his horse nearer to hers. Neither he nor Billy knew a great deal about ranching, but they were certainly willing to learn. Addie had been unable to resist their boyish enthusiasm for the job when they had ridden out to the ranch nearly a month ago and said they were looking for work. Like Trent, they were willing to work for room and board until there was money coming in once more, and Addie realized that they probably had no place else to go. Her father had often teased her about her soft heart, she recalled with an inner chuckle.

"I hope we'll find more than we did the last time," she answered him with a faint smile. Thank goodness the wind had died down, she mused, her eyes scanning the frozen landscape as they rode. The wintertime task of going out on the range to make certain the cattle weren't starving or freezing to death was both necessary and grueling. The cattle had a mindless, obstinate tendency to stand placidly in the snow, shivering and hungry, rather than try to find food. What was more, Addie thought with a brief sigh, the stubborn creatures even lacked the instinct to eat the snow for the desperately needed moisture.

Within minutes, she and the others had come upon a sizable herd of the lean, rawboned longhorns. The animals' hides were crusted heavily with the snow, their muzzles dripping tiny icicles. Addie dismounted beside the men, and the hands began chopping through the glazed snow and ice so that the cattle could drink from the small pond around which they were clustered. Silas and Addie started checking to see if the animals were branded, and they were satisfied when they found that the majority of the herd bore the brand of the Rolling L.

"They look healthy enough, don't you think, Silas?" remarked Addie, her cheeks reddened by the cold, her hazel eyes sparkling.

"Yes, Miss Addie, they do," he agreed with a soft laugh. He quickly sobered as he added, "But this here was only the first snow of the winter. Come spring, there's no tellin' how many will still be alive."

"Perhaps we'll get lucky," she said flippantly, though she knew as well as Silas that the worst was yet to come. But, she optimistically reflected, the longhorns were a tough breed. Rangy and muscled, they were the survivors of vast herds the Spanish *conquistadores* had driven across the hostile land many years earlier. "Well, I suppose we've done all we can do here for the day. Let's get going," she finally decreed, striding back toward her patiently waiting horse.

"Where to now, Miss Addie?" Billy questioned, he and Clay mounting up beside the two older men. Their breaths were a visible fog in the frigid morning air, and Addie suddenly frowned as she paused to wonder if it would remain below freezing for the entire day.

"We'll head farther south for a while. I'd like for us to get a look at as many of the Rolling L stock as possible today," she replied, tugging her gloves more securely onto her hands.

"It might be best if we stopped long enough to build us a fire in a while," Silas wisely suggested, noticing the effect the cold was already beginning to have on everyone.

"All right," Addie readily agreed. "We'll stop and make camp when we spot the next herd." Reining her horse about, she led the way to the south, the five of them swiftly traversing the gently rolling landscape that boasted endless acres of thick prairie grass.

Less than an hour later, the coffee was boiling in the pot over the blazing, crackling fire that had been built within the shelter of a grove of cottonwood trees. Addie gratefully inhaled the strong aroma, then began withdrawing the food Esther had wrapped in thread-bare linen napkins before she had packed the small bundles inside the woven hamper. There were sour-dough biscuits spread with freshly churned butter, miniature, individual pies loaded with meat and beans, as well as a generous supply of sugar with which to sweeten the black coffee, the sugar being a special treat because of its high price and scarcity.

"Coffee's ready," Silas announced. Addie and the men moved closer to the fire's warmth, all of them appreciative of the heat given off by the smoking blaze.

"You still planning for us to clear those dead trees tomorrow, Miss Addie?" Trent suddenly questioned, his solemn gaze catching hers as they carefully sipped the burning hot liquid.

"I suppose so. Unless we get more snow," she replied, peering overhead at the heavy cover of ominous gray clouds. "If we do happen to get more, I think it might be best to spend the day chopping firewood." She returned her gaze to Trent, and, with only the slightest hint of a smile on her face, she asked, "Is there any particular reason for your wanting to know?" The soft, crunching sound made by the small herd of cattle nearby was quite audible in the stillness of the cold air, and the popping of the burning wood was the only other noise to be heard as the four men and one woman remained companionably about the fire.

"Thought you might be able to make do without me for a couple of days. I've got some business to attend to," he responded evasively.

"I don't suppose a couple of days will matter much. As a matter of fact," she said, her gaze now moving to include Billy and Clay as well, "why don't all of you take a couple of days off? Christmas is less than two weeks away, and you might want to go into town, to Turner's, and see about choosing some new pairs of boots."

"But, we . . . we ain't got any money, Miss Addie," Clay hesistantly declared, coloring slightly as if the pitiable state of his finances was something of which to be ashamed.

"Then consider it my Christmas gift to you. You and Billy and Trent. You've all worked extremely hard and, well, let's just say you deserve some sort of special compensation."

"But how are you gonna—" Billy tactlessly started to ask, only to be interrupted by his beautiful young employer.

"I may not have the cash, but Mr. Turner has made it clear that he will generously extend to me all the credit I need." It was a foolish act of extravagance, she knew, but she wasn't in the least bit sorry she had made the offer. The boots the men were wearing were now in a sorry state, and wouldn't they be able to work better if more properly attired? This she stubbornly told herself even as her voice of reason chided, *Adelaide, you're a softhearted idiot!*

"That's mighty kind of you, Miss Addie," Clay murmured, obviously touched by her generosity. Billy merely responded with a broad smile and a nod, while Trent remained silent. Whether his silence stemmed from disinterest, a wounded sense of pride, or neither, Addie could not tell.

"Rider's comin'," Silas suddenly announced, staring past Addie's head. She and the others immediately turned about, eyeing the lone horseman with increasing curiosity.

"Who else would be out here on Rolling L land on a day like today?" Addie wondered aloud, her eyes narrowing slightly as the rider approached. He had apparently glimpsed the white smoke curling upward from their fire, she surmised as she waited for his identity to be revealed.

"More than likely just someone passing through on his way to town," offered Billy, raising the tin cup to his lips once more.

"Then he'll be in for a big disappointment when he discovers he's traveling in the wrong direction!" Addie wryly observed. Her lips curved into a faint smile, but the smile rapidly faded into a look of horrible realization as the rider drew closer.

"Looks like a stranger to me," Clay declared, for they could make out the lone horseman's face by now.

"Well, whoever he is, he'll be welcome to share our fire and a cup of coffee," Silas asserted. Then he added, "Ain't that so, Miss Addie?"

For the second time in the space of less than twenty-four hours, Addie was rendered totally speechless. What in thunder was he doing here? she resentfully asked herself, staring at the tall, undeniably handsome rider with narrowed, flashing hazel eyes. She had successfully managed to put him from her mind, and now here he was, riding nonchalantly up to her and her men and shattering the protective barrier she had erected about her thoughts and emotions!

"Good day to you," Daniel called as he slowed his mount to a walk. "I spotted the smoke and thought I'd

67

ride on over and take a look," he casually explained, drawing the whiskey-colored animal to a halt. He was wearing a sheepskin and leather coat, heavy gray wool trousers, and his black boots. His steely gaze caught Addie's, but, as it had done the previous day, it hastily moved away again. "Mind if I share your fire for a spell?"

The four men surrounding Addie instinctively glanced at their young boss, mildly surprised when she did not respond to the stranger's simple request. Following several moments' silence, the oldest man took it upon himself to answer.

"Not at all," Silas replied with his customary good humor. Then he added, "Might as well have some of this here coffee while you're at it."

"Much obliged," stated Daniel, swinging down lithely from his new, hand-tooled saddle.

"You're not from around these parts, are you, mister?" Clay amiably queried, passing Daniel the tin cup Silas had just filled.

"The name's Daniel Jordan, and I've just recently settled near here." He nodded gratefully at the younger man as he took the cup and immediately raised it to his lips to take a swallow of the hot brew. Addie, meanwhile, resolutely kept her eyes from moving to him. She appeared to have developed a great and sudden interest in the fire, for her gaze never wavered from the dancing flames.

"I'm Clay Miller. This here's Billy Kendrick, Trent Evans, and Silas Fremont," he announced, a quick sweep of his hand including the others he named. "Oh, and this here's our boss, Miss Addie." The tone of his voice noticeably altered when he turned to indicate the silent young woman standing beside him. It was obvious that he held Addie in the highest esteem, a fact not lost upon an inwardly amused Daniel. It was also obvious that the young man knew little about the social graces, for he had introduced the only woman last.

"I'm very glad to make your acquaintance," responded Daniel, smiling briefly at Clay as the two of them shook hands. His smile was considerably slower and broader when he turned to Addie. "I am particularly honored to make your acquaintance, ma'am." He gallantly tipped his hat as he inclined his head in her direction, revealing the thick, wheat-colored hair beneath the protection of his spotless tan Stetson.

Addie was thereupon placed in somewhat of a quandary. If she attempted to ignore him, her men would think it singularly odd and uncharacteristic, for it had always been her way to offer a greeting to any passing stranger, to offer the hospitality that was an unspoken law in Texas. On the other hand, she furiously reasoned with herself, if she responded with an outward display of warmth and friendliness, she knew without a doubt that it would please Daniel Jordan immensely, something she most assuredly did not wish to do! She had no desire to be the source of his smirk of triumphant amusement.

"Mr. Jordan," she finally chose to quietly murmur, nodding curtly in his direction. If her men thought her behavior odd, then so be it!

Daniel's eyes glowed with an unfathomable light as Addie turned her attention back to the fire. He proceeded to exchange more brief smiles and hand-shakes with the other men. Only Trent failed to acknowledge his smile, but nevertheless he wordlessly shook the taller man's hand when it was offered.

"How far from here's your place?" Trent unexpectedly asked a second later, his brown eyes narrowing imperceptibly as he peered at Daniel over the rim of the cup from which he was drinking.

"Not far," Daniel drawled lazily, already anticipating the inevitable questions to follow.

"And just how far it that?" the black-haired man relentlessly probed, prompting Addie to glance at him with a look of puzzlement in her eyes. There was something in Trent's voice, an inexplicable edge that seemed to indicate immediate dislike for the man who had joined them at the fire.

"Say," Billy suddenly interjected, a thoughtful frown on his boyish features, "you ain't by any chance the one . . . I mean, you ain't—"

"If you're trying to ask me if I'm the 'damn Yankee' who bought the Ferguson place," Daniel interrupted with a faintly mocking smile on his face, "then the answer is yes, I am."

Five pairs of eyes stared at him in stunned disbelief. Trent, Billy, Clay, and Silas were taken aback by the stranger's perfunctory willingness to admit to his "crime," while Addie was startled at his rather sardonic, nonchalant treatment of the situation. Didn't he realize he was treading on dangerous ground? she silently wondered. Didn't the infuriating man realize what a terrible mistake he had made in coming to Texas at all?

"Well now," remarked Trent with a short, humorless laugh, "I'm surprised you had the guts to admit it." His eyes narrowed into a menacing squint, and his dark,

70

hawkish features tightened. "We don't need no Yankee son of a bitch on Rolling L land—"

"Trent!" Addie hurried to intervene, her tone sharp and authoritative. "There's to be no trouble," she quietly insisted, her solemn gaze meeting his blazing one. She shot him one last telling glance before rounding on a calm, impassive Daniel and declaring in angry, clipped tones, "It was unwise of you to come here, Mr. Jordan. I think it's best if you move on now."

"It's your land," he responded with a slight, unconcerned nod. Addie bristled beneath his piercing stare then grew even more incensed when he took his time about leaving. She glared at him as he leisurely tossed the remaining trace of coffee from his cup, then offered the cup back to a wide-eyed and speechless Clay. "Miss Addie," he said as he tipped his hat to her again. She was certain that she detected a touch of sarcasm in his deep voice and a secret amusement in his twinkling gray eyes, and her lips tightened into a thin line of displeasure as she watched him turn and saunter away.

He had already mounted up again and was reining his horse about when his gaze caught hers for one charged moment. An invisible current passed between them as they faced one another across the short distance. Addie was dismayed to feel her cheeks flaming, and she could have sworn she heard a soft chuckle escape his lips before he gently spurred his horse and rode away with a maddening lack of haste.

"Well, how do you like that?" Billy muttered with a shake of his head. "If that don't beat all, the way that Yankee comes—"

"I'd prefer that we not discuss Mr. Daniel Jordan,"

71

snapped Addie, the expression on her beautiful face quite stormy. She spun about on her booted heel and marched toward her horse, leaving the four men to stare after her in bewilderment.

"Guess she didn't take to him much," Clay observed with a crooked grin.

"Come on. There's work to be done and time's awastin'," Silas declared with a sudden frown. He, too, was puzzled by Miss Addie's strange behavior, but it was still nobody's business but Miss Addie's. If she felt the need to confide in him, then he'd gladly listen, just as he'd done since she was old enough to talk.

"Damned bluebelly," Trent ground out, kicking snow on the fire as they prepared to leave. Neither Clay nor Billy said another word as they followed Silas to their horses and swung up into the saddles. Soon the four men and one woman were on their way once more, heading farther south in an attempt to find more Rolling L stock.

Addie groaned inwardly as she rode, silently berating herself for allowing Daniel to affect her, for allowing her feelings to get the better of her in front of her men. It was almost as if he had planned the "accidental" encounter! she fumed, tucking the woolen scarf more securely about her neck as she eased up on the reins. The horse beneath her snorted and lowered his head, his rider's tenseness apparently causing him distress.

"Easy boy. Easy," she soothingly murmured, reaching down to pat the animal's smooth neck. Easy, her mind echoed. Her own nerves were in need of such advice. It would do her no good to react with such angry resentment every time she saw Daniel Jordan,

72

for there was no telling how long he was planning to stay.

And she, Adelaide Caton, was bound and determined to make certain that the man who had once broken her heart never again played even a minor role in her life. But, she reflected as a sigh escaped her lips, her determination was going to be sorely tested, for it appeared that Daniel was equally determined to plague her with his disturbing presence.

Five

"I hate to leave you here all alone, honey. Why don't you just come on along with us?" Esther suggested in a soft, persuasive tone, flinging the heavy scarlet cloak about her broad shoulders. Clad in her best two-piece suit of light brown wool, she was looking forward to the day in town with rapidly increasing anticipation, for Silas had promised to allow her the entire afternoon to spend browsing in the handful of shops. The simple fact of their lack of funds would not hinder Esther's enjoyment in the slightest, since she rarely spent a day away from the ranch.

"No, thank you," replied Addie with a warm smile. "There's more than enough to occupy my time here." And, she silently added, it would be a nice change to be alone for a while.

"I was hopin' maybe you'd come along to Turner's and help the boys pick out those new boots you promised them," Esther remarked with a sudden frown, leaving no doubt as to what she thought of Addie's impulsive generosity.

"You and Silas can take care of that for me. Just tell Gil to add them to the list. We've already so much owing, I fail to see how the boots will make that much difference."

"When are you finally gonna let that nice, young Mr. Foster call on you?" the older woman abruptly demanded.

"And when are you finally going to realize that my personal life—" Addie began to admonish for what she told herself must be at least the hundredth time.

"What personal life?" Esther broke in, giving an expressive shake of her kerchief-covered head. "You ain't had no personal life, Miss Addie Caton. And I don't know why you won't let no man call on you!"

"Esther, why must you keep bringing up that same, tired, old subject?" she asked wearily.

"Because it ain't natural for you to keep so much to yourself like you been doin' since long before your daddy passed on."

"It's perfectly natural if it happens to be what I choose to do!"

"Your mama wouldn't like it none," observed Esther, frowning again. "She wanted you to be a lady, like her. What do you think she'd say if she was to see you gone all wild and tryin' to pretend you ain't no female at all—"

"I'm sure Silas is becoming quite impatient by now. You'd best be on your way," Addie coolly interrupted, her temper rising. Wishing to avoid the disagreeable subject Esther was apparently determined to pursue, she turned and began climbing the stairs. She could almost feel the older woman's eyes upon her, and she was relieved a few moments later when she heard the front door of the house close.

Wandering into her room, she heaved a sigh as she sank down upon her bed and stared toward the window. It had continued to snow off and on throughout the night, though the occasional flurries had not as yet deepened into anything like the major storm that was still predicted by some of the old-timers such as Silas. Nevertheless, it was a bitterly cold and dispiriting sort of day, and Addie momentarily regretted her decision to remain at home alone.

It would have pleased Esther to no end if I had told her that I had agreed to allow Gil to escort me to the Christmas dance tomorrow night, she mused with a faint smile. Gil Foster worked for his uncle at the mercantile, and he and Addie had become friends during the past several months since his arrival in town. The two of them often sat together during the Sunday morning services at church, and Gil had frequently tried to persuade Addie to allow him to call upon her at the ranch. But, until now, she had displayed little interest in the young man's persistent attentions. And, she reflected, she had only agreed to attend the dance with him because it was to be the first Christmas celebration in town since before the war.

She knew very little about Gil, save for the fact that he was originally from Tennessee and had been seriously wounded while fighting for the Confederacy. He was a quiet man, only four or five years older than herself, and seemed to be a particularly fine person. Not precisely what one would consider handsome, he was nonetheless attractive, with his light brown hair and deep blue eyes. He was tall and slender, an amiable young man who was already well liked by his

77

fellow townspeople.

If he's so nice, then why on earth don't I feel more pleased and flattered by his attempts to court me? she asked herself in confusion. Have I truly done what Esther accused me of? Have I tried to pretend I am not a woman at all?

"Don't be a blasted fool!" Addie crossly exclaimed, abruptly rising to her feet. Never one given to such soul-searching introspection, she berated herself for wasting time on such nonsense, and she marched back downstairs and into her father's study.

Decorated in an undeniably masculine fashion, the room contained a number of pieces of massive, polished oak furniture. The draperies at the single large window were of deep red velvet, and the colorful rugs scattered about the bare wooden floors had been braided by Esther several years earlier. There were shelves lined with books on either side of the stone fireplace, the very books from which Addie had been taught to read by her beautiful, well-educated mother.

She now hastened to light a fire, anxious to chase the lingering chill from the cramped but intimate interior of the room, a room which still seemed to be dominated by her father's presence. No one could deny the fact that Will Caton was a strong person, she thought with a slight, ironic smile. Even in death, the Rolling L continued to be run the way he would have wanted, the way he had taught his only child to do.

Once the kindling had sparked and the fire began blazing to life, Addie stood and drew the edges of her knitted shawl more closely together. She had taken a bath and washed her hair earlier in the morning, and she was now clad in an old, faded, calico dress that barely resembled the lovely gown it had once been. Her dark, shining hair hung loosely about her shoulders, making her look even younger than her twenty-one years. Addie, however, cared little about her appearance for the moment, for she was planning to spend the remainder of the morning going over the ranch's account books.

Settling herself in the ladder-back chair at her father's large, multi-drawered desk, she opened the thick ledger and impatiently turned the yellowed pages until she came to the place where she had made the last entry. Debits, debits, nothing but debits! she silently complained, scanning the growing list of unpaid expenses. The only credit listed on the page was dated more than a month ago, the last time any Rolling L stock had been sold.

Will Caton had believed in parting with some of his cattle only twice a year, immediately after spring roundup and then just before winter set in. It was his peculiar way of doing business, fondly mused his daughter, but it had kept the Rolling L going year after year nonetheless. But now, she told herself with a rather desperate little sigh, there was no decent market, no way to bring in the amount of capital required to make the ranch prosperous once more.

"What are we going to do?" she wondered aloud, putting the ledger aside as her countenance grew pensive. After no more than a minute had elapsed, she rose to her feet and wandered aimlessly over to the window. Perhaps I should have gone to town with the others after all, she reflected, distractedly fingering the smooth red velvet of the draperies. What good was it going to do her to concentrate on the accounts when it would change nothing?

It puzzled her, this uncharacteristic feeling of restlessness. Though she was not what one would call a starry-eyed optimist, neither was she as pessimistic as she had suddenly appeared to have become. What was troubling her? she asked herself. Was it the ranch's difficulties, or something else?

The answer eluded her as she started to turn away from the window, only to have her attention caught by movement glimpsed out of the corner of her eye. Immediately pressing closer to the window, her widened gaze sharply scanned the grounds in front of the house. She was startled, as well as a little alarmed, when she heard a loud, insistent knock on the door an instant later.

Addie hurried away from the window and into the front entrance hall, pausing briefly to lift down a rifle from the mounted rack on one wall of the study, having been taught that it was always best to be prepared. As she stepped to the door she smiled to herself, for her first thought had been of the Comanches and Kiowas who had long ago terrorized the area. But none of the farmers or ranchers this close to town had been bothered by any of the tribes since before the war, and, besides, she mused, Indians didn't make their presence known by knocking at the front door!

Grasping the rifle in one hand, she unlocked and eased open the heavy wooden door, hearing the hinges creaking softly as she peered around the door's edge. The beautiful hazel eyes widened again, flashing in recognition of the tall man who stood alone upon the weathered step.

"Daniel! What . . . what are you doing here?" she

breathlessly demanded, swinging the door wide open to confront him squarely as a faint, rosy color suffused her astonished features.

"I came to deliver something I had intended to give you the other evening," he stated quietly, his own heart beating wildly. Would he ever stop experiencing such a surge of mingled love and desire whenever he saw her? he wondered with an inward smile. His steely gaze swept up and down her softly curved form, unusually well revealed by the tight calico dress. "Well, aren't you going to ask me inside?" he quipped mockingly, favoring her with a disarming grin.

"How did you know—" she irritably began, only to break off abruptly. She had been going to ask him how he knew she was alone at the ranch, but decided against it. "What is it you claim to be delivering?" she demanded instead, still clasping the rifle in one hand.

"If you've any plans to use that thing," remarked Daniel, nodding to indicate the gun, a light of undisguised merriment in his gray eyes, "then you'd best do it now." He was looking every inch the handsome young rancher this morning, attired in a pair of heavy denim trousers, polished leather boots, a gray flannel shirt that matched the color of his eyes, his sheepskin and leather coat, and the felt hat upon his head. Addie silently cursed herself for the sudden light-headedness she was feeling.

"Will you please just give me whatever it is you came to give me and then take yourself off," she insisted impatiently. She did, however, lower the gun, leaning to prop it in the corner behind the door. Clutching the shawl tightly about her like a shield, she raised her chin a trifle higher, her proud gaze meeting Daniel's with an undisguised challenge reflected in the flashing hazel depths.

"Where are your men, Addie?" he unexpectedly asked, seemingly unaware of the fact that he was still standing in the bitter cold. There was just the ghost of a smile on his face now, and Addie visibly bristled beneath his unwavering stare.

"You knew they were gone, didn't you?" she accused, still refusing to allow him entrance. "You wouldn't have come here if you hadn't known I was alone!"

"I had no idea you were here alone, Addie," he softly denied, his deep voice holding a trace of huskiness. "But, if we are indeed alone, then this would be the perfect opportunity for us to have a talk."

"We've nothing to discuss," Addie stubbornly countered, realizing she was behaving childishly but unable to help it. She began closing the door again, conscious only of the fact that she didn't want to be alone with Daniel, didn't want to talk to him without someone else nearby. She gasped in surprise when he masterfully strode inside, effortlessly forcing the door open before closing it behind him. Addie was helpless to prevent his high-handed actions, but she exclaimed in angry indignation, "How dare you! You have absolutely no right to come barging in here, Daniel Jordan! Get out of my house at once!"

"Not until we've had that talk," he responded with maddening, self-assured calm. Removing his hat, he made it painfully clear to Addie that he intended to stay, no matter what she said to the contrary. She realized bitterly that she had no choice but to hear him out.

"Very well," she haughtily conceded, "what is it you

wish to discuss?" As she unconsciously tossed her head, her chestnut tresses fanned about her like a gleaming, silken curtain, and it was a moment before Daniel answered.

"I was entrusted with a letter for you. As I said, I meant to give it to you the other evening, but things didn't go quite the way I expected." Addie felt unaccountably flustered as he gazed down at her, and she spun about on her heel and moved hastily back into the study, as if she could somehow escape the disturbing look in Daniel's glowing eyes.

"Where is the letter?" she demanded, whirling back around to face him, then catching her breath upon a gasp when she perceived that he was standing mere inches behind her. Towering above her, he once again made her feel smaller, more uncertain of herself, and her anger with him rapidly increased.

"Right here," he murmured, reaching inside his coat and withdrawing an envelope sealed with wax. "It's from my sister, Carrie," he added, watching Addie's face closely.

"Carrie?" she repeated in surprise. Her dearest friend, the friend she had not seen since . . . but no, she wouldn't think of the night she had left St. Louis. She had received a few letters from Carrie during the first months of the war but had never answered any of them. Because Carrie was Daniel's sister, she couldn't bear to be reminded of him, couldn't maintain her friendship with one of his family without agonizing over their painful, bitter separation . . .

"She knows about our marriage, Addie. I told her about it some time ago," Daniel quietly revealed, noting the deep sadness which shadowed her beautiful features. "As soon as she discovered my plans to come here, she insisted upon my delivering this letter to you." The golden firelight danced across Addie's face, casting a shimmering glow onto her dark tresses, and Daniel longed to reach out and draw her to him, longed to erase the pain reflected in her bright eyes. But he exercised admirable restraint, telling himself that now was not the time.

"Is she . . . is she well?" Addie questioned, fighting back the tears which she was determined to deny.

"Well enough," he replied with a brief smile. "You know Carrie. Nothing can destroy her enthusiasm for life." He smiled again, his tanned, rugged countenance appearing younger and more vulnerable, more like the Daniel she had once known. Shaking off such thoughts, she took the letter he held out to her, then seemed to forget all about him as she sank down onto a carved bench near the fire and swiftly tore open the envelope, anxious to survey its contents.

Daniel unbuttoned his coat and shrugged it off, then took a seat in an oversized rocking chair near the bench where Addie sat totally engrossed in the letter. He leaned back and patiently waited, watching the array of varying emotions which played across her face. The burning logs popped and crackled, but the room was otherwise cloaked in an oddly charged silence.

Finally, Addie raised her head. She clasped the letter tightly in one hand as she stared unblinkingly toward the flames.

"How long has Carrie been a widow?" she asked Daniel, her voice barely audible as she continued to face the fire.

"It's been nearly two years now since Alan's death."

So, Addie reflected, Carrie had married that other tall young Cavalry officer, the one who had accompanied Daniel to the dance all those years ago. From what Carrie had written, she and Alan Rogers had shared a deep love for one another until his death. They had been afforded two years together, two years during which they actually spent less than a month as husband and wife.

"But, dearest Addie," Carrie had gone on to say in her letter, "don't pity me. Alan and I considered ourselves much more fortunate than others. At least we were able to spend a few short weeks together. And I would not have traded those brief, precious days for a lifetime with someone else."

Brief, precious days. The words echoed in Addie's mind, for didn't they also describe what she and Daniel had shared before the war had torn them apart?

"Now that my brother has explained things to me, I am no longer so distressed that you answered none of my letters," Carrie wrote near the end of the letter. "I must confess, however, that I was terribly hurt when I heard nothing from you in reply. And I am still unenlightened as to exactly what happened to separate you and Daniel. But you were and will always remain my special friend, Addie. I can only pray that we will be able to see one another again someday. I will also pray that you and Daniel are able to resolve your differences, whatever they are." She had finished by sending her friend warmest regards, then signing the letter, "Your loving sister, Carrie Jordan Rogers."

Sister? Of course, Addie suddenly recalled, Carrie was her sister-in-law. She was, after all, still legally married to Carrie's older brother.

"Carrie is very fond of you, Addie," Daniel quietly remarked, his own gaze moving to the fire. "She mentioned the possibility of a visit to my new ranch some time in the near future."

"Is . . . is the rest of your family well?" Addie murmured, her mind still spinning with thoughts of Carrie.

"My brother, Robert, was fortunate enough to escape injury. We lost another brother-in-law by the name of Jeb Harris, who was married to my sister, Susan. Jeb fought for the Confederacy."

"Your own sister's husband?" she asked in disbelief, finally glancing in his direction.

"Missouri was nearly split in two by opposing views, Addie," explained Daniel, leaning forward to rest his arms upon his knees as he clasped his hands together and met her gaze. "There were a great many who fought for the South."

"But didn't your family, I mean, didn't the rest of you—"

"Hate Jeb for choosing to fight against us?" he finished for her. He slowly shook his head, his handsome face wearing a grim expression as he said, "No, we didn't hate him. He was a good man, a man who followed his own beliefs and principles."

"Just as you followed yours?" she couldn't refrain from demanding, an unmistakable edge to her voice.

Daniel didn't answer but instead rose to his feet and slowly approached her. Addie abruptly stood as well, despising herself once again for the weakness she experienced when he paused directly before her, so close they were almost touching.

"Why didn't you send word to me before I reported for duty, Addie? Why didn't you try to contact me? Was it simply because of my position in the war, because of the stand I had chosen to defend? Was it merely because we suddenly found ourselves on opposite sides of a conflict that should never have been?" The words came tumbling forth from his lips, as if they had been trying to escape for a long time and were now set free. His eyes were gleaming dully, his handsome features solemn as he stared down at her.

"We were enemies," she replied in a voice seemingly devoid of emotion. Her eyes sparkled with unshed tears as she hastily averted her gaze. "I could not change the way I felt any more than you could. As I told you then, I am part of my homeland. And my homeland has been vanquished by you and your comrades. Defeated and broken, but not dead. Never entirely destroyed," she concluded in a hoarse whisper, her eyes mirroring the fire's blaze.

"What of the vows we made to one another four years ago, Addie? Did they mean nothing to you?"

"They meant everything to me!" she feelingly responded, her gaze flying to meet his again.

"Not everything," he quietly disagreed. "Was it your father who taught you to put all else above love, Addie?" he suddenly demanded, his voice growing harsh.

"My father had nothing to do with what happened between us!"

"Didn't he?" Daniel sardonically retorted, one eyebrow raised in a mocking gesture. "Didn't he have something to do with the fact that you neglected your duties as a wife in order to please him, in order to maintain the fierce, fanatical pride in your family's honor?"

"How dare you!" stormed Addie, infuriated almost beyond reason. "How dare you talk about a man you know nothing about! My father was one of the finest men who ever lived, which is a damn sight more than I can say for you, Daniel Jordan! Why, you're nothing more than a...a damned bluebelly, a Yankee bastard!" she lashed out, her temper raging out of control.

"And you, dearest Adelaide, are every inch a woman, in spite of your efforts to deny it!" he ground out then startled her by suddenly grasping her shoulders, his hands tightening upon her soft flesh.

"Let go of me!" she furiously commanded, her own hands raised to push frantically at his broad chest.

"Perhaps it's time someone reminded you what it is to be a woman," Daniel huskily proclaimed, aware that Addie's impassioned struggles were entirely useless against his superior strength.

"It would take a better man than you!" she countered rashly, the chestnut locks tumbling wildly about her flushed face as she twisted and squirmed. She raised her foot to deliver a punishing blow to his booted shin, only to find herself being lifted bodily upward, her feet kicking helplessly as they left the floor.

Daniel imprisoned both of her arms as he yanked her close, holding her against him with one powerful arm while the other clasped her flailing legs and effectively stilled her violent struggles. She gasped in mingled fear and furious indignation as he cradled her like a mere babe, his arms like bands of steel about her outraged softness.

"You've become a wildcat, my love," he appreciatively observed, his voice low and deceptively even, "a beautiful, gloriously untamed wildcat."

"Let go of me, damn you!" she wrathfully commanded, twisting futilely. Her eyes blazed at him, narrowing as they sent almost visible, murderous daggers flying toward him. His head relentlessly lowered and she gasped softly, a scream of protest welling up deep in her throat as his lips triumphantly captured hers.

His kiss, at first hard and bruising, gradually became warm and persuasive, and Addie felt herself overcome by the bewildering sensations which she had long since forgotten. She was shocked at her body's traitorous response as she stilled within Daniel's forceful embrace, all her resistance rapidly melting away with the force of his devastatingly seductive assault.

She soon began returning his tenderly demanding kisses with an answering passion, her soft curves yielding and pressing instinctively closer against his muscular leanness. Her arms were suddenly released, and they moved with a will of their own to entwine about his neck as her lips parted beneath his.

Addie was only dazedly aware of the moment when Daniel gently lowered her to the braided rug in front of the flames which only added heat to their own rapidly escalating desires. She gasped yet again when his lips trailed a fiery path across her face to the slender curve of her silken throat, and it seemed as if his mouth branded her wherever it so provocatively caressed.

Then his hands were at the buttons of her calico bodice, the fabric of which strained across her rounded breasts where the gown had become too tight for her ripening, womanly form. Before she quite knew what was happening, his long fingers had deftly liberated the buttons from their corresponding loops to reveal Addie's full, rose-tipped bosom covered only by the thin white cotton of her chemise.

In that small part of her mind which was still capable of rational thought, Addie desperately realized that she shouldn't be letting Daniel touch her with such intimate boldness, shouldn't allow him to kiss her with his skillful, controlled passion. What was happening to her? she breathlessly wondered, her head in a dizzying whirl.

For four years she had staunchly quelled such deep yearnings, such disturbingly sensual impulses. How could she do this now? How could she degrade herself in such a humiliating manner? After all, though they were still legally married, she was no longer Daniel's true wife. He was the man she had vowed never to allow back into her well-ordered life, that conquering enemy who had never truly loved her!

"No!" she found the strength to protest, frantically clutching at the edges of her bodice as she abruptly pulled herself into a sitting position. Her beautiful, stormy countenance was suffused with a rosy blush as she began to struggle in renewed defiance, battling her own confusing emotions as well as the hands that sought to subdue her once more.

"Addie," Daniel murmured in a deep, vibrant tone, endeavoring to soothe her as she furiously struck out at him with tightly clenched fists.

"Take your hands off me!" she vehemently demanded, wrestling vigorously within his iron grasp. Her breasts swelled above the low, tucked neckline of her chemise, and Daniel's gaze was irresistibly drawn to the sight of her pale, enticingly rounded flesh, his eyes feasting hungrily upon her only partially concealed charms. Addie gasped in embarrassment when she noted the direction of his intense stare, and she jerked violently away from him with a muttered curse, scrambling to her feet and furiously attempting to draw the edges of her bodice more closely together across her heaving breasts.

She had never been in such a furor before, never in the entirety of her young life, and she could only stand proudly, imperiously erect for several long moments as she searched in vain for the proper words with which to give vent to her raging anger. Refusing to admit that at least a tiny portion of her wrath should be directed toward herself, she glared venomously across at him as he slowly climbed to his feet and stared wordlessly down at her, his gray eyes filled with an unfathomable light.

"Get out of my house!" she finally spat, her rising voice not quite steady. She trembled with the force of what she told herself was her hatred for Daniel Jordan.

"I'm terribly sorry to have wounded your pride, Addie," he declared in a decidedly unapologetic manner, the faint smile which was now in evidence on his handsome countenance causing her to experience the powerful urge to slap his clean-shaven, sun-bronzed cheek. It was as if he had read her mind, for he said an instant later, "I'd strongly advise against any further physical contact on your part, for it would only serve to compel me to respond in an equally physical manner."

"Oh, how I hate you!" fumed Addie.

"Only a few short minutes ago you were politely

inquiring after my family's health," he noted wryly, finding it considerably difficult to refrain from touching her when her spirited beauty was so alluringly heightened by her fury. "You're a strong, passionate woman, Adelaide Caton Jordan, and you need a strong, passionate man to tame you, to teach you—"

"I need no man! And most particularly, I do not need you!" Addie ground out, whirling around now and flouncing from the room, her calico skirts rustling in soft accompaniment to her angry movements as she turned the corner and disappeared back into the entrance hall. She marched to the front door, wrenched it open, then called out, "Either you leave my house this very minute, Mr. Jordan, or I shall indeed put this rifle to good use!" Snatching the gun from its resting place in the corner, she once again held it defensively in one hand.

It was only an instant later when Daniel appeared. His eyes gleamed almost savagely as he swiftly crossed the distance in long, purposeful strides. Addie's hazel eyes grew round as saucers when he advanced upon her with a set look to his face, a look that definitely signaled danger.

"What the devil do you think you're doing?" she fiercely demanded, frowning darkly when he reached out and took hold of the rifle.

"You don't need a gun to keep me away from you," he muttered tightly, easily wrenching the weapon from her defiant grasp as she indignantly protested his actions. "You've already erected more than enough barriers between us without the need of any outside assistance!" Returning the rifle to its resting place behind the opened door, he faced Addie again, his warm gray eyes boring into her widened hazel ones. "We both know why I've come to Texas, Addie. What's going to happen is inevitable. You might as well face the truth now." With those startling, mysteriously foreboding words, he took his leave, striding out into the winter morning with his hat and coat clutched in one hand.

Addie stood framed in the doorway, unmindful of the fact that the cold wind was sweeping over her, and she watched as Daniel donned his coat, replaced the hat atop his head, then swung up into the saddle of the horse he had left tied to a post. It appeared he never spared her so much as a glance as he reined about and rode away, heading toward the town which lay only a few miles to the east.

Finally, she took a step backward and slammed the door with resounding force. A most unladylike oath escaped her lips as she spun about and swept angrily into the study once more, moving to a position near the fireplace, where she stared unseeingly into the golden flames.

Daniel's last words spun about in her head, seizing control of her tumultuous thoughts. She was totally confused as to their meaning and even more puzzled by the fact that she had merely stood there listening to them without reacting with the fiery response she had intended for their speaker.

Why had he come to Texas? Why had he purchased the very ranch which bordered hers? There was one thing of which she was certain, and that was the fact that he had done it for a specific reason. Was she, herself, the reason? Had Daniel truly come all that way, perhaps bought property he didn't even want, just so that he could be near her?

But then, she attempted to reason with herself, there could be no truth to that possibility, for Daniel Jordan didn't love her. And, her mind insisted, she didn't love him. What had once been between them was now long buried, buried in the past where it belonged. Their love—if they had ever truly loved each other—had long since been destroyed. So why had Daniel come?

"Damnation!" she quietly muttered, sinking down onto the bench. When her gaze fell upon the braided rug before the fire, her cheeks flamed with bright color. Humiliation washed over her yet again as she recalled what she now considered her wanton behavior, and she became even more distressed when she perceived the way her unbuttoned bodice still gaped to reveal a goodly expanse of her rounded bosom.

Jumping up from the bench, she ran from the study and up the stairs to her room. She hastily peeled off the calico dress and vigorously tossed it aside, watching with narrowed eyes as the faded gown landed in a heap on the polished wooden floor.

Much later in the day, long after she had exchanged a loose-fitting woolen dress for the tight calico, Addie was still plagued with anguished memories of the way Daniel had kissed her and the way she had surrendered following only a token resistance. And, although she despised herself for her weakness, she couldn't help softly touching a finger to her lips, lips which still seemed to tingle from the hard pressure of Daniel Jordan's warm, demanding mouth.

Six

Addie's fingers lightly smoothed the folds of the lavender silk, her touch lingering on the delicate fabric with something akin to wonderment. Brocaded in gray velvet, with short, gathered sleeves, full double skirts, and a scooped, rather daring neckline which displayed a fashionably bared bosom and shoulders, the exquisite ball gown had been neatly tucked away within the protective confines of a large trunk these past several years, along with the other beautiful dresses and various accessories she had worn before the war. All of these treasures had been given to her by Will Caton following a sudden attack of conscience he'd suffered shortly after her seventeenth birthday.

Her undergarments, which were equally as fine and delicate as the lavender silk, had also been retrieved from the trunk. The chemise was edged in spidery lace, the pantalettes trimmed with dainty ruffles, and the multitude of starched petticoats, which were now substituted for the unwieldy crinoline she had once worn with the gown, were the snowiest white muslin and also edged with frills. Since her waist had remained small, she had no need of a corset, a fact for which she now gave silent thanks.

A transformation had certainly taken place, she mused, uncertain as to whether or not she was pleased with the results. Her shining tresses were massed just slightly above the nape of her neck in a flattering array of long curls which cascaded onto the creamy flesh of her shoulders. It was an infinitely more feminine style than she usually affected. In fact, she silently observed, releasing her breath upon a faint sigh, the entire effect was undeniably feminine. She frowned, however, as she critically eyed the way the gown molded her soft curves to perfection.

"Might as well be one of those painted doxies in town!" muttered Addie in growing trepidation, unjustly comparing herself to the flock of "soiled doves" who had recently taken up residence in one of Fort Worth's former saloons. Why, she didn't look like herself at all. It was as if a stranger stood in her place, a beautiful young lady who appeared to belong anywhere but out on a struggling cattle ranch!

Why should I be taking such pains with the way I look tonight? she silently queried, drifting away from the mirror. After all, it wasn't exactly as if she hoped to impress anyone, was it?

She certainly harbored no secret romantic designs when it came to her escort for the evening. Gil Foster was a very likable young man, but it wouldn't have mattered if he had been the most charming fellow in all of Texas. She was still a married woman, she dully reminded herself, and she wasn't free to become involved with anyone else. At least not until you've filed for and been granted a divorce, that nagging voice in the back of her mind interjected.

"Miss Addie?" Esther's raised voice broke in to draw her out of her silent reverie. Addie hastily opened the bedroom door, calling downstairs in response.

"Yes, Esther? What is it?"

"That nice, young Mr. Foster's just driven up! You'd best be gettin' a move on!" The black woman was poised near the foot of the staircase, grinning broadly to herself as she peered out through the curtains at the small window beside the front door. Addie sighed audibly and shook her head as she stepped from her room onto the upstairs landing, a look of annoyance evident on her slightly flushed countenance.

"You'd think this was the first time a gentleman had ever come calling!" she irritably muttered, her hands gently clutching the folds of her gathered skirts to lift them out of the way as she carefully descended the staircase.

"Well, it's the first gentleman's come callin' around here in many a day!" responded Esther, turning to face her young mistress now. She drew in her breath with a gasp, and her brown eyes widened in obvious amazement at the startling sight they beheld.

"What's the matter?" Addie sternly demanded, unconsciously tugging at the scooped bodice of the silk dress in an effort to cover a bit more of her exposed flesh.

"Why, honey, if you ain't almost the very picture of your mama!" She beamed in satisfaction as her eyes swept up and down the younger woman's slender

97

curves, so flawlessly and stylishly attired. "I never thought I'd see the day when you wore that dress again!"

"There is nothing special about this particular gown," Addie stiffly remarked, wishing she'd never decided to wear the blasted thing. She mused that she was little better than a fool, a primped and puffed up sparrow who was trying to look like a peacock! True, she had worn such finery before the war, but it had been done under protest even then, and only to please her father. But her father was gone and the war was over, so why in heaven's name had she decided to make such a spectacle of herself? she wondered, her uncharacteristic nervousness rapidly increasing.

"Just wait till all the folks in town see what you been hidin' all these years." Esther spoke with a soft chuckle. Addie opened her mouth to offer a suitable retort, but Gil's knock upon the front door silenced her. She watched as Esther hastened to open the door.

"Good evenin' to you, Mr. Foster," said Esther as she stepped aside to admit him.

"Good evening, Mrs. Fremont," he cordially returned, sweeping his hat from his head as he stepped inside the comforting warmth of the house. His blue eyes softened as he turned his gaze upon Addie, who still stood immobile at the foot of the staircase. "Good evening, Miss Addie," he ventured, apparently not at all amazed to see her dressed as she was. He smiled warmly in her direction, prompting Addie's nervousness to flee as she returned his smile. He was so nice and attractive, she thought, eyeing the tall, slender young man in his sober black suit. Not the sort of man to make her heart do flip-flops, but there was more to life than that, she staunchly concluded.

"Good evening, Gil." She turned toward an astutely observant Esther, shooting the older woman a meaningful glance.

"Well, it's high time Silas and me were gettin' ourselves to that party of ours," Esther suddenly announced, smoothing down the skirts of her slightly faded red calico dress. "You and Miss Addie have yourselves a real good time," she said to Gil as she started ambling out of the entrance hall, pausing momentarily in the doorway of the kitchen to bestow another irrepressible grin upon Addie. The younger woman responded with an imperceptible narrowing of her hazel eyes and felt relieved when she and Gil were finally left alone.

"I hope you don't mind my saying so, Miss Addie, but you're looking exceptionally well this evening," proclaimed Gil. His blue eyes sparkled with visible admiration. "I'm very honored that you consented to attend the dance with me."

"We might as well get something settled between us right now, Gil Foster," she unexpectedly asserted, her chestnut curls bouncing riotously as she gave a brief nod. Her steady gaze met his rather puzzled one squarely, and there was a faint smile playing about her lips as she said, "There's no need for you to bother with flattery and compliments and the like with me. I can assure you that I'm not the sort of woman who's impressed with the honeyed words a man speaks! I believe the two of us have already developed a close enough friendship to dispense with such tiresome amenities, and I should like to think that we might continue to be honest with one another."

Gil appeared somewhat startled at first, but it was only a matter of seconds before he smiled and shook his head in appreciative amusement. His blue eyes twinkled merrily at her as he asked with a quiet laugh, "Has anyone ever told you that you're an extraordinary lady?"

"Not often enough, I dare say," she retorted with a soft chuckle of her own. Stepping forward, she lifted her woolen cloak down from the pegged hall tree near the door. Gil was there beside her in an instant to help her on with the dark blue capelike garment that was hooded and had wide pagoda sleeves. Addie was well covered by the soft, flowing wool as she and Gil stepped outside into the frosty evening air, their breaths fogging in the prickling cold.

They were soon on their way to town, sitting companionably close together in the buggy Gil had borrowed from his uncle. Several snuggling layers of blankets lay across their laps to aid in protecting them from the chilling wind, a wind that was beginning to increase in velocity with each passing hour.

"I do believe we're going to have that storm Silas has been predicting," remarked Addie, glancing up speculatively at the sky. She pulled her hood down a bit, more toward her face. Her cheeks were rosy with the cold, and there was a thin coating of tiny snowflakes glistening on the dark blue surface of her cloak.

"Do you have very harsh winters here?" inquired Gil, snapping the reins lightly across the horse's back. His hands were encased in warm leather gloves, and his pleasant features were also faintly reddened by the cold.

"Sometimes, though not what the Yankees would consider harsh, I'm sure." The image of Daniel's handsome, mocking face flashed into her mind, and she cursed herself for thinking of him. Forcing a bright smile to her lips, she declared, "I suppose your winters varied in Tennessee, too. You know, my parents were from Tennessee."

"Were they?" responded Gil in mild surprise. "I'd like it very much if you'd tell me something about them. It seems that your father's name is still frequently mentioned in town."

"That's because he lived here for so long. I think he knew practically everyone within fifty miles," she offered with a brief smile. "He first came to Texas to fight with Sam Houston back in '36, but it wasn't until several years later that we settled here." She silently recalled the story she'd heard so many times, the story of how Will Caton had settled on a farm in East Texas after that first war, on the five hundred acres the Republic had awarded him for his service. And he didn't even meet the beautiful, well-bred Lilah Ashford until he returned to Tennessee for a visit some six years later.

"How was it you and your family came to live here?"

"Papa left Mama and me alone on the farm—with Silas and Esther, of course—while he took himself off to fight against Mexico in '48. When he came back, we discovered that he had already made his decision to move us to Fort Worth, though there wasn't actually a town here at the time. He had managed to find a buyer for the farm and had already acquired the first few hundred acres of the Rolling L."

101

"This area must have been rather wild back then."

"It most certainly was," she confirmed with a soft laugh.

"I suppose the Fremonts have been of considerable help to you since the death of your father," he observed, frowning slightly in concern as he took note of the thickening snow flurry.

"In all likelihood the ranch would have gone under by now if not for them."

"They're fine people," opined Gil, "very fine people. Were they your slaves before the war?"

"They were born into slavery but were freed by my father immediately after his marriage to my mother." The Ashfords, she reminisced to herself, had been of the landed gentry. Her mother had told her of the magnificent plantation near Memphis that had been her girlhood home. The Catons, on the other hand, had been humble dirt farmers. Lilah's parents had forbidden their beloved daughter to marry Will Caton, but she had defied them. Silas and Esther, who had been with the Ashfords since before Lilah's birth, were given to the newlyweds by Addie's grandfather, who claimed he wanted no daughter of his to begin a new life with nothing to her name. The Ashfords, however, had given them nothing else.

"Was your father opposed to slavery?"

"He detested the notion of one human being owning another."

"I see," Gil murmured thoughtfully. Following a few moments' silence, he asked, "Have you ever visited any of your kinfolk back in Tennessee?"

"No. All of my grandparents died many years ago. And my parents chose not to maintain contact with any

102

of the other family, not at all surprising under the circumstances, I suppose."

"You mean you've never even met any of your relatives?" he questioned in disbelief.

"Only one—a cousin of my mother's who lives in St. Louis. I visited her for a short time while attending school there a few years ago." Her husband's face swam before her eyes once more, and she unconsciously stiffened beside Gil.

"Are you cold?" His eyes mirrored his genuine concern.

"A little," she hastily replied, mentally consigning the vision of Daniel Jordan to the devil.

"It won't be long now. We're almost there," Gil assured her, flicking the reins again in order to increase the horse's pace. "I come from a very large family," he then told her. "I can't remember a time when there weren't at least a dozen children running about my mother's house!"

"And are they all still back in Tennessee?"

"Those who are still alive," he answered quietly, his attractive countenance growing solemn.

Addie wanted to ask him to elaborate upon his intriguing statement, but the two of them suddenly glimpsed the lights of the town in the near distance, and their conversation turned to the evening's celebration.

There were more than a dozen wagons and buckboards in front of the old wooden courthouse, the unfinished stone building standing empty and roofless beside its more simple counterpart. Gil assisted Addie in alighting from the buggy then handed the reins to Kyle Townsend, whose father owned the town's only livery stable. The animals were to be sheltered there while their owners attended the long-awaited holiday dance.

"Looks like we're gonna have a full barn tonight," remarked Kyle, nodding a greeting in Addie's direction.

"I'll save a dance for you," she responded with a teasing smile.

The boy colored and countered with a begrudging grin, murmuring, "Aw, hell, Miss Addie, I ain't gonna come to no dance!"

"You shouldn't speak to Miss Addie that way, Kyle," Gil gently admonished. Addie linked her arm through his as they began moving toward the doorway, but she spared a conspiratorial wink for Kyle before disappearing inside.

Pausing in a small room just within the brightly lit building, Gil helped Addie remove her cloak before drawing off his own coat and hat. He hung their things beside other such garments on one of the numerous pegs high on the wall, then he turned back to Addie to gallantly inquire, "Shall we proceed inside to the festivities?"

"I . . . I suppose so," she replied uneasily, her earlier apprehension returning to plague her again. She hastily tugged at the revealing bodice once more, oblivious to her escort's suppressed amusement at her actions, then proudly lifted her head and strolled into the main room beside Gil.

The fast-paced music, enthusiastically played by four older men on their fiddles and harmonicas, drifted outward over the handful of couples who were promenading about the dance floor. Addie noted that the room had been cleared of nearly all its furnishings in preparation for the celebration, and there were lamps hanging everywhere to provide the needed illumination. Several tables were covered with gaily colored gingham and calico tablecloths and laden with a mouth-watering assortment of food and drink. A huge, iron, potbellied stove gave off a comforting warmth that helped chase most of the chill from the spacious room. The bare wooden floors had been cleaned and polished, and still smelled pleasantly of lemon oil and beeswax.

More than a dozen of Addie's friends and neighbors stood in the far corner, chatting and drinking punch together. However, nearly every head in the room turned the moment Addie stepped inside with Gil. She stood with her beautiful face faintly blushing, and her hand instinctively tightened on Gil's arm as she felt so many pairs of eyes upon her.

"Merciful heavens! Is that Miss Addie?" a young woman leaned close to whisper to her speechless partner. Attired in a simple dress of homespun cotton, she gazed in awe at the silken finery the usually plainly clad Adelaide Caton was wearing.

"Why, I'll be damned! Ain't she the prettiest thing!" a masculine voice appreciatively declared above the strains of "Sweet Betsy From Pike." There were several accompanying comments as Addie moved forward onto the dance floor with Gil, painfully aware of the fact that she looked exceedingly different from the Miss Addie her friends had previously known.

"I don't suppose they'd have stared any less if I had come traipsing in here without a stitch on," she muttered with more than a touch of displeasure, her body stiff within Gil's arms as he began whirling her about in the movements of the dance. She noted the way everyone's openly astonished gazes were still fastened upon the two of them.

"They're just a bit surprised, that's all." Gil spoke comfortingly, smiling down at her. "You must admit, you don't look quite the same tonight."

"May I take that to mean that you and everyone else in this room think my appearance tonight is some sort of miraculous improvement?" There was a slight edge to her voice, and she immediately felt ashamed for snapping at the kindly young man.

"Not at all," he amiably disagreed, his steps graceful and well executed. "You happen to be a very beautiful woman, Miss Addie. It matters little what sort of clothing you choose to wear."

Addie smiled benignly up at him, once again telling herself that here was a nice young man, a true Southern gentleman who would make some fortunate girl a wonderful husband. *Husband,* her mind perversely echoed, presenting another perplexing vision of a tall, handsome man with wheat gold hair. Why did she have to think of him at a time like this?

The dance ended shortly thereafter, and Gil escorted Addie over to join the group in the corner. Ike Henry was there with his wife, as was Gil's uncle, Jonas Turner. Thomas Bowman and John Hayward were also in attendance, along with a number of men and women, most of whom Addie had known for several years. Following a long-established custom, the children were enjoying their own celebration at the nearby church.

"You certainly look lovely tonight, my dear," Ella Henry remarked as Gil and Addie approached. A

106

petite woman of perhaps fifty years, her thick hair was still as dark as a raven's wing. She stepped forward to give Addie an affectionate hug.

"Thank you, Ella," murmured Addie, her tenseness beginning to dissipate now.

"Will would be proud to see you looking so pretty, Miss Addie," added Ike, his bearded face smiling fondly down at her.

"Seems that you're the luckiest man here tonight, Gil," declared John, his wife nudging him sharply in mock affront. Harriet Hayward was as thin and fair as John was dark and heavyset, and the two of them were both generally kind and good-natured.

Addie was greeted warmly by everyone, as was her escort. She and Gil were talking and laughing easily with others in the group when a sudden hush fell upon the heretofore loudly jovial assembly. Even the four musicians ceased their lively efforts, prompting the puzzled gazes of the nearly one hundred people in the room to fix upon them before swiftly darting to the uninvited newcomer who had sauntered forward to pause in the doorway.

"What the hell—" Ike furiously muttered, breaking off as his wife's hand moved upon his arm. Although Ella and most of the others at the gathering had never met the tall, gray-eyed man, they were not totally unaware of his identity. Nearly everyone, it seemed, had already been privy to a detailed description of the Yankee by this time.

Addie's beautiful face paled as she stared toward the doorway. It took only a brief moment for Daniel's searching gaze to find her. They stared at each other across the crowded, almost totally silent room, their eyes irrevocably drawn to one another while Addie struggled to regain her breath. Dear Lord, she frantically thought, what now?

"He's got no right to be here," Thomas gruffly decreed. He and Ike and John nodded at each other in silent, purposeful agreement, then began striding forward to confront the intruder. Their wives judged it wisest to refrain from attempting to stop them, and the crowd instinctively cleared a path for the grim-faced men, who were now joined by at least a dozen others, as they made their way across the dance floor.

Addie tore her gaze away from Daniel, watching with breathless anticipation as the menacing group of men approached him with dangerous calm. Her mind was spinning, her pounding heart assailed by a myriad of tumultuous, conflicting emotions.

Why does he stand there as if nothing is happening? she wondered, almost angrily eyeing the way Daniel remained motionless and apparently unconcerned. What had prompted him to place himself in such unnecessary danger? she asked herself in stunned bewilderment.

A low murmur could be heard rising from the crowd now, but Addie was oblivious to everything but the sight of Daniel standing fearlessly in the doorway, the look on his tanned, rugged face inscrutable. She vaguely noted the expertly tailored dark suit he wore, the perfect whiteness of his linen shirt, the careless necktie below his snowy collar. He had never appeared more handsome, or more thoroughly disturbing. The memory of his powerful arms about her, of his demanding lips upon hers, flashed unbidden to her mind, and she felt an involuntary shiver run the length of her spine.

"Are you going to leave peacefully, or do we have to use force?" Ike Henry ground out with barely controlled rage. He had paused mere inches away from Daniel as the other men formed an intimidating semicircle behind their leader. All of them glared at the Yankee with ruthless intent reflected in their narrowed eyes, but he appeared unimpressed.

"It was my understanding that this was to be a celebration of Christmas, an affair open to anyone in this area who cared to attend," Daniel replied with studied nonchalance.

"It's a celebration for friends and neighbors in these parts. But not for you," Ike reiterated.

"I happen to be a neighbor," the younger man casually pointed out. His gaze met Addie's once again, and there was a ghost of a smile curving his lips as he stared at her across the room.

You blasted idiot! she silently berated him, her hazel eyes flashing expressively. Don't you have any idea of the trouble you've gotten yourself into by coming here tonight?

Feelings ran high against the former enemy, and most Texans had not yet put aside their prejudices. They had been beaten down for four long years and would continue to see Daniel Jordan only as the hated intruder they deemed him to be this night, reflected Addie. She released a slightly ragged sigh, causing Gil to glance down at her with a worried frown. He himself was more than a trifle concerned at the turn of events, and he pondered the potentially explosive situation. His hand briefly pressed Addie's arm before he suddenly began making his own way forward through

109

the crowd.

Addie stared at his retreating back in surprise, wondering what he hoped to accomplish by interfering. She knew with a certainty that he wouldn't become a part of the threatening group, for he had never joined them in any of their similar activities before.

If something didn't happen to stop Ike and the others, there was every possibility that Daniel Jordan would come to physical harm. And that, she realized as the startling truth dawned on her, she could not allow to happen, even if it meant publicly defying her friends.

"I'll tell you one last time, Jordan. Either you leave now or we'll damn well make you leave!" gritted Ike, his hands doubling into fists at his sides. The men behind him took a step forward, but Daniel continued to display nothing but a quietly determined calm.

"I have no intention of leaving yet," he stated, his voice deep and resonant and steady. There was no fear in his eyes, only a certain resignation.

The couples in the room stared at him in mingled anger and confusion, for his behavior was totally disconcerting. What did the fool Yankee hope to gain by facing up to so many? they wondered.

"Then you'd best prepare yourself, you addlepated son of a bitch!" one of the men with Ike growled. He and the others had just begun advancing on Daniel when Gil Foster maneuvered his way to the front, taking a defensive stance beside Ike.

"There's no call for violence," Gil firmly contested. His words were met with a rumble of disapproval from the crowd of onlookers. Addie walked slowly toward the doorway now as well, acutely conscious of the way Daniel's steely gaze was riveted upon her as she drew closer.

"This don't concern you, Foster!" Thomas Bowman wrathfully insisted.

"Just move aside," commanded Ike.

"Can't you see that what you are doing is wrong?" Gil attempted to reason with the group of men, men whose antagonism and hatred shone from their eyes and suffused their faces with dull color. "This man hasn't done any harm by coming here," he said, nodding his head to indicate the tall, silent Yankee. He didn't even know the man, but it mattered little to him. What mattered was trying to prevent needless bloodshed. There had been more than enough of that these past several years.

Daniel's eyes narrowed a fraction as his gaze moved to the slender young man who had apparently appointed himself the voice of sanity. The fellow had been with Addie when Daniel first walked in and saw her, so it was logical to assume that the two of them were together. That thought provoked a surge of jealousy to well up deep within him, though he mastered his emotions and focused his attention on the unpleasant situation at hand, a situation he had fully expected.

Addie made her way to Gil's side, noting the unfathomable glow in Daniel's eyes before she swiftly averted her gaze from his. Gil glanced down at her in mingled surprise and disapproval, but she ignored him as she whirled about to face her many friends.

"Gil Foster's right!" she declared with a challenging look on her beautiful young face. Her words prompted startled gasps and expressions of puzzled amazement from the numerous people in the crowd who were astonished to hear Miss Addie speaking in defense of the Yankee.

111

"Now, now, Miss Addie, you'd best just step aside," Thomas suggested, not unkindly.

"Why?" she shot back at him, her color high, her hazel eyes blazing. "So that you and the others can do something that you'll only live to regret? I don't want this man here any more than you do," she feelingly proclaimed, still refusing to look at Daniel, "but that doesn't mean I want any of you to force him to leave!" She was, however, experiencing a strong inclination to use force against him herself.

"Haven't we had enough of hatred and violence?" Gil quietly addressed the crowd, a faintly perceptible sadness shining forth from his blue eyes. "We've all come here tonight to celebrate Christmas, haven't we? Why don't we try to remember the significance of what is supposed to be a peaceful celebration?" A long period of silence followed, during which Ike and the men continued to focus their belligerent gazes upon Daniel. But, they did not make any further moves in his direction, and Addie breathed an inward sigh of relief.

Harriet and Ella and several other wives appeared to take Gil's words to heart, for they now approached their husbands and stood waiting expectantly. The musicians struck up another familiar tune, and it wasn't long before the majority of the dancers had resumed their activities, their eyes still frequently moving to the group near the doorway.

"Come on, Ike. You haven't even danced with your own wife this evening," said Ella, a silent plea in her eyes as her husband visibly hesitated. Finally, he muttered an unintelligible oath and reluctantly led his wife onto the dance floor. The other men followed his example, leaving only Gil and Addie with Daniel.

112

"I think it's highly advisable that you take your leave now," stated Gil as he turned to face the man who was several inches taller than himself. Daniel's handsome face wore a faint smile as he responded in a voice brimming with sardonic humor.

"Much obliged."

"Why don't you come to your senses and get out of here?" Addie fairly hissed as she rounded on him, her eyes flashing angrily up at him. "You're a fool for ever daring to show your face here tonight, Daniel Jordan!"

"Do you know this man, Miss Addie?" asked Gil in surprise, a slight frown creasing his attractive brow.

"The lady and I are neighbors," Daniel explained before Addie could answer, his eyes never leaving her fierily blushing countenance.

"Are you ever going to leave?" she quietly raged at him, her hazel glare sending invisible daggers at his head.

"Not until I get what I came for," he replied with another hint of a smile, his own eyes glowing like molten steel.

"And just what is it you came for?" demanded Addie. Gil peered closely at her before transferring his gaze to Daniel. The music swelled to a crescendo at that point, but Addie heard him reply in a low voice that was barely audible.

"The motive for my presence here is a simple one. I came to dance with my charming neighbor."

"You . . . you must be out of your mind!" she gasped in scornful disbelief.

"Perhaps," murmured Daniel, smiling with what she conceived to be smug audacity.

The two of them appeared to have momentarily

forgotten Gil's presence, but they were reminded of it an instant later when he quietly asserted, "We'd best be getting back to the dance, Miss Addie." He was feeling oddly discomfited by the brief exchange between Addie and the Yankee, though he told himself the source of his uneasiness must surely be nothing more than concern for the fact that the three of them were attracting unwanted attention. Cupping his hand beneath Addie's elbow, he was intent upon leading her away, but she appeared to relegate him to oblivion yet again as she turned back to confront Daniel once more, uttering in a low, furious tone, "Why don't you cease this ridiculous game of yours and get out of here?"

"Not until you've granted me a dance." His face wore an expression of unflappable determination, and his eyes were alight with fearless resolve. Addie opened her mouth to offer him a scathing refusal, but Gil swiftly intervened at this point.

"I believe the lady has already made her wishes known. In order to avoid further trouble, I suggest you forget your intentions of joining in the celebration and take yourself off." His hand applied gentle but firm pressure to Addie's elbow as he turned away, but she surprised him by jerking her arm free, her eyes flashing in annoyance.

"I don't believe the lady wishes to go with you," Daniel mockingly observed.

"I'm not going to dance with you, damn it!" Addie whispered fiercely, her silken skirts rustling softly as she whirled to glare up at him again. "Now get the hell out of here!"

"I'll leave on one condition," he countered, folding his muscular arms against his broad chest, his sun-

114

bronzed features appearing even more golden above the whiteness of his linen shirt.

"You're not in a position to be making demands," Gil broke in, his displeasure with the turn of events rapidly deepening. He had spoken in the man's defense, but he suddenly found himself wishing he had not.

"And just what the devil is that condition?" Addie inquired with biting sarcasm.

"I'll take my leave this very moment," revealed Daniel, his warm gaze sliding over her with intimate boldness before meeting the multicolored fire of her eyes, "if you'll go with me."

Seven

His words were followed by a highly charged silence. Addie, who was initially flabbergasted by his amazing proposition, could feel her face coloring as her temper flared to a dangerous level. Gil, on the other hand, appeared to be thoroughly bewildered at what was taking place. Only Daniel maintained his outwardly impassive composure, the merest hint of a smile playing about his lips as he waited for the furious reaction he knew Addie would provide.

"You must be insane!" she raged, finally giving voice to her anger. Her dark curls danced about the silken curve of her shoulders as she lifted her chin in almost haughty defiance, her firmly rounded breasts heaving with indignation as they swelled above the edge of her scooped bodice. Gil took a step forward as if to lay hands upon Daniel and grimly murmured, "You've gone too far!" His attractive features mirrored his own increasing ire, and Addie swiftly intervened, placing her hand upon his arm, her fingers tightening in a silent request for restraint.

"You know that what you ask is impossible!" she protested to Daniel in a vibrant tone, her voice scarcely heard above the music. "Why are you doing this?" she went on to demand in a hoarse whisper.

"Either you come with me, or I remain," he reiterated complacently, ignoring her question and thereby prompting her to release an angrily impatient sigh.

His words and actions combined to throw her into a quandary, for she was well aware of the fact that if he remained at the dance much longer there would be, in all likelihood, further trouble with Ike and the other men. But, she hastily reasoned with herself, if she agreed to go with him— No, she wouldn't allow her thoughts to turn to anything other than the unpleasant situation at hand!

"Miss Addie, I suggest that we return to the dance now," Gil broke in on her dizzying contemplation, his voice deep and commanding. "And you, sir," he said, addressing Daniel as he valiantly attempted to quell the rising tide of fury threatening to overpower his better judgment, "would do well to remember that it is considered particularly ungentlemanly to attempt to use a lady to extricate yourself from a difficulty of your own making!" His eyes widened then quickly narrowed when Daniel merely laughed softly, and Addie hastened to intervene once more.

"Very well, Mr. Jordan," she unexpectedly capitulated, visibly startling her escort, "you may take me home."

"Miss Addie—" began Gil, frowning deeply.

"I'm terribly sorry, Gil," she declared sincerely, "but this is the only solution." She squared her shoulders and raised her proud chin a trifle higher as she marched resolutely past the two men, her full skirts gently swaying as she disappeared through the doorway. Gil paused a moment to direct a narrowed, telling look at Daniel before taking off after Addie.

Daniel Jordan smiled inwardly, his gray eyes glowing with secret triumph as he turned and followed. The musicians took a welcome break a short time later, and the talk amongst the revelers centered on the puzzling scene enacted by Miss Addie, Jonas Turner's nephew, and the Yankee.

"I cannot allow you to do this," Gil insisted as Addie flung her cloak about her shoulders.

"I told you, it's the only way." She heaved a sigh as she gazed up at him, catching sight of Daniel out of the corner of her eye. "He's simply going to drive me home. Esther and Silas will probably be there by now," she pointedly remarked, her eyes glancing sideways to make certain Daniel had heard. He responded with a slight inclination of his head in her direction, one eyebrow raised in mocking unconcern. Her face wore a mutinous expression as she watched him don his own coat and hat.

"I think it would be better if you didn't involve yourself in this matter, Miss Addie," advised Gil. "But, in any case, I'm going to come with you," he asserted, reaching for his coat now as well.

"Don't be absurd!" retorted Addie. "There's no sense in your driving all the way back out to the ranch under the circumstances. I'll be perfectly safe, Gil," she reassured him, smiling briefly up into his visibly anxious countenance. "Please feel free to call upon me again soon." Bestowing one last warm smile upon him, she headed for the front door, tugging the hood of her cloak upward to rest upon her shining curls. Daniel began moving wordlessly after her, but a darkly scowling Gil momentarily blocked his path.

"Simply because I didn't want to stand by and watch you set upon by a bloodthirsty mob doesn't mean I'll allow you to get away with anything like this ever again!" he tersely warned. "And if you dare to behave in an unfitting manner—"

"The lady doesn't belong to you," Daniel curtly interrupted, his handsome features looking quite grim.

Catching sight of the way the two men stood glaring militantly at one another, Addie muttered a curse and said, "If we're going to leave, Mr. Jordan, then let's be on our way!" She flung open the door and stepped outside, shivering at the blast of cold air which met her with such unexpected force. Daniel's eyes glittered dangerously before he abruptly strode away as well, leaving Gil to stare after them in furious, helpless frustration.

"Wait here," Daniel instructed, neither receiving nor expecting a response as he crossed the street to retrieve his horse from the livery stable. Addie remained mulishly silent when he returned to hitch the animal to the rather dilapidated buckboard he had discovered in the barn on his new property.

When he started forward to assist her into the weathered, snow-covered conveyance, she gathered the voluminous folds of her skirts and petticoats and unceremoniously scrambled up to the seat by herself. There she sat, staring stonily ahead, only her beautiful, sparkling eyes giving evidence of her turbulent emotions. Daniel chuckled softly to himself and lithely climbed upward beside her, his capable hands slapping the reins and guiding the single horse down the white-blanketed street.

"Looks like the storm's worsening," he conversationally remarked, not the least bit surprised when his beautiful, albeit unwilling, traveling companion said nothing in response. "I've heard a few predictions about this winter. Seems that it's supposed to be a particularly difficult one." He reached a hand down to fling a layer of blankets across their laps, a tiny frown creasing his brow as he told himself that it was a good thing they had a relatively short distance to traverse that night. The visibility was gradually lessening, and drifts were taking shape along the gently rolling landscape.

Addie was inescapably conscious of Daniel's warm, masculine body beside her, his lean, muscular thigh pressing against her silken skirts beneath the blankets. Still so thoroughly incensed with him her mind could scarcely formulate anything approaching a rational thought, she was nonetheless moved to speech before they had traveled far from town.

"What made you do it?" she demanded in a low, vibrant voice, clutching at the edges of her cloak to draw the protective wool more closely about her. She was cold and furious, covered with snow, and certainly in no mood for flippant discussion. Daniel wisely sensed this, so he answered her without preamble, his gaze briefly catching hers.

"Something like that was necessary, Addie. I had to make it clear that I don't intend to be intimidated. I've no intention of hiding, of letting them believe their threats and animosity frighten me."

"You"ll only make things worse," she prophesied, her anger far from easing. "And, in the end, they'll kill you!"

"Would that make such a difference to you?" he softly parried.

Her storm-filled eyes flew to his face, and she suddenly experienced a strong impulse to plead with him to leave, to save himself from the repercussions she knew to be inevitable if he remained. Instead, however, she frowned deeply and replied, "It's your life. If you choose to throw it away in such a foolish manner, then it's no concern of mine!"

"Isn't it?" he mockingly retorted, his own eyes glowing dully again. "You'd be a widow then, Addie. You'd be free to marry someone else. Hasn't the idea even occurred to you?"

"It's none of your blasted business whether I've entertained the notion or not!" she furiously countered.

"It's my business," he firmly disagreed, his jealousy flaring to the surface once more. "I'm still your husband, like it or not. And until our marriage is legally dissolved, you've no right to encourage the attentions of anyone, including your gallant escort of tonight."

"Just who the hell do you think you are?" Addie indignantly retorted, her voice rising in the silence of the frozen countryside. "You're the last person in this world who can tell me what to do!" She was so infuriated, she actually thought fleetingly of leaping down off the moving buckboard, but then she sensibly realized that she'd only risk freezing to death even if she did manage to escape injury.

"Perhaps," Daniel murmured with a faint smile. "But you and your friends are going to have to realize, sooner or later, that I intend to stay here. I intend to become a part of this community. And I certainly don't intend to sit idly by and watch you engage the affections of another man while you're still married to me."

"Why should it matter to you?" she bitterly responded. "I've neither seen nor heard from you in more than four years, remember? What was once between us is long dead. I've a perfect right to make a new life of my own!" She shifted abruptly upon the wooden seat, presenting her back to him as she stared unseeingly outward over the passing scenery.

"Not yet. For now, my dearest Addie," he quietly insisted, his long fingers tightening upon the reins, "you do not have the right."

"Is that why you came to the dance?" she questioned, twisting back around to confront him. He turned his head slowly toward her, his gaze unflinching as hers blazed up at him. "Did you plan all of this in order to ruin my life again? If so, it won't work! I'll see anyone I please, do anything I please, do you hear?" He did not offer her a reply, but she glimpsed the veiled look of almost savage displeasure in his gray eyes before he focused his attention on guiding the buckboard closer to the buildings of the Rolling L which were now faintly visible in the distance.

As soon as they stopped in front of the house, Addie threw off the blankets and gathered up her skirts once more as she prepared to alight, but Daniel surprised her by quickly seizing her arm. She attempted to jerk free, but his grip remained firm and unrelenting.

"What the hell do you think you're doing now?" she demanded. "Don't you think you've caused enough trouble for one night?" She twisted futilely in his grasp. "Have you lost what little sense you were given? Don't you realize that I never want to see you again?" He remained silent, his features inscrutable as she continued to struggle. Raising her face to his, she sighed in mingled anger and exasperation. "Whatever it is you've obviously decided you've got to say to me, say it now and get it over with! I'm near to freezing now!" she finished with a toss of her head, disturbing the thin layer of snow which covered her hood.

"Let's go inside," he finally said, releasing her arm as he jumped down and started around to where she sat. "I'll be in just as soon as I see to the horse." He was standing before her now, his hands already reaching for her while she stared down at him in astonished disbelief.

"Are you truly out of your mind?" she gasped. "I don't want you to stay one second longer! And that particular fact aside, what am I supposed to tell Esther and Silas about your being here?"

"Whatever you please," he nonchalantly replied. "However, I don't believe they've returned yet. There's no sign of any lights within the house." His hands were closing firmly about her slender waist before she could do anything to prevent his action, and she suddenly found herself being lifted up from the wooden seat and then down to the ground, the majority of her laced, high-topped leather boots nearly disappearing into the several inches of snow covering the ground just below the front steps.

"You are damn well not going to come inside my

house!" she declared in haughty defiance, swiftly moving away from him and starting as hurriedly as possible up the steps.

"We'll discuss it just as soon as I put the horse in your barn," pronounced Daniel, apparently undaunted as he turned and began unhitching the cold and weary animal. Addie directed a venomous glare at his broad back before she flounced inside, slamming the door with resounding force after her.

What am I going to do? she wondered with a sudden feeling of near panic. Esther and Silas would be home soon. How in heaven's name will I explain Daniel Jordan's presence here?

I won't have to explain a blasted thing! she staunchly decided. I'll simply have to manage to get rid of him before the Fremonts return. But how?

Releasing another sigh of intense annoyance, she removed the snow-laden cloak and headed for the kitchen. Her face and hands were tingling with cold, and she scurried about to light a fire in the stove. That particular task done, she glanced hastily toward the back door, her face wearing an expression of nervous anticipation.

Daniel appeared at the rear entrance a few moments later, striding confidently inside without first pausing to knock. After removing his hat and coat, he turned to face a rigidly composed Addie, the decidedly unwelcoming look in her expressive hazel eyes leaving no doubt as to her true feelings concerning his presence.

"It's coming down pretty heavy out there now," he announced, moving closer to the warmth of the stove. "I don't believe those people of yours are going to be traveling at all until there's a break in the storm." He paused a moment, then asked, "By the way, are your men still gone? I saw no evidence of life in the bunkhouse."

"How dare you go snooping around my property!" she snapped, immediately realizing how childish she sounded. Don't do this, don't let him know how distressed you are at being alone with him again, her mind sternly commanded. "It so happens that the hands are attending a celebration of their own," she frostily revealed, then added sharply, "but they should also be returning at any time now." She knew it wasn't precisely the truth, for the men weren't actually due to return from Dallas until the following morning, but it suddenly seemed wisest to allow him to believe otherwise.

"Aren't you at least going to offer me a cup of coffee?" he asked with a quick, disarming grin.

"If I do, will you agree to leave immediately afterward?" she shot back at him.

"I give you my word that I'll consider it," he replied, smiling briefly once more. Addie hesitated, fixing him with a speculative glance, then heaved another sigh and set about filling the coffeepot with water from the pump at the sink. Daniel stood and watched, his gaze moving up and down her well-displayed curves with an appreciative lack of haste. When she turned about to place the pot upon the stove, she caught the unmistakable gleam of desire in his smoldering gray eyes, and she colored rosily as she set the heavy pot down with a loud clatter.

"And just what the devil do you think you're staring at?" she angrily demanded, bristling as his gaze remained unwaveringly upon her.

"You look beautiful tonight, Addie," he told her softly, his voice deep and resonant. "It reminds me of the first time I ever saw you." He took a step closer, the glow in his eyes striking an inexplicable apprehension in her pounding heart.

She swallowed a sudden lump in her throat before responding in a slightly unsteady voice, "I . . . I'd prefer it if you didn't mention the past ever again!"

"It's still a part of us. Memories, both good and bad, will always remain with us," he quietly observed, taking yet another step closer. "But not all of our memories are bad, are they, Addie?" he asked, his voice barely above a whisper now as he stood gazing down at her with his eyes looking more than ever like molten steel, his handsome face wearing an unfathomable expression that only served to increase her inner anxiety. "Don't you ever think back to what it was like between us in the beginning?"

"I don't think about it," she firmly declared, dismayed to feel herself fairly trembling at his close proximity. She was painfully aware of the clean, masculine scent which emanated from him, and she found herself once again recalling, with disturbing vividness, the impassioned kiss they had shared the day before.

It was as if Daniel had read her thoughts, for he said, "You can't forget it, can you? What we once had together can never be totally erased from your mind."

"All I remember is the heartbreak, the sense of betrayal. I remember how ashamed I was that I had allowed myself to be so blinded by nothing more than . . . than pure animal lust!" She abruptly turned away from him, her dark, thick curls flying wildly about her face and bared shoulders. "You can have your cup of coffee. Then I want you to get off my ranch!" she coldly decreed, refusing to look at him again as she hastily whirled and started for the doorway. A loud gasp escaped her lips as her arm was unexpectedly seized and she was spun back around to stand gazing up in stunned astonishment at a strangely grim-faced Daniel.

"Nothing but lust, Addie?" His voice was low and whipcord sharp. "If it was nothing but lust, then why the pain and sense of betrayal? And if it was nothing but lust, then why not ease the loneliness of these past four years with more of the same?" Before she could escape, his arms wrapped about her like bands of iron, and his head lowered as his lips ruthlessly captured hers in a searing kiss. She struggled against him, moaning her outrage deep in her throat as she endeavored to wrench her mouth away from his. One of his hands fastened in the abundance of chestnut curls at the back of her head, his other arm easily holding her about the waist as she frantically pushed and squirmed. Remembering a defensive maneuver her father had once taught her, she attempted to raise her knee to deliver a punishing blow to Daniel's groin. Though hampered by her full skirts and petticoats, she nonetheless managed to bring her leg upward. But he seemed to possess lightning-quick reflexes, and he easily deflected her kick by lifting her off her feet, then clamping her so tightly against his muscular hardness that she could scarcely breathe. She moaned again as his lips continued their hard, demanding assault upon hers. Finally, just when Addie was convinced she was about to surrender to total, immobilizing panic, she

128

found herself released, her booted feet making almost jolting contact with the floor again. She stared wordlessly up at Daniel for several long seconds, her hair tumbling riotously from its pins, her beautiful features appearing quite flushed and agitated. Her eyes, however, narrowed and blazed at the man who stood gazing down at her with outward calm, and only the imperceptible narrowing of his own glowing eyes offering evidence of his turbulent emotions.

"Oh, how I hate you!" she finally seethed. Before pausing to reconsider the dangerous impulse, she raised her hand and slapped him forcefully across one tanned cheek, her palm stinging fierily as she then swept past him and flew from the room. She had already reached the foot of the staircase before Daniel ground out a savage oath and gave chase, catching her before she had climbed more than halfway up the steps. "Let go of me, damn you!" she cried, fighting against the hands that gripped her slender waist.

He ignored her, however, as he merely twirled her about and lifted her again, effortlessly tossing her over his broad shoulder and moving with steady and assured strides up the darkened staircase. Addie beat viciously upon his hard-muscled back, her long hair streaming about her face and nearly trailing the polished surface of the steps as she was swiftly carried to the upstairs landing. She kicked and writhed futilely, screaming and cursing at the top of her lungs, desperately hoping that Esther and Silas would return without further delay.

It was as if Daniel instinctively sensed which room belonged to Addie, for he opened the door to her bedroom and crossed to the four-poster bed, dumping

129

his loudly protesting burden unceremoniously upon the cushioning softness of the quilt-covered feather mattress. She furiously scrambled to her knees as he quickly lit a candle beside her bed. Then he returned to the door with leisurely determination, closed and locked it, and negligently tossed the key aside to land atop the dressing table a short distance away. By this time, Addie had bounced off the bed and was hastily searching about the room for something to use as a weapon, her fingers gratefully closing upon a long-handled button hook.

"You come near me again, Daniel Jordan, and I'll use this!" she asserted, her voice holding a touch of shrillness. Her full breasts were threatening to spill over the edge of her silken bodice as she held the button hook in one hand, her other hand impatiently sweeping the hair from her flushed face. Daniel mused to himself that she appeared every inch the beautiful wildcat he had proclaimed her to be—an untamed, wholly desirable wildcat who had driven him to the limit.

"It won't do you any good, Addie. We both knew that this was inevitable." He began edging forward, slowly and purposefully, as if he were some sort of splendidly masculine animal stalking his prey. Addie breathlessly retreated a step and held the button hook a bit higher.

"The only thing that's inevitable is the fact that I'll kill you if you touch me again!"

"As if you could with that ridiculous thing," he wryly noted. "But you wouldn't kill me even if you were holding a gun," he insisted, still advancing upon her as she continued to back away. "As much as you've tried to convince yourself that you hate me, you never will. We're in each other's blood, Adelaide Caton Jordan, and there's nothing either of us can do about it. Not even four long years can totally destroy the powerful bond between us." Mere inches separated them now.

"There's no bond between us!" She gasped audibly as her back came into contact with the wall beside the bed. Her eyes were wide and full of desperation, and her fingers tightened about the button hook as she nearly cried aloud in helpless frustration.

"Isn't there?" he softly murmured before lunging forward and knocking her hand aside, sending the button hook clattering noisily to the bare wooden floor. His powerful arms locked about her as she made one last frantic attempt to escape. "Go ahead and try to forget the past, Addie," he huskily remarked against her ear as she still refused to surrender. "You can try all you like, but I'm going to make you remember a part of it that can never be denied."

"Then this is the reason you came here, isn't it?" she hoarsely demanded. "You came to force yourself upon me, to humiliate me! It's nothing more than revenge you want!" She flailed and kicked, but to no avail. Dear Lord, she frantically pleaded, please let Silas and Esther get here before it's too late!

"Revenge?" he echoed, his low voice sounding a trifle harsh in the semi-darkened confines of the room, the only source of light being the wavering flame of the candle. "No, dearest Addie, revenge is a wasted motivation," he muttered then effectively ended all discussion between them when he swiftly bent and lifted her high in his arms, his lips claiming hers once more as he moved to the bed. He lowered her to the quilt, imprisoning her as he placed his own body atop hers.

Addie began to struggle with renewed strength the

131

very instant her back touched the mattress but was thoroughly dismayed to feel herself growing light-headed with a long-denied yearning that was blossoming to life deep inside her very soul as Daniel's lips moved persuasively, seductively upon hers. He was demanding a response with his warm, intoxicating mouth as his hands skillfully unfastened the buttons at the back of her lavender dress, while keeping her pinned beneath him.

His kiss deepened, his tongue masterfully plundering the sensitive recesses of her mouth, and his hands smoothed against the silken contours of her shoulder blades as he slipped the edges of her dress downward. Her struggles slowly eased, her senses reeling, and she was shocked to realize she had suddenly begun returning his urgent kisses with an answering passion of her own. Instinctively she arched against him. Gone were all thoughts of how she would explain Daniel Jordan's presence in her house, much less in the privacy of her own bedroom, should the Fremonts return soon. She could think only of the wild, overpowering excitement that sent her buried desires spiraling upward. Her arms seemed to have developed a will of their own as they clasped him tightly to her soft curves.

"Addie," he whispered her name, his lips trailing a fiery path across her flushed face as she gasped softly. His fingers now lingered at the graceful curve of her neck before impatiently moving to the fine white linen of her chemise, the only remaining barrier between his ardent caress and her pale, beautifully formed breasts. Within seconds, the strings of the delicate garment had been untied and the fabric brushed aside to free the rounded, rose-tipped flesh.

Her breasts tingled with anticipation as she heard him release a soft, appreciative sigh. No matter how desperately she tried to tell herself that what she was doing was madness, that it would only cause her further pain, she was powerless to resist the dizzying whirl of sensuality Daniel had so adroitly created. Thus, she was left to gasp once more as his warm fingers gently touched her breasts, his lips soon following to bestow gentle, provocative kisses along an imaginary path leading in a circular pattern across the straining peaks before traveling to the shadowed softness between.

Addie drew in her breath sharply as her fingers curled into his soft, thick hair, and she stifled the cry which rose to her lips as his mouth trailed to fasten about one of her dark pink nipples, his tongue seductively encircling the rosy tip, his lips gently suckling.

Four years! her mind dazedly reminded her, her entire body alive and trembling with the force of her reawakened passion. It had been more than four years since she had allowed herself to behave this way, to forget all else save this wonderfully abandoned ecstasy that left her weak and trembling. And it had been Daniel who had first initiated her into the world of such delights, Daniel who had taught her what it meant to be a woman. Was it truly happening again? It was suddenly as if all those years had never been, as if the war had never been, as if they were once again secret newlyweds who could not get enough of each other.

Soon, however, all such thought, indeed all thought, was once again forgotten as she surrendered to the conquering pressure of Daniel's lips. When he moved to tease at her other breast, his hands also moved to push her chemise and dress even farther downward and to tug at her lace-trimmed drawers until she was rendered entirely naked, totally vulnerable to his searing, desire-filled gaze.

"You're even more beautiful than I remembered," he murmured, startling her as he suddenly pushed himself up with his elbows and proceeded to divest himself of his own clothing while standing beside the bed, towering above her and making her feel a strange, more forceful aching. She could only watch in breathless fascination as he first tugged off his boots, then unbuttoned and removed his shirt. Her widened eyes were drawn to the bronzed skin of his muscular chest, and she appeared almost hypnotized when his hands moved to the waistband of his trousers. His trim waist was revealed, tapering down into lithely muscled thighs which bespoke obvious power. But it was the undeniably aroused masculinity between his long legs that drew her rapt attention as he finished undressing. She felt the hot color flooding her already flushed cheeks and a sudden, burning sensation in the very pit of her stomach.

It was enough to awaken her from her momentary trance. She swiftly rolled to her side upon the bed, a look of highly perplexed consternation on her lovely face. But Daniel's arms shot out to prevent her escape, prompting her to shriek in renewed outrage, "No! I'll not give in to you, Daniel Jordan! I'll not allow you to steal away what little pride I have left!" She beat at the hands which held her, her hair tumbling wildly about her naked curves like a billowing chestnut curtain.

"The last thing in the world you need is pride,

Addie," he mockingly quipped, easily subduing her by positioning himself atop her once more. She gasped audibly as his bare flesh made contact with hers, and she wriggled almost violently beneath him. The curse which rose to her lips was silenced when his lips descended to claim the faintly swollen softness of hers once more, his lean, virile body pressing her down into the mattress.

She moaned quietly against his mouth when his warm fingers touched her at the moist, secret place between her thighs, and she was hardly aware of it when her silken, quivering limbs opened to him. His other hand moved to the mass of dark hair which fanned out across the gaily colored squares of the quilt, his fingers fastening within the thick, fragrant curls.

In spite of Daniel's efforts to prolong the highly delectable torment, he soon found he could no longer contain his own blazing hunger, and his hands lowered to grip Addie's firmly rounded buttocks while his hardness pressed against her feminine passage. She uttered a faint, rather strangled cry when he sheathed himself within her soft, velvety warmth, and her arms clutched him feverishly against her as he began a slow, rapidly escalating rotation of his firm hips.

Her breath was coming in short gasps as she clung to him, their bodies moving together in the ultimate intimacy. Her head tossed restlessly upon the quilt as she gave herself up to her soaring passions. She gasped loudly when the bursting fulfillment took hold of her, dimly aware of Daniel's own sharp intake of breath before he collapsed against her.

Addie felt as if she were floating. Her body remained weak and languid as Daniel eased himself upward, then lay silently beside her, one powerful arm still flung across the pale, gleaming smoothness of her slender waist, his other arm tenderly pillowing her head. It took her several long moments to regain her breath, and she suddenly became acutely aware of the fact that her husband's steely gaze was riveted to her face. She could feel his eyes upon her, could feel his arm tightening a bit across her naked body, and the realization of what had just occurred hit her with full, abrupt force.

"Damn you!" she hissed, jerking upright in the bed.

"Damn the both of us, I suppose," he retorted, a half-smile curving his lips as his sun-bronzed arm remained draped across her softness. His face appeared so devastatingly handsome—and so triumphantly smug! Addie resentfully told herself.

"Let go of me!" she wrathfully commanded, twisting against his arm as she tried to swing her legs off the bed.

"I think we ought to talk first," he insisted, refusing to relinquish his hold.

She cast him a venomous glare as she bitterly reminded him, "Esther and Silas could be here any minute now! Haven't you done enough harm as it is?" She used both of her hands in an attempt to pry his arm loose, then nearly toppled to the floor when he unexpectedly released her. Sliding off the bed, she snatched up the discarded lavender dress and under-garments, holding them before her like a shield as she whirled about to confront him again. There was an intense light in his gray eyes, and a shadowed, inscrutable look crossed his features as he stared up at her from where he still lay upon the bed, his magnificent body spread without shame before her.

Her cheeks flamed again as she forced her gaze to remain fixed upon his face.

"Get out of my house, and get off my ranch!" she ordered imperiously, one arm flinging outward emphatically toward the door.

Daniel's eyes took in the sight of her barely covered, disheveled loveliness, and he visibly hesitated. Telling himself that now was not the time to try to discuss anything with the indignant firebrand he so desperately loved, he nevertheless found it difficult to battle against the temptation to make love to her again before taking his leave. He had waited so long, had dreamt of the moment when she would be his once more. It hadn't been exactly as he had planned, but it had proven something to him. Addie still cared. She still cared, at least in some small way. He was convinced that she couldn't have responded to him the way she had if she didn't feel something for him. And that was enough to provide him with renewed hope and determination, enough to make his heart sing with the promise of certain success.

"Very well," he finally acquiesced, rising slowly from the bed with a lithe, masculine grace. He noticed the way Addie hastily averted her gaze as he stood to his full height before her, and he smiled to himself. She waited in obvious impatience while he leisurely pulled on his clothing and boots. Her hands were trembling upon the silk as she clutched it about her nakedness, and she was certain that she would never be able to live with the humiliation which washed over her.

"I'll leave now, Addie," he announced, sauntering to the door at last. He retrieved the key and unlocked it, then paused before stepping through the doorway.

"But you know that I'll be back." Flashing her a brief, disarming smile, he turned and left her alone in the room, his boots clumping softly upon the steps as he moved down the staircase.

"You set one foot on my place ever again, Daniel Jordan, and I'll—" she loudly threatened, breaking off when she heard the unmistakable sound of the front door closing. Sinking back down upon the bed, she despised herself for the hot tears which filled her sparkling eyes. Nearly a full minute passed before she hastily rose again, and, following a sudden impulse, she padded over to the window.

Her eyes could barely make him out through the white blur of snow as she watched him leading his horse from the barn. The storm, she numbly observed, was apparently beginning to let up a bit. It meant that in all likelihood Esther and Silas would be home soon. Their delayed return had proven to be both disastrous and fortunate, for she still had no idea what she would have said to them if they had found her alone with Daniel.

Daniel. Would she ever forget the shame of surrendering to him tonight? Would she ever be able to erase from her mind the burning memory of his impassioned kisses, his breathtaking caresses?

Jerking away from the window, she returned to the bed and threw herself facedown upon its rumpled softness. For the second time in less than a week she burst into a veritable torrent of weeping, though even her wrenching sobs were unable to vanquish the bewildering pain in her heart.

Eight

"Damnation!" breathed Addie, taking note of the aromatic black liquid oozing from beneath the lid of the coffeepot and streaming down its sides to form a sizzling puddle on the newly scrubbed surface of the cookstove. Rushing forward to prevent further disaster, she muttered another oath when she accidentally touched her fingers to the scalding liquid, and she whirled to snatch up a towel with which to grip the hot handle of the pot. It was at this inopportune moment that Esther and Silas came bursting through the back doorway, both of their faces registering a combination of relief and renewed concern as they caught sight of their young mistress.

"The Lord have mercy!" Esther gasped, scurrying across the kitchen to lend unwanted assistance with the coffeepot.

"Please, just get out of my way!" snapped the younger woman as she successfully lifted the dripping pot and hurriedly transferred it to the sink.

"Are you all right, Miss Addie?" demanded Silas,

closing the door behind him now. Like Esther, his outer garments were coated with glistening white flakes and his kindly face was somewhat chapped by the cold.

"Of course I'm all right!" Addie impatiently replied, then hastened to ask, "Why shouldn't I be?" She turned away from the sink, her eyes bright and sparkling, her features becomingly flushed. She met the worried gazes of the other two with a faintly challenging air as her fingers unconsciously tightened the belt at her waist. Her nightgown and wrapper had been donned shortly after she had finally managed to compose herself, though she had first scrubbed nearly every inch of her flesh until it was pink and glowing. It was as if she had been endeavoring to obliterate all memory of Daniel Jordan's caresses upon her body, but she knew that she had failed miserably. The image of their shocking intimacy continued to haunt her even now, in spite of the fact that she was desperately trying to conceal any evidence of her inner, tempestuous emotions.

"Gil Foster came to tell us about what happened at the dance," explained Esther in a low voice, her eyes narrowing slightly as they fastened unwaveringly upon Addie's face. "He told us about what that Yankee did, about how you agreed to come on home with him. Said we was to get back and see about you right away." She began tugging off her damp cloak, the corners of her mouth turning down into a frown. "That Yankee, he didn't do nothin'—"

"Don't be ridiculous!" Addie indignantly interrupted. "It was foolish of Gil to send you hurrying back here," she declared in a calmer tone. "Mr. Jordan simply brought me home." Seizing the towel once more, she presented her back to Esther and Silas and began mopping at the spilled coffee.

"Sounds like that new neighbor of ours put himself smack-dab in the middle of a hornet's nest tonight," remarked Silas, shrugging out of his coat and hanging it on a hook beside Addie's dark blue cloak. He took the scarlet cloak his wife handed him and did the same with it. "Yes, sir, I do believe we're gonna have ourselves another little war right here in these parts."

"What do you mean?" demanded Addie, wrinkling her nose at the black, soggy mess she had made of the clean, white towel. She finally allowed an insistent Esther to take over with the cleaning, and she faced Silas with a faintly puzzled frown.

"Seemed like there was a whole bunch of us leavin' town soon as the storm let up a bit. And I heard tell there just might be some trouble over that Jordan feller's showin' up at the dance." He shook his head as he took a seat at the table and ran a hand through his thick, grizzled hair. "Folks don't take kindly to those that push in where they ain't wanted. But, just the same, I hope they don't hurt him none."

"Are they . . . are they planning to do something tonight?" questioned Addie, her voice deceptively level. Could it possibly be that she had only made things worse by leaving with Daniel? Were Ike and the others truly bent on avenging what they evidently perceived as an unforgivable transgression on the part of the man they viewed only as a hated adversary?

"Don't know for certain," admitted Silas, briskly rubbing his hands together in an effort to warm them.

"They'd be mighty foolish to go traipsin' about in this weather!" commented Esther, efficiently preparing another pot of coffee. She set it on to boil, then moved

141

to take a seat at the table beside her husband. Addie appeared quite preoccupied as she sank into a chair as well. "Are you sure you're all right, honey?" the plump, maternal woman queried, reaching out an affectionate hand to Addie's shoulder. "It's a shame you had to be caught up in the middle of all this. I think it was a real good thing you did tonight, leavin' with that man to save his hide. Gil Foster seemed to think so, too."

"Did he?" she murmured, her mind in a whirl. Daniel would be all alone against many if they did indeed ride against him tonight, she was thinking. The arrogant, impossible, infuriating man might even be killed. And, she reflected, no matter how much she despised him for what he had made her do just a short time ago, she still couldn't turn her back and knowingly allow him to be harmed. For some mysterious reason, she felt somewhat responsible for him, though she once again cursed herself for what she considered to be her weakness.

"Are you goin' on up to bed?" asked Esther as she watched the other woman rise to her feet.

"Saddle Old Buck for me, will you, Silas?" Addie instructed, ignoring Esther's question. She had already crossed to the doorway when both of the Fremonts voiced their disapproval.

"You can't go ridin' about in this!" protested Esther.

"It won't do you no good, Miss Addie," argued Silas. "If you're set on headin' off to where I think you are, it won't do you no good."

"What are you talkin' about?" queried his wife in obvious bemusement. "Where is it you think she's goin'?"

"Possibly to help prevent that war Silas mentioned," Addie supplied, then was gone.

"You ain't gonna let her go off on a night like this, are you?" Esther demanded of her husband, following after him as he moved to don his hat, coat, and gloves once more. Her brow was creased with a frown of mingled concern and exasperation.

"There ain't much I can do to stop her," he answered with a faint sigh of resignation. Smiling briefly, he took Esther's hand between both of his as he added, "But don't you worry none, old woman. I'll be there to make sure she don't come to no harm. I reckon I've done a fair enough job of lookin' after her all these years." He leaned forward and softly brushed his wife's plump cheek with his lips before opening the back door and striding out into the frozen night.

Esther pursed her lips, her head shaking at both her husband's irresistible charm and her young mistress's headstrong nature. Telling herself that she'd never be able to figure out the two of them in a hundred years, she ambled over to the window and peered anxiously outward at what little bit of gleaming white landscape she could discern in the blanketed darkness.

Minutes later Addie and Silas were on their way, the two of them well bundled against the cold and lightened flurry of snow as they rode toward Daniel's ranch. It wasn't particularly hazardous for either of them to be out riding in such weather, for they knew the countryside well, and their destination lay less than a mile away. Nevertheless, Addie experienced a sharp pang of apprehension as her fingers tightened on the reins.

Daniel reached the boundaries of his property without incident, his thoughts still centered on what had happened earlier between himself and Addie. Once

143

again, a slow, satisfied smile rose to his lips, and his gray eyes gleamed in remembrance.

A sudden noise drew his attention, and his sharp gaze darted toward the outline of the buildings which lay just ahead as he pulled the horse to an abrupt halt. His perceptive eyes caught movement, and he now saw nearly a dozen men on horseback galloping away from the direction of the barn, the hoofbeats muffled in the soft snow.

His hand reached instinctively for the gun inside his coat, and he withdrew the Colt pistol at the same moment he jumped lithely from the buckboard. Then, stealthily approaching the rear of the barn, he paused and listened. What he heard was a strange crackling noise, the sound of flames licking at one side of the old building. The telltale smoke began curling upward from the tinned roof as the fire blazed higher and higher.

He ground out a savage curse as he hurried to the front of the weathered structure, his only thought for the moment the rescue of any stock that might be trapped within its smoke-filled interior. Flinging open one of the heavy wooden doors, he charged inside. Following a hasty search, during which he was satisfied to see that the night riders had at least possessed the decency to allow the livestock to go free, he was just spinning about to escape the thick, choking heat and smoke when his gaze fell upon the unmistakable form of a man's body lying in the far corner.

Rushing to the unconscious man's side, Daniel knelt upon the hay-strewn floor and rolled him to his back. His eyes widened in immediate recognition, but he gave the man's identity no further thought as he grasped the

144

front of his buckskin coat and pulled him upward, positioning his own shoulder to support the bleeding man's weight. Daniel's lips compressed into a tight, thin line as he managed to lift the burly fellow. Then he slowly made his way back to the front of the barn toward the beckoning safety outside, the thickening smoke stinging his eyes as he blinked rapidly in an effort to gauge the remaining distance to the doors.

"Look!" exclaimed Addie, abruptly pulling up on the reins as she pointed ahead to the rather eerie, golden glow on the horizon. "Dear God, I think we're too late!" she whispered hoarsely, her voice heavy with emotion. Digging her heels into the horse's flanks, she urged the animal inexorably onward, a grim-faced Silas in her wake.

The two of them arrived upon the scene just as Daniel was lowering the still-unconscious form of Ike Henry into the bed of the buckboard. The barn was fully ablaze by this time, its four walls being rapidly consumed by the relentless flames. Daniel could only watch in helpless fury, his handsome features tightening savagely as he stepped around to snatch up the blankets on the buckboard's seat. He whirled in defensive readiness as the two riders approached, his hand returning to his gun. Smiling sardonically, he lowered the hand to his side when the faces of the two were revealed in the fiery light.

"Well, well, if it isn't more of my charming neighbors come to pay a visit," he remarked with biting sarcasm, intently watching as Addie hastily dismounted and hurried forward to peer down anxiously at the man she glimpsed lying in the buckboard. "Did you want to get a closer look at the damage to my ranch, Addie?" he asked softly. Silas swung down from the saddle as well, though he remained silent and still a short distance away.

"You bastard!" Addie furiously proclaimed, raising her stormy face to his. "What have you done to him?" she demanded, nodding curtly downward.

"Although I believe I would have been entirely justified in inflicting any punishment upon one of the men who apparently just finished putting a torch to my property," he mockingly countered, the look in his eyes growing hard, "I didn't lay a hand on him. It appears that his friends—and yours—" he added with a harsh edge to his voice, "were ignorant of his presence inside the building."

"They wouldn't have left without Ike!" she vehemently denied, frowning darkly as she bent to examine the gaping wound on the side of the man's head.

"Believe what you will," he tersely responded, "but the fact is that your friend here's got a nasty gash, and probably a concussion. He'll need medical attention without delay."

"I know that, damn it!" Addie muttered in high temper, her eyes flashing. "We can take him to the Rolling L for now. It's the closest place between here and town. Silas can ride for the doctor in the meantime." She spoke more calmly.

"Whatever you say, Miss Addie," retorted Daniel, ignoring her wrathfully indignant glare as he spread the blankets across the prone figure of Ike before climbing up to take his place upon the seat once more. Snapping the reins, he drove away, a grim expression on his handsome face as he threw one last glance at what remained of his barn, realizing that it would be nothing more than a smoldering pile of ashes by the time he returned. And, he silently vowed, his steely gray eyes narrowing again, he would return.

Addie waited until the buckboard rolled a short distance away, then turned to stare at the roaring blaze for several long moments. An array of conflicting emotions played across her face before she spun about and marched to where Silas stood patiently holding the reins of their gently snorting horses.

"You'll need to fetch Doc Bennett," she solemnly instructed, grasping the saddlehorn as she placed her foot in the stirrup and swung her other leg across the comfortably worn leather strapped to the animal's back.

"You want me to tell Mr. Henry's missus what's happened to him?" Silas thought to ask, following her example as he mounted up as well.

"Yes," Addie replied with a heavy sigh, already reining about to follow after Daniel. "I suppose Ella will have to be told. She'll more than likely want to come back out with you, too. You'd best be on your way." She shifted in the saddle as she added, "And have a care to yourself." He smiled briefly as he nodded quickly in her direction. Murmuring a soothing word to his horse, he wasted no further time in heading off toward town.

Addie easily caught up with Daniel's buckboard a short time later. Peering closely at the man lying so still and lifeless in the wagon's bed, she repeated a silent prayer on his behalf.

"I'm sure he'll be fine," Daniel startled her by saying.

147

Her widened gaze hastily traveled to his impassive features, only faintly visible in the darkness as she moved along the snow-covered trail beside him.

"Will he?" she countered with resentful sarcasm, stiffening in the saddle. She glanced away from the disturbing, unwavering stare he turned upon her.

"Tell me something, Addie," he commanded in a low voice. "Were you disappointed to find that your marauding friends did nothing more than burn my barn?" He lightly flicked the reins in an effort to increase the weary animal's lessening pace. The snow had all but ended by this time, but it felt as if the temperature had dropped somewhat. Fortunately, the wind was gusting only occasionally, though it sent involuntary shivers down their backs when it chose to exert its chilling power.

"That doesn't even deserve an answer!" she scornfully declared, her color heightening again.

"I can't say you didn't warn me, can I?" he offered with a brief, mocking smile. "But their efforts still won't achieve the desired results." He lapsed into silence again when Addie didn't answer, and he did not make another attempt at conversation. Ike moaned softly beneath the blankets a few times as he struggled unsuccessfully to regain consciousness, and Addie was profoundly relieved when she finally glimpsed the welcoming light streaming forth from her house.

Esther had apparently been watching for them, for she quickly flung her cloak about her ample shoulders as she came scurrying out through the front doorway, a lantern held high in her hand. She rushed to Addie's side as soon as the younger woman dismounted.

"Silas stopped long enough to tell me you was

bringin' Mr. Henry," she breathlessly explained. "I got a bed fixed up for him in your daddy's study. I figured it'd be easier not to try and take him on upstairs."

"Thank you, Esther," Addie murmured with a preoccupied air. She hurried forward to offer assistance as Daniel began cautiously lifting and sliding Ike's body to the rear edge of the buckboard.

"Just stay clear!" he snapped at her, his knees bending imperceptibly beneath the strain as he hoisted the large man to his broad, capable shoulders and began moving toward the house. Addie jerked away the hands she had stretched outward in a gesture of help, visibly bristling at his authoritative tone. Esther bustled back up the steps in his wake, holding the lantern even higher in an attempt to illuminate his path. When Addie crossed the threshold and stepped briskly into the study an instant later, she saw that Daniel had eased his burden upon the oversized chaise near the desk. Esther had already thoughtfully provided the warmth of a fire, and she now raced to the kitchen to fetch the bandages and bowl of freshly boiled water she had prepared.

Ike moaned again, his head tossing restlessly upon the smooth velvet as his eyelids fluttered open. They swept closed after a brief moment, and it was with obvious difficulty that the older man struggled against lapsing into unconsciousness once more.

"You're going to be all right, Ike," Addie reassuringly pronounced, her voice soft and mellow as she knelt solicitously on the floor beside her friend. "Doc Bennett will be here soon. And Silas will let Ella know where you are." Putting a gentle hand on his shoulder, she felt tears starting in her eyes as she now clearly viewed the jagged wound near his left temple. In spite of his efforts, Ike slipped into blissful darkness once more.

Daniel's steely gaze softened as he watched the way Addie touched the injured man, the way she unashamedly displayed affection. He could feel his heart twisting at the thought that she had once treated him with even more love and respect. And, he told himself with a set look to his handsome features, he was bound and determined for things to be that way again.

"You did this to him!" Her accusing words broke in on his reverie. Their gazes met and locked in silent combat as Addie drew herself up to her full height before him. Daniel's initial reply was cut off, however, as Esther returned to the room.

"I ain't never gonna understand how grown men can act so senseless!" she muttered as she carefully began dabbing at the dried blood surrounding Ike's wound.

The two younger people stood wordlessly facing one another for the space of several long seconds before Daniel suddenly announced in a low voice, "I could use that coffee I was promised earlier." His gray eyes gleamed with a meaningful light when he noted the telltale blush rising to Addie's cheeks. "I'll be waiting in the kitchen," he added, the ghost of a smile lurking about his finely chiseled lips as he turned and leisurely sauntered from the study. Addie was dismayed to feel a sudden tremor deep inside as she watched him go, her eyes unconsciously moving to his trimly rounded hips and lean, powerful thighs. A vivid, albeit unbidden image of his magnificent, naked body rose to the forefront of her mind.

"How did this happen, honey?" Esther's quiet words

150

rescued her from the disturbing recollection.

"I don't know," replied Addie with a faint sigh, sinking into a chiar as she met the other woman's gaze. "When Silas and I got there, the barn was on fire and Dan . . . Mr. Jordan," she hastily amended, "was loading Ike into the buckboard."

"Then you was right about that little war," Esther murmured, half to herself. Having finished cleansing the wound as best she could, she applied a neat fold of clean white bandages to Ike's head. "Well, that's about all I can do for now," she concluded, rising slowly to her feet and adjusting the blankets about the unconscious man. "It don't look near as bad as I first thought, but it ain't good that he's still not come to yet."

"I know," responded Addie with another sigh. Reaching upward, she pulled the hat from her head, freeing the abundant chestnut curls which came tumbling down about her shoulders. She leaned forward, still clasping the brim of the hat as she rested her arms upon her knees. "I hope the weather holds until Silas gets back with the doctor." Her gaze traveled from Ike's pale face to the softly roaring fire before she rose to her feet and began pacing restlessly about the room.

"Why don't you take off that coat of yours?" suggested Esther, fixing the younger woman with a searching look. There was a decidedly pensive expression on Addie's lovely countenance as she shrugged out of the coat and tossed it negligently onto the chair she had just vacated. "And don't you think you ought to go on out to the kitchen and see to your guest?" she gently admonished.

"Guest?" repeated Addie in mild confusion. Her

expression rapidly changed to one of mutinous displeasure. "If you're speaking of Mr. Jordan, then may I remind you that he is here merely because of an unpleasant incident which has left Ike Henry gravely injured!"

"That don't make no difference," Esther stubbornly insisted, her tone more maternal than ever. "The man's your guest just as long as he's in your house." Her stern frown eased as she said, "You go on out to the kitchen, honey. I'll stay here and keep a watch over Mr. Henry."

Addie opened her mouth to refuse but apparently conceded defeat as she heaved an exasperated sigh and marched resolutely from the study and toward the kitchen. Once out of Esther's line of vision, however, she slowed her steps to a halt, hesitating just beyond the doorway leading into the room where she knew Daniel Jordan waited.

Taking a deep breath of determination, she squared her shoulders and lifted her head proudly, staunchly telling herself that she was fully prepared to do battle. For, she reflected with a nagging touch of uneasiness, a battle undoubtedly awaited her. She intended to make a few things clear to the man who had brought such turmoil into her life, long ago as well as of late. And she also had every intention of making certain he understood that what had happened between them earlier in the evening would never, never occur again!

Daniel looked up from the table where he sat sipping his coffee when Addie swept disdainfully into the room and purposefully closed the door behind her. She spared him only a passing glance as she crossed to the stove and poured herself a cup of the fragrant brew. Furious with herself for the weakness which assailed her in his presence, she whirled to face him with her hazel eyes flashing in obvious defiance, a few drops of coffee spilling from the rim of the cup as she stiffly moved forward to take a seat opposite the man who patiently watched and waited.

"Any change in his condition?" Daniel finally asked. His own hat and coat were resting in the chair beside him. It was a moment before Addie raised her eyes to his, and when she did so, she was startled at the powerful, invisible current which passed between them. Glancing quickly away, she focused her gaze on the faint curl of steam rising from the cup of hot liquid.

"He's still unconscious," she begrudgingly answered, tossing her head slightly to rearrange a stray lock of hair which had fallen perilously close to the cup she was fingering.

"You still believe I'm the one responsible for his wound, don't you?"

"Well, aren't you?" she harshly demanded, her eyes blazing as they met his squarely now. "Even if you didn't actually hit him, it's still your fault!"

"Oh?" he remarked with a faint, sardonic smile. "And what kind of reasoning did you use to make that rather odd deduction?"

"All of this has happened because you came here! When are you going to realize that there will only be more of the same if you don't leave?"

"When are you going to accept the fact that I'm not going to leave?"

"Are you so set on remaining because you believe . . . because you think that we . . . that you and I . . ." she angrily faltered, coloring rosily beneath his mocking scrutiny.

"What do you think?" he evasively countered, lifting the cup to his lips once more, though his eyes never left her face.

"I don't know what the devil to think!" she hotly retorted, fighting the sudden temptation to fling the rapidly cooling contents of her cup into his handsome, maddening face. It would be more fitting to aim quite a bit lower toward a more appropriate part of his anatomy! she mused resentfully. "All I know is that what happened between us tonight was a terrible, humiliating mistake! And it will for damn sure never happen again!" Her breasts heaved with indignation beneath the heavy flannel shirt she wore, and she gasped inwardly as Daniel's gaze moved to linger boldly upon the rounded curve of feminine flesh before returning to her stormy face.

"Won't it?" he taunted in a voice barely above a whisper.

His words so infuriated her that she scarcely knew what she was doing as she jumped to her feet and actually surrendered to the impulse to toss the now-warm coffee directly into his lap. She gasped aloud as her eyes widened, at first in amazement at her own actions, then in astonishment when Daniel merely rose slowly to his feet, the coffee a darkening stain on his denim trousers. He took a step closer, towering above her, while she could only stand transfixed, literally holding her breath in expectation.

"You of all people, dearest Addie, should know that physical violence only breeds more of the same." His tone was deep and resonant, and the expression on his face totally inscrutable. Addie numbly took a step backward, obviously quite confused at his puzzling reaction. Her confusion was swiftly replaced by renewed fury when his hands closed upon her shoulders and he drew her toward him, his hard, sinewy arms enveloping her before she could give voice to her protest. She pushed mightily against him, but he smiled softly down at her as she remained imprisoned within his powerful embrace. "The next time will be different, Addie," he quietly proclaimed, his glowing eyes leaving little doubt as to his meaning. "After all, it's been four long years. Our private time together should be savored."

"There won't be any more 'times'!" she uttered fiercely, a cutting edge to her voice as she attempted to keep her tone low so that Esther wouldn't hear. She angrily realized that she couldn't very well rant and rave at him without arousing suspicion regarding their relationship. But she certainly wasn't going to allow him to manhandle her without a struggle, Esther or no Esther!

"Ah, but there will," asserted Daniel, chuckling softly as she directed a scathing glare up at him. "What happened between us tonight was a mere taste of things to come." With that, his lips descended upon hers with almost bruising force. His arms tightened about her like a vise, leaving her little choice but to lie passively against him, for she still had no desire to create a loud stir and thus bring Esther rushing into the kitchen to see what all the commotion was about.

Pressed so closely to his lean hardness, she was embarrassingly aware of his surging desire. Her pulses raced alarmingly as his lips moved upon hers with undeniably masterful skill, and she was left softly gasping for breath when he released her with perplexing abruptness.

"Unless the two of us wish to find ourselves in a decidedly awkward situation, I'd best take my leave now," Daniel remarked with a wry grin, his eyes alight with passion and a touch of amusement. He turned to draw on his coat and settle his hat upon his thick, golden hair. Addie was unusually silent, her own gaze both troubled and angry as her fingers clutched at the back of a chair. "Please offer my apologies to Esther for leaving without an introduction."

"Aren't you even the least bit concerned about the condition of the man lying unconscious because of you?" she irrationally flung at him.

"It will be easy enough to make inquiries in town tomorrow. I firmly believe he'll pull through, Addie," he told her in a more serious vein. "But, as much as you want to blame me, I think you know—"

"I only know that nothing has been the same since you had the contemptible temerity to come here!" she feelingly interrupted, her eyes sparkling brightly.

"And nothing will ever be the same again, not with you," he quietly declared. A ghost of a smile curved his lips as he added, "I changed your life once before, though we harbor different opinions as to either the value or the significance of my role. And I'm going to change your life again. Only this time there will be no doubt as to whether or not it was for the better." With that astounding, confident statement, he turned and opened the back door, flashed Addie one last disquieting look before leaving, then gently pulled the door closed behind him.

It wasn't long before she glimpsed his buckboard rolling past the kitchen window, momentarily illuminated by the light streaming outward through the glass. Her legs suddenly gave way beneath her, and she grasped at the table for support as she eased herself into the chair again. She stared unseeingly toward the back door for the space of nearly a full minute before she happened to glance downward and take note of the slight dampness which darkened portions of her shirt and woolen skirts, a visible reminder of the coffee she had tossed in Daniel's lap.

Muttering an extremely unladylike curse, she left the kitchen and headed back to the study, persistent thoughts of Daniel bringing a frown to her beautiful countenance even before she crossed to the chaise and peered closely down at Ike Henry's pale, drawn features. Esther wordlessly moved to Addie's side, placing a comforting arm about the younger woman's faintly trembling shoulders.

Nine

The injured man was pronounced well enough to travel by late afternoon of the following day, though the doctor delivered a stern caution regarding any undue stress or physical activity. Ike had indeed suffered a concussion, and he would now be forced to ride home in the bed of the wagon his wife had driven out to the Rolling L.

"I appreciate your coming back out to look in on Ike again," Addie graciously thanked the bespectacled, dark-haired man she was escorting to the front doorway.

"That's what I'm here for," Doc Bennett dryly quipped, then smiled down indulgently at the young woman he had known for more than half of her life. "And as for you, my dear Miss Addie, I'd advise against any further late-night excursions in this weather. You're looking a bit pale yourself."

"Am I?" she flippantly retorted, hastily averting her eyes from his scrutinizing gaze. She stepped past him and opened the door, then glanced up into his slightly frowning, ruddy-skinned features. "Thanks again. I hope you and your family have a nice Christmas. If you happen to be out this way again before then, stop by and Esther will see that you get one of her sweet potato pies to take home to those kids of yours!"

"Would you care to tell me what it is that's troubling you, Addie?" he surprised her by asking, his eyes full of compassion. When she hesitated, he smiled crookedly and added, "Or would you prefer that I mind my own business?" Placing his hat atop his head, he began fastening the buttons on his coat with one hand, while his other hand clutched the black leather bag that was his trademark.

"Well, I . . . that is, I don't . . ." she stammered indecisively, not at all certain what to say to him in response. Why are you behaving like such a fool? she chided herself in a burst of renewed annoyance.

"Never mind," the doctor good-naturedly directed, turning about and crossing the threshold. "If you ever need to talk to someone, you know I'll be more than happy to listen," he said as he descended the steps and climbed into the buggy he always used to make his rounds. "If I don't see you before next week, a very merry Christmas to you!" He tipped his hat to her, then flicked the reins and drove away at a moderate pace, the buggy's wheels leaving a marked trail in the snow.

"Give my love to Beatrice!" Addie called after him, smiling to herself as she thought of the woman who was so amazingly like her husband. Closing the door, she hesitated a moment before returning to the study, distractedly moving a hand to her forehead. When she wandered back into the room, she found that Ike was already sitting up on the chaise and drawing on his

160

buckskin coat. Ella was standing before him, fussing over the bearded man in spite of his repeated efforts to refuse her continuing, persistent offers of wifely assistance.

The two of them had apparently reached a standstill when Addie entered the sunlit room. She chuckled softly, drawing their attention to her as she moved to take a stance at the fireplace. After stretching her fingers toward the comforting warmth of the well-tended blaze, she turned about to face them with a sobered expression and she earnestly remarked, "I'm glad Doc Bennett said you were doing so well, Ike. You had all of us pretty worried last night."

"Yes, and he's got his own wife pretty worried right now!" Ella interjected with mock sternness, fixing her husband with a frown. "Perhaps you can reason with him, my dear," she said to the younger woman as she released a heavy sigh. "I'm trying to tell him that simply because the doctor has given him permission to go home it doesn't necessarily mean that he's recovered enough to leap up and start running about like a—"

"Didn't you say something about fetching me a bite to eat before we leave?" her husband gruffly interrupted. Ella subjected him to a quelling look as she clamped her mouth shut and took herself off, leaving an unrepentant Ike to grin across briefly at Addie, who suppressed an answering smile.

"She's only concerned about your welfare, you know," she mildly reproved, moving to take a seat in the chair nearest him, her skirts rustling softly. Attired in a simple but attractive gown of pale blue wool, her chestnut curls pulled back with a ribbon, she appeared much younger than usual, and Ike found himself thinking back to the first time he had seen her, all those years ago. Since that time, he had come to look upon her much like his own daughter. And, he mused, his heart twisting at the recollection, he had once even cherished hopes of his only son and Adelaide Caton . . .

"I've got something to say to you, Miss Addie," he declared in a low voice, pausing to noisily clear his throat. "It's . . . it's about what happened last night." His lined, bearded countenance became suffused with a dull color, prompting Addie to stare at him in puzzlement.

"Last night?" she echoed. "Ike," she then told him, experiencing a sudden uneasiness, "you don't have to tell me . . . you don't have to explain anything to me."

"I want you to know." His eyes were clouded with pain as he paused again. When he spoke this time, it was mostly in a low monotone, as if he were forcing himself to do something necessary but distasteful. "We wanted to show Jordan that we didn't aim to take any of his damned Yankee insolence, that we weren't going to let him get away with coming in here to take over like it was his due for chancing to be on the winning side. It was bad enough finding out that Ferguson had sold his place to one of the enemy," he muttered grimly, "though I'll allow you can't hardly blame a man for needing the money to make a new life for himself."

"The Fergusons were in a bad situation," Addie quietly reminded him. "They were faced with little choice in the matter."

"I know that. And that's why none of us tried to do anything about it before Jordan came here. We didn't think he'd ever actually have the guts to show his face in these parts. But it wasn't any time at all until we saw he

162

was even worse than what we had expected. Him and his blasted arrogance! Then, finding out he'd been one of those who was responsible for killing my boy . . ." His voice trailed away, and it was a visible struggle for him to resume. "The way he barged in at the dance last night was the final straw. You know how folks around here feel. The last thing we wanted was to live side by side with a damned bluebelly!"

"It was the last thing I wanted, too," murmured Addie, reflecting that her own reasons involved a great deal more than the simple fact of Daniel Jordan's loyalties in the recently ended conflict.

"So, we decided to teach him a lesson. We had in mind to try to scare him away, to show him we were dead serious about our threats to force him out. Only, everything backfired, didn't it?" he concluded, his voice sounding rather distant. He reached up a hand to stroke absently at the coarse bristles of his beard, his eyes narrowing as his expression grew pensive.

Addie was silent and still, feeling at a loss for words. When she did speak, she attempted to mask her inner confusion with a forced smile. Rising to her feet, she strolled across to stand before the heat of the fireplace again. She raised a hand to the thick oak mantle and leaned into the warmth.

"Well, there's no use in lamenting the fact that things didn't work out quite the way you planned," she remarked lamely, her back turned toward Ike. Daniel's face swam before her eyes. "But, tell me, Ike," she requested, her gaze focusing upon the dancing flames, "how did you come to be lying unconscious in that barn?"

"I suppose I haven't offered much of an explanation

163

about that yet, have I?" he observed with a faint, rueful smile. "It's not something I'm proud to admit. I'd gone on into the barn with a torch, telling the others that I'd catch up with them. We knew Jordan would be showing up at any moment, and I just . . . well, I just thought I'd make certain the job was done right. I'd no sooner climbed up into the loft when the boards gave way beneath me—something I should have had sense enough to suspect, seeing as how the damned thing was so old and all. The last thing I remember is falling and hitting my head on the edge of the ladder."

"You were unconscious when Silas and I got there," softly recalled Addie, the flickering blaze mirrored in her shining eyes.

"When I found out this morning that it was Jordan who got me out of there . . . instead of letting me roast alive . . ." He cleared his throat again, and his face wore a fierce scowl as he shifted uncomfortably upon the chaise. "That Yankee son of a bitch has put me in one hell of a position!"

"What do you mean?" she asked, turning slowly about to face him, her arms crossing against the rounded curve of her bosom.

"He saved my life," Ike stated simply, then released a long, resigned sigh. "No matter what he is, no matter what he's done, I can't raise my hand against a man who saved my life."

"Then you and the others won't be—"

"No," he broke in, "we won't be riding against him any longer."

"You mean you're actually going to accept him?" she questioned in stunned amazement, her gaze wide and faintly bewildered. Could it really be that because of one undeniably moral act on Daniel Jordan's part that a man such as Ike Henry, a man so very embittered by the war and its devastating toll upon his own family, would now be willing to live in peace with one of the enemy?

"Accept him?" repeated Ike, his tone rising sharply. "I'll damn sure never accept him! But this is a question of honor, Miss Addie," he explained with more composure. "Though I'll never be able to look upon him as either friend or neighbor, neither will I do anything to interfere with him or his ranch. That's the least I can do after he saved my life," he concluded with another deep scowl.

Addie speechlessly stared across at him, her features still reflecting the confusion his words had created within her. Looking quite dubious, she nonetheless forced another bolstering smile to her lips as she declared, "My father always said you were quite a man, Ike Henry!"

"He is that," agreed Ella, appearing in the doorway now with a tray in her hands. She lowered the tray to a small table beside the chaise before placing her hands on her hips and narrowing her eyes at her husband. "I'll have you know that I expect you to eat every bite of this food!"

Ike's brow cleared, and he chuckled softly at his petite wife's domineering tone. Addie smiled inwardly as she watched the two of them exchange a look of mingled affection and marital understanding. For some unknown reason, however, she also experienced a sharp, decidedly unsettling twinge of discontent.

*   *   *

Later, after Addie's guests had taken their leave, she climbed the stairs to her room and hastily changed into her working clothes. Having decided to venture outside for a word with the ranch hands, she made her way into the kitchen, where she paused to draw on her outer garments. Esther was occupied with her daily bread-baking, but she immediately set aside her task and turned her attention to the other woman as she rinsed the flour from her hands.

"Silas said you was to meet him out in the barn soon as you got a chance."

"Oh?" responded Addie with a slight frown. "Did he say what it was he wanted?" She buttoned her coat and pulled the hat low on her head, then began tugging on the thick leather gloves.

"Somethin' about wolves," Esther replied, drying her hands on a towel. She stood near the stove, her plump features reflecting a certain preoccupation as she glanced toward Addie. "I was sure glad to see Mr. Henry's gonna be all right."

"Yes. Doc Bennett said he should be fully recovered within a couple of days." The subject brought Daniel to mind again. Why did she always have to be reminded of that man? she asked herself in exasperation. Was there no escape from thoughts of him?

"Well, it seems to me that folks around her ought to stop all this foolishness about burnin' barns and the like," Esther emphatically pronounced, punctuating her words with a brisk nod. "Yankee or no Yankee, it ain't right."

"There wouldn't have been any need for such 'foolishness' if a certain bluebelly had stayed where he belonged instead of—" Addie began to assert crossly, a

166

hot, angry color rising to her face as her eyes flashed with brilliant fire. She broke off abruptly when she perceived the way Esther was staring at her, apparently quite surprised at the younger woman's unexpected vehemence.

Releasing an audible sigh, Addie marched to the back door and hastily made her exit, directing her purposeful strides toward the barn. The golden rays of the late afternoon sun fell upon her head, and she appreciatively raised her face to its soothing warmth. The skies were vividly blue and cloudless, and the only remaining evidence of the recent storm were the several inches of snow which still covered the rolling, tree-dotted landscape.

"Esther said you wanted to see me," she remarked to Silas as she entered the barn and found him critically inspecting a loosening horseshoe on one of the well-groomed animals. She waited, watching while he murmured softly to the horse as he released its foreleg. "What's this about wolves?" she then asked with a slight frown.

"Clay and Billy found what was left of a calf when they rode out after gettin' back from Dallas this mornin'," he informed her, straightening up and administering one last gentle pat upon the animal's neck. "Looks like we're gonna have to do ourselves a bit of huntin'."

"Damnation!" muttered Addie, her face tightening with increased displeasure. Impatiently whipping the hat from her head, she twisted the single braid of shining chestnut hair farther upward upon her head, then covered the thick, lustrous mass with the broad-brimmed hat once more.

Silas, meanwhile, was watching her closely, telling himself that there was something bothering Miss Addie, something other than the unfortunate matter of the wolves who grew even bolder during the cold months and began fearlessly stalking the cattle. Yes sir, he silently mused, his heart aching for whatever it was that troubled her, he knew Miss Addie, and he knew somethin' was sure causin' her worry.

"I thought maybe I'd take Trent and go on out tonight to see about gettin' us a few of them varmints," he announced, returning to the problem of the wolves.

"Where is Trent now?" she asked, feeling strangely detached. Suddenly, the image of Daniel's barn engulfed in flames came unbidden to her mind. He would have no shelter for his horses, no place to store the hay so desperately needed in the winter. But what concern is it of yours? she silently berated herself.

"Him and the boys have gone on out to see if they find anythin' else. Said they'd be back before dark." Addie said nothing in reply but instead stared down thoughtfully at the hay-covered ground inside the barn. When she finally raised her head, she startled Silas by instructing him to hitch Smokey up to the buckboard and toss a couple of bales of the sweet-smelling hay into the bed.

"You plannin' to drive out and feed some of the stock?" he asked in puzzlement. "There's no call for you to do that. The boys've already taken care of—"

"I'm not going to feed our stock," she firmly interrupted, then raised her chin in an unconscious gesture of defiance. "I . . . I want you to take the hay over to Mr. Jordan."

"You do?" It was obvious that her words threw him

168

into further confusion.

"It's the least we can do. After all," she pointed out, as if endeavoring to convince herself as well as him, "we're his nearest neighbors, aren't we? No matter how I feel about the man, I can't stand by and watch his horses starve!"

"Beggin' your pardon, Miss Addie, but he can get all the hay he needs over in the next county," Silas reminded her.

"Yes, but he doesn't know that!" she countered with yet another sigh. "You can tell him when you take him the hay. But, in the meantime, he'll need this now," she insisted, nodding toward the bales stacked nearly as high as the vaulted ceiling. "I thought you'd approve of the neighborly gesture, Silas," she added, a bit perplexed at his apparent disapproval. "You're usually the first one who expresses the willingness to extend a helping hand to anyone in need."

"Yes, ma'am, I reckon that's true," he murmured, turning away to set about following her instructions.

"Why the objections then?" Addie demanded persistently.

"Well, Miss Addie," answered Silas, his own expression growing thoughtful. "It's like this. Seems like that Yankee ain't brought nothin' but trouble with him. And, most of all 'cause of what happened last night, I don't want to see you get mixed up in all the trouble," he admitted, his kindly features appearing quite solemn.

"You needn't worry about me," she quietly responded, touched by his concern on her behalf. "I'm well able to take care of myself."

"That don't make no difference!" he argued with

uncharacteristic vigor. "Mr. Will and Miss Lilah always said I was to look after you. And I'm tellin' you, there's nothin' but trouble ahead if you have anythin' more to do with that there Yankee." Then, as if he'd already said too much, he turned away again and quickly led Smokey out of the barn.

Addie folded her arms across her bosom and shook her head, consternation written on her beautiful face. It distressed her to see Silas so bothered by the situation. It was as if he sensed the underlying complications between herself and Daniel, she mused, wandering aimlessly toward the doorway.

Daniel. Why was she actually trying to help him, in even the smallest way? Because, she defensively reasoned with herself, it was the only decent thing, the only honorable thing to do under the circumstances. It was the way she had been taught to behave, wasn't it?

"And just what the hell do you think he's going to make of your foolish generosity?" she wondered aloud, trying to visualize Daniel's reaction to the simple gift of hay. Then, realizing that she was talking to herself again, something she had never done until quite recently, she uttered a curse and strode from the barn.

Addie was upstairs in her bedroom in the early hours of the evening when she heard Esther calling for her. Descending the staircase, clad only in a warm flannel wrapper, she stepped into the kitchen to find Silas shrugging out of his coat. The delectable aromas of the various dishes Esther would serve them that night pleasantly filled the room that had always been Addie's favorite.

"Yes, Esther, what is it?" she asked, nodding briefly in Silas's direction before facing his wife. In all actuality, she was quite anxious to hear Silas's account of his errand to Daniel's ranch, but she had no intention of allowing her impatience to be seen by the two older people.

"Silas has some news for you," Esther replied, ambling past Addie as she carried the coffeepot and two cups to the table.

"Oh?" remarked Addie, feigning only casual interest. She took a seat at the table and accepted the cup Esther offered her. Her long, flowing hair was still damp from her bath, her cheeks becomingly flushed.

"He wouldn't take it, Miss Addie," Silas told her, folding his lean form into a chair.

"What do you mean, 'he wouldn't take it'?" she demanded a bit sharply.

"I took the hay on over to him, just like you said. Told him it was just somethin' to see him through till he could get on over to the next county and get a load of his own. I was tellin' him where to go to get it when he cut me off, sayin' he was much obliged but didn't need it."

"Didn't need it?" echoed Addie in utter bewilderment.

"That's what the man said. Come to find out," explained Silas, "there was a whole stack of fresh hay 'round on the other side of his cabin. It turns out a couple of his other neighbors had brung it over a while ago."

"Well, I wonder who . . ." she began, her voice trailing away as it suddenly dawned on her that the startling account of what Daniel Jordan had done for

Ike Henry would most likely have been spread all over town by this time. She was constantly amazed at how rapidly news traveled.

"I think some folks was feelin' a mite guilty for their part in last night's mischief," Esther opined, her line of thought evidently paralleling Addie's. Pouring her husband a cup of steaming black coffee, she added, "It's good to hear there's still some that's got a conscience."

"Did he . . . did he say anything else?" Addie inquired of the man opposite her as she carefully sipped the hot brew, her mind drifting back to the unpleasant scene that had taken place in the kitchen the previous night, and most particularly the incident involving the same liquid she was drinking at the moment.

"Yes, ma'am, he did," Silas answered readily enough but then appeared somewhat hesitant about delivering the message he had been charged with giving his boss.

"Well, what was it?"

"Mr. Jordan said I was to tell you that he appreciated the little bit of hay you sent over, but that you could take your charity and keep it for those with more virtuous intentions."

She was certain her face turned at least a dozen shades of red. Her eyes narrowed and blazed. The audacity, the blasted insolence of the man! Addie inwardly raged. She became further infuriated when she met the curious stares of both Silas and Esther.

"What did he mean by that?" Esther wondered aloud, frowning down at Addie as she set the coffeepot on the polished surface of the table.

"I think . . . I think the man believed the remark to

172

be humorous," she stiffly declared, envisioning all sorts of appropriate retribution for his offensive mockery.

"I guess it just goes to show you," remarked Esther, turning away to see to the food cooking on the stove, "that what us folks thinks is funny and what them Yankees thinks is funny ain't one and the same."

"Is that the only message Mr. Jordan requested that you give me?" Addie coolly asked Silas, successfully concealing the explosive state of her temper.

"That was the only one." He drained his cup then stood up and began drawing on his coat again. "I better get on out to the bunkhouse and let Trent know we're goin' huntin' tonight," he told her, relieved that she didn't appear nearly as upset with Jordan's peculiar message as he'd thought she might be.

"Supper's almost ready, so you just make certain you get yourself back inside in time to eat it!" commanded Esther, casting him a look of mock ferocity. He responded with a broad grin, then headed back outside.

It wasn't until much later in the evening, long after Addie had retired to the privacy of her room, that she allowed herself to dwell upon the insulting message Daniel had sent to her via Silas. Her palm fairly itched to slap his handsome, arrogant face again, and she vowed that she would think of some way to pay him back for his outrageous impudence!

Finally sliding beneath the covers of her bed, she tossed restlessly as she sought an elusive position of comfort. She was suddenly, starkly reminded of the shameful intimacy she had shared with Daniel upon that very bed, and she groaned inwardly as her face flamed in renewed embarrassment.

Rolling to her side, she clutched at the pillow which cushioned her head, her fingers tightening almost convulsively in its softness. She was thoroughly dismayed to feel a dull ache starting in the very pit of her stomach and spreading slowly outward, an ache that owed its origins to something she dared not name.

Ten

Christmas came, and Addie had neither seen nor heard from Daniel in nearly a week. His silence both confused and unnerved her, though she was loathe to admit that she was even the least bit curious about it. But her dreams each night were filled with disturbing memories of a steely-eyed, golden-haired man who seemed to be forever mocking her, laughing at her, a man whose fiery touch she had nonetheless been unable to resist.

She determinedly shook off the latest dream as she made her way downstairs on Christmas morning, attired in a very flattering, simply tailored dress of bottle green flannel, its high neck and small collar folded under and the resulting opening filled in with a bright red kerchief. Her appearance prompted Esther to remark, "Honey, you sure do look like you got the holiday spirit!"

Addie smiled warmly in response, sweeping farther inside the kitchen and pausing to tie on a clean white apron. "You look quite festive yourself," she pro-

175

claimed, nodding at the two-piece scarlet wool suit the older woman was wearing. "Now, what can I help you with?" she asked, her hands on her hips as she surveyed the multitude of pots and pans scattered about the stove and table.

"Well, I already done most of the cookin', but you might set yourself down and peel me a few potatoes." Addie was quite willing to oblige, and it wasn't long before she had gathered up a bowl of potatoes and a sharp knife and had applied herself to the task.

She and Esther conversed amiably as they worked, though the two of them wisely refrained from mentioning anything about a certain neighbor. Addie had resolutely decided to avoid all thought of Daniel Jordan that day, for it was the first Christmas since the end of the war, and she was determined to make it a pleasant, untroubled celebration.

When the four men filed into the dining room a few hours later, their eyes widened in appreciation at the mouth-watering array of foods awaiting them. As was the tradition, the ranch hands were to share Christmas dinner with their employer in the main house. It was a time-honored custom practiced by nearly every rancher in the state.

"Clay, Billy, the two of you sit there," directed Addie, pointing to indicate their places at the long, rectangular table, its dark oak surface covered with a spotless linen tablecloth. "And Silas, you're to sit there beside your wife, of course," she instructed with a brief smile.

"Where do you want me, Miss Addie?" Trent Evans quietly asked, waiting close beside her as she stood at the head of the table. He and the others were dressed in their best shirts and trousers, their new boots polished, their faces scrubbed and clean-shaven for the occasion. Trent's brown eyes narrowed slightly as he secretly took note of the way Addie's dark curls caught and reflected the light of the overhead lantern.

"There," she stated, nodding at the seat to the right of hers, the place usually reserved for special guests. Although she would actually have preferred for either Clay or Billy to sit beside her, she knew it was Trent's due as the hand who had been at the ranch the longest.

Trent smiled faintly at the honor accorded him, quite pleased that she had so favored him before the others. Silas was at his other side, with Esther occupying the seat at the opposite end from Addie.

"That's got to be the biggest damn turkey I ever—" said Clay, hungrily eyeing the perfectly browned specimen on the table before him.

"Shall we say grace now?" Addie interrupted with a rather austere frown in his direction, though her hazel eyes sparkled in secret amusement. She waited until everyone had bowed their heads before she repeated the same prayer of thanksgiving she said every year at that time, another quaint tradition established by her late father.

It wasn't long until the hands were well on their way to devouring every single scrap of the roast turkey, and Addie smiled to herself with a feeling of deep satisfaction. The Rolling L had managed to make it through yet another year, she mused, and she was convinced that the ranch would continue to survive, no matter what misfortunes lay ahead.

She was just lifting another forkful of cornbread dressing to her mouth when she was startled by a loud, insistent knock at the front door.

"Now who could that be?" remarked Esther, frowning as she prepared to rise and answer the door.

"I'll get it," insisted Addie, standing and negligently tossing her napkin to the table. Her face wore a look of mild curiosity as she stepped into the entrance hall, and she thought to herself that it certainly was unusual for anyone to come calling on that particular day. Her hand reached to turn the brass knob, and she swung open the door with a polite smile rising to her lips.

"Merry Christmas, Addie," proclaimed Daniel, smiling softly down at her.

"You!" she exclaimed in astonishment. Then she quickly lowered her voice as she furiously whispered, "What are you doing here?" Her annoyance swiftly increased as she felt a strange fluttering deep inside.

"I thought since this was our first real Christmas together—"

"We're not *together!*" she waspishly interjected, keeping her voice low.

"—that I would stop by and wish you a merry Christmas, which I have just done," he finished, good-naturedly completing the explanation as if she had never spoken.

"Well then, since you've done what you came to do, you'll be on your way again!" She attempted to close the door in his face, but the large, booted foot he placed squarely upon the threshold prevented her success. Glaring reproachfully up at him, she harshly demanded, "What is it now?" She glanced anxiously back toward the dining room, and Daniel smiled mockingly at her obvious concern that they would be overheard.

"Why don't you simply invite me inside?"

"We happen to be enjoying our Christmas dinner at the moment!"

"I haven't eaten yet," he informed her with a low chuckle, his gray eyes twinkling merrily down at her.

"You were not invited!" she pointedly reminded him, her own eyes sending invisible daggers at his head. "Now will you please leave?"

"Miss Addie?" Esther's voice called from the other room. "Who is it, honey?"

"Just a minute!" Addie hastily tossed over her shoulder. Turning her stormy gaze upon Daniel again, she indignantly whispered, "Remove your foot at once!"

"Unless you want to create that scene you're so hoping to avoid," he quietly countered, an ironic smile on his handsome face, "I'd suggest you agree to come outside with me for a moment."

"Come outside with you?" she repeated, stunned by his suggestion. "I most certainly will not!"

"Then I'll simply have to stand here in the doorway while your dinner, not to mention your house, grows cold," asserted Daniel with an unabashed grin.

His words provoked Addie to mutter a blistering oath, but the tall man before her appeared totally unscathed. One of his eyebrows was raised in sardonic expectation as he waited for her to make her decision. It seemed to Addie that he looked supremely confident as to her choice, a choice between giving in to him and being forced to explain to the others that the Yankee was staying for Christmas dinner. She capitulated with an ill grace, spinning about on her heel and flouncing away from him as she went to present some sort of explanation to Esther and the men.

"I'm afraid you'll all have to excuse me for a short time. I . . . I have a bit of business to take care of," she offered rather lamely, raising her chin a trifle as she stood framed in the doorway of the dining room.

"Business? On Christmas Day?" retorted Esther, her plump features reflecting her extreme disapproval.

"Is it somethin' I can take care of for you, Miss Addie?" Silas generously asked, already laying aside his fork.

"No, thank you," Addie quickly replied, smiling weakly across at him. "Please, continue with the meal. I shouldn't be long." She turned and left them staring curiously after her, and she could hear Esther's voice murmuring something about how inconsiderate some folks were when it came to timing.

Daniel was awaiting her return in the front doorway, and he pulled the tan Stetson lower on his head as he watched Addie fling her woolen cloak about her shoulders. He refrained from offering her assistance, knowing full well that she would only refuse. Finally, she swept wordlessly past him with as much dignity as she could muster, leaving him to pull the door softly to before he turned and followed.

"All right, why did you insist that I come out here?" Addie haughtily demanded, rounding on him as soon as she reached the bottom step. The day had dawned cold and cloudy, but there was fortunately no sign of any further storms. The hard, frozen ground was still blanketed with a thin coating of snow, the majority of it having already melted during the past week.

"I wanted to give you your Christmas gift," he replied with unfaltering equanimity, smiling down at her again. Addie, however, was not amused.

"What?" she raged. "I've no time to waste on such foolish sentiment, especially when I feel anything but sentimental about you, Daniel Jordan!" She whirled about and was angrily gathering her skirts to march back up the front steps when he seized her arm and pulled her gently but firmly to a halt.

"The least you can do is accept my gift with something approaching politeness," he admonished in a low tone, his deep voice laced with a touch of his own rising anger. In the next moment, however, amusement flickered briefly over his handsome face. "I can assure you that it's a simple enough thing to grant, accepting a gift from your own husband."

"You're not my husband!" she hotly denied, jerking her arm from his grasp.

"Let's not waste time debating that particular issue right now," he responded in a conciliatory tone. His expression sobered and his eyes gleamed dully as he said, "No matter how you feel about me, I don't think it's too much to ask that you come to the barn and see what I brought you."

Anything he asked was too much! Addie resentfully told herself, her beautiful face appearing quite mutinous as she stood poised for flight upon the step and waged a silent battle with her conflicting emotions.

It was Christmas, a time for making peace with one's enemies, a time for forgiveness, her conscience reminded her. Yes, but what if forgiveness hadn't even been asked for? she angrily mused.

Still, she admitted with an inward sigh, her bitterness toward him should at least be set aside for this one day. No matter what ill feelings she harbored for the man who was apparently set upon wreaking utter havoc in her life, it certainly could do her no significant harm to treat him with mere common courtesy.

Drawing herself regally erect, she faced Daniel with a distrustful look as she reluctantly acquiesced. "Oh, all right!"

"Then come to the barn with me," he commanded with a brief smile, taking her arm again.

"Why to the barn?" she warily demanded, nevertheless allowing him to lead her along.

"Because that happens to be where I left your gift," he evasively answered, quickening their approach to the tin-roofed building. Addie eyed him suspiciously, but she watched in silence while he eased open one of the huge wooden doors. She gasped in surprise as her startled gaze fell upon the tiny bundle of energy which came bounding exuberantly out of the barn, its tail wagging excitedly.

"Why, it's a dog!" Addie breathed in amazement.

"Well, I'm glad we were able to settle that issue so easily," Daniel quipped wryly. He was rewarded with a withering glance, but he ignored it as he bent down a moment to carefully seize the squirming, multicolored puppy and present it to Addie for her inspection.

"Where did you get him?" she stiffly asked, instinctively reaching out a hand to stroke the puppy gently upon his soft, fuzzy head. His big brown eyes looked up at her so appealingly that she couldn't resist smiling faintly in response. All else was momentarily forgotten as she murmured softly to the irresistible, floppy-eared animal. She was unaware of the way Daniel's steely gaze softened and glowed as he watched her.

"I bought him from the boy at the livery stable in

town a couple of days ago," he told her, his hands still holding the puppy aloft while Addie lightly stroked its head.

"From Kyle Townsend?"

"Yes. When I told him I was looking for a good cow dog, he said he had just the thing. He happened to mention that the pup's sire was reputed to be the best cow dog in all the county."

"Did Kyle also happen to mention that he's reputed to be one of the biggest liars in all the county?" Addie sardonically observed, raising her eyes to Daniel's face now.

"Who? The boy, or the dog?" he quietly teased, his steady gaze filled with irrepressible humor. Addie was dismayed to feel a sudden flip-flop in her stomach, and she attempted to mask her perplexing emotions with an attitude of renewed irritation.

"I must be getting back inside now." She bestowed a final pat upon the puppy's head as she proclaimed, "I'm afraid I won't be able to accept your gift."

"Why not?"

"Because . . ." she began, searching for an explanation, "because he'll only get underfoot around here!" She knew it was a lie, and that a dog would be quite useful around the ranch. Their last dog had died more than a year ago, and they'd simply never bothered to replace it, mainly because of Addie's attachment to the old hound that had been more of a pet than a work dog. She was unable to deny to herself that she would like nothing better than to accept the puppy Daniel had brought her, but she didn't want to give him any reason to assume that she had softened toward him in even the slightest way.

"He'll learn to stay out of the way," Daniel insisted, making it clear that he had no intention of accepting her refusal. His eyes looked so very gray against the tanned skin of his face, she vaguely thought, then mentally shook herself.

"I'm sorry, but—" She started to offer her objections once more but broke off when he thrust the puppy into her unsuspecting arms.

"As you said, you'll need to be getting back inside." He politely tipped his hat to her, smiling once more before sauntering unconcernedly past her as he headed back toward the horse he had left tied to the hitching post in front of her house. Addie stared speechlessly after him for several long seconds before striding hurriedly to catch up.

"Daniel Jordan—"

"Never mind about asking me to join you for dinner now, Addie," he cut her off with a mocking grin as he swung up into the saddle. "I've got other plans."

"Why, you . . . you egotistical son of a—" she indignantly sputtered, battling the childish urge to stamp her foot in temperamental frustration.

"Merry Christmas, Addie," Daniel masterfully broke in yet again then blithely reined his horse about and rode away at a leisurely pace, leaving Addie to glare venomously at his retreating back.

She unconsciously hugged the softly whining puppy to her breast before turning about and climbing the steps with a preoccupied air. Her mind was in a dizzying whirl when she entered the dining room again, and she had apparently forgotten about the warm bundle she was cradling as she wandered toward the table.

"I was beginnin' to think you'd never get back—" Esther started to chide with a deep frown, her eyes growing round as saucers when she glimpsed the ball of fur hidden just within the folds of the cloak Addie had neglected to remove. "What on earth have you got there?" she loudly demanded.

"What?" Addie murmured as if in a trance. She glanced up at the other woman as if only just becoming aware of her surroundings. "Oh, this," she replied, withdrawing the puppy from the protective wool and holding it securely with both hands. "It's a dog, of course."

"A dog?" repeated Esther in astonishment.

"I been thinkin' we could sure use us another dog around here," Silas commented with a broad grin.

"He don't look like much, does he?" Clay blurted out, eyeing the tiny animal with youthful disdain. He and Billy were finishing the last bits of food on their plates, and they eagerly awaited the pumpkin pie Esther had promised them for dessert.

"Where'd you get him, Miss Addie?" Trent surprised her by asking, his hawkish gaze fixed unblinkingly upon the wriggling puppy in her grasp.

"Well, I . . . I . . ." she faltered, feeling quite discomfited as she observed the way everyone was staring at her with open curiosity. Her eyes glistened in visible defiance as she evenly declared, "Mr. Jordan gave him to me." It was best to tell them the truth now, she thought, for they would in all likelihood discover it eventually, especially if Daniel had mentioned to Kyle that he intended the puppy as a gift for her. The man did nothing but cause her trouble!

"Mr. Jordan? Well, why in heaven's name did that

man go and give you a dog? And why didn't you ask him to come on inside?" interrogated Esther.

"The dog was a simple gesture of . . . of holiday good will, and I didn't ask him inside because I had no wish to share Christmas dinner with him!"

"But—" the older woman started to argue, only to be silenced by a firm, quelling glance from her husband.

"Leave her be, Esther. Miss Addie's done what she thought best." Addie cast him a grateful look, pleased to see that he, at least, apparently agreed with her decision.

"It would've spoiled things to have that bluebelly in here," ventured Billy, pushing his plate away at last and releasing a long, contented sigh.

Addie smiled faintly at him, but her smile rapidly faded when her gaze moved to catch the tight-lipped expression on Trent's face. He didn't raise his eyes to hers, but she could see the way his fingers clenched about his fork, could almost feel a rigidly controlled violence emanating from his dark features.

Glancing sharply back at Esther, she was further discomfited by the silent reproof she read in the other woman's unwavering stare. Well aware of Esther's beliefs regarding dutiful hospitality to one's neighbors —or even strangers, for that matter—she was annoyed to experience a twinge of remorse for the way she had treated Daniel.

"What you plannin' to do with that thing?" Esther suddenly queried, gesturing toward the animal now lying still and sleepy eyed within Addie's arms. Without waiting for a reply, she said, "You'd best be gettin' back to your dinner before it gets stone cold."

Addie gazed heavenward in total exasperation for an

instant before wheeling about and sweeping from the room again, her brisk movements bespeaking the worsening condition of her already frayed nerves. Marching out of the house and back toward the barn, she frowned down at the warm bundle of fur, musing that it was odd how such a little thing could create so much added complication.

The puppy seemed to have read her thoughts, for it raised its tiny head and softly licked Addie's hand. And, in that moment, the gift's giver mattered little, for the heart of its recipient, evidently quite susceptible to brown-eyed, multicolored dogs of questionable parentage, melted entirely.

"I'm glad you decided to come with me," declared Gil, smiling warmly down at Addie as he escorted her from the small wooden church located near the town's square. "It's nice having someone like you to share Christmas with, Miss Addie."

"But you have family here," she reminded him, allowing him to assist her into the buggy. "Your aunt and uncle seem quite fond of you," she added as she settled the folds of her cloak about her. Gil paused to give her a faintly quizzical look before stepping around to the other side.

"It's not quite the same," he murmured dryly, climbing up to take hold of the reins. Snapping the long leather straps together above the horse's back, he guided the buggy away from the other vehicles and horses awaiting their owners in front of the church. The special Christmas evening service had been well attended, and Addie's spirits were a good deal higher than when Gil had come for her less than two hours before . . .

Gil was slightly early when he arrived at the Rolling L, and when Addie invited him inside the house for a cup of coffee and a slice of Esther's pumpkin pie, he appeared quite pleased by her gracious welcome. She had made a point of stopping by to visit with him at the mercantile twice during the past week, for she still felt quite guilty about the disastrous ending of their outing together the night of the dance. It was also the main reason she had agreed to accompany him to church that night, she recalled to herself as she waited for him to remove his hat and coat.

"It's a small miracle there is anything at all left of Esther's pies after Clay and Billy finished with them," Addie remarked with a low chuckle, leading the way toward the kitchen. She was unaware of the way Gil's eyes narrowed and shone as they feasted appreciatively upon her lustrous curls before being drawn irresistibly downward to the gentle sway of her rounded hips beneath the soft flannel of her skirts. His lips momentarily compressed into a thin, tight line, but he schooled his features to remain impassive as Addie swung open the door to the kitchen. "Esther? Esther, Mr. Foster's—" she began, breaking off when she saw that the other woman had mysteriously disappeared from the room. "Now where on earth could she have gone? She was here only a moment ago, just before you drove up."

"I don't want to put you to any trouble about the pie and coffee, Miss Addie," he gallantly insisted.

"It's no trouble at all," she replied with an airy wave of her hand. "Go ahead and have a seat while I see about putting on a fresh pot of coffee." Gil was amused at her commanding tone, but he hid the smile which rose to his lips as he did as she'd bid.

She was in the process of filling the coffeepot with water from the pump when the back door opened and Esther bustled hurriedly inside. Holding something in one hand, she paused to close the door before she turned about and took notice of the other occupants of the room.

"Well, good evenin' to you, Mr. Foster!" she declared, beaming at Gil. "And a merry Christmas to you, too!" Casting only a brief glance in Addie's direction, she raised a hand to lower the hood of her cloak.

"Thank you, Mrs. Fremont," Gil politely responded, rising to his feet and moving to help her remove the cloak. "I hope your own Christmas has proven to be a happy one." He took the woolen garment and transferred it to one of the pegs beside the door. Esther murmured her thanks, then turned to Addie at last. A sudden frown creased Addie's brow as she finally glimpsed what Esther held.

"What are you bringing him in here for?" demanded Addie.

"Well, I was thinkin' that the little mite would be gettin' too cold out there in that barn, and I . . . well, I thought it'd be best to bring him on inside for a spell," Esther finished a bit defensively. Stooping closer to the floor, she released the wriggling animal, grinning broadly as she watched it scamper straight toward Addie.

Gil smiled as Addie bent and scooped the dog into her arms, her expression softening as she tenderly stroked its head. He was touched by the warm glow in her eyes, and his smile deepened as he and Esther exchanged fondly indulgent looks, both of them silently musing that their Miss Addie seemed younger and more vulnerable than usual.

"He's an affectionate little fellow, isn't he?" observed Gil, stepping forward for a closer inspection of the newest addition to the Rolling L stock. His own hand instinctively moved to pet the dog as he casually asked, "Where did you get him?"

When Addie visibly hesitated, Esther rushed in to supply, "That new neighbor of ours rode over with him just today."

"New neighbor?" echoed Gil in bemusement.

"Yes," Addie reluctantly admitted, hastily averting her gaze, "Mr. Jordan."

"Oh," murmured Gil. "I see." Addie peered up at him then, noting the barely perceptible color rising to his attractive face, the faint glimmer of displeasure reflected in his deep blue eyes. And once again she felt a rising irritation, an irritation that never seemed to be far from the surface of late and always centered on Daniel . . .

She had been relieved that Gil hadn't included the subject of the puppy in their conversation on the way into town. But now, as they drove homeward in the crisp night air, the three-quarter moon casting a silvery glow over the winter landscape, an obviously preoccupied Gil startled her by saying, "You know, Miss

Addie, I'd no idea you and Jordan were on such good terms now."

"Mr. Jordan and I? We most certainly are not!" she adamantly denied, emphatically tossing her head so that the hood of her cloak fell back to reveal her silky chestnut tresses. She was puzzled to feel Gil stiffening beside her.

"I'm glad to hear it," he stated with an indefinable edge to his usually pleasant voice.

"Oh? And why is that?" Addie was unable to refrain from asking.

"The man is trouble. But it's much more than that." He fell silent for a moment, lifting a hand up to settle his hat more firmly upon his slightly waved, light brown hair. Battling the temptation to reveal the extent of his burgeoning regard for her, he deemed it wiser to admit only to a touch of jealousy. "To be honest, I don't like the thought of Jordan coming around your place too often. In fact, I suppose it wouldn't matter who my rival was," he concluded with a rather sheepish grin.

"Rival? What are you talking about?"

"Well, it's simply that if you and I are going to begin seeing one another on a regular basis, I'd take it kindly if you wouldn't allow anyone else to come calling on you."

"Is that so?" Addie crisply responded, her hazel eyes shooting sparks. Gil was quite taken aback when she rounded on him. "First of all, Gil Foster, Daniel Jordan is not 'calling' on me, as you so delicately put it! I thoroughly despise the man, so there's no possible way he could ever be considered any man's rival when it comes to my affections! And secondly, you have absolutely no right to dictate to me whom I should or should not see! Neither you, nor any other man, will ever own me!" She threw herself back against the buggy's cushion, furiously jerking her hood upward to cover her shining hair once more.

"I assure you that I meant no offense, Miss Addie," Gil apologized, still appearing stunned. Flicking the reins, he sought to quicken the horse's pace as Addie turned her fiercely sparkling gaze outward over the suddenly blurred countryside. Dashing impatiently at the hot, confused tears filling her eyes, she cursed herself for behaving so emotionally, for unjustly raging at a largely innocent Gil.

She was going to have to do something about Daniel Jordan, and soon, she grimly vowed, for she couldn't go on this way much longer. She desperately wanted things to return to normal, to be the way they were before he forcibly came charging into her life!

"I'm going to change your life again," he had emphatically promised. Well, she was going to see to it that he regretted the day he decided to come to Texas, the day he decided to so rudely destroy the serenity of her world!

Eleven

The horizon was ablaze with color, the dawn just breaking, as Addie guided her horse away from the barn and headed out toward the range. The rising sun cast a pale, yellow-orange glow upon the land, where a newly fallen snow signaled the beginning of yet another period of fierce winter weather. It was the first day of the new year, and Addie told herself that, if determination counted for anything, the next twelve months would be considerably better than the last.

But, she thought as a soft sigh escaped her lips, she would still have to think of a way to be free of Daniel Jordan in order to accomplish her goal of a return to peace, a return to the relatively calm orderliness she had known just before the war, before she had ever journeyed to St. Louis and met a tall, dashing young cavalry officer . . .

Mentally shaking herself, she shifted in the saddle, her gaze scanning the almost blinding whiteness of the countryside as she rode. Everything was quiet and still, she noted with satisfaction. She had always reveled in the freedom and privacy she was afforded on her early morning rides. This was her land, the land she loved, the land that had become such an integral part of Adelaide Caton.

Adelaide Caton Jordan, a tiny voice at the back of her mind perversely amended. How could she ever hope to be free of a man to whom she was still legally, if not emotionally, bound?

The question remained unanswered as a sudden movement caught her eye. Peering closely at the small grove of trees a short distance away, it took only an instant for her to ascertain that it was no longhorn that had drawn her gaze, but rather a lone wolf, soon followed by others of his pack as he emerged from the leafless, ice-coated cottonwoods.

Addie reached for her rifle, cautiously withdrawing it from its scabbard fastened on one side of the saddle. Recalling that the men had found the remains of several head of stock during the past couple of weeks, she was intent upon bringing down as many of the predators as she could. Trent and Silas had managed to exterminate half a dozen so far, she grimly reflected, but it appeared their efforts had had little effect on the ever-worsening problem.

She had always been an expert shot, and she now raised the gun to her shoulder and took careful aim as she murmured low words of command to her mount. The horse seemed to have understood, for it remained calm and motionless while its rider sighted her target and squeezed gently on the trigger. The shot rang out with almost deafening force, shattering the stillness of the frigid dawn air.

Addie gasped as her horse abruptly shied, its

reaction totally unforeseen, and she desperately sought to bring it under control again. The animal, however, reared violently, one of its back hooves disappearing into a treacherous, hidden gopher hole beneath the concealing blanket of snow. Stumbling and whinnying in alarm, the horse frantically attempted to regain its balance as a helpless Addie could only hold tight to the saddle horn with one hand, while her other hand clutched both the rifle and the reins.

"Whoa there, Twister! Whoa, boy!" she pleaded, relieved to feel the animal righting itself, then distressed as she realized that he was limping. He snorted softly as he favored his right foreleg, prompting Addie to hastily dismount and inspect the damage. "Hold still, boy," she quietly directed, impatiently sliding the offending weapon into its scabbard once more before bending down to tenderly brush the snow from the horse's leg.

Stripping off her warm leather gloves, she frowned darkly when she viewed the way Twister was unable to place much weight upon the injured shank, and she gently touched and probed the sensitive area before rising to her feet again.

"Damnation!" she muttered, furious with herself for having been the cause, albeit indirectly, of the horse's misfortune. Irritably reflecting that she should have known better than to fire a gun while sitting astride the occasionally skittish Twister, she chided herself for behaving like a complete jackass as she consolingly patted the animal's neck. "Well, boy, I suppose we'd best see about getting you back home."

But the Rolling L, she unhappily realized, was quite some distance from where she and the horse stood alone in the snow, the dead wolf's comrades having immediately fled at the sound of the gunshot. Not wishing to risk aggravating the horse's injury, Addie deemed it wisest to settle for making it to the closest neighbor's place instead. Then she would send back to her own ranch for Silas and another mount.

Her speculative gaze swept the frozen landscape as she gathered up the reins. The nearest ranch was just beyond the hill to the west, she vaguely remembered, her eyes abruptly widening as a look of total dismay crossed her face.

Daniel's place! The Ferguson ranch was the nearest to hers, only a short walk from the spot where she stood with the injured horse. And the Ferguson ranch now belonged to Daniel!

She couldn't go there. She couldn't simply appear on his doorstep at this early hour of the morning. And she certainly didn't want to place herself in the disturbing position of being completely alone with him!

In spite of her immense reluctance, in spite of all her emotion-charged arguments, she knew that she had no choice. It was a question of her cherished horse's well-being, not her own wounded pride. She truly had no choice, she begrudgingly concluded with an inward sigh of deep displeasure.

"Come on, Twister. Take it easy, boy. It isn't far," she murmured to the limping animal as she slowly led it forward. They passed the wolf Addie had shot, its eyes glazed, its features hideously contorted in death as its blood became a bright red stain upon the glistening snow. Addie turned away from the grotesque sight, her mind preoccupied with thoughts of what she would say to Daniel, of what his reaction would be to her appearance.

It wasn't long before her worst fears were realized. His words to her as she stood upon the threshold of his cabin were every bit as mocking and insulting as she had dreaded they would be.

"Well, well. Good morning to you, my dearest Mrs. Jordan. I was wondering how long it would take before your curiosity got the better of you!" He was smiling crookedly down at her, a faint shadowing of dark blond beard evident on the lower half of his handsome face, his thick, wheat gold hair still tousled from the sleep her knock had interrupted a few seconds earlier. He had hurriedly drawn on a pair of denim trousers, but the lithely muscled upper portion of his magnificent form—the broad, sun-bronzed chest and equally tanned arms—was quite bare, irrevocably drawing Addie's widening gaze before she grew angry and visibly bristled.

"You . . . you are absolutely insufferable!" He merely chuckled low in response, his gray eyes brimming with humor. "Aren't you at least going to ask me what I'm doing here?" she snapped.

"If you'd like to tell me."

"I knew it was a blasted mistake to come here!" she feelingly announced, spinning about on her booted heel and preparing to stalk away in disgust.

"Wait a minute, Addie," Daniel good-naturedly commanded, his hand shooting out to close about her wrist and pull her to a halt. "What is it? What brings you here at such an hour?" he asked more seriously.

Addie's eyes continued to flash, but she nevertheless turned about to face him again as she stiffly replied, "It's my horse. He's hurt his leg."

"Where is he?"

"In the barn. I didn't think you'd mind if I borrowed a bit of your hay." At the thought of hay, her anger returned, for she remembered all too well the way he had refused her generous offer of the two bales several weeks earlier.

"Oh, so you noticed I have a barn once more. And no, I don't mind at all about the hay," he responded with another brief smile. "If you'll give me a moment, I'll get dressed and go take a look at that horse of yours."

"There's no need for that. It's plain to see that he's strained one of his forelegs. I'd simply like to borrow one of your mounts so I can ride back to the Rolling L and fetch Silas."

"I see." He opened the door a bit wider and smiled again. "Forgive my lack of manners, Addie. Won't you please come inside?"

"No!" she hastily refused, then relented enough to add, "Thank you. I'd like to be on my way, if you don't mind." She did not meet his gaze, but instead stared past his head toward the smoldering ashes in the stone fireplace inside his cabin.

"You could at least come inside for a cup of coffee before setting off again," Daniel insisted, his voice deep and resonant. He seemed oblivious to the cold as he stood framed in the doorway, towering above Addie, who remained adamant about taking her leave.

"No. Would you please just tell me which horse you'd prefer that I take?"

"What's the matter, Addie?" Daniel asked, his tone soft and faintly sarcastic. "Are you afraid of what might happen if you stay long enough for coffee?"

"The hell I am!" she indignantly countered. "I'm not afraid of you, Daniel Jordan!" Her eyes flew to his, and she caught her breath upon an inaudible gasp as she viewed the disturbing, unfathomable light in those steely depths.

"Well then?" he murmured, his attitude offering a definite challenge.

Addie visibly hesitated. The last thing in the world she wanted was to be forced to prove to Daniel, and to herself, that she was immune to his undeniably virile, masculine charm! And yet, she reasoned with herself, her infinite pride rising to meet the challenge, why not show him that he had no hold over her, that simply because he had managed to overpower her better judgment once before, he would not be able to do so again?

"All right," she staunchly declared, her head held high as he stepped aside to allow her entrance. "I'll stay long enough for a cup of coffee," she decreed, tugging off her hat and moving to stand before the dwindling spark in the fireplace. Daniel closed the door and turned to look at Addie, his eyes glowing anew when he noted the single chestnut braid reaching to her waist, the aristocratic lines of her beautiful profile as she gazed downward at the dying embers.

"I'll get the fire going again before I see to that coffee," he told her, leisurely closing the distance between them as he headed for the fireplace. Addie, however, felt a sudden, unaccountable nervousness at his approach, and she abruptly wheeled away, striding rapidly to the curtained window while Daniel smiled to himself at her obvious unease. Placing a handful of kindling atop the ashes, then adding several small logs, he soon had the blaze flaring healthily once more. "Why don't you take off your coat and gloves? It should be warming up in here within a few more minutes," he said, rising to his feet and moving toward her again.

"When did you finish the new barn?" she questioned, endeavoring to remain casual and composed. Taking his advice, she removed her warm outer garments and placed them on a table below the window.

"The day before yesterday. I've hired a couple of older boys to help out around here. Besides erecting a new barn, they've also helped me do wonders with the cabin, in case you haven't noticed. The bunkhouse is our next project." He paused before her. "Since I am fully aware of the fact that my attire is somewhat . . . lacking," he remarked in obvious amusement, "I'll take a moment and get myself properly dressed. Why don't you have a look at the rest of the cabin? It's changed considerably since I first came here." Without waiting for a reply, he took himself off, leaving Addie to stare after him, her eyebrows pulled together in a faintly perplexed frown.

Why is he being so damnably pleasant? she wondered, her eyes sparkling in annoyance as she crossed her arms against her bosom and moved away from the window. Before she quite knew what she was doing, her steps were leading her about the much-altered interior of the large cabin. Just as Daniel had said, the place had been restored to a fair representation of its former condition and revealed the same charm it had displayed when it had been brand new, so many years ago.

The floors and walls had been cleaned and painted,

the windows scrubbed until the glass was spotless and clear. Numerous pieces of sturdy yet tasteful furniture filled the various rooms, and the spacious kitchen contained a new cookstove and sink. There were even new curtains at all the windows, she noted in surprise, marveling at the fact that a man had attended to such detail.

"It's quite a bit more homey, don't you think?" asked Daniel, appearing in the doorway to the kitchen. True to his word, he was now fully dressed. And yet, Addie was forced to admit, he was every bit as dangerous as before!

"It's definitely an improvement," she allowed, glancing quickly away from him. Touching a hand to the new stove, she hastily retrieved it and announced in a voice that was not quite steady, "I . . . I'm afraid I won't be able to stay for that coffee after all. It's getting late and—"

"Late? Why it's barely past dawn."

"Yes, but Esther and Silas will begin to worry," she insisted, frantically searching for a way to extricate herself from the increasingly uncomfortable situation without losing her dignity. Why, oh, why was she letting him get to her like this? she scornfully chastised herself.

"You won't be that much longer," he nonchalantly countered, crossing the room to fetch the coffeepot from the sink. "This may surprise you, Addie, but I make a fairly decent cup of coffee."

There was only a hint of a smile on his face, but Addie was afforded a glimpse of the irrepressible merriment in his eyes. He was laughing at her again! she furiously reflected. He was apparently quite aware

201

of her discomfort and was actually enjoying it!

"Keep your damned coffee, Daniel Jordan!" she cried wrathfully, whirling away from him and bolting from the room. He easily caught up with her, his gaze burning into hers as he forced her around to face him.

"What are you so afraid of, Addie? Is it me? Or could it possibly be yourself?"

"Take your hands off me!"

"Haven't we played this little scene before, my dearest wife?" he taunted. His expression grew solemn as he declared in a low, vibrant tone, "You're always running way from me, aren't you, Addie? You ran away from me more than four years ago, and you're still running. Do you truly believe you'll ever be able to run far enough?"

"I don't know what the hell you mean!" She twisted within his grasp, frightened of her own response as she felt the treacherous weakening of her body. He was so close, his head lowered and mere inches from her own, his eyes boring into hers as if he would see into her very soul.

"You know exactly what I mean!" he harshly disagreed, shaking her slightly for emphasis. "Wake up, Addie! Damn it, woman, come to your senses and see that what we had . . . what we *have* together can never be totally denied!"

"I see nothing but the despicable fact that you are trying to force your will upon me once again," she coldly responded, raising her chin in defiance as she became totally rigid beneath his hands.

Experiencing a sharp anxiety as she noted the grim set of her husband's jaw, Addie trembled inwardly as he dully stated, "So be it then." His words were as completely devoid of emotion as hers had been full of haughty scorn, and his hands abruptly dropped from her shoulders as he wordlessly turned away. He had taken only a single step when Addie's voice rang out with razor-sharp clarity.

"I shall not be borrowing a mount from you after all, Mr. Jordan. I would prefer to walk the entire distance home rather than be beholden to you!" she icily asserted, snatching up her things and preparing to flee.

"Beholden to me?" Daniel contemptuously echoed, slowly facing her again. "Don't you realize, dearest Addie, that you are already quite 'beholden' to me?"

"I . . . I sure as hell am not!" she fervently denied.

"Yes, you are. Or perhaps you simply choose not to remember that I was the one who taught you what it is to be a woman?" he softly remarked, purposefully goading her, his mouth twisted into a boldly derisive smile.

Addie stared up at him in stunned amazement, not at all certain she had heard him correctly. But when she viewed the mocking gleam in his eyes and the unmistakably taunting light therein, she became overwhelmed by the force of her blazing, tempestuous emotions. Without another word, she launched herself at him, her tightly clenched fists beating wildly upon his broad chest as her explosive temper was goaded beyond control.

Daniel wasted no time in enclosing her within his iron embrace, a look of undeniable satisfaction on his handsome face as he now sought to subdue the beautiful, furious young woman who seemed quite intent upon doing him bodily harm. Addie found herself effectively imprisoned, and yet she continued to kick and squirm in helpless rage while her captor merely held fast and patiently waited for admirable strength to wane.

"Release me!" she ground out, her features becoming brightly flushed. Her arms were pinned at her sides, and her booted feet were apparently inflicting inconsequential damage as her skirts flew about her furiously thrashing legs.

Daniel responded with a low chuckle, his obvious enjoyment of the situation provoking Addie to renew her struggles. Then, before she guessed his intent, his lips captured hers, shocking her into momentary immobility. The next instant, however, she twisted her head, tearing her lips from his as her eyes blazed up into his unconcerned stare.

"If you don't let go of me, I'll . . . I'll . . ." she spat at him.

"Scream?" he mockingly supplied. "Or perhaps level a thousand curses at my head? It doesn't matter what you do, Addie." To prove his point, he kissed her again, and she was thoroughly dismayed to feel herself weakening beneath the onslaught of his seductive assault. The deep, unnamed longing returned to plague her, but she made one last, desperate attempt to conquer it as she wrenched her mouth from the dangerously arousing warmth of his.

"Damn you! Let go of me!" she venomously demanded.

"This time I'm going to show you what our reunion should have been like in the first place," Daniel huskily vowed, prompting Addie to gasp in rapidly increasing alarm.

"No!" Her sparkling eyes were wide and full of fear,

though the panic she experienced was caused by the way her body trembled with what she recognized to be a forceful, dizzying surge of desire. The meaning of his words was beyond her comprehension, she dazedly thought, but she knew in that moment that she was completely powerless to resist him. For weeks now, ever since he had reentered her life and had begun methodically destroying the protective barriers she had erected around herself, she had been denying the immensely potent attraction which still existed between them. Now she choked back a sob of defeat, and hot tears burned her eyelids as they swept closed.

Daniel seemed acutely aware of her unspoken surrender, for his hold upon her suddenly relaxed. His arms freed hers before his hands seized her about the waist and urgently pulled her close again. Addie breathlessly met his intense, glowing gaze as his head lowered with a studied lack of haste, his mouth triumphantly claiming hers in a gentle kiss that swiftly grew more ardently inflamed.

His lips moved upon hers with infinite tenderness even as his searing kisses demanded her response. Addie could scarcely breathe as her arms lifted to entwine about his strong neck, tugging him even closer against her highly sensitive curves. Her lips parted beneath his, and she moaned quietly into his warm mouth when his fingers moved to caress the soft mound of her breast beneath the layers of wool and linen. His other hand cupped a firmly rounded hip, gently squeezing as she melted against his lean hardness.

She did not protest when he began unfastening the buttons of her blouse, or when the soft woolen garment was discarded, tossed aside to float unnoticed to the bare wooden floor. His lips roamed feverishly across the smooth contours of her face, returning to the inviting curve of her mouth as his fingers now deftly unbuttoned her skirt, its gathered folds slipping downward to land in a heap about her ankles. Her denim riding knickers soon followed, leaving her clad only in her chemise and flannel underwear.

Daniel released her long enough to bend and lift her high in his muscular arms, then effortlessly carried her to the darkened privacy of his bedroom a short distance away. Addie knew a moment's panic when he lowered her to the softness of his bed and knelt to tug off her boots.

"No . . . I . . . I can't!" she hoarsely whispered, desperately trying to stop him as he began easing off the last boot. Her eyes flashed in renewed confusion, and she rolled to her side on the bed as Daniel successfully removed the boot and allowed it to drop to the floor.

"You can't prevent it, Addie," he quietly proclaimed, blocking her only escape route as he stood in the doorway and reached up to start removing his own clothing. Addie lay still and watched in mesmerized silence as he quickly drew off his shirt and trousers, then took a seat on the edge of the bed to take off his thick wool socks. She seemed oblivious to the chill of the room, and her heart pounded wildly when Daniel turned about to face her again, wearing nothing but his own long winter underwear.

She knew there was no use in trying to leave, in trying to fight against what she now realized was the inevitable. Daniel Jordan did indeed wield a certain, unexplainable power over her, though she told herself her reaction stemmed from nothing more than mere physical desire. Lust. She pronounced the word in her mind. She was surrendering to nothing more than lust, and she knew that she would hate herself for it afterward. But now, she breathlessly admitted, she could not summon the strength to resist any longer!

"Loosen your hair, Addie," Daniel softly commanded, slowing rising to his feet beside the bed, his burning gaze lingering on her rosily blushing countenance as she sat upright on the quilt. As if she were in a trance, her fingers hastened to obey, carefully unwinding the long, single braid. Gently shaking her head, her graceful movements caused the gleaming chestnut tresses to fan about her face and shoulders in glorious disarray. She gasped inwardly at the flare of visible hunger she saw reflected in Daniel's eyes as she waited in breathless anticipation, her pulses racing with alarming speed.

She was puzzled when his hands clasped her elbows and gently but firmly drew her to her knees upon the bed, yet she could find no voice with which to question him. She trembled anew when his warm fingers slowly, provocatively untied the ribbon at the top edge of her simple linen chemise and then slid the thin fabric upward. Her arms seemed to rise of their own accord, and she shivered slightly as her breasts were left totally bare, her camisole joining Daniel's discarded clothing on the floor.

His gray eyes appeared to kindle with an even fiercer light, and his hands reached out to close tenderly, appreciatively over the full, rose-tipped peaks. Addie felt increasingly light-headed as his fingers smoothed over her breasts before trailing downward to begin easing off her long underwear. Within seconds, she was entirely naked, the fitted flannel drawers bunched about her knees. Trembling almost violently now, she watched as Daniel removed the last remaining barrier of his own clothing before kneeling upon the bed as well, his superbly fashioned masculine form revealed in all its magnificent glory.

The dim illumination inside the small room owed its origins to the pale streaks of golden sunlight filtering in through the curtains at the window near the iron bedstead, but the light was more than adequate for Daniel and Addie as they faced one another on the quilt-covered feather mattress. The atmosphere was highly charged, and Addie felt her emotions straining to a fever pitch, convinced that she would faint dead away if Daniel didn't take her soon.

Her wholly delicious agony, however, was far from over, for her husband's hands returned to her breasts, his long fingers curling erotically over the quivering white flesh, his skillful lips soon following. Addie moaned low in her throat when his head bent and his mouth closed upon one of the rose-tipped peaks. As his tongue swirled hotly, seductively about the sensitive nipple, his hands moved to tightly clasp her firmly rounded buttocks. Her fingers clutched at the rippling muscles of his shoulders, and she experienced such an overwhelming weakness that she would have fallen if not for the fact that he supported her body with his own.

His lips followed an imaginary, fiery path across her lavender-scented skin to tease at her other breast, and his fingers tightened upon the soft, silken flesh of her well-shaped derriere, intimately molding her lower body against his hard, undeniably aroused masculinity. Addie drew in her breath sharply as her femininity was pressed boldly to the throbbing instrument of his passion and his mouth began sucking tenderly yet greedily at her breast.

The next thing she was numbly aware of was the fact that he was lowering her to the mattress and turning her upon her side as he tugged the flannel underwear from about her knees and slipped it off. She gasped anew and her cheeks flamed crimson when he bent to brush the backs of her knees with his mouth, his lips gently nudging and faintly nipping as they traveled up the smooth white flesh of her slender thighs then lingered at the delectable roundess of her naked bottom.

He gently turned her upon her back once more, and her eyes flashed with an answering passion as they met Daniel's fiery orbs, so much like molten steel at that moment. He placed his body atop hers, and her arms welcomed him, her lips boldly inviting the warm caress of his own once more. He was more than happy to oblige, and their whirling emotions were sent soaring heavenward as they kissed and tasted, stroked and explored, until it become impossible to deny themselves the ultimate union any longer.

Addie surrendered to the wild abandon he evoked as she strained upward against Daniel's gentle fingers, the secret womanly flesh concealed beneath the tight chestnut curls at the apex of her thighs yearning for and gratefully receiving his touch. His fingers continued their pleasurable torment as he positioned himself above her, his maleness demanding entrance, then plunging into her velvety, honeyed warmth. She thought she would die with the tumultuous sensations assailing her, and she moaned again, her head tossing restlessly upon the pillow.

"Addie, my sweet wildcat," he murmured against her ear, the slow rotation of his hips swiftly increasing in tempo.

"Daniel," she could only whisper tremulously in response, her eyelids fluttering closed once more as she clutched him feverishly against her, her legs moving of their own volition to wrap about his waist as he moved faster and faster, taking them both higher and higher.

A faint cry escaped Addie's lips when the bursting fulfillment took hold of her, almost in unison with Daniel's low moan of release. The two of them were left breathless and numb, and it was fully half a minute later before he slid off her and lay at her side, his arms drawing her unresistingly within his warm, slightly moist embrace.

Neither of them spoke for what seemed like the space of several minutes, but was in actuality little more than one. Addie was the first to break the silence.

"Damn you," she muttered, her tone lacking conviction.

"Again?" Daniel sardonically quipped, chuckling softly as he hugged her tighter, her dark curls tumbling riotously about her flushed face. "Dearest, beautiful, sharp-tongued Adelaide. How you stir a man's blood!" he contentedly remarked, his fingers tenderly sweeping the tangled hair from her forehead.

"And how you . . . you . . . you confuse me!" she feelingly countered, unconsciously stiffening within his arms, even as her head rested upon his broad shoulder and her troubled gaze fixed upon the gentle rise and fall of his bronzed chest. "I never thought I'd see you again, Daniel Jordan." She spoke with a sigh, then frowned before adding, "And you have made my life an absolute misery ever since you came here!"

"Ah, but it's a splendid misery, isn't it?" he retorted, his deep voice smooth and vibrant in the stillness of the room. Addie was certain she could feel him smiling in smug triumph as he said, "Some things will never change between us, Addie."

"Everything changed between us long ago," she quietly insisted, her look of displeasure deepening. "There's no way we can ever go back."

"Do you think that's what I want?" he asked with a slight furrowing of his own brow, his hold upon her soft, naked body tightening. "No, Addie, I have no wish to go back. We're different people than we were four years ago. I don't want to try to live in the past. I want only to dwell upon the present, to concentrate on building upon what we have now."

"What we have now?" she repeated. Her expression became one of renewed defiance as she declared, "We have nothing but mere physical attraction, and—"

"Then you feel nothing else for me?" he lightly demanded. "Can you honestly claim that your heart has remained completely untouched by what just occurred?"

"It is none of your concern whether I choose to claim anything or not!" She sat bolt upright in the bed, facing him with a stormy look on her beautiful face, her eyes flashing their multicolored fire.

"Why did you want me to make love to you, Addie?" he started her by asking. As he eased himself up into a sitting position beside her, his handsome face remained inscrutable, his gaze unflinching as it met the fury of hers.

"I . . . I . . ." she tried to answer, faltering beneath his stare. She was acutely aware of the fact that the two of them were still entirely naked, and it took great strength of will for her to refrain from glancing at his splendid, exposed form.

Daniel, it seemed, chose not to practice the same restraint, for his eyes swept up and down her voluptuous curves in a leisurely, audacious scrutiny, which prompted her to grasp the nearest edge of the quilt, fling it up over her nakedness, then clutch it against her bosom like a shield. "I allowed what . . . what just happened between us to take place because I believed it would get you out of my system once and for all!" she furiously asserted.

"And did it work?" he inquired, one eyebrow cocked as a smile tugged at the corners of his finely chiseled lips.

"Yes!" she exclaimed, a shrill note creeping into her voice.

"Liar," he softly accused, leaning back against the pillow again as he placed his hands beneath his head. Before she could offer him a suitable retort, he mockingly ventured, "Is your horse's leg truly injured, Addie? Or did you perhaps invent such an excuse in order to see me again? After all, it's been a week since you last saw me, and nearly two since the night of the dance, when we—"

"Oh, how I despise you!" she fervently cried, battling the sudden impulse to strike him across his handsome, insolently smirking face. Fully realizing that such

212

action would only provoke him to further insult, she settled for muttering a savage oath as she jerked back the quilt and swiftly bounced off the bed.

Bending over to retrieve her undergarments and boots, her temper flared even more dangerously when she heard Daniel boldly observe, "You have a magnificent body, Addie, perfectly fashioned for loving. You should put it to such use more often, now that I'm here to—"

"How dare you!" she indignantly cut him off, drawing herself rigidly erect as she attempted to drape the linen and flannel about her as protection from his smoldering gaze. Her eyes glistened with unshed tears, and her voice sounded bitter as she tersely uttered, "Thank you very much, Mr. Jordan, for reminding me what a conceited bastard you truly are! You can rest assured that you will never again have the opportunity to . . . to humiliate me! I feel nothing but shame at my own behavior, though it's just as well that this episode occurred, for it will lay to rest any deceptively pleasant memories which might have lingered between us!" With that, she spun about on her bare heel and swept from the room, her demeanor quite proud in spite of her lack of attire.

Daniel remained in the bed until he heard the front door slam with unnecessary force a short time later. Then a slow smile rose to his lips as he stood and began donning his clothes again. Readily admitting to himself that he had purposely goaded Addie into anger once more, he reasoned that he had done so simply because he preferred to have her boiling mad rather than coldly indifferent. He was determined to draw all of his recalcitrant wife's innermost feelings for him to the

213

surface. And, if her continuing tendency to take offense at every turn was any indication at all, he mused, her affection for him—however vigorously denied—ran every bit as deep as his own for her.

Lending an ear to the inner voice which urged him to try a different approach, he reflected that perhaps it was time to reveal the truth to Addie, to tell her that he had never stopped loving her and that it was for this reason alone that he had gone to such lengths. But, he thought with a heavy sigh, was she ready to accept the love he offered? Was she ready to forget the bitterness of the past and admit that she still loved him as well?

His thoughts returned to the impassioned intimacy they had just shared. Warmly enveloped in contented visions of their future lovemaking, for he was certain there would be other times, he finished dressing and directed his long, easy strides toward the barn.

Twelve

Just as Daniel had suspected, Addie was obstinately heading back to her ranch on foot. He spurred his horse after the lone figure traipsing across the hard, snow-covered ground, guiding his gently snorting mount close beside her as he said in a conciliatory tone, "Come on, Addie. I'll take you home."

"No, thank you!" came the expected refusal. Her proud, beautiful features were suffused with a dull color, and numerous strands of shining chestnut hair tumbled rebelliously downward from beneath her felt hat. Refusing either to pause or glance up at the man on horseback, Addie kept her steps measured and swift as she continued marching across the sun-drenched whiteness of the land.

"Climb up behind me, Addie. There's no sense in risking pneumonia in order to make a point," Daniel insisted reasonably, tugging on the reins as he drew his horse to a halt. Swinging lithely down from the saddle, he caught up with Addie again and purposefully blocked her path. "You don't have to prove anything to

215

me. And I can't allow you to make yourself ill because of what I said." Fully prepared for her to force her way past him, he was instead mildly surprised when she merely stood and confronted him squarely.

"Why should the state of my health be of any concern to you?" she cynically countered, a faint shadowing of inexplicable pain evident in her challenging gaze.

"Don't you know, Addie?" he solemnly murmured, his voice soft, his eyes boring into hers as he towered above her. "Don't you realize yet why I came to Texas, why I went to so much trouble arranging to purchase the ranch next to yours, why I made it my business to discover every single thing I could about you before entering your life again?" His expression softened, and he smiled gently down at her as he studied her face. "I think you know, Addie. In your heart, you know."

She suddenly found herself at a loss for words. As she stared up at him in breathless confusion, her mind was awhirl with conflicting thoughts and emotions. Her initial annoyance with him rapidly diminished, but she soon began experiencing an irrational fury in its place.

"Is that your eminently charming way of telling me that you still care for me?" she finally responded, her voice laced with bitter sarcasm, her eyes blazing up at him once more. "And do you truly expect me to believe such an obvious untruth?"

"Why do you judge it to be an untruth?" he quietly demanded, her words creating a sharp ache in his heart. Although he firmly reminded himself that the time wasn't right, he nonetheless found himself impulsively adding, "Is it so impossible to believe that my feelings

216

for you could have endured the bitter separation of these past four years?"

Addie's eyes widened in stunned amazement at his words. Could it be that he was actually saying he loved her? The word "love" had never crossed his lips these past few weeks, she dazedly recalled. Indeed, she told herself, he had displayed nothing more than a desire to taunt her, to make her life miserable! And yet . . .

"I—" she started to reply, not at all certain of what she would say.

"We'd best be on our way," he curtly interrupted, taking a negligent hold upon her arm as he turned back to his horse. Surprised to experience a sudden twinge of disappointment, she did not utter a protest as Daniel swung himself into the saddle and extended a hand to help her up behind him. Forced to clasp him about the waist in order to maintain her balance astride the galloping horse, she was painfully aware of the way her thighs were pressed so tightly against the hard muscles of his hips, and her discomfort with such an embarrassingly intimate position rapidly increased. The relatively short ride to the Rolling L was passed in heavy silence.

Upon reaching Addie's ranch, Daniel patiently waited for her to explain Twister's predicament to a visibly concerned Silas. He was certain he could see the relief written on her face when Silas insisted, "There ain't no use in you goin' all the way back there, Miss Addie. Like as not, Twister'll need to stay put for a few days till that leg of his heals. If that's all right with Mr. Jordan here, that is," he said, turning a respectful eye to the younger man.

"He can remain at my place as long as necessary,"

Daniel generously agreed. Addie refused to meet his searching gaze, and it was with a mumbled "thank you" that she turned and disappeared inside the house, leaving the two men to mount up and be on their way.

Once he had gone, Addie pondered Daniel's perplexing words, words that he appeared to have immediately regretted uttering to her. What did he mean when he mentioned that his "feelings" could have possibly endured? Were they deep feelings or perhaps only a lingering fondness for the woman who had once been his secret bride?

Indeed, she concluded with an unconscious sigh, his words could mean nothing more than the latter, for there remained the inescapable fact that he had not even attempted to contact her during all those years. He apparently had put her from his mind and his heart until he suddenly, mysteriously chose to seek her out once more.

Convincing herself that his motives had nothing whatsoever to do with true and noble emotions, she sighed again and slowly trudged up the stairs to her room. As she swung open the door, her gaze fell upon the quilt-covered bed. The disturbing memory of her earlier, wanton behavior returned to hit her full force, and it was with a vengeance that she proceeded to strip off every stitch of clothing she was wearing and call down to Esther to fetch hot water for yet another bath.

"From what I hear, nearly everyone got a notice," John Hayward remarked with a fierce scowl, his heavyset features coloring lightly. "It's downright robbery, that's what it is! We've already paid more taxes than any of those blasted thieves had a right to demand from us!"

"I know," Gil sympathetically murmured. "But I don't see that you have any choice. Like before, either you pay, or your lands will be confiscated." He stood behind the counter of his uncle's store, his gaze swiftly moving to the lovely, obviously distressed countenance of the woman standing beside John. "I'm sorry, Miss Addie. Sorry I had to be the bearer of such ill tidings."

"It certainly isn't your fault," she assured him with a faint smile, her eyes remaining clouded with worry. "You simply distribute the mail. You have no control over its contents." Damn the carpetbaggers! she silently raged. She and the other landowners in Texas had already paid exorbitant amounts of money for so-called "taxes." Though the war had ended, the new laws had become another scourge to plague the state.

"Will you be able to pay, Miss Addie?" John softly asked, laying aside his own troubles as he turned a genuinely concerned face to his young friend.

"I . . . I don't see how," she admitted with a brisk shake of her head. "What about you?"

"It will mean using land script, I'm afraid," he replied sadly. He, like everyone else, detested the notion of using so much as a square foot of his land to pay what he considered the bitterly unfair amount the new state government had assessed him. But what else is there to do? he mused with an inner sigh of resignation.

John departed a short time later, leaving Gil and Addie momentarily alone inside the store. She was obviously preoccupied with the news she had just received, but Gil was quite content simply to stand and look at her for the numerous seconds she remained silent, her gaze fastened on the dusty wooden floor. It was rather dark inside the store, and the lamplight caused the various boxes and barrels to cast odd shadows, but Addie seemed totally oblivious to her surroundings.

"How the devil are we going to get enough this time?" she wondered aloud, her voice scarcely above a whisper. There just wasn't any cash left, she grimly reflected, especially after those fiscal agents for the Confederacy had confiscated at least a tenth of all money and goods during the last desperate months of the war. But, she staunchly told herself, that had been different, different for the simple reason that she had believed, and still believed, in the cause of the Confederacy and had never begrudged what little she could give to aid her homeland.

"Is there anything I can do to help?" Gil gently offered, his blue eyes shining as she glanced up to meet his gaze.

"There's nothing anyone can do," she despondently murmured, sighing audibly. Then, forcing a smile to her lips, she said, "But I appreciate the offer, Gil." She would have been startled to learn that his thoughts were miles away from the disagreeable subject of taxes, and she did not notice the way his eyes feasted hungrily upon her smiling lips.

"Miss Addie—" he began, only to break off and take a deep breath before continuing. "I have a little money put aside, my pay from the . . . from the war, as well as what I've earned working for my uncle. I'd be honored if you'd accept it." His attractive, gentlemanly features were quite earnest, and Addie felt a sudden constriction of her throat as tears came unbidden to her eyes.

220

"Oh, Gil," she breathed, finding it difficult to speak. She was so touched by his generosity, she didn't glimpse the tall man who had just that instant appeared in the open doorway.

"It would make me very happy if you'd accept it," Gil reiterated, his attention focused solely on the young woman before him. Though she was attired in her plain, everyday wool and flannel, he could still envision the way she had looked the night of the dance, and the recollection brought a pleasantly warm sensation to his heart.

"You know I must decline," Addie finally answered, impulsively reaching out and taking his hand between both of hers. "You are a good and true friend, Gil Foster, and I'll always be grateful for the offer. But I can't take your money."

"Why not?" he asked with a faint, puzzled frown.

"Mainly because I do happen to value our friendship. But that isn't the only reason. We Catons are a proud lot, you see," she explained with a soft laugh, releasing his hand and retrieving her hat from atop the cluttered counter. "There's no way I could ever accept charity."

"You could consider it a loan then."

"No, Gil, I'm afraid I can't accept that, either. But don't worry," she lightly declared, tugging on her hat and preparing to leave. "I'll think of some way to meet the deadline. The Rolling L has survived much worse than this. And I'm not about to allow it to fail now!" Flashing him one last, grateful smile, she turned about and headed for the doorway, her steps abruptly halting when she came face to face with the man who had been watching her for the last several minutes.

221

"Good afternoon, Miss Caton," said Daniel, his voice brimming with mocking politeness. His piercing stare and his faintly curved lips combined to make a suddenly disconcerted Addie blush fierily.

"What are you doing here?" she snapped resentfully, forced to tilt her head back in order to peer narrowly up into his tanned countenance.

"This is the first chance I've had to get to town since the start of the new year. It seems I was getting a bit low on . . . coffee," he replied, his smile widening. "I hope the year started off as pleasantly for you as it did for me, Miss Addie."

Her eyes flashed with indignation and her cheeks flamed, but her reply was cut off as Gil chose this moment to interject, "I've got some mail here for you, Jordan." His own color appeared a bit heightened above the white linen of his collar, and there was a visible tightness to his features as he shot Daniel a sharp look.

Addie attempted to move past the man blocking the doorway, but he refused to step aside. Extremely annoyed, she realized that he had no intention of allowing her to leave until he had finished telling her whatever was on his mind. Abruptly folding her arms across her chest, she impatiently challenged, "Well? What is it?"

"I thought you might like to know that Twister's leg is much improved," he informed her, his expression quickly sobering. "In fact, I think you'll be able to take him home within the week." Addie felt a sharp twinge of guilt, for she had scarcely given the horse a thought during the past several days. She had been doing her absolute best to prevent all reminders of what had happened two days ago from entering her mind.

"Thank you," she murmured stiffly. "I'll send Silas over to fetch him on Saturday." She relented enough to gaze directly into his eyes as she solemnly added, "I want you to know that I . . . I appreciate your allowing Twister to remain in your barn. And I give you my word that I'll think of some way to repay you."

"There's no need for that," Daniel responded with a slight shake of his head. As always, Addie mused, he was so totally masculine, so undeniably handsome, his leather and sheepskin coat fit his broad shoulders to perfection, and his heavy denim trousers molded his hard-muscled hips and legs. In short, she told herself with an inner scowl, the infuriating, arrogant man was irresistible, and his presence brought a certain weakness to her body even now.

"Nevertheless, I shall repay you," she stubbornly proclaimed, relieved when he finally removed his tall frame from within the doorway. She hastily exited the store, certain she could feel Daniel's eyes upon her as she marched down the muddy boardwalk to the spot where she had left her horse and buckboard waiting.

"What was that you said about mail?" Daniel casually inquired, turning his attention to Gil at last. He sauntered toward the counter with an easy, self-assured grace, the merest hint of a smile on his face as he met Gil's faintly belligerent gaze.

"Here," muttered Gil, reaching below the counter and withdrawing the envelope with Daniel's name scrawled on it. He watched closely as the other man negligently tore it open, unfolded the paper within, then leisurely scanned its unpleasant contents. "Since you're new to this part of the country," remarked Gil,

223

"you probably aren't aware of the new tax laws."

"On the contrary," Daniel affably disagreed, folding the paper again and stuffing it almost indifferently into his coat pocket. "I made it a point to research all the new laws and regulations before coming here."

"This newest tax law doesn't actually have anything to do with laws or regulations. It's come without warning, in addition to being severely unjust. Most of the folks won't be able to pay," supplied Gil with a deeper frown. His gaze narrowed as it flew to the taller man's. "Will you?"

"That happens to be none of your business, Foster," he answered in a low, even voice, "But, yes, I'll be able to meet the tax requirements." Smiling sardonically, he quietly asked, "Does that particular news disappoint you?"

"Why should it matter to me?"

"We both know why."

"Because of Miss Addie," Gil finally admitted, nodding curtly. "The lady has already expressed a profound dislike for you, Jordan. Why then do you continue to force your presence on her?" he tersely demanded.

"That, too, is none of your business."

"Anything that concerns Miss Addie concerns me as well!"

"Oh?" Daniel remarked with a cocked eyebrow, his tone deceptively unconcerned. Within his steely gaze, however, there gleamed an intense, almost savage light. "And why is that?"

"Because I plan for the lady in question to become my wife," proclaimed Gil, giving voice to his feelings for the first time.

He was both angered and surprised when Daniel chuckled softly and stated, "That's not too likely."

"I suppose you think you'll somehow bring about a complete transformation in Miss Addie's feelings for you?" Gil harshly questioned, his voice edged with sarcasm.

Daniel's eyes glowed, and his lips compressed into a thin, tight line as he curtly parried with, "You can save yourself a great deal of heartache, Foster, if you heed me now. Adelaide Caton will never belong to you."

Before Gil could digest his prophetic words, Daniel had spun about on his booted heel and was striding through the doorway once more.

Addie sank into the chair at her late father's desk in the study, her troubled gaze fixed unseeingly upon the ledger books, papers, and other items strewn about the polished surface of the massive piece of oak furniture. She had already searched without success through the numerous drawers and pigeonholes, and now she released a long, rather desperate sigh.

"There has to be some way!" she determined aloud. But she knew how difficult it had been to make the other tax payments and how much deeper in debt the Rolling L became after each such demand. Where was the money to come from this time? she asked herself, her expression becoming even more troubled.

Rising to her feet, she strolled over to the fireplace, her thoughts inexorably drifting back to her brief confrontation with Daniel earlier that day. She reflected that although the vexatious little scene had lasted only a few moments, seeing him again had affected her more than she cared to admit.

"I brought you some coffee and biscuits, honey," Esther announced, sweeping inside the room and placing the tray she carried atop the desk. "You ain't had nothin' to eat since this mornin'. I declare, I don't know what's gotten into you! You used to have a healthy appetite," she observed with a brisk shake of her head, her black curls covered with a bright red kerchief.

"Thank you," Addie murmured, apparently still quite preoccupied as she turned slowly away from the warmth of the fire and reassumed her seat at the desk.

"You gonna tell Esther what it is that's troublin' you?" the older woman asked kindly, loving concern reflected in her wide brown eyes.

"I'd rather not discuss it right now," insisted Addie in a low voice. She had already decided not to worry Silas, or Esther, or the ranch hands with the news just yet, at least not until she was totally convinced there was no hope left.

"Well, just so long as you know I'm here to listen," Esther asserted, reluctantly taking her leave, her eyes flitting back to Addie's faintly pale countenance several times before she returned to her work in the kitchen.

Once Esther had gone, Addie took only a quick sip of the coffee before beginning another search through the desk. Realizing that she hadn't the vaguest notion of what she was hoping to find, she nonetheless started rummaging through the drawers again, determined that she would find something with which to solve the latest dilemma facing her ranch.

Nearly half an hour later, her search had once more

226

proven fruitless. She had managed to locate only old receipts and bills, and a handful of Confederate paper money that was now entirely worthless. If she could think of no way to raise the needed cash, then she, like her friend John, would be forced to pay with land script.

"Oh, Papa!" she cried. With tears filling her eyes, Addie lowered her head to her crossed arms resting on the top of the desk. Unless a miracle occurred, she would be forced to give up most of the land her father had worked so hard to tame. Her parents, like all the other homesteaders in the area, had battled Indians, fires, drought, illness, and had endured all sorts of trials and tribulations in order to carve a place for themselves in the wilderness that had become Fort Worth.

And now, she told herself, fiercely blinking back the tears which threatened to spill over at any moment, she faced the heartbreaking prospect of seeing her parents' dream of a sprawling, prosperous cattle ranch being destroyed forever. Soon the land they had intended as a legacy for their descendants would have to be handed over to the enemy which called itself the new government in Texas.

Courage, Adelaide! she staunchly commanded herself, dashing angrily at the salty drops of moisture glistening in her eyes. This newest battle had just begun, and she had no intention of giving in without a fight!

Twisting resolutely about in the chair, she started to rise, only to find her skirts caught on something. As she tugged briskly, she found it puzzling that a fold of the fabric near the hemline remained imprisoned, and she

227

slid out of the chair to kneel upon the floor. Frowning in bemusement, she finally succeeded in extricating her skirts from what appeared to be a sharp metal object projecting from the inside base of the desk.

The lamplight from above provided barely adequate illumination, and only as she leaned closer to the floor was she able to ascertain that the piece of metal seemed to be a tiny lever. She found that easing it upward caused a small drawer directly below the lever to swing outward, revealing a secret compartment that she had never known to exist.

Addie was startled to see it, and she experienced a strange hesitation before putting her hand inside the drawer and taking hold of its contents. Discovering papers of some kind, she cautiously climbed from beneath the desk and rose to her feet, immediately stepping nearer to the light.

She gasped in stunned amazement as she perceived that her own name was written on what was obviously the envelope of a letter. She held two such envelopes in her hand, and she saw that the second was addressed to her as well. Both of them, she quickly noted, had been opened.

Why had her father never told her about the secret compartment? she silently wondered. And why were letters meant for her, letters she was certain she had never seen, concealed within the drawer?

Reflecting that the handwriting seemed vaguely familiar, she opened one of the envelopes noting that the paper was yellowed and the ink smudged in several places. The date at the top of the single page was July, 1861. Hastily turning the paper over, she gasped again and her eyes widened in shock as they fastened upon the signature—*Daniel Jordan*.

"Daniel!" she numbly whispered. Feverishly turning the letter again and reading from the beginning, she became alternately chilled and warm, her breathing quite irregular.

"My dearest wife," he had begun—

It is my sincerest hope that this letter finds you in good health. Though I experienced no little difficulty, I was able to obtain your address from your cousin, Miss Hamilton, who asked that I send you her love. But that is not the reason I am writing. I have been unable to forget the bitterness of our parting, Addie. While we remain on opposite sides, I assure you that I am attempting to understand your beliefs and actions. I would have you do the same on my behalf. I can only pray that you have not forgotten the love we share. You are forever in my heart, my love, and I cannot believe that your feelings have undergone such an alteration that your own heart has irreversibly hardened against your husband.

Addie paused and took a deep, steadying breath, the tears returning unbidden to her eyes as she turned the paper and continued reading.

Our separation is painful for me, but I hold fast to the hope that we will be reunited in the near future. However, I do not know when I will be able to return to St. Louis. And as long as the present conflict continues, there will exist no possibility of my being able to join you at your home. So, my dearest Addie, all I ask of you now is that you respond to this letter, that you tell me your love for your husband is as strong as his for you. You can write to me in care of my sister in St. Louis; I have included the address in the event that you have lost it. I will write to you again, but I do not know when conditions will permit the letter to find its way to you. I love you, Addie. And I remain

—here he signed it, "your devoted husband, Daniel Jordan."

Sinking down into the chair, Addie stared at the paper in her hand, the words blurring as her tears obscured them. But she did not allow herself to lose control, and, instead, took up the second letter and rapidly scanned its contents. It was dated several months later than the first one—December, 1861.

"My dearest wife," he had called her once more—

Christmas is near, and I cannot help but think of you. I had hoped to hear from you by now. Although I know that there can exist any number of reasons for your silence, I entreat you one last time to answer my letter. You never have been out of my thoughts, never have lost your cherished place in my heart. The war shows no sign of ending, and I am afraid it will be an unfortunate number of months before we can even hope for peace. But in the meantime, my love, I continue to pray for your well-being. Though I am unable to divulge my location, I trust that you will indeed send a letter to me via Carrie. As ever, I love you.

And I will always be your devoted husband,
Daniel Jordan.

So, Addie dazedly told herself, Daniel had not been lying after all. He had written to her twice, just as he had claimed. And he had told her that he loved her, that he would always love her.

A stricken look crossed her face when she suddenly realized that it must have been her father who had intercepted the letters and read them, then hidden them in the secret drawer. Will Caton had known about her marriage, had known that she was married to one of the enemy.

Why had he never told her that he knew? she agonized, her mind awhirl with a myriad of turbulent, conflicting emotions. Why had he allowed her to believe him ignorant of her unhappy secret? And, most of all, why had he kept the letters hidden from her?

"Why did you do it, Papa?" Addie murmured aloud, feeling so miserable and confused that she actually began to wish she had never found the letters. Why had fate been so cruel as to allow her to find them now? she bitterly asked herself. Her father was no longer there, could not answer the multitude of questions his actions had brought to her mind. And, she mused with an inward sigh, Daniel Jordan had changed. He was no longer the same young man who had written her those letters.

Her father's motives more than likely had stemmed from pride, she sadly decided, experiencing a sharp feeling of betrayal. He had kept Daniel's letters from her, letters that might possibly have changed the course of her life.

Rising from the chair, she clutched the letters in her hand and moved toward the fireplace again, her tear-filled eyes mirroring the dancing flames. She once again could see Daniel's face as it had been all those years ago, could see the pain in his eyes when she had told him she would never forgive him for his loyalties in the war.

Then an image of her late father's face intruded. She recalled the way he had taught her to put pride and honor above everything. Her love for Daniel had been set aside because of pride and honor, she realized, her stare fixed unwaveringly upon the fire.

There was a sharp, twisting pain deep in her heart, and she stifled the sob which rose to her lips as she spun about and started blindly from the study, instinctively seeking the privacy of her bedroom. She had no sooner reached the foot of the staircase, however, when a loud, insistent knock sounded at the front door.

"Damnation!" she muttered crossly, swiping with a vengeance at the tears coursing down her brightly flushed cheeks. Though tempted to have Esther answer the knock and announce that her mistress was indisposed, she instead hastily composed herself and turned to the door, stuffing the letters into the deep side pocket of her woolen skirt.

Her beautiful face paled considerably when she swung open the heavy wooden door and stared up into the unusually solemn features of the last person on earth she wanted to find upon her doorstep at that moment.

Thirteen

"I'd like to talk to you, Addie," proclaimed Daniel, frowning inwardly as he glimpsed the remaining evidence of her tears.

"This isn't . . . this isn't the right time to—" Addie faltered in visible confusion, unconsciously raising her hand to smooth back the loose tendrils of dark hair curling about her face.

"What I've come to discuss is very important," he firmly interrupted, sweeping the hat from his head as he strode past her and inside the house. Unable to find the will to argue with him, she quietly closed the door and turned about, dismayed to feel her eyes filling with tears once more as her thoughts returned to the letters. Swiftly moving away from Daniel's piercing gaze, she furiously blinked back the returning tears and led the way into the study.

"I hope this won't take long," she stiffly remarked, her voice sounding strangely distant as she took a seat upon the bench near the fire. "There are several matters which require my immediate attention."

"Then I'll get right to the point," he replied, shrugging out of his coat before bending his tall, muscular frame into the oversized wing chair a few feet away. "Like you, I received a statement of new land taxes today."

"I would have thought that since you fought for the North you would be exempt from the same demands imposed upon us." Daniel's eyes imperceptibly narrowed as he watched the firelight playing across her proud features, noting the way her thick, shining tresses reflected its comforting glow.

"I'm a citizen of Texas now," he reminded her, a faint smile curving his lips. His perceptive gaze flitted briefly to the paper-strewn desk in the corner of the room. "I heard that most of our neighbors won't be able to make the payment."

"Why should that concern you?" Her voice held a touch of resentment.

"I'm concerned about one neighbor in particular," he declared, his smile rapidly fading.

"Oh?" she retorted, striving to make her voice sound disinterested. Every time she glanced at his face, she envisioned the way he must have looked when he had written her those letters so long ago. Experiencing a sudden light-headedness, she placed a hand on her temple.

"What's wrong, Addie?" Daniel sharply demanded, his brow creasing with a genuinely concerned frown as he leaned forward in the chair. "Are you troubled because of the taxes?"

The taxes? her mind echoed. She hadn't given the matter a second thought since discovering Daniel's letters. Rising abruptly to her feet, she stood before the fireplace, presenting her back to the man who seemed forever destined to disturb any semblance of order in her life!

"Yes. The taxes," she murmured, her voice scarcely audible. She was amazed at the way his simple display of concern prompted her heart to beat faster.

"I have a proposition to put to you that I believe will solve a problem facing both of us."

"You mean you won't be able to pay, either?" queried Addie in surprise, momentarily inclining her head toward him.

"I've got the cash," he revealed with an almost imperceptible shake of his own head. "What I need is something entirely different. That's why I'm here. You see, I strongly suspect that your ranch is in a financial bind." He paused an instant before casually announcing, "I'm prepared to advance you the necessary money."

Addie's hazel eyes widened in disbelief as she wheeled about to face him again.

"What?" she breathlessly exclaimed.

"I'll give you the cash to pay your taxes," Daniel patiently repeated, his expression perfectly serious.

"Do you honestly believe I'd ever take so much as one blasted cent from you?" Addie indignantly responded, her eyes flashing angrily at his presumption.

"If you'll allow me to explain—"

"The hell I will!" she furiously broke in. "How dare you offer me charity, Daniel Jordan!" Her hands were clenched into tight fists at her sides as she lashed out at him, and she fought the sudden, powerful temptation to march from the room. Though she didn't understand why, she felt deeply hurt by his offer.

"Damn it, woman, will you be quiet long enough for me to explain?" Daniel startled her by harshly commanding. Then he rose to his feet and swiftly closed the distance between them. Addie glared up at him defiantly, opening her mouth to offer him a scathing retort but gasping instead as his hands closed tightly upon her shoulders, his own temper rising. "Must you always take offense at everything I do or say?" he wearily chided, his eyes glistening coldly. Addie experienced a faint twinge of apprehension as he towered somewhat menacingly above her.

"Very well, what is your explanation?" she managed to ask disdainfully, raising her chin to create an air of bravado. Although she remained totally rigid and unyielding beneath his hands, her heart pounded erratically.

"The money won't be a gift. I'll want something in return," he stated evenly, his hands slowly, reluctantly, dropping from her shoulders.

"And what is it you want?" she demanded frostily, her eyes meeting his in a silent challenge.

"I want you to become my partner," he told her, another ghost of a smile emerging on his rugged, sun-bronzed countenance as he studied her beautiful, rebellious counterpart.

"Your . . . your partner?" she echoed in astonishment.

"Strictly a business arrangement, of course," he sardonically quipped, his eyes sparkling with humor now. "The simple fact is, Addie, you need cash to pay your taxes. And I, on the other hand, need someone who knows the country, someone who is knowledgeable about cattle ranching, to help me get my own ranch in order. I happen to believe such an arrangement would be the perfect solution for both of us," he concluded.

"Oh, you do, do you?" With her hands on her hips and her cheeks brightly flushed, Addie bristled at what she perceived to be his infuriating, supremely confident assumption that she would wholeheartedly embrace his ridiculous proposition, that she would naturally be in agreement with his assessment of the situation! "It so happens that I find your reasoning in this matter to be absolutely incomprehensible! Wherever did you get the addlepated notion that I would agree to such an arrangement?"

"Don't fly off the handle until you've at least rationally considered it," he blithely directed, a disarming grin tugging at the corners of his mouth. "When you've finished this latest display of the intimidating Caton temper," he added, a mocking gleam in his clear, gray eyes, "you'll be able to realize that my proposition is the only solution."

"I'll find another way!" she defiantly asserted, flinging herself back down upon the fire-warmed bench, her full, gathered skirts swirling gently about her. Her stormy gaze was drawn back to the dancing flames, their wildly irregular movements matching her frenzied pulse.

"I'm afraid you're going to have to make a choice, Addie. You'll have to decide which is worth more— your damnable pride, or your land," Daniel evenly observed, his voice smooth and resonant. Staring down intently at his wife's angry, perplexed features, he waited in silence for her answer. His gaze traveled

237

slowly, lovingly, from her sun-streaked chestnut locks, to the flushed, silken contours of her face, then lower to where her undeniably provocative, firmly rounded breasts were gently heaving beneath the soft linen of her blouse. A veritable flood tide of love and longing suddenly threatened to overwhelm him, forcing him to exercise iron control, to remain motionless and quiet, though his eyes smoldered with unquenchable desire.

"But you don't know anything at all about ranching!" Addie finally opened her mouth to vehemently protest, her gaze flying upward to confront his. "And even if you did, the last person on earth I'd want to have as a partner is you!"

"How many other such offers have you received?" he swiftly countered.

"You know as well as I do that no one around here has any cash!"

"I do," Daniel pointedly reminded her, an unholy light of amusement evident in his eyes.

"A Yankee's blood money!" snapped Addie. Without warning, her arms were abruptly seized, and she gasped as she was unceremoniously hauled upward to find her startled, slightly fear-tinged eyes gazing directly into Daniel's narrowed ones. She blanched inwardly at the savage gleam reflected there.

"For the last time, Addie, the war is over!" he ground out. "You're so damned willing to forget all the good things that happened between us in the past, so why not finally let go of the bad as well?" Releasing her arms just as unexpectedly as he had ruthlessly gripped them, he spun about and snatched up his coat, his long, angry strides leading him to the doorway. Turning to her one last time, he curtly announced, "I'll allow you the remainder of the day to make up your mind. You can expect me first thing in the morning to hear your decision." With that, he was gone, and the ensuing silence was broken only by the rapid opening and closing of the front door and the sound of his boots clipping lightly down the front steps of the house.

Addie sank slowly onto the bench once more, her head spinning alarmingly. She was still sitting before the fire, her eyes staring blankly toward the window, when Esther entered the room a short time later.

"I didn't aim to eavesdrop, Miss Addie, but I heard some of what Mr. Jordan said to you," the older woman admitted, taking a seat on the bench beside Addie. "You plannin' to take him up on that offer?" she gently probed.

Addie blinked rapidly as she transferred her gaze to Esther. Damnation! she silently cursed. She had forgotten all about Esther's being in the house. Finding those blasted letters had driven everything else from her mind! A feeling of dismay washed over her when she realized that Daniel had made mention, however vague, of the fact that they had known one another in the past.

"What exactly did you hear?" she queried sharply.

"Well, I heard him tellin' you that he had enough money to pay his own taxes. I heard him say that he wanted the two of you to become partners. And I heard that last part about him comin' back in the mornin' for your answer."

"So you know about the new taxes?" Addie responded with a question of her own, sighing heavily when Esther merely nodded. "To tell the truth, I don't know what to do. I was hoping there was some way I

239

could raise enough cash . . . but I've exhausted every possibility."

"That's why I was thinkin' that maybe you might just want to accept Mr. Jordan's offer," Esther carefully suggested, wisely sensing the other woman's inner turmoil. "It sounds to me like he's got a pretty good idea of—"

"Oh yes, Mr. Jordan's got plenty of good ideas!" she broke in with bitter sarcasm, hastily rising to her feet and wandering aimlessly back to the desk. She stood frowning pensively at the mountain of paper she had created, and her hand seemed to move with a will of its own as it returned to finger the contents of her skirt pocket. Once again, the problem of the taxes was pushed to the back of her mind as her thoughts centered on the letters. No matter how desperately she tried, she could not prevent them from taking precedence.

Noting the faraway look on Addie's face, Esther quietly left the room. Thoughts of Daniel Jordan were foremost in her own mind, for she had heard more of his conversation with her young mistress than she had revealed to Addie. And she had chanced to be standing in the front entrance foyer when he had put hands upon the young woman and spoken harshly to her. Esther told herself that Miss Addie wasn't the sort who would allow a man to do such a thing, unless he were more than just a neighbor, more than the Yankee stranger she and the others believed him to be.

"Somethin' here just ain't right," Esther muttered to herself as she disappeared into the kitchen again.

*   *   *

Addie, Silas, and Esther stayed up until the wee hours of the morning, jointly endeavoring to think of a way out of the Rolling L's financial difficulties. There was much discussion about how many head of cattle it would take to raise the required amount of cash, but eventually they realized that even that possibility was hopeless because of the weather. They wouldn't be able to round up enough stock until the spring. The price was down to four or five dollars a head, and there was no indication that the local market would improve in the near future. Furthermore, they were aware of the fact that the Eastern markets, where the Texas ranchers had once sold hides to leather goods manufacturers and beef to the U.S. Army, would not be opening again for quite some time. And they could not afford to wait.

The following morning, a weary Addie sat alone in her room and reflected upon the miserable night she had spent. After finally bidding the Fremonts a good night and taking herself off to bed, she had felt absolutely bone weary. In spite of her exhaustion, however, sleep had proven strangely elusive.

Though she had refused to surrender to the urge to read Daniel's letters once more, their contents had continued to play havoc with both her thoughts and emotions. It kept occurring to her that her husband had cared enough to write to her upon two separate occasions, and that he had put aside his own pride in order to make the first overture toward reconciliation.

Also spinning around in her head had been the realization that her father had purposely kept the letters from her. It caused her a great deal of pain to think that he had discovered her shameful secret and never told her, that he had remained totally silent upon the matter, even when he had known he was going to die. She and her father had always been so close, and yet they had each harbored a secret, a secret involving the same man.

How did she truly feel about all that she had discovered? Addie now asked herself, rising from her seat at the mirrored dressing table and drifting toward the doorway. Had the restless, contemplative night changed anything at all?

"Breakfast is ready!" she heard Esther's voice ring out as she opened her bedroom door and started down the stairs. It was a pleasantly crisp January morning, with only a few puffy clouds dotting the lightening sky, and Addie mentally promised herself to make time for a private ride later in the day.

"Morning, Esther," she said, smiling faintly as she entered the kitchen and took a seat at the small table. "Where's Silas?"

"Fetchin' more firewood. Said he'd be back in time for his eggs," Esther cheerfully replied, glancing across at the younger woman, then taking a second look. "You sure do look pretty this mornin', honey!" Her grin broadened as her lively brown eyes appreciatively swept up and down the length of Addie's velvet-clad form. "What you all dressed up for?"

"Don't you have anything better to do than pay such absurdly close attention to the state of my attire?" Addie crossly retorted, immediately regretting her harsh response. Her features slowly relaxed into a smile as she sighed and wryly explained, "I thought I'd try to look my best when facing the enemy."

"Enemy?" repeated Esther, momentarily puzzled.

242

"Oh, you mean Mr. Jordan?"

"Precisely," murmured Addie, unconsciously smoothing the folds of the pale blue gown. Though high necked and fashioned along rather severe lines, it was quite becoming, its simplicity providing a subtle tribute to her admirable figure. "If I must admit defeat, then I'd prefer to do it while hopefully appearing undaunted!"

"It ain't no defeat, what you're aimin' to do, Miss Addie. It's just the only way to save the ranch."

Addie digested Esther's words of consolation as she carefully sipped her coffee. She was still appalled at the notion that she was actually planning to become Daniel Jordan's partner, that she was going to be indebted to the very man who had turned her life upside down. And yet, just as Esther had pointed out, it had to be done for the sake of the ranch. She wasn't going to allow herself to think about anything other than saving the ranch.

Later, as she restlessly paced the floor of the study while awaiting Daniel's arrival, her thoughts once more turned to the letters she had found the day before. Would she never be free of the past? she unhappily reflected, finally settling into a chair and staring anxiously toward the window.

Drawn out of her silent reverie by Daniel's knock on the front door—readily identifiable by its distinctive forcefulness—Addie took slow, measured steps as she moved to answer it. Inwardly, however, her heart was racing.

"Good morning, Addie," he declared in a low, steady voice, following his usual custom of crossing the threshold without waiting for an invitation to enter. He

243

paused to remove his hat and coat before turning back to his uncharacteristically silent wife. Smiling faintly, he remarked unexpectedly, "I noticed the pup near the barn. By the way, what did you name him?"

She stared blankly up at him for an instant before reluctantly answering, "Silas suggested we call him Rascal." Why in heaven's name was he wasting time on small talk? she irritably wondered. Didn't he have any idea of how impatient she was to get this confrontation over with? He probably knows quite well! she then mused, her mouth tightening into a thin line of displeasure.

"Rascal," he echoed with a quiet chuckle. "It probably suits him." His smile faded as he extended his arm and gestured toward the study. "Shall we begin our discussion?" There was only a trace of mockery in his tone, but it was more than enough to provoke an already tense Addie to exhibit a flash of anger.

"The sooner we talk, the sooner you leave!" she sharply retorted, whirling about and loftily sweeping past him into the study. She braced a hand against the oak mantle above the fireplace as he followed and moved to stand beside her. Shooting him a resentful look, she tossed her long braid of chestnut hair over her shoulder before insisting, "Will you please sit down?"

She was nonplussed when he merely turned and stepped to the doorway of the study again, his movements quite unhurried as he proceeded to close and lock the double doors. That done, he returned to the fireplace and stood gazing down at her with an unfathomable, though nonetheless disturbing, light in his eyes.

"Well, what is your answer, Addie?" he calmly

244

demanded, his handsome face totally inscrutable. His thick hair appeared even lighter above the dark plaid of his flannel shirt, and Addie was dismayed to feel herself remembering the tight golden curls which covered the broad expanse of his chest, the line of wheat-colored fluff which narrowed and tapered downward to . . .

Certain he could see her face burning, she hastily looked away and folded her arms tightly across her bosom as she replied in a slightly tremulous voice, "I . . . I think there are a few points we should discuss first." Suddenly she felt warm all over and told herself it was only the heat of the blazing fire which caused her body to experience an abrupt rise in temperature.

"All right," Daniel quietly agreed, his eyes never leaving hers as she turned back to face him squarely.

"First of all," began Addie, softly clearing a sudden lump in her throat, "do you have any idea what kind of money it will require to pay the taxes on my ranch?"

"It doesn't matter. I've got plenty."

"It will take more than a thousand dollars in cash!"

"I told you," he responded with another faint smile, "I've got plenty. I can advance you as much as you need."

"And just how the devil did you come to be so blasted wealthy?" she challenged, her eyes widening as they met his steely gaze.

"It wasn't difficult. I had four years of pay set aside by the end of the war. There simply wasn't much to spend it on during all that time."

Addie started to make another remark about the manner in which he had earned his pay, but she thought better of it when she recalled his somewhat violent reaction of the night before. Frowning deeply, she moved past him and over to the desk, her gaze fixed upon the soft glow of the lamp in the corner. "If I were to agree to this 'arrangement,' what would you expect in return for your money?" she finally asked, her eyes clouding with rapidly increasing dread. Surely he wouldn't demand that she . . . she give herself to him as part of the payment! Addie feverishly reasoned.

"An equal partnership. Which means I would be entitled to half the profits from the cattle drive."

"Cattle drive? What cattle drive?" she sharply questioned, her expression one of total bewilderment as she spun about to face him again.

"The one we're going to plan for the spring," he replied enigmatically, slowly closing the distance between them.

"How long have you been prone to these lapses in sanity?" Addie sarcastically queried. "There haven't been any successful cattle drives since before the war!" There had been one local man, she silently recalled, who had attempted to drive to Shreveport back in the fall. But Captain Daggett's drive had proven to be disastrous, and he had been able to clear only six dollars profit per head.

"Nevertheless," asserted Daniel, his steps halting as he stood close beside her once more, "we're going to plan one. But we'll discuss all the details about that when the time comes. Right now, the issue is whether or not you're going to accept my offer."

"But you still don't know anything at all about ranching! For instance, are you aware of the fact that we don't have even the vaguest idea of how many head of cattle we own? Thousands of them wandered off their home ranges during the war. No one's been able to

246

have a decent roundup for four years now. There's no way of knowing exactly how many bear the Rolling L brand or how many unbranded offspring are out there!"

"I know it won't be easy, but I'm willing to take my chances. With you as my partner, I'll learn. And I can assure you that I'm a quick study," he declared with another smile, his eyes glowing as they caught and held her confused gaze.

"You know good and well I have no choice, don't you?" she reproachfully charged, a pale color rising to her face once more. Sweeping regally past him again, she paused before the window and whirled about, her eyes sparkling defiantly as she crisply announced, "Very well. We'll become business partners. We'll split the profits from the cattle right down the middle. You'll be expected to do your share of the work, to hire your own hands for the roundup in the spring. In return, my taxes will be paid and I'll advise you on any matters which require my attention. However," she added, sending him a silent warning with her narrowing gaze, "there is one more thing—something we might as well get clear between us now."

"Oh?" Daniel murmured sardonically, sauntering forward in leisurely pursuit yet again.

"Our . . . relationship is to be strictly business. The partnership between us has nothing whatsoever to do with our personal feelings, or with the highly disagreeable fact that we are still legally husband and wife. As a matter of fact, I fully intend to remedy that unfortunate situation as soon as possible!" Her eyes widened as he moved closer and closer, and the inexplicable breathlessness she had frequently experienced in his presence returned once more.

"Aren't you ever going to face the truth?" he softly demanded, disregarding the way her beautiful countenance visibly bristled with renewed irritation. "You know as well as I do that we'll never be free of each other. I think the time has come for both of us to openly admit that particular fact. As I've said before, the bond between us is simply too powerful to destroy."

"For the last time, there is no bond between us!" she desperately cried, furious with herself for the way her body trembled as she attempted to direct a rebellious glare at this man who was mere inches away, the one man who could make her feel the despicable weakness she now experienced. Thoughts of his letters returned unbidden to her mind, and a sharp aching gripped her heart as she recalled the words of love he had written to her.

"Keep telling yourself that, dearest Adelaide. Perhaps, in twenty or thirty years' more time, you'll finally be able to convince yourself." His low, rather husky voice was brimming with indulgent humor, and Addie could only gaze helplessly up at him as his arms closed about her and pulled her tenderly against his lean warmth, his lips claiming hers in a kiss that was gentle in its insistence, a kiss that effectively melted any resistance she might have attempted.

Her arms were suddenly clutching him tighter, her full breasts making stimulating contact with his muscular chest as his lips moved upon hers with tantalizing slowness. His hands moved downward to caress and mold her velvet-covered buttocks, intimately pressing her soft curves against his masculine hardness.

Addie's head was spinning, and the familiar yearning built to a fever pitch as Daniel's lips tasted and teased at hers. His fingers curled with fierce possessiveness about her derriere, and she was effortlessly lifted upward into his impassioned embrace.

Drawing in her breath sharply, she felt herself being lowered to the chaise below the curtained window, the graceful curve of her back sinking into the velvet cushions as Daniel knelt beside her, his lips refusing to relinquish hers. His hands now moved to her high-necked bodice. There he impatiently unfastened enough of the small pearl buttons so that his warm fingers could sweep aside the lace to close gently about one of her breasts, still covered by the delicate cotton of her chemise. She gasped at the highly erotic sensation he created as his fingers kneaded her sensitive flesh, tenderly brushing the rosy peak jutting against the thin fabric.

Addie grew alarmed at the spiraling intensity of their embrace, and she frantically pushed against him, freeing her lips long enough to breathlessly whisper, "No! We . . . we can't! Esther—"

"Will not disturb us," he masterfully finished, his head lowering with purposeful intent once more. "Besides, I locked the door, remember?" He soon made it clear that he intended to kiss away all objections, and she was offered little recourse as she surrendered to the flaming passions which so thoroughly engulfed her.

Shocked by the fact that she was actually allowing Daniel to make love to her in her own house again, that the two of them were sharing such wanton intimacy while Esther was in another room under the same roof, Addie nevertheless became lost in a world of blazing ecstasy with the only man who had ever been able to make her forget all else but this purely physical pleasure.

Her emotions, however, did not remain untouched. The fire in her blood was well matched by the undeniable rhapsody in her heart, and she gave herself willingly, boldly, to Daniel, the memory of what they had once shared brought vividly to the forefront of her mind by the fateful discovery of his letters. It was almost as if the past four years had never been, as if she and Daniel were once again secret newlyweds joyously exploring one another's bodies, the sense of forbidden adventure only serving to heighten their mutual desire.

Daniel's insistent mouth traveled to the creamy swell of her breasts above the lacy edge of her chemise, his lips branding her exposed, silken flesh. Addie gasped again, her slender figure curling tightly within his thick, golden hair as she instinctively arched beneath him, straining to offer even more of her womanly curves for his delightfully sensuous caresses. His hands began urgently bunching her velvet skirts, inching them upward so his fingers could loop into the waistband of her pantalettes.

She felt a cool rush of air upon her feverish skin as the pantalettes were pulled downward over her hips, then drawn completely off and tossed negligently to the floor. Daniel placed the length of his hard body atop hers now, and it was with rapidly increasing fervor that his lips returned to claim hers once more. The pale rays of sunlight filtering through the curtains directly above them cast a warm, hazy glow across the lovers as they gloried in their impassioned abandon.

Addie's hands moved boldly downward to glide over

the hard muscles of Daniel's hips beneath the denim of his fitted trousers, and she found herself unashamedly desiring that there be no barriers of clothing between them. There was no time to achieve her wish, however, as their passions escalated to the outermost limits of tolerance. His fingers momentarily deserted the tingling softness amid the silky triangle of chestnut curls between her thighs to swiftly unfasten the opening of his trousers. A faint, unintelligible cry broke from her lips when he expertly sheathed himself within her welcoming moistness. She clutched him to her as if she were drowning and he were the only means by which she could be saved.

The final blending of their bodies bordered on searing perfection, their temptestuous, breathtaking completion occurring in rapturous unison. Addie was forced to bite at her lower lip in order to stifle the faint scream which formed in her throat as her mind whirled and her senses soared.

She was left stunned and dizzy, and it took several long moments before Daniel regained enough of his own composure to ease himself up and away from her. Feeling languid and weak, she could only lie still and watch as he slowly stood and refastened his trousers. The volatile intimacy they had just shared provoked a combination of mingled embarrassment and supreme satisfaction deep within her, and she could feel her cheeks crimsoning as Daniel turned his unwavering gaze upon her. She hastily sat upright and pulled the unbuttoned edges of her bodice closed, modestly tossing her skirts back down about her shapely, stockinged limbs.

"I didn't mean for things to go that far, Addie," he

softly admitted, though his handsome face exhibited absolutely no sign of remorse. His eyes were so full of love that a suddenly discomfited Addie quickly averted her own shining gaze.

"It . . . it was every bit as much my fault as yours," she responded with admirable honesty, her voice not quite steady as she sought to regain control of her breathing. Her long braid of hair lay draped across one shoulder, its gleaming strands now appearing in some disarray.

"Addie, I—" Daniel began, only to break off as he obviously changed his mind about what he was going to say. Addie's expectant gaze was drawn irrevocably back up to his, and she was startled by the sudden flip-flop of her stomach and the abrupt tightening in her chest.

"Please," she managed to utter, a slight catch in her low voice, "let's . . . let's not talk about what happened. It's over and done with."

"Is it?" he whispered, his eyes seeming to bore into her very soul. He forced himself to turn away at that point. Taking up his hat and coat, he paused before Addie once more, his heart turning over in his breast at the sight of her sitting so confused and forlorn-looking upon the chaise, the sun's golden rays turning her hair into a blaze of color. It took every ounce of self-control to keep him from pouring out his heart to her right then and there, to keep from telling her that he loved her more than ever. Not yet, he firmly told himself. He wanted her to come to him of her own free will, to love him with no restraints, no barriers from either the past or the present. He realized that it would require continued patience and endurance if he wanted to win

Addie—all of her—back.

"I'll be going now, but I'll stop by again within a couple of days," he quietly declared. She could only stare numbly up at him, her eyes clouding with a myriad of emotions as she silently watched him stride to the doorway. After unlocking and opening the doors, he left her with no parting words.

Addie released a heavy sigh. Her wandering gaze fell upon the pantalettes lying in a heap on the floor beside the velvet chaise. Muttering a halfhearted curse, she snatched them up and escaped from the disturbing confines of the study, seeking tearful refuge in the private sanctuary of her bedroom.

Fourteen

The anticipation Addie experienced as a result of Daniel's parting words was a constant source of perplexity to her throughout the following week. He had declared his intention of returning in a couple of days, she mused in growing annoyance toward the end of the week. It had been nearly four, and still there was no sign of him.

Telling herself that she should be grateful for his absence, she attempted to focus her thoughts and energy on the business of running her ranch. The worse month of the winter appeared to have already passed, for most of the days were now cold and clear, with only an occasional mild rainstorm upsetting the balance. All evidence pointed to an early spring, and Addie eagerly awaited the first true roundup of Rolling L cattle in years.

With Trent, Clay, and Billy to help, she was convinced that the sale of her stock would yield more than enough to repay Daniel. She refused to give credence to his mention of a cattle drive, considering it no more than an extremely remote possibility. Drives were too risky in a financial sense, besides being too dangerous, she reflected, which only went to prove how ignorant her new partner was when it came to the business of raising and selling cattle.

Addie rode into town on Friday afternoon, some five days after she had last seen Daniel. A brief visit to the courthouse had put her in a high temper, and she immediately headed for the mercantile where she found Gil alone and in the process of closing up for the day.

"Why, Miss Addie!" he remarked in pleasant surprise, his attractive face visibly brightening when he caught sight of her in the doorway. "I didn't know you were planning to come into town today," he added as he finished donning his coat and hurried forward, his smile rapidly fading as he heard her first words.

"Were you aware of the fact that John Hayward is going to lose all of his land?" Her beautiful features were quite stormy, and her eyes sparkled with a militant light.

"He stopped by the store a day or two ago," responded Gil, nodding grimly.

"It's just so blasted unfair!" raged Addie, pulling off her hat and pacing about distractedly. "He said he was going to have to use land scrip to pay his taxes, but I had no idea he was going to lose the entire ranch!" Her hair tumbled willfully from its pins and her cheeks flushed brightly as she vented her anger and frustration through several well-chosen words for the ones responsible for such injustice.

"How did you find out about it?" Gil quietly asked.

"I was over at the courthouse and just happened to

overhear a couple of men discussing the Haywards' misfortune. Oh, Gil, we can't allow them to lose everything!"

"I know. I wish there were something I could do to help." He placed a comforting hand upon her arm, saying, "Come on. I'll drive you home."

"There's no need for that," she protested with a curt toss of her head, still quite distressed at the news she had heard.

"I insist. I've been wanting an opportunity to speak to you in private again," he revealed, leading a pensive, acquiescent Addie outside. He paused to turn the key in the lock before escorting her down the boardwalk to where she had left her mount's reins looped securely around the hitching post. It wasn't long before Gil and Addie were sitting close together in his uncle's buggy, her horse tied behind as they headed toward the winter sun which was sinking below the western horizon. "I hope you don't mind my asking, Miss Addie, but have you been able to think of a way to pay your own taxes?" Gil inquired, sincere concern shining from his blue eyes.

There was an imperceptible tightening of Addie's features, and she hesitated a moment before reluctantly answering, "Yes, Gil, I have."

"Are you also going to have to pay in land scrip?"

"No. Fortunately I won't have to surrender any of the Rolling L's land. You see," she explained, choosing her words carefully, "I . . . I have taken on a partner. He's agreed to pay the taxes." Of course, she bitterly reminded herself, he still hadn't fulfilled any of his promises, including the one to return within two days' time. She had a sneaking suspicion that the impossible man wanted to keep her on pins and needles, that he wanted to have her fairly itching with curiosity about his absence!

"And who is this partner of yours?" Gil questioned levelly as he flicked the reins.

"Does it really matter?" Addie evasively parried, knowing full well that Gil harbored a certain animosity for Daniel Jordan. And she was partly to blame for it.

"I suppose not. But I think I've got a pretty good idea."

"Oh? And how is it you have any idea at all?"

"To be honest, Silas let it slip when you sent him in for supplies a few days ago," Gil rather sheepishly confessed.

"If you already knew about it, Gil Foster, then why pretend ignorance?" Addie crossly demanded, reaching up to briskly tug her hat lower over her forehead.

"I guess I just wanted to hear it from you. It's still difficult to believe that you're tied up in a partnership with a man you profess to despise." He turned a faintly scowling face to her, and Addie was startled by the immense displeasure she read in his eyes. "You didn't have to agree to go into business with him, did you? I don't understand how you could accept his assistance when you refused mine," he softly accused.

"You're right," pronounced Addie in clipped tones, "about its being something you wouldn't understand."

"Please don't be angry with me. It's simply that I . . . I care a great deal about you. And I hate seeing you trapped in a partnership with a man like Jordan."

Addie said nothing in response, and the silence hung heavy between them for the next several moments. Suddenly the spoked wheels of the buggy bounced across an unavoidable rut in the dirt road, jostling the vehicle's occupants and unceremoniously throwing them into even closer contact with one another. Before Addie quite knew what was happening, Gil's arm was about her shoulders. Sharply turning her face to his, she was in the process of opening her mouth to make it clear to him that she was in no need of such support, when his lips swooped down upon hers. His action was so totally unexpected that she was shocked into momentary immobility, her body soft and pliant against the slender tautness of his.

It was only an instant later, however, when she recovered her poise and pushed violently at his chest. Her eyes were blazing fiercely as she jerked away, her bosom heaving in anger. Her infatuated companion, on the other hand, appeared comically bewildered.

"Damn it, Gil! Why did you do that?" she demanded, her voice rising sharply as she felt the telltale color rushing to her face.

"It seemed like the natural thing to do, I suppose," he explained uneasily, his eyes dull as he directed his gaze straight ahead. They were nearing Addie's ranch now.

"Natural? What the devil is so natural about—" she started to argue, only to clamp her mouth shut abruptly. Following a brief hesitation, she continued in a calmer vein. "It shouldn't have happened, Gil. I thought you understood that the two of us are friends, nothing more." She was greatly disturbed by the sudden realization that Gil's mild, somewhat proper kiss didn't hold a candle to Daniel's ardent, intoxicating embrace. Why did he have to plague her every waking moment? she sourly mused. Forcing her attention back to the issue at hand, she suggested in a

259

conciliatory voice, "Let's just forget about it."

"I can't forget about it," Gil quietly disagreed. He was furious with himself for mishandling the situation. He had wanted nothing more than to spend some time alone with the woman he had already given a place in his heart. Cursing inwardly, he told himself that for all her apparent toughness, Miss Addie was a lady and should be treated as such, should be gently wooed. He had behaved little better than a rutting schoolboy!

"Nevertheless," Addie sternly decreed, "you'll have to try." They were slowing up before her house now, and she turned to Gil with a tentative smile. "Would you care to stay for dinner?" She didn't want to think about what had motivated his kiss, didn't want to have to face any further emotional turmoil at the moment. It was a simple mistake on his part, she told herself, and should be forgotten.

"You . . . you're not angry with me?" he asked in disbelief.

"Not at all. You're a good friend, Gil Foster, and I have no intention of ruining our friendship because of outraged maidenly modesty!" Gathering up her skirts, she jumped down from the buggy and set about untying her horse's reins. A very confused Gil remained seated only a second longer before climbing down as well and hurrying to offer his assistance.

His impulsive kiss returned to her thoughts frequently throughout the evening, in spite of her efforts to allow the matter limited attention. By the time Gil took his leave, Addie was reluctantly forced to face the truth. Her friend apparently believed himself in love with her. There simply had been too many clues—the way his eyes had fastened so adoringly upon her

260

throughout the meal, the way his voice had been almost like a gentle caress whenever he spoke to her. There was other evidence as well, she sadly concluded, recalling the times they had been together.

Though it occurred to her that she should feel flattered to have such a nice young man in love with her, the realization only served to cause her disquiet. She knew that she could never return Gil's love. And, even if she did care for him as he seemed to care for her, she was still legally married to Daniel. When was she going to stop procrastinating and set about obtaining a divorce? she asked herself as she disconsolately left the house and headed toward the barn to check on Rascal one last time before retiring to her own bed for the night.

Holding the lamp high, she opened one of the huge double doors and stepped inside the cold, dark building, a tender smile forming on her lips as her gaze fell upon the pup, all curled up in the hay in a corner of Twister's empty stall. Reminded of her horse, she was also forcibly reminded of the man in whose barn he had spent the past several days.

A vivid image of their last, wildly amorous encounter rose to take control of her thoughts, and a nagging sense of shame washed over her once more. It was, however, quickly overpowered by an alarming sensation of deepest yearning, yearning to be held in his strong arms again, to be kissed until she literally begged for the ultimate release . . .

"Adelaide, you're a hypocritical fool!" she muttered aloud, but she was surprised to realize that her self-admonishing tone held little conviction.

Tomorrow is Saturday, she suddenly mused, slowly

turning about and strolling back to the doorway. She had planned to send Silas over to Daniel's on Saturday to fetch Twister home. But now she decided that Silas wouldn't be the one to go. Her lips compressing into a thin line, she told herself that she'd had enough of waiting, that she would demand some answers from her infuriating partner without further delay.

Who the hell did he think he was, she silently fumed, forever making her wonder when he was going to condescend to pay her a visit? After all, the partnership had been his idea, not hers. True, she admitted as she climbed the stairs to her room at last, she was going to benefit from the arrangement. So was he. But only if she didn't decide to call the whole thing off!

Her troubled dreams that night were filled with alternating visions of Gil and Daniel. As in stories of old, Gil was clad in spotless, shining armor and seated astride a beautiful white horse. A gentle, soft-spoken knight, he sought to court her with his gallant reverence, only forgetting his vows of chivalry long enough to bestow an impulsive, nonetheless chaste kiss upon her expectant lips, a kiss that failed to ignite even a spark of desire within her breast.

Daniel, on the other hand, was the epitome of the black knight, his handsome, mocking face smiling wickedly at her as he swept her up before him on his magnificent, black-as-midnight stallion, then thundered away with her to his dark, formidable castle high upon an equally forbidding mountain. She was scorched by his insolently seductive gaze, and a scream of mingled fear and excitement escaped her lips as his skillful hands soon rendered her completely naked and swept up and down her trembling curves in a bold, arrogant manner, his hot-blooded caresses and in-flamed kisses provoking such an intense degree of near painful ecstasy that she would have swooned if not for the powerfully muscled arms which held her . . .

Addie awoke gasping for breath, a fine sheen of perspiration coating her softly quaking body. Her eyes were round as saucers as they hastily glanced toward the window, where she noted the pale light of the dawn touching the cold, frosted glass. Tossing back the covers with a vengeance, she slid from the warmth of her bed, padded across to the dressing table, and quickly lit a candle.

Her gaze was still anxious as she sank down on the cushioned bench and faced her reflection in the mirror. Dear God, she prayed in desperation, what am I to do? I can't go on this way! For four long years I've tried to convince myself that Daniel Jordan was completely out of my life, completely out of both my heart and mind. But I seem totally helpless to prevent thoughts of him from invading every facet of my existence, even my dreams. Worse yet, I can't seem to control this fierce longing to be seduced by him again and again!

Nothing had been resolved by the time Addie saddled a horse and started off toward Daniel's ranch. She had eaten a quick breakfast, endured Esther's freely expressed objections as a result, and firmly rejected Silas's offer to ride along with her. The other men were out on the range, which afforded her the luxury of being completely alone as she traveled the short distance to the old Ferguson place.

She was spared the humiliation of being greeted by a

half-naked Daniel this time, for he was already up and about, his long strides taking him out of the barn just as Addie reined her mount to a halt before the cabin. Irrationally bristling as she saw his lazy smile and unhurried approach, she chose not to dismount. Instead, her voice rang out in the stillness of the crisp air as she tersely announced, "I've come to get Twister."

"I thought you were going to send Silas," he amiably countered, halting at her side. As he negligently pushed his hat back upon his golden head, his eyes twinkled merrily up at her.

"And I thought you were going to be back in a couple of days!" she blurted out, then could have bitten her tongue for allowing him to hear what sounded to her like nothing more than childish annoyance. Schooling her lovely countenance to remain proudly composed, she spoke in a steadier voice. "I had believed that you were going to return before now to discuss the various details of our partnership."

"I apologize for any *inconvenience* my tardiness has caused," Daniel replied solemnly, another smile twisting at the corners of his mouth, "but I've been busy. Besides, I thought it best to allow a period of time to pass before calling on you again."

"Are you aware of the fact that the taxes are due next week? You could at least have bothered to find the time to fulfill the obligation you—"

"I've already fulfilled the obligation," he blithely interrupted, casually rearranging the hat upon his head again. "Your taxes have been paid. I've been meaning to ride over and deliver the receipt."

"You . . . you mean you paid them and didn't even

tell me?" she sputtered in disbelief.

"I'm telling you now. The truth is," he quietly declared, the light of humor rapidly fading from his steely gaze, "I was going to tell you yesterday afternoon. But then I happened to see Gil Foster's buggy in front of your house. What's more, I also happened to see the two of you walking up the front steps of your house together," Daniel noted wryly. "I certainly didn't want to interrupt any *conversation* the two of you were having."

In all actuality, he grimly recalled, he had found himself in the throes of a rapidly escalating, jealous rage at the thought of another man pursuing his beloved wife. And it had required a great deal of restraint to keep from bursting into Addie's house and revealing the truth of their relationship to Gil. But he had consoled himself with the assurance that Addie wasn't the sort of woman to encourage one man while married to another. On the contrary, he mused, staring up into her visibly surprised features, he knew very well that she had all she could handle with the husband who was so determinedly pursuing her.

"You mean you were spying on me!" she wrathfully accused, her eyes flashing down at him as her fingers tightened on the reins. "How dare you! You don't own me, Daniel Jordan!"

"Don't I? Have you forgotten that there are laws concerning a husband and wife, Addie? Unwritten laws as well as written ones." A faint scowl appeared on his face as he grimly added, "Under the law, a man's allowed to exact revenge for betrayal by an unfaithful wife and her lover."

Immediately jumping to the conclusion that Daniel

was insinuating that she was guilty of adultery, Addie felt her temper flaring to a dangerous level. Drawing herself rigidly erect upon her horse, her eyes narrowed and blazing, she ruthlessly taunted, "But what if the wife has been deserted by her husband, ignored by him for four long years? Shouldn't the poor woman be allowed to take a lover in order to ease the loneliness? Should she be forced to deny her . . . her femininity during such an unforgivably long period of time?" Hot tears blurred her vision as she attempted to guide her horse away, her heels already digging into the animal's sleek flanks.

Daniel's long fingers closed upon the trim flesh of Addie's waist, and he unceremoniously hauled her off the horse before she could escape. The startled animal snorted loudly and leapt forward, leaving his rider helplessly imprisoned in the iron grasp of the tall, steely-eyed man who glared so savagely at his squirming captive.

"If I thought there was one ounce of truth in what you said—" he ground out, abruptly breaking off. His hands moved from her waist to her upper arms as her struggles unexpectedly ceased.

"What if it is the truth?" she defiantly sneered, unable to comprehend what was driving her to such rashness. "Was I truly supposed to sit and wait for you for all those years? Did you really expect me to remain true to a man who no longer loved me?" There was a sharp catch in her voice, and bright color stained her cheeks as she stared up at him through her tears.

Daniel met her stormy gaze with deadly calm. She took a shuddering breath, then stood quiet and still before him, only a slight trembling of her arms detectable beneath his hands. He saw her chin rise in an unconscious gesture of resistance, and her eyes seemed to reflect a fierce pride in spite of the luminous drops of moisture clinging to her thick lashes. When he finally spoke, it was in a voice deceptively low and even.

"I loved you, Addie. Whether you choose to believe me or not, I loved you with all my heart. I even wrote you—"

"I know all about the letters!" she cut him off, not pausing to consider the significance of what she was revealing.

"You know about the letters?" echoed Daniel in surprise. His hands tightened on her arms. "Then you realize that I didn't lie to you. And if you read them, you also realize what was in my heart when I wrote them. How can you doubt the sincerity of my feelings?"

"Because—" she began weakly, only to have him interrupt with barely contained violence.

"Damn it, Addie! I tried to stop loving you. God knows, I tried! But it was no use. Your beautiful face was always there to haunt me, the memory of your sweet body next to mine always testing me beyond endurance! You have no idea what it was like to lead my men into battle after bloody battle, always wondering if that day would be my last upon this earth, always longing to see you, to hold you, one more time!" Abruptly releasing her arms, he spun away with a muffled, blistering oath before facing her again, his handsome face slightly flushed beneath his tan, his gray eyes suffused with a fierce, unfathomable light.

"You don't know what war does to a man, Addie. It makes each second with the woman he loves the most precious thing in all the world. It makes him forget all about pride and honor and principles, makes him realize that the most important thing is spending his life with the only person on earth who can love him as he needs to be loved, the only person he can love as she needs to be loved in return. Don't you understand?" he demanded feelingly, again insistently gripping her shoulders. "Loving you is something that's an inseparable part of me!"

"No, I . . . I don't understand," she hoarsely whispered, her own gaze sparkling with a combination of shock and confusion as she slowly shook her head. "I don't understand how you can say that you love a woman, and yet fight against everything she holds sacred—her home, her family, her only chance for happiness with the man she loves!" Her breathing was shallow and ragged as she choked out, "I wasn't in danger of losing my life in a battle, Daniel. I nearly died of a broken heart. There were times when I would have given anything, anything at all, to see you, to talk to you, to have you hold me again. But I didn't die of a broken heart, did I?" she bitterly finished, her tears now coursing freely down her stricken face. She attempted to pull away from him, but he held fast.

"Why didn't you write to me, Addie?" he sharply questioned, his own voice full of undisguised pain.

"What was I to say? Everything had already been said between us, remember? What was there left to say?"

Raising her tear-streaked countenance to the rugged lines of his, she gasped softly as he harshly responded with, "You could have said you still loved me! When I didn't hear from you, when you failed to answer my letters . . . I was undeniably hurt, but I still refused to abandon all hope. Only the war prevented me from seeking you out," he concluded with a heavy sigh, his eyes glowing dully.

"None of this matters, don't you see? What's done is done," Addie declared wearily, averting her swimming gaze as she stared toward her contentedly grazing horse a short distance away.

"It matters," Daniel solemnly asserted, placing his finger beneath her chin and forcing her to look up at him again. "I love you, Addie. Nothing has ever been able to change that. And I came here to discover if you still loved me as well. I believe you do."

"I . . . I don't!" she fearfully denied, her head shaking emphatically. The trembling of the soft flesh beneath his hands increased, and he smiled a tender half-smile.

"I've been a patient man. Some people would say I've had the patience of a saint. But I'm no saint. I'm all too human, Addie, a flesh-and-blood man. And I want you to be my wife again." Her astonished gaze, flying upward to his, was full of alarm. "I'm going to do everything in my power to win you back. I'll continue to be patient for as long as it takes. But heed me well, Addie," he commanded, his tone indicating that he was completely confident of his victory. "You're mine. You've been mine from the first moment we met. I can't erase the pain of these past four years, but I promise you I'll do my damnedest to be the kind of husband you need, the kind of husband who will love you as you deserve to be loved. So I'll wait. But rest assured that you will be my wife in every way again. And know that such a time isn't that far off in the future."

"Do you think it's just the past that's between us?"

269

cried Addie. "No, Daniel. The past is indeed irreversible, but the present is every bit as much a barrier. I've gotten along very well without you all these years. I certainly haven't needed an arrogant, domineering male around in order to run my ranch! And I sure as hell have no intention of allowing myself to be ordered about by a husband who suddenly decides to show up and make unwarranted demands!"

"Demands?" Daniel echoed softly. "I've made no demands."

"Made no demands?" she furiously repeated, successfully jerking away, her eyes shooting fire. "Why, you . . . you have constantly . . . stalked me, Daniel Jordan! You have . . . have used my own body against me, made me do things of which I am unbearably ashamed!" charged Addie, her face blushing rosily beneath her broad-brimmed hat. Though she had dressed that morning in the most unattractive, functional clothing she owned, she nevertheless appeared eminently desirable to Daniel.

"Which only supports my case. You couldn't respond to me the way you do unless you still loved me, Addie," he insisted, slowly inching closer. It seemed to Addie that he loomed threateningly over her, and she instinctively retreated a step.

"That's . . . that's not true!"

"It's the truth, all right. Only you're too blasted stubborn to admit it!" He raised his hands as if intending to touch her again but apparently changed his mind. She watched with stunned amazement, and more than a touch of relief, as he merely wheeled about and began striding back toward the barn, almost

270

casually tossing over his shoulder, "I'll get Twister for you."

Addie blinked rapidly, dashing impatiently at her tears. Following only an instant's hesitation, she scurried toward her horse and quickly mounted up. By the time Daniel reappeared, leading Twister by the halter, she sat white-faced but composed in the saddle.

"I don't think he'll have any further trouble with that foreleg. You can fetch his saddle the next time you're over this way," stated Daniel, sauntering forward to hand the reins up to Addie.

"I won't be coming this way again!" she stiffly retorted, looping Twister's reins about her saddle horn.

"Yes you will," he complacently disagreed. "We're partners now, remember? You'll have to force yourself to face me again, and often."

"We can't be partners! Not after what's been said here today!"

"What's been said doesn't change a thing as far as the business arrangement between us is concerned. I've paid the taxes on your ranch, and now the two of us are in business together." He paused, peering up at her with a strange light reflected in his steady gaze. "But now you know how I feel, Addie. Now you know that I'm not going to rest until you totally belong to me again, body and soul." The expression on his handsome face was inscrutable, but there was a faintly perceptible tightening about his mouth.

Before she could reply, his hand rose and connected gently but firmly with the muscled rump of her mount. The horse took flight, whinnying in outrage, and Twister followed obediently behind. Addie muttered a

271

vicious curse and urged the animal beneath her to an even faster pace. The ride home was completed in almost record time, and she guiltily spent the hour afterward rubbing down the weary, sweat-coated horses while her tears mingled with the warm water in the bucket at her feet.

Fifteen

"There's nothing anyone can do, Miss Addie," John Hayward sadly conceded, lighting his pipe and puffing gently. Although the tall, heavyset man appeared resigned to his fate, there was deep pain mirrored in his brown eyes. He and the daughter of the man who had been his closest friend sat together in the simply furnished but comfortable parlor of his house, some three days before the deadline to pay his taxes.

"But where are you and Harriet going to go? What are you going to do?" Addie worriedly questioned, distractedly fingering the handle of the coffee cup John's wife had earlier presented to her.

"Well, I thought we might head on back to Austin. I've got a brother who operates a flour mill down there. Thought I might see about getting a job with him."

"It's just so damned unfair!" she adamantly decreed.

"Yes, it is. But knowing that won't change anything. We've been working this place nigh onto fifteen years, and now all we can do is stand by and watch it stolen right out from under us. I'd be lying if I didn't say it's tearing me apart to lose my land, Miss Addie," John admitted with a heavy sigh, then philosophically added, "but, I don't aim to let it beat me down entirely. You see, as long as Harriet and I have each other, we'll manage somehow. Life's not always been kind to us, but we've always managed." His heartfelt words brought a sudden rush of tears to Addie's eyes.

"Don't give up hope yet, John. There's still time to think of something. Your friends aren't going to admit defeat without at least putting up one hell of a fight!" She realized that her defiant exhortation would bring him little comfort, and it was with a heavy heart that she took her leave a short time later.

The air seemed filled with the scent of approaching rain as Addie swung up into the saddle, and she took a moment to peer speculatively up at the ominous gray clouds churning overhead. A frown creased her brow when she realized she might not make it to her ranch before the impending storm broke. The Rolling L was several miles to the south of the Haywards' place, and she silently berated herself for wasting so much time in town before heading out to speak with John. A clap of thunder rang out, prompting her to reach down and smooth a hand along Twister's neck.

"Easy, boy. I'm afraid we're in for a soaking," she murmured, buttoning her coat against the damp, chilling wind that was now beginning to swirl about them with rapidly increasing force.

She was less than half the way home when another rider approached. Her hazel eyes narrowing as she endeavored to ascertain the man's identity, she needed no more than a brief second to recognize his unmistakably masculine bearing, the way he sat so tall

274

and self-assured in the saddle. Her pulses leapt, and she thought back to that day, less than a week ago, when he had uttered those words—words of love and determination—which had never been out of her mind since.

Against her will, she had softened toward him that day. It both startled and puzzled her that suddenly she was no longer able to conjure up any residual feelings of either hate or betrayal. The memory of his declaration of love, however urgently uttered, continued to burn within the deepest recesses of her brain.

But, Addie reflected with an inner sigh as she watched him move relentlessly nearer, she still felt only confusion as far as her own emotions were concerned. When would the turbulent maze of thoughts that had once been her well-ordered mind return to normal?

"What are you doing here?" Addie immediately demanded as he drew to a halt before her, forcing her to tug on the reins of her own mount.

"Heading back home," Daniel replied with a disarming grin. "Hoping to outrun the storm, the same as you."

"Neither one of us is going to meet with success if you don't get out of the way!" She didn't want to be alone with him, didn't want to talk to him. She needed more time to think, to try to decide what she was going to do.

"I've got something to tell you, Addie—" he began, his sentence left unfinished as lightning flashed overhead. The two of them were forced to soothe their snorting, apprehensive horses as the accompanying thunder rumbled menacingly. Daniel's eyes reflected a growing concern, and he turned back to Addie to suggest, "I know of an old cabin nearby where we can go to get out of the rain while we talk."

"It isn't raining yet!" she retorted. The words were no sooner out of her mouth when the heavens opened up and began pelting them with large, chilling drops that lightly stung their exposed skin. Shooting Daniel an angry, resentful look, she frowned and asked crossly, "Well, where the devil is this place of yours?" Not certain whether or not she truly heard him laugh softly in response, she swiftly followed after him as he urged his horse toward the abandoned homestead he had found while leisurely roaming the countryside a few weeks earlier.

What had once been a well-tended farm was now nothing more than a smattering of weathered, abandoned shacks, but neither Addie nor Daniel felt any inclination to be critical as they left the animals in the partially roofless barn, then hurried inside what remained of the cabin to seek shelter from the storm.

The darkened sky allowed little light through the barren windows, but Daniel quickly located a half-filled tallow lamp which had been overlooked by its departing owners, and he soon had it flickering to a strengthening glow. Addie, meanwhile, stood shivering uncontrollably, for the downpour had left her very nearly soaked to the skin, her woolen skirts having absorbed the moisture much like a sponge.

"We'd best see about getting a fire started before we catch our deaths," asserted Daniel, masterfully taking control of the situation as he began searching through the various items which littered the mud-caked floor.

Crossing her arms tightly against her chest and valiantly fighting back the tremors, Addie proceeded to conduct her own search in the other rooms. She returned a few minutes later, her arms laden with the splintered remains of a chair, presenting them to Daniel with a stiffly worded, "Here. That's all I could find." He smiled and took the wood from her, adding it to the surprisingly large pile of broken furniture he had already collected and placed in the stone fireplace.

"Well, at least we won't freeze to death for an hour or two," he noted wryly, kneeling down to light the old, yellowed newspaper he had discovered tacked to one of the walls.

As he leaned forward to nurture the budding flame, Addie's gaze was irrevocably drawn to the broad shoulders outlined by his coat, and to the powerful leanness of his hips and thighs which seemed molded by his damp trousers. She watched in rapt attention while he cupped his hands about the minuscule blaze in an effort to shelter it from the wind whistling in under the poorly hinged door. Why had she come with him? she asked herself. Why hadn't she done what she usually did—braved the storm and ridden homeward?

"It appears that you took quite a drenching," he ventured as he rose to his feet a short time later, satisfied that the wood had finally caught fire. His eyes swept critically up and down her shivering form before returning to her rosy-cheeked countenance. "You'd better get out of those wet things."

"What about you?" she shot back, resentfully noting that he seemed to have miraculously escaped any serious dousing from the storm.

"Come on. You can put on my shirt till your things are dry," he casually directed, ignoring her question. Her proud features were visibly mutinous, which prompted him to smile mockingly as he added, "If it will

277

make you feel any better, I promise to turn my back!" Chuckling quietly, he began drawing off his coat.

Addie hesitated. She was cold and miserable, and she wanted nothing more than to be warm and dry. But the thought of being alone with Daniel while wearing nothing more than his shirt caused her to feel suddenly flushed all over.

"I don't really think—" she started to decline.

Daniel cut her off with, "Don't be childish, Addie. Either you take off those clothes, or I'll take them off for you." An audible gasp escaped her lips as her widening eyes flew upward to his face. Glimpsing the serious intent in his steely gaze, she threw him a venomous look but nevertheless stood obediently awaiting the gift of his shirt. When he removed it and negligently tossed it in her direction, she hesitated only a fleeting moment before taking it and hastily retreating to another room.

The rain beat noisily upon the cabin roof as the fire blazed comfortingly inside. Daniel took a seat on the floor in front of the fireplace, and, clad only in his trousers, he rested his arms upon his bent knees and warmed himself before the softly crackling flames. There was a faintly pensive expression on his face as his gaze moved frequently to the doorway through which Addie had disappeared, and a slow smile curved his finely chiseled lips.

When she finally gathered enough courage to return to the fire—driven by cold as much as rebellious pride—Addie snatched up her wet things and staunchly quickened her steps, padding barefoot across the dirty wooden floor and defiantly ignoring Daniel's amused stare altogether as he rose to his feet. Her hands were

278

not quite steady when she knelt to spread her clothing on the floor beside the hearth, but she turned purposefully to the man towering above her as she stood again.

"You mentioned that there was something you wanted to tell me," she remarked coolly.

Daniel, musing to himself that she had never looked more youthful or vulnerably desirable, suppressed a grin at her slightly incongruous appearance. The shirttail reached almost to her shapely knees, and the too-long sleeves were rolled up above her elbows. Though the oversized garment hung loosely upon her small frame, Daniel's eyes were drawn to the outline of her firmly rounded breasts rising and falling gently beneath the soft blue flannel. Her long, flowing hair curled damply about her face and shoulders, and her eyes were wide and luminous as she gazed up at him.

"It will wait," he replied unconcernedly, taking a seat on the floor again. Addie had little choice but to sit beside him. A spark of amusement shone in his eyes as he watched her arranging the folds of the shirt in an effort to cover more of her exposed limbs. "What were you doing out on a day like this?" he asked, taking up a stick to poke at the fire.

"I fail to see how that's any of your business!" She shifted uncomfortably upon the hard wooden floor, edging closer to the flames as a sudden draft swept across her scantily clad form.

"I ran into Ike Henry in town today. He told me that John Hayward is going to lose his land." Her eyes flew to his in surprise.

"Why would Ike think you would be even the slightest bit interested in such information?"

"I didn't ask," Daniel replied with another faint smile. "The thing is, he did tell me, and I want you to know that I'm sorry to hear about it. I gather he's a friend of yours."

"Yes," she murmured, staring at the fire once more. "He and my father were very close. John and Harriet came here not long after we did." His words of sympathy had unnerved her, though she certainly didn't understand why. It was then that a remote possibility suddenly occurred to her.

No! she told herself, allowing her sense of pride to sway her. She couldn't ask him such a thing! In the next instant, however, she realized that her own feelings were not important, that helping John and Harriet was all that truly mattered. She would simply have to swallow her pride and ask. But, she then agonized, what would she do if he refused?

"It sounds like the storm might be easing up a bit," she heard Daniel say, his deep voice drawing her out of her silent, decidedly perplexing contemplations. Turning toward him, she met his still faintly amused gaze squarely and took a deep breath.

"I . . . I have something I'd like to discuss with you," proclaimed Addie, dismayed to feel her face coloring again. He merely stared expectantly across at her, and she paused to clear her throat quietly before continuing. "Since you're already aware of John Hayward's unfortunate situation, there's no need for me to elaborate upon it too much. He's going to need almost three hundred dollars to pay his taxes. There's no way for him to raise that amount of money in such a short period of time. His friends, including myself, would like to help him, but we simply don't have the means to do so. And that . . . that's where you come in," she finished in a rush, quickly averting her gaze in embarrassment.

"Do I?" he responded with a faint, crooked grin.

"Yes. I want to ask you . . . I was hoping you . . ." she stammered in growing discomfort. Raising her eyes to his, a certain defiance returning to glow within their hazel depths, she finally blurted out, "I want you to give John the money for his taxes!" It was as if she were daring him to refuse, to chide her for her presumptuous demand. And she was vastly relieved when he did neither.

"And what am I to receive in return?" he solemnly inquired, tossing another piece of wood on the fire.

"It will only be a loan," she hastened to assure him. "He'll be able to repay you, with interest, after roundup. And I know he'd be forever grateful to you. John's a proud man, but I don't think he'll let his pride stand in the way of his keeping his land."

"Do you honestly believe he'll accept my assistance?"

"He will, after I talk to him. I know I can convince him. You'll get your money back in a few months' time," she reiterated, vaguely noting the way the firelight played across the ruggedly handsome contours of his face and the splendidly muscled planes of his bare chest. "And I . . . I would consider it a sizable favor if you were to agree."

This last statement was met with an imperceptible narrowing of Daniel's eyes. Addie waited in breathless anticipation, watching as he slowly rose to his feet and moved to stand at the window, directing his unfathomable gaze outward at the continuing storm. When he spoke, his voice was low and even.

"All right, Addie. I'll do it—but not as a favor to John Hayward. I'll do it for the simple reason that it obviously means so much to you." He turned around to face her, the expression on his sun-bronzed countenance quite somber, though his gray eyes softened as they fell upon her again. "Whatever matters to you, matters to me as well."

His words brought a flutter to her heart and unexpected tears to her eyes. Hastily looking away, she softly declared in a slightly tremulous voice, "I'm grateful to you, Daniel." Numbly realizing that yet another wall of the barrier she had erected about herself had come crashing down as a result of his generosity, she felt her entire body trembling. She held her hands out toward the warmth of the fire, vividly aware of the way Daniel was staring across at her so intently. She was also aware that she was now experiencing an overwhelming urge to have him take her in his arms and chase the chill from her body with the sort of blaze only he could so skillfully create within her!

"I don't want your gratitude, Addie," he huskily asserted, striding forward to seize her arms and lift her up before him. She felt the familiar weakness assailing her at the first touch of his hands, and she knew that it was only a matter of time before she would be willingly surrendering to his deliciously impassioned caresses, his wildly seductive kisses . . .

She was stunned when he abruptly released her and took a seat before the fire again, leaving her standing with an aching sense of disappointment, as well as an inexplicable feeling of defeat.

Why hadn't he kissed her? she dazedly wondered,

staring down at his golden head in bemusement. For more than a month now, the impossible man had been forcing his attentions upon her at every turn! Indignantly reflecting that in the past his arrogant man-handling had always led to something of a more intimate nature, she flounced away and marched to the spot at the window Daniel had just vacated. Thunder rumbled overhead, and another torrent of rain pounded on the cabin roof as Addie's turbulent thoughts whirled.

With feminine perverseness, she suddenly decided to exert the power she was confident she possessed. All reason fled as her emotions took control. Whirling back around, she returned to take up the stick Daniel had used to poke at the fire. While he merely sat and stared deeply into the flames, she leaned over to imitate his earlier actions, bending at the waist so that the man beside her was afforded a tantalizing, eye-level glimpse of the silken curves beneath the flannel shirt.

Daniel, who had previously assured Addie that he was only flesh and blood, found his gaze irresistibly drawn to the enticing roundness of his wife's naked derriere. The sight brought his smoldering desire for her—desire that was never far from the surface—surging upward. He smiled to himself, for he knew full well what she was doing. And, despite his firm resolve not to be the one to initiate any further lovemaking between them until she had pronounced the words of love he so impatiently longed to hear, he good-naturedly, and wholeheartedly, succumbed to her not-too-subtle attempts at seduction.

"Without a doubt, dearest Adelaide, you've got the prettiest backside I've ever seen," he remarked, rising to his feet and taking hold of her shoulders to turn her toward him. "And you deserve to have it soundly spanked for all the thoroughly wicked thoughts it's creating within my head!" he added with mock ferocity, his eyes twinkling irrepressibly as he looked down into her fierily blushing countenance.

"What . . . what do you mean?" she lamely queried, unable to meet his gaze as she now experienced a certain embarrassment for her bold, wanton display.

"I mean that you are a beautiful, desirable woman, and if you want me to make love to you, all you have to do is come right out and say so."

"Why, you . . . you—" she furiously sputtered, only to be effectively silenced by the pressure of his lips upon hers. His tongue plundered the moist, sweet recesses of her mouth, and his hands worked their delectable magic as they swept up and down her supple curves. Within seconds, the flannel shirt was discarded and the last of Daniel's clothing joined Addie's on the floor.

Soon the two of them were entwined before the fire atop the scant cushion of discarded clothing, their kisses growing rapidly more inflamed. Daniel's warm fingers hungrily explored the secret, womanly places of Addie's quivering form, and she met his passion eagerly, her own caresses becoming more and more bold.

Suddenly rolling to his back, he was now beneath her, and she gasped softly at the unfamiliar position in which she found herself. She had no time to contemplate any awkwardness she might have experienced, however, for his hands lifted her slightly upward and forward, and his lips closed greedily upon the rosy nipple of her full breast. She moaned, her own fingers clutching at his head, curling tightly within the thick, wheat-colored hair that smelled faintly of wood smoke.

"Oh, Daniel!" she breathed, his mouth suckling tenderly at her other breast now, his hands molding the firm mounds of her bottom as the tip of his manhood rubbed provocatively against the tingling place between her smooth thighs. She drew in her breath sharply, oblivious to the drafts which swept across her naked back. The deep yearning she felt within her became a consuming flame as her heart pounded in her ears.

A flash of lightning illuminated the window, but both Addie and Daniel ignored the storm raging outside as they created a powerfully sensual tempest of their own in the fire's glow. Before long, she felt herself being lifted again, and she uttered a hoarse cry as he sheathed his hardness within her velvety warmth. Her movements soon matched his, and the tempo of their union became increasingly frenzied as his hands held her about the hips and she rode atop him in glorious abandon. Countless emotions exploded within her head when they both reached the pinnacle of satisfaction, and she could do nothing more than collapse weakly upon his chest as he strained upward against her.

In the languid aftermath of their volatile passion, Addie lay cradled against her husband, the fire warming one side of her body while the heat of Daniel's virile form warmed the other. She felt thoroughly contented and sated, and, for some unknown reason, happier than she had felt in a long time.

"I love you, Addie," Daniel quietly declared, his lips

285

tenderly brushing against her forehead.

"Do you?" she responded, a rather plaintive note in her tremulous voice.

"You know I do." His arms tightened possessively about her.

"I don't know what to think, what to believe." She sighed, snuggling closer against his muscular leanness. "I only know that I . . . I seem to be a different person whenever I'm in your arms. The whole world seems to fade away . . ." she murmured, her voice trailing off into confused silence.

"That's the way it should be," he observed with a low chuckle, an indulgent light shining forth from his eyes as he tipped her face up to his. "For two people who love each other, that is."

"Oh, Daniel, if only we could go back to that time when we were so young and foolishly ignorant of what was to come!" she earnestly declared. "If only—"

"When are you going to realize that it's only today that's important, my love?" he gently interrupted, placing a tender kiss upon her cheek. She sighed heavily, her head returning to rest upon his chest. They lay in thoughtful silence for several more seconds, until Daniel said, "Much as I would enjoy nothing more than holding you like this forever, it's getting late. And unless my ears deceive me, the storm has abated." He reluctantly drew away and stood up, quickly donning his trousers as protection against the cold air. Addie's clothing, though still damp, was much drier than when she had removed it, and she also set about getting dressed.

When Daniel opened the door a short time later, he was satisfied to note that the rain had tapered off into nothing more than a drizzle. He turned back to Addie with a soft, teasing smile.

"Maybe we'll be fortunate enough to get caught in another storm the next time we chance to meet while out riding." Although she initially bristled at his remark, she couldn't help but find his ironic humor infectious, and she smiled grudgingly in response. Outlined in the doorway, the gray light filtering through the thick cover of clouds at his back, Daniel seemed to Addie even taller than usual, and more roguishly irresistible . . .

A shot rang out, its loud report shattering the stillness of the misty afternoon. Addie could only watch in horrified shock as Daniel cursed and grabbed at his left arm, then spun about and flung himself at her, forcefully knocking her to the floor beneath him. His right hand instinctively reached for the gun in his coat pocket, and he withdrew it and held it in defensive readiness, wincing with the sharp pain which raced through his injured arm as he eased himself up and toward the window.

"Daniel!" breathed Addie, rolling over and stealthily moving across the floor to his side. Her rifle was propped in the corner near the window, and she hurriedly snatched it up. "Do you see anyone?" she whispered, scrutinizing him as he peered cautiously through the streaked and broken glass. She frowned as her gaze fastened on the blood seeping through the ragged tear in the sleeve of his coat.

"There's a lone rider in the distance, but I can't tell who it is," he tersely answered, clenching his teeth against the searing pain. "He's heading away."

"Who would do such a thing?" she wondered aloud,

her fingers tightening upon the gun.

"I can think of any number of people," Daniel responded with a short, humorless laugh as he turned away from the window. Returning the pistol to his coat pocket, he told a visibly shaken Addie, "Whoever it was, I don't think he'll be coming back."

"But he . . . he tried to kill you!"

"I'm not so sure about that," he muttered, his mouth tightening into a thin line as he carefully shrugged out of his coat. Addie set aside her own gun and hurried to bring the lamp closer, her beautiful face a mask of genuine concern. "Looks like he wasn't much of a marksman," observed Daniel. The bullet had torn through the outer flesh of his forearm but had apparently inflicted no serious damage. The wound was bleeding profusely, however, and Addie wasted no time in partially disrobing again, hurriedly removing her coat and shirt in order to use the soft cotton of her chemise to bind Daniel's arm.

"You'll need to have Doc Bennett take a look at this as soon as possible," she pronounced, breathing an inward sigh of relief that the makeshift bandage appeared to succeed in temporarily stanching the flow of blood.

"That won't be necessary," he disagreed, his eyes glowing as he watched her button her soft linen shirt.

"Don't be an idiot! That wound might not look like much, but infection could set in, and then you'd find yourself in a fine mess!" she vigorously admonished, drawing on her coat and tossing her head so that her long, gleaming hair swirled about her shoulders.

"Would it matter so much to you, Addie?" Daniel lovingly taunted, reaching out to grasp her wrist. It was obvious that his words threw her into consternation, and he relented with a brief smile, saying, "We'd better get going. I don't know who the hell it was who decided to use me for target practice, but I certainly don't intend to wait around for more of the same." He was thinking of Addie's safety, not his own, and in actuality he was more concerned about the incident than he was willing to admit to his wife. It enraged him that someone had endangered Addie's life in order to issue what he believed to be no more than a warning of some kind, a warning undoubtedly meant for him.

"Do you think it's safe for us to leave now?" she questioned apprehensively.

"We've got to get home before dark. Don't worry," he reassured her, pulling her against him for one last embrace. "I don't think he'll try anything else today." He kissed her, then led her out through the open doorway toward the barn, the lingering drizzle coating them with tiny droplets of moisture. They mounted quickly and headed in the direction of Addie's ranch, their gazes continually watchful as they urged the horses into a full gallop.

Sixteen

"No!" cried Addie, her own voice jolting her awake. She came abruptly upright in the bed, her eyes wide and full of numbing terror. The horrible vision of a bullet tearing through Daniel's heart and leaving him to crumple lifelessly to the ground had forced its way into her dreams. Her entire body trembled beneath the quilt, and she felt a decidedly queasy sensation in the pit of her stomach.

It was only a bad dream, she reassured herself, sinking back down upon the pillow—a nightmare brought on as a result of the actual shooting which had occurred earlier that day. Dream or not, she thought as a very real sigh of relief escaped her lips, its effects were still uncomfortably tangible.

Recalling the way Daniel had smiled so warmly at her before taking his leave that evening, after he had gallantly allowed Esther to fuss over his injury to her heart's content, Addie's discomfort increased tenfold. He was such a handsome, strong, principled man, she mused—the kind of man even her father would have approved of . . .

Don't be ridiculous! she scornfully chided herself. Will Caton would never have approved of his only daughter's marrying one of the enemy! But, she then reflected with another sigh, he didn't seem like the enemy any longer. He was simply Daniel, the man who could make her feel so vibrantly alive, so intensely feminine, the man who was solely responsible for drastically changing her life, not once but twice.

Thinking of the awful dream again, she pondered its significance. She couldn't deny that her heart had nearly stopped when she had seen Daniel shot. And realizing that he could still be in danger, that there was every possibility the violence against him would be repeated, made her body's trembling worsen.

What was she to do? In the days that followed, she continued to tell herself that she couldn't even consider acknowledging herself to be his wife again, yet, at the same time, she was vividly aware of the fact that she couldn't bear to think of life without him!

Addie's emotional dilemma was brought to a startling climax less than three weeks later. It had all begun when she had driven the buckboard into town to fetch some supplies, and her thoughts had drifted back to the day when she and Daniel had been together in the deserted cabin, the day he had received the wound that had now healed completely.

That had been the last time he had so much as touched her, she mused with a deep frown. She had seen him four times since, but he had remained bewilderingly distant on each occasion, stopping by the

Rolling L merely to discuss matters pertaining to the upcoming roundup. He hadn't even mentioned the subject of a cattle drive again, she suddenly realized, confused about his silence.

She had frequently caught herself worrying about the exasperating man, though she now perversely decided to try to prevent any personal thoughts of him from entering her mind. He had professed his love for her, and yet he was suddenly behaving as if the two of them had never shared anything more than their blasted business partnership!

"Afternoon, Miss Addie!" called Harriet Hayward. She ambled forward as Addie smiled and drew up alongside the boardwalk in front of the newly reopened hotel.

"You're looking well, Harriet," proclaimed Addie, gathering up her skirts and lithely climbing down from the buckboard. Negligently looping the reins about the brake handle, she turned to her friend and asked, "How is John?" She tugged off her hat and smoothed the wayward chestnut curls from her face. As she did so, the bright sunlight beating down upon her head turned her hair into a blaze of color.

"John's fine. Looking forward anxiously to the early spring we're supposed to have," Harriet said with a laugh. The expression on her thin, kindly face sobered slightly before she sincerely asserted, "I don't know what we'd have done without you, dearest Addie. You and Mr. Jordan will never know how truly grateful we are."

"Now, Harriet, you and John have already thanked me quite sufficiently! And Dan . . . Mr. Jordan told me about the visit John paid him. I'm only glad that husband of yours finally agreed to go along with the arrangement."

"My man is among the stubbornest, but he's no fool," quipped Harriet. She and Addie talked together for several more minutes, until Harriet reluctantly declared that she had best be getting on with the numerous errands which had brought her to town that day. The two women parted with a brief embrace, and Addie's mood was considerably improved as she turned away to head toward the mercantile.

"Addie?" a soft, feminine voice hesitantly ventured behind her. "Addie, is that you?"

She spun about, the voice sounding vaguely familiar to her ears. Her eyes widened in her amazement, and she seemed rooted to the spot as she faced the petite redhead who had just exited the hotel.

"Carrie?" she whispered in disbelief.

"Oh, Addie, it is you!" cried the other young woman, wasting no further time before sweeping forward to fling her arms enthusiastically about her former schoolmate. "Why, I scarcely recognized you!"

"What are you doing here?" Addie joyfully demanded, warmly returning her friend's hug before drawing away to study Carrie's beautiful, lightly freckled countenance. "I . . . I didn't know . . . Daniel didn't tell me you were coming!"

"Of course not. I wanted to surprise you!" she responded with an engaging laugh. Her bright red curls bounced and her green eyes sparkled as she linked her arm companionably through Addie's and said, "Oh, there is so much I want to tell you, so much I want to ask you!"

"When did you arrive?" questioned Addie, still in a daze.

"Yesterday. Charity and I came on the stage. You see, we traveled from St. Louis to San Antonio with my Aunt Millie, who was going to visit her husband who is stationed there, and then Charity and I decided to come to Fort Worth a few days earlier than planned. You should have seen my brother's face when the two of us arrived on his doorstep!" she supplied in an energetic rush, her pleasant laughter ringing out again as she began leading a slightly bemused Addie into the hotel.

"But what are you doing here in town? And who is Charity?" Her head was in a whirl as she sank gratefully into the velvet-upholstered chair opposite Carrie's inside the gaily decorated lobby. Her shining gaze swept up and down her friend's elegant form, and she noted how well the slightly buxom young woman looked in her black-and-white-striped dress trimmed in dull cherry red, and the white straw hat with small red and white plumes.

"Well, we couldn't very well stay out at Daniel's place, now, could we? Imagine, two females trying to cohabitate in such close quarters, and with that brother of mine besides!" She giggled, leaning forward and grasping Addie's hand. "And Charity—Charity Bransom, that is—is an old friend of the family. She's resting upstairs in her room at the moment. Charity was a couple of years ahead of us at Miss Kent's. In fact, she and Daniel—" she began, only to break off rather mysteriously and change the subject. "Oh, Addie, how are you? I must say, the years have only enhanced your beauty, though I doubt very seriously if either Miss Kent or your cousin Martha would have approved of your attire!" she teased good-naturedly, her small, gloved hand indicating the loose-fitting flannel shirt and drab woolen skirt beneath Addie's masculine, buckskin coat.

"I'm fine," replied Addie with an indulgent smile, inwardly marveling at the other woman's irrepressible vitality. "And fine silks and satins are hardly suitable for running a ranch!" She grew solemn as she quietly asked, "And you, Carrie? How are you? I . . . I read the letter you sent with Daniel. I was so sorry to hear about Alan. I had no idea . . ." she murmured, her voice trailing away as a sudden wave of guilt washed over her. She should have written Carrie, should not have allowed her disastrous relationship with her friend's brother to drive her into what must have seemed uncaring silence.

"It honestly doesn't tear me apart any longer. It's been so long, and yet it doesn't seem that it's been any time at all. But, I'm all right, dear Addie," Carrie assured her, squeezing her hand for emphasis. "I'm getting on with my life, just as Alan would have wanted."

"It's so good to see you again, Carrie," Addie feelingly proclaimed, a slight catch in her voice as she and her friend embraced again. They were both fighting back the tears when they rose to their feet a few moments later and strolled out of the hotel together.

"Daniel had promised to escort me out to see you this evening," revealed Carrie, her hand moving gracefully upward to secure her hat as a sudden gust of wind threatened to send it flying.

"He never gave me any clue about your visit." She felt a surge of anger toward him for his unfailing ability to keep a secret.

"Don't blame him," said Carrie, as if she had read the other woman's thoughts. "He didn't want to keep you in the dark, but I begged him to allow me to surprise you. And, to tell the truth, I wanted to see for myself how the two of you were getting along." They began moving down the boardwalk toward the mercantile now, oblivious to the curious and admiring stares the petite woman was receiving from the predominantly male passersby.

"What do you mean?" Addie evasively countered.

"Well, since my brother finally revealed to me that the two of you are married—"

"Were married," corrected Addie.

"Daniel didn't say anything about a divorce," Carrie responded with a pensive frown.

"There hasn't exactly been a divorce," her friend admitted. "But I still intend to seek one as soon as time and circumstances allow!" Her words sounded unconvincing, even to herself.

"Time and circumstances? Why, Addie, it's been more than four years now!"

"I'm well aware of that fact. But, if you don't mind, I'd rather keep your brother out of the present conversation," she firmly insisted.

"Very well," Carrie amiably agreed. "After all, I intend to spend a good deal of time with you, and you can be certain Daniel's name will surface in our heart-to-heart discussions sooner or later!"

They paused before the doorway of the mercantile now, and Carrie released her hold upon her hat in order to lift her full skirts out of the dust which caked the threshold. It was as if the Texas wind had been waiting for such an opportunity, for it proceeded to whip the plumed bonnet from her head, sending it tumbling unceremoniously back down the boardwalk.

Gil Foster, who had happily glanced up to see Miss Addie standing in front of the store, was already hurrying forward to greet her when his eyes fell upon her charming companion. He came to an abrupt halt, his blue eyes full of something akin to wonderment. He stood thus for the space of several awestruck seconds, then suddenly came to life once more as the young vision's hat was torn from her flaming curls.

Rushing past the two women in gallant pursuit of the errant feminine concoction, he successfully retrieved it and brought it back to its exceedingly grateful owner, who favored him with a dazzling, dimpled smile. Gil swallowed hard and spared only a passing glance for Miss Addie before his gaze fixed unwaveringly upon her friend's lovely, pixieish face.

"Thank you," Carrie warmly declared, taking the hat from his hands with another smile. "I suppose it was rather foolish of me to wear the silly thing on such a windy day!" She raised her lively green eyes to his and experienced something of a shock as she felt an invisible current passing between the two of them.

"Not at all," murmured Gil, a quizzical expression on his own attractive features and a faint flush rising to the skin just above the collar of his white linen shirt.

"Good afternoon, Gil," interjected Addie. "I'd like you to meet a dear friend of mine, Mrs. Carrie Rogers. And Carrie, I'd like to present Mr. Gil Foster, another friend."

"The pleasure is all mine, Mrs. Rogers," Gil politely murmured, his eyes clouding with disappointment at the news that the delightful young lady was a married woman.

"Mr. Foster," returned Carrie, nodding graciously in his direction and oblivious to the fact that her suddenly trembling fingers were crushing the plumes of her hat. Musing that Gil Foster's eyes were the bluest she had ever seen, she shook her head slightly as if to clear her thoughts, tearing her gaze away from the tall gentleman's stare and transferring it to the woman at her side. "Addie, perhaps I'd better return to the hotel. Charity should be well rested by now, and my brother will be coming to call upon us soon." Though she didn't understand why, she was now experiencing a sudden need to escape the man's presence. There was a queer sensation in the pit of her stomach.

"Your brother?" echoed Gil.

"Mrs. Rogers's brother is Daniel Jordan," supplied Addie, silently noting Gil's frown at the news. "I would like it very much if you and Miss Bransom and . . . and your brother came to supper tonight," she requested, directing her invitation to a strangely pale Carrie.

"Of course we'll come," agreed her friend. Inclining her head briefly toward Gil, for she could not bring herself to meet his gaze again, she bestowed one last hug upon Addie before taking her leave. Her dainty, high-topped boots connected briskly with the rough-hewn boards of the walk as she quickly made her way back to the hotel.

Addie was left alone with an oddly pensive Gil, who seemed to be awakening from some sort of trance as he hastily cleared his throat and escorted her inside the

299

store. Neither of them mentioned Carrie as they went about their business, Addie ordering the various foodstuffs she had come to fetch, and Gil efficiently gathering the supplies. Their talk centered upon nothing more personal than the weather, which they both agreed was unusually mild for February, and the upcoming roundup which every rancher in the area eagerly anticipated.

By the time Addie left town and headed back to the Rolling L, her mind was literally spinning with thoughts of the afternoon's events. She was stunned by Carrie's unexpected appearance in town. And a lingering annoyance with Carrie's brother brought a tight-lipped expression to her face and a returning blaze to her eyes as she flicked the reins and guided the buckboard along the rutted wagon road.

Esther attacked the preparations for the evening meal with even more than her usual zeal. Having expressed profound delight when Addie informed her that they would be entertaining guests at supper, she continued to make no secret of her enthusiasm for the fact that her young mistress had finally begun inviting friends to the Rolling L again.

"No sir, they ain't gonna be able to resist Esther's chicken and dumplin's!" the older woman proclaimed with an accompanying chuckle as she flew about the kitchen, apron strings flying.

"Who is it that's comin'?" asked Silas, sipping his coffee and grinning at his wife's whirlwind movements.

"Two young ladies from back East, and that Mr. Jordan." She began slicing the potatoes she had peeled earlier, humming a lively tune as she worked.

"Mr. Jordan?" repeated Silas in mild surprise, his voice also holding a touch of disapproval.

"Now don't go takin' that tone, old man!" his perceptive wife reproved with a knowing frown. "It ain't up to us to decide who Miss Addie invites to supper! Besides," she opined, flashing him a conspiratorial grin, "I got an idea he and our Miss Addie are more *friendly* than either of them's willin' to let on."

"What makes you say that?" he sharply queried, his kindly brown eyes reflecting a deepening concern. The more he saw of Daniel Jordan, the more he liked the man, but that still didn't mean he wanted to see his beloved employer get tied up with a man who seemed only to cause her inexplicable unhappiness. He had watched the two of them together, and he knew without a doubt that there was indeed something between the two of them, something that went far beyond their opposing loyalties in the war . . .

"Us womenfolk knows these things, that's all!" Esther enigmatically parried, resuming her preparations as well as her humming. Silas merely sat and frowned thoughtfully into his coffee cup.

Meanwhile, the subject of their discussion was upstairs in her bedroom, muttering impatient oaths as she tried to choose from the meager collection of dresses she considered suitable for the evening's affair. Asking herself why the devil she should waste so much time on something as unimportant as her attire, she agonized over her decision nevertheless. Finally settling upon an apple-green and white figured silk with a tight waist and very full gathered skirts, she wrinkled her nose as she realized that a faint smell of cedar hung about the gown, the result of many years spent inside the large trunk.

"Oh, who the devil cares?" she muttered aloud in defiance, spinning away from the bed to start undressing. Musing that it was a good thing she'd already had her bath that day, she tossed her skirt and blouse into the chair before her dressing table, then donned the fitted silk. After wrestling successfully with the tiny mother-of-pearl buttons up the back, she turned to the gilded mirror and adjusted the bodice about her bosom and shoulders.

What would Daniel think when he saw her in the gown? she found herself wondering. She hadn't worn such finery since the night of the Christmas dance, the night the two of them had . . .

Memories of the intimacy they had shared that night—the first since their brief period as newlyweds so long ago—still brought a rosy blush to her cheeks. And the times they had shared passion since had also left indelible prints upon her mind. Why hadn't he made any such overtures in the past few weeks? she asked herself again.

Though it was a source of great embarrassment to her, she knew that she ached for Daniel's touch, and the wild stirring in her blood only grew stronger each time she thought of him. And yet, she realized, uncoiling her thick hair and taking up the hairbrush to methodically brush the tangles from the lustrous chestnut locks, it seemed that the yearnings deep within her breast went far beyond mere physical desire. She longed to have him speak words of love to her again, to tell her once more that he had always loved her and would never stop . . .

"You're a fool!" she muttered to her reflection. Her fingers tugged almost painfully at her hair as she recoiled it and fastened it into a chignon at the base of her graceful neck. Why did she want to hear declarations of undying love and devotion from a man who had done nothing but cause her grief?

Only grief? a voice at the back of her mind challenged. Hadn't she known great, vibrant joy when he kissed her, when he stroked her curves with such wonderfully torturous expertise? Hadn't she felt a strange twisting of her heart that stormy day at the cabin when he had protectively covered her body with his after being shot? And weren't her dreams still troubled with recurring nightmares concerning her fears that he would be injured again?

Her eyes widened, then swept closed. She remained in this state for the space of several moments, until, finally, she mentally shook herself and hastily exited the room. Valiantly attempting to force her thoughts elsewhere, she descended the stairs and stepped into the kitchen to help Esther.

Addie flew to answer the knock at the front door, unconsciously smoothing the stray tendrils of hair at her temples as she took a deep, steadying breath. She swung open the door to find a beaming Carrie, a somber-faced, dark-eyed woman at her side, and a faintly smiling Daniel, whose gaze immediately captured hers.

"Oh, Addie, your house is lovely!" exclaimed Carrie, planting an affectionate kiss on her friend's cheek before sweeping inside. The other woman favored

303

Addie with a distant, decidedly unfriendly ghost of a smile as she entered, leaving an oddly expectant Daniel standing alone in the doorway.

"Won't you come inside?" Addie politely offered, her pulse racing alarmingly at the sight of his handsome, mocking face.

"Do you realize that this is the first time you've ever actually asked me inside?" he sardonically noted, lowering his voice so that only she was able to decipher his words. He moved forward with slow, unhurried steps, removing his hat and unbuttoning his coat as he stepped into the entrance hall. He was wearing a simple but impeccably tailored black suit, and Addie threw him a quelling glance before quickly turning to her other guests.

"Addie, this is Charity Bransom. Charity, this is Addie Caton, a dear friend of mine who was once also a schoolmate at Miss Kent's," Carrie announced, eager to complete the introductions.

"Welcome to the Rolling L, Miss Bransom," said Addie, her voice lacking warmth as she responded to the faintly hostile gaze Charity turned upon her.

"Thank you, Miss Caton." Even her voice was cold and distant, Addie silently observed, watching now as Daniel gallantly offered to assist Charity in removing her cloak. Charity Bransom was a tall, slender brunette whose figure was flawless and her attire enviably elegant. She was wearing a gown of peacock blue velvet, banded in lighter blue with white tassels, and her raven curls, arranged in the popular waterfall style, were trimmed with narrow white satin ribbons. Her features were a trifle sharp but undeniably aristocratic, and the smile she was turning upon Daniel was obviously calculated to enchant.

"What in heaven's name is that delicious aroma?" demanded Carrie merrily, drawing Addie out of her disturbing preoccupation. She smiled at the petite redhead, taking Carrie's hand in hers as they began moving toward the dining room, though she didn't fail to notice how Daniel's eyes softened as he drew Charity's arm through his and followed after them.

"I'm afraid Esther is rather immodest when it comes to her chicken and dumplings!" revealed Addie with a soft laugh, taking a seat at the head of the table, the polished surface of which had been covered by a spotless white linen tablecloth. Carrie chose the seat to her right, and Daniel pulled out the chair to Addie's left for Charity, who settled her velvet skirts about her with a graceful flourish. The fact that he chose the seat farthest away from hers provoked Addie to what she recognized as irrational annoyance, a reaction she couldn't seem to prevent.

Esther, as if on cue, bustled out of the kitchen a moment later, proudly carrying the huge bowl of what she deemed her culinary triumph. It wasn't long before the table was laden with accompanying bowls of creamed potatoes, biscuits, custard pudding, and apple fritters.

"My, but you do eat heavily here, don't you?" Charity remarked with a faint, unmistakably critical grimace on her aristocratic countenance.

"Perhaps," replied Addie with an edge to her own voice, "but then, we work hard out here." She didn't miss the fond looks Charity and Daniel exchanged as her words apparently fell on deaf ears, and she felt a sudden, unfamiliar emotion rising within her breast.

"Daniel told us that you're expecting to have an early roundup," said Carrie, helping herself to a surprisingly hearty portion of potatoes. "I'm so glad we'll be staying long enough to see it. I don't know a great deal about ranching. I was quite young when we left our own place and moved to St. Louis to live with my aunt and uncle."

"You lived on a ranch?" Addie questioned in surprise.

"More of a farm, actually, wasn't it, Daniel?" answered Carrie, looking to her brother for elaboration upon the subject.

"A combination of the two," he supplied, his gaze finally moving from Charity to Addie.

"You never told me—" Addie started to say, her eyes silently accusing him of some sort of deception. She caught herself, however, and glanced back to a watchful Carrie, unaware of the way Charity's well-formed lips tightened into a mild frown of displeasure. "There really isn't much to see during a roundup, at least not that I think you'd be interested in. Roping and branding might be exciting to some, but such pursuits probably wouldn't be what you'd call fascinating!"

Laying aside her fork in order to take a sip of water, Addie nearly choked when Charity observed with a perceptible sneer, "I suppose you personally take part in these . . . activities, Miss Caton." Her brown eyes moved with leisurely disdain across Addie's tanned form.

"Of course. I've been taking part in these particular *activities* since I was a child. And I learned to ride almost before I could walk. You see, Miss Bransom," Addie stated in a voice laced with biting sarcasm, "there isn't much use for *helpless* females in this

306

country. Although girls are taught the more domestic skills, they're also taught how to hunt and dress meat, herd cattle, chop wood, butcher hogs—"

"How nice," Charity frostily interrupted, dull color staining her cheeks. Daniel remained unusually silent, though his eyes glowed as he watched the subtle battle taking place. Carrie appeared a trifle perplexed, however, and she hastened to intervene.

"I told Addie that you also attended Miss Kent's Academy, Charity." She regretted her choice of subject a moment later as Charity again directed her words toward Addie.

"I heard that you were forced to leave after only a short time in our fair city, Miss Caton. That would naturally explain why we never chanced to meet before now. But what a pity you were unable to complete your education. I've found that my years at Miss Kent's have proven quite beneficial to me."

"I had already received a more than sufficient education at home," Addie curtly replied. "And I seem to recall Carrie's telling me that you were a few years ahead of us at school, so there's no reason why our paths should have crossed."

Her words were met with cold-eyed silence, and Daniel finally interjected, "Addie, I've got some news concerning the cattle drive. If you don't mind, I'd like to stop by tomorrow and discuss it with you." There was a visible challenge in his steely gray eyes, and Addie resentfully mused that this was the first time he had so much as mentioned a cattle drive in weeks. It was also the first time he had bothered to ask her if she minded whether or not he stopped by! Inwardly she fumed. She could only assume that his deceptive display of gentlemanly behavior was for Miss Charity Bransom's benefit!

"You're planning a cattle drive?" Charity broke in, turning to him with a feigned show of interest.

"Yes. And since Miss Caton and I are business partners, there are naturally matters which require discussion between us," he casually explained. His business partner irritably wondered why he felt compelled to explain anything to the snobbish bundle of useless femininity seated next to him.

"You sound as if you consider the drive a sure thing," Addie remarked crossly, tossing her napkin to the table as she suddenly found herself without appetite.

"It is. As a matter of fact, I already have everything arranged. But I'll tell you all about it tomorrow." He, too, indicated that he had finished eating by negligently pushing his empty plate away. Carrie, the only one who had enthusiastically sampled Esther's cooking, declared that she and Charity were eager to see the rest of the house. Refraining from announcing that she knew damn well Charity hadn't the least interest in seeing the rest of the house, Addie dutifully led the way from the dining room and up the stairs. Daniel sauntered into the fire-warmed study, and there was an inscrutable smile on his handsome face as he leaned against the oak mantle and complacently awaited the women's return.

Seventeen

Following the departure of her guests, Addie was left with a fairly smoldering anger, in addition to another, less recognizable sensation. Daniel's behavior had been undeniably proper, which should have pleased her but did not; Charity's had become more openly antagonistic; and an ever-pleasant Carrie had overcompensated for her companion's unfriendliness with her endless, albeit good-natured, chattering.

Putting a hand on her forehead, Addie finally joined Esther and Silas in the kitchen. Both individuals immediately sensed the younger woman's troubled mood, and they wisely refrained from questioning her about the outcome of the evening.

"Silas," said Addie, obviously preoccupied as she took a seat beside him and gratefully accepted a cup of freshly brewed coffee from his solicitous wife, "I'd like your honest opinion about something."

"What is it, honey?" he gently questioned, his lined face displaying his usual loving concern.

"Would it truly be possible for us to have a cattle

drive this spring?"

"Well," he murmured, apparently pondering the matter, "I guess that all depends on where you're plannin' to drive your stock."

"I don't know," she confided, smiling wanly. "Mr. Jordan seems to think it's all settled, though. There's no denying we could get a much better price farther east, or even farther north. But I don't see how we could hope to succeed with all the obstacles in our way."

"I ain't never been on a drive, Miss Addie," admitted Silas, "but I wouldn't rule it out just yet. There just might be somethin' to Mr. Jordan's idea." He had heard that one could get forty to fifty dollars a head back East, which was ten times what the local market would support. The more he turned it over in his mind, the more the thought of a drive appealed to him. "You say you don't know where Mr. Jordan's got in mind to head the stock?"

"He's coming over tomorrow to discuss it with me," Addie replied, releasing a soft sigh as she took one last sip of coffee and rose to her feet. "You outdid yourself on the supper, Esther," she complimented, her soft voice holding unmistakable pride. The older woman enveloped her in a deeply affectionate embrace before Addie took herself off to bed, though her sleep offered only a brief respite from her troubles.

She awoke feeling considerably refreshed, however, and set about her morning chores with a lightened heart. There had been no dreams to disturb her night's rest, no visions of Daniel to cause her disquiet. Striding out to the barn after breakfast, she went to Twister's stall and gently stroked the animal's silken mane.

"Mornin', Miss Addie." The sudden sound of Trent's voice alarmed her, for she hadn't realized he was inside the barn. Her gaze moved to where he was tightening the cinch on the saddle of his mount a few feet away. "Thought you might like to know that Clay and Billy found an early calf yesterday afternoon."

"They did?" she responded in obvious pleasure. Then her dawning smile faded into a frown, and she asked, "Well, why didn't you tell me yesterday?" As he stood and faced her, she noted uncomfortably that his dark eyes roamed briefly up and down the length of her body.

"I would have done that, Miss Addie, but you were busy with Jordan and those two ladies he brought out here with him." There was a barely perceptible edge to his voice, but Addie's ears caught it.

"I see," she murmured in a low tone, moving to saddle Twister. "Where are Clay and Billy this morning?" she asked, forcing an affable note into her own voice. Smoothing the blanket across the horse's sleek back, she glanced up to meet Trent's piercing stare.

"I figured I'd send the two of them on out to look for any other calves that might have dropped early. If this stretch of good weather holds, we'll be able to have ourselves a roundup before too much longer." Leading his horse from its stall, he paused before a suddenly uneasy Addie. "I was hopin' maybe you'd ride out with me today, Miss Addie."

"I'm sorry, Trent, but I've got some business to attend to," she declined with a faint smile, tossing her hand-tooled saddle atop the blanket and making a pretense of adjusting one of the stirrups. She didn't

311

know why, but Trent had changed. There always seemed to be a hidden meaning in his words whenever he spoke to her now. She had tried to tell herself that she was imagining it, but his next statement only substantiated her belief that his attitude had undergone a puzzling alteration.

"I don't think you should spend so much time with that Yankee, Miss Addie. I heard tell there're some folks who ain't prepared to forgive and forget so easily. You shouldn't go and get yourself mixed up with a no-account bastard like that!"

"Damn it, Trent, you have absolutely no right to tell me what to do!" snapped Addie, her eyes flashing at his uncharacteristic insolence. "I hired you on as a hand, not as a guardian!" she harshly reminded him, refusing to be intimidated by the dangerous gleam in his hawkish eyes.

"I know that, but I just thought—" he attempted to explain, only to be abruptly cut off.

"You're not paid to think—only to take orders!" She regretted the insulting remark as soon as it crossed her lips, but she didn't feel like apologizing at that moment. Leading Twister out of the barn, she chose to ignore Trent's parting words.

"You're the boss, Miss Addie, but that doesn't mean you can stop me from worryin' about you." He stood and watched until she had swung up into the saddle and ridden away, his eyes narrowing as she soon became nothing more than a tiny speck upon the horizon.

She had decided, while vigorously scrubbing her skin during her morning bath, that she would be the one to pay a call to discuss the cattle drive with Daniel. Remembering all too well what had occurred the last time the two of them had been alone together in her father's study, she told herself she certainly wouldn't allow a repetition of that particular episode!

She passed several head of Rolling L cattle as she rode, and her anticipation regarding the impending roundup increased. Was it truly possible that they could drive the longhorns to a better market? she wondered, a glimmer of hope budding deep within her as she seriously contemplated the idea. If they could just get twice as much as they had originally counted on, the financial status of her ranch would be back on solid ground at last.

The morning air was crisp and cold, and Addie was grateful for the sunshine which warmed her as she guided Twister across the golden hills and valleys of the late winter landscape. Reaching the boundaries of Daniel's ranch, she found herself drawing to a halt in sudden hesitation.

Would Daniel be there at all? she asked herself. Perhaps he had risen early and had ridden into town to be with his sister and their "old friend." She was certain Charity Bransom had been much more than a friend to Daniel, and the thought gave her little comfort as she frowned darkly and urged the horse to continue its even-paced canter.

Smoke was curling upward from the chimney as she tugged on the reins and dismounted before his cabin. As she raised her hand to rap briskly upon the front door, her ears detected the sound of someone chopping wood. She directed her steps to the rear of the log building and, as she had expected, discovered that it was Daniel who wielded the axe. Glimpsing movement out of the corner of his eye, he turned to face her with a

313

roguish grin on his face.

"Well, good morning, partner! I wasn't expecting you." Lifting the axe and skillfully imbedding it in the center of the massive stump he used as a chopping block, he drew on his coat and moved toward her. "What brings you here so early in the day? You haven't been shooting at wolves again, have you?" he mischievously teased, his eyes sparkling with amusement.

"I came by to discuss the cattle drive you're apparently so convinced we're going to participate in!" she tersely explained, a disturbing recollection of the openly admiring glances he had bestowed upon Charity the night before prompting her anger with him to return.

"I didn't think you'd be able to contain your curiosity for very long," he told her with a low chuckle, moving toward the back door of the cabin. "Come on inside." He didn't wait for either her acceptance or refusal as he strode inside. Addie hesitated only an instant before following after him.

"I'd consider it a great favor if we didn't waste time on small talk!" she coolly requested, closing the door and watching as he sauntered across to the stove and poured two cups of coffee. "I came to discover precisely what arrangements you claim to have made for a drive."

"Not 'claim to have made,' dearest Addie," he mildly corrected, stepping over to the table near the spot where Addie stood. He set the cups before him as he bent his tall frame into a ladder-back chair, glancing up at her with another faintly mocking smile. "You may as well sit down and drink this." She did so, but with ill grace.

"Exactly what have you got in mind for our stock?" she demanded a bit impatiently, wincing slightly as her tastebuds encountered the hot, bitter brew. "You call this coffee?" she complained, pushing the cup away from her with another expressive grimace.

"I suppose I did learn to drink it a trifle strong while in the Cavalry," he responded with an easy laugh. "But it sure as hell kept us awake whenever the situation required." He carefully sipped from his own cup, his gaze meeting hers and holding it for several long, silent moments. Addie was the first to look away. "Now, about the cattle drive," he began, folding his arms across his broad, flannel-covered chest. "It's quite simple, really. If we can manage to get our stock to Missouri—to Sedalia, to be exact—there's a buyer ready and waiting to pay us good money for as many head as we can deliver."

"What do you consider 'good money'? And just who the devil is this buyer of yours?"

"We'll get nearly fifty dollars a head. That's ten times what we'd be forced to sell for here in Texas. And the buyer happens to be an old acquaintance of my uncle. I've already been in contact with him, and he's counting on us to show up sometime in late spring."

"Do you have any idea what you're talking about when you mention a drive? To get to Missouri, we'd have to cross Indian territory! And if you're thinking of following the old Shawnee Trail, just how do you plan to get us past the blockade? Or do you even know anything about the Texas fever quarantines that closed the trail?"

"Of course I know. I happen to be from Missouri, remember?" he answered with a brief, mocking smile curving his lips. "But I believe we can do it nonetheless. It's worth a try, isn't it? You already know what a paltry amount you'll get for your cattle here."

"All right then, let's say you've already thought about all the obstacles we'll face. Have you given any thought to who you're going to get to drive the herd, who you're going to hire as trail boss, drovers—" she vehemently argued, not wanting him to guess how very much his idea had begun to appeal to her.

"Drovers are no problem. There are scores of young men eager for the opportunity to go. And, as for a trail boss, I'm going to fill that particular position myself."

It was obvious that his words were a shock to her. "You?" she blurted, her eyes widening in stunned disbelief. "What in blazes do you know about leading a cattle drive?"

"A good deal more than you apparently think I do," he quipped ironically. "I don't intend to trust our stock to anyone else but myself, Addie. I have every confidence that I'll be able to get the herd through."

"Then you might as well know right now that I intend to come along as well!"

"Don't be ridiculous," he said with a disapproving frown.

"Ridiculous? Why, you arrogant, bullheaded son of a—" she lashed out, breaking off as she abruptly stood and wheeled away in an attempt to control her raging temper. When she faced him again, her eyes were blazing, her voice deceptively low and even. "If you'll recall, Daniel Jordan, when you first proposed this business arrangement between us, it was partly because you said you needed to learn about ranching from an expert, namely myself. In all honesty then, may I ask who would be a better choice to have along on a cattle drive?"

"It isn't that I don't think you're competent," reasoned Daniel, rising to his feet and approaching her with a strange glow in his eyes. "It's just that a cattle drive is no place for a woman, especially a woman as young and disturbingly lovely as yourself!" He paused mere inches away, staring deeply into her stormy gaze.

"And I suppose a ranch is no place for a woman either!" she bitterly challenged. "I've been running the Rolling L ever since the death of my father two years ago! There's no one more qualified than myself to take those cattle to Missouri! You seem to forget that not all of the members of the *weaker sex* are as frivolous and useless as that fancy piece of fluff you brought to my house last night!"

"What does Charity have to do with this?" he demanded with a maddening grin on his handsome face.

"If that's the sort of woman you want, Daniel Jordan, then I don't know why the hell you've been wasting so much time with the likes of me! I could never be like that, nor would I ever have even the slightest desire to be!" she irrationally raged. As she drew in her breath sharply upon an inward gasp, it suddenly dawned on her that she was jealous of Charity Bransom, jealous of the woman's poise and sophistication, jealous of the way Daniel had looked at her. Her anger didn't stem merely from a profound dislike for the woman, but more from a powerful, decidedly unpleasant emotion she had never known before the previous night.

"No," Daniel softly agreed, his hands closing gently

317

upon her stiffening shoulders, "you could never be like that, Addie. And I'd never want you to be." Her eyes flew to meet his, and she felt a sudden lump in her throat at his tender words. Even though she sensed that his hands sought to console and not arouse, it was the first time he'd touched her in so long, and the surge of desire she experienced sent her into a state of utter confusion.

"I . . . I've got work to do at home," she faltered, moving hastily away. She pulled her hat atop her chestnut curls, turned about, and headed for the doorway. "I'm sure we'll be discussing the drive repeatedly throughout the next several weeks. I promise you that I'll think it over in the meantime." Her hand had already closed upon the door handle when Daniel strode forward and pulled her back into his strong arms.

"Why do you always turn away, my love?" he softly asked, holding her close while his gaze burned downward into hers.

"Because what happens between us . . . it frightens me!" she cried, as if ashamed to admit it. "I've never felt like this before, and I don't like it!" It was all too true, she reflected miserably. She was confused and bothered and jealous and wanted him so much it hurt!

"There's nothing to be frightened of," he assured her, his head moving lower to allow his lips a slow, provocative descent to claim hers. Within seconds, Addie's answering passion had been ignited to a fever pitch, and she swayed weakly against him as his arms supported her. She was left with an unfulfilled aching when he released her after only one searingly rapturous kiss. "If you want me to make love to you this time,

318

Adelaide, you'll have to ask me," he huskily commanded.

"What?" she gasped out, her face flushed and incredulous.

"I want to hear you say it. I want to hear you say you love me as much as I love you, that you want me as much as I so desperately want you!" It took all his strength of will to keep himself from crushing her within his embrace once more, but he knew that he must remain firm in his resolve. For three weeks now, he had been purposefully aloof. Now he wanted the two of them to come together without any barriers between them, to come together in the secure knowledge that their love for one another was even stronger than before.

"Do you truly believe you can use this . . . this reprehensible blackmail as a means to force me to say that I love you?" charged Addie, her eyes filling with hot, angry tears. "If you ever were to hear such words from me, it would be because I felt them in my heart and most certainly not because I had been spineless enough to surrender to such despicable tactics!" With that, she whirled away and flung open the door, her long, furious strides leading her around to the front of the cabin. Daniel soon heard the muffled sounds of hoofbeats as she urged Twister into a gallop and rode away.

Cursing himself for a fool, he sighed heavily and moved restlessly back to the table. He stared down at the two coffee cups, and his gray eyes kindled with anger, an anger directed at both himself and the beautiful, headstrong woman he loved.

"Damnation!" he ground out, then laughed aloud an

319

instant later at the realization that the wrathful expression was the same one Addie used so frequently. Moving outside once again, he resumed his task at the chopping block, engrossed with thoughts of how he was going to break through Addie's final defenses. It was still only a matter of time, he reassured himself.

For Addie, the next few days passed in a disagreeable haze. Carrie's visits were the only bright spot in her emotional darkness, and she gave silent thanks for her friend's presence. It was the end of February now, and the good weather continued, with only one cold and rainy day to dampen everyone's spirits. That particular day, however, was the one on which Carrie chose to hire a buggy at the livery stable to drive herself and Charity out to Daniel's place for a surprise visit.

"I most certainly will not accompany you!" vowed Charity, poised just inside the hotel entrance and eyeing the light rain with haughty distaste. "I have no intention of allowing myself to arrive wet and bedraggled upon your brother's doorstep!" As much as she wanted to see Daniel again, she most definitely did not want to present a less than perfectly groomed appearance. Of course, she spitefully mused, if her competition lay strictly within the local ranks, with Miss Addie Caton serving as a fair representative, then she had absolutely nothing to worry about!

"Please come, Charity," coaxed her petite friend. "We've been here nearly a week now, and we've yet to visit Daniel's ranch on our own!"

"Absolutely not. I prefer to remain here at the hotel and await your brother's visit. You know very well that he is planning to call upon us this very evening."

"Yes, I know that," Carrie responded with exaggerated patience, "but I thought he would enjoy it if we called upon him instead." Despite several more attempts at persuasion, Carrie admitted defeat. Finally declaring in exasperation that she would go alone, she left a sternly disapproving Charity and flounced out onto the muddy boardwalk, opening her ruffled parasol as protection against the rain.

Reflecting that she might as well stop to visit Addie on her way out to Daniel's ranch, her steps were quite lively and determined as she marched to the livery stable at the far end of town. The streets of Fort Worth were virtually deserted on such a soggy morning, but one tall young gentleman was in the process of opening his uncle's store when he glimpsed the lovely redhead sweeping past the front windows.

Gil felt an almost violent stirring of his senses as his eyes fixed unwaveringly upon Carrie. He had found his thoughts straying to her on more than one occasion during the past several days. Curious about the absence of her husband, he had wanted to question Miss Addie about her friend but had been afraid such inquiries would seem improper. Now he forgot all about the social amenities as he hurriedly shrugged on his coat and hastened out the door in pursuit.

His disappointment was obvious when he discovered that the feminine object of his interest had vanished, but he brightened again as he caught sight of her driving a buggy out of the livery stable a short distance from the mercantile. It was then that he found himself in a quandary, for how could he hope to engage her in conversation when she seemed so intent upon driving away?

The solution to Gil's dilemma took a startling form. As Carrie's buggy rolled past the courthouse directly across the street from where her admirer stood avidly watching her, one of the wheels unexpectedly sank into a deep rut filled with an astonishingly large amount of muddy water. The brown liquid splashed unceremoniously across Carrie's silken skirts, causing her to gasp loudly in surprise and relax her grip upon the reins. The horse—a usually tame roan mare—was spooked by Carrie's faint shriek of distress as she viewed the stain which darkened her gown, and the animal suddenly reared, whinnying and snorting before lurching forward.

Believing that the mare was preparing to bolt, Gil rushed swiftly across the mud-slicked street, his hat flying off his head to land in a puddle, his hands reaching out to grip the animal's harness in an attempt to steady it. Carrie, however, was under the impression that she had everything well under control, and her lovely face wore an expression of indignant outrage as her unwanted rescuer forced the horse, which had moved scarcely ten feet, to a halt.

"Take your hands off that animal at once!" she imperiously directed, tugging firmly upon the reins as the mare quieted. Gil, who had expected quite the opposite reaction, turned to her with a stunned look, oblivious to the rivulets of moisture which coursed down his face.

"I beg your pardon?" he responded, his words an obvious question. The rain plastered his light brown hair to his head, and his eyes reflected his bemusement

322

at her apparent displeasure with him.

"Was that absurd display of flamboyant bravado for my benefit, or someone else's?" she scathingly snapped, her eyes like two pools of liquid green fire as they swept up and down Gil's muddied form.

"I had merely thought to assist you," he calmly asserted, his unflinching gaze meeting hers. As Carrie glimpsed the honesty in his vividly blue eyes, she grew ashamed of her temperamental outburst. She was just opening her mouth to offer him a sincere apology when he bowed stiffly and said, "Good day to you, Mrs. Rogers." He spun about on his booted heel and began striding back through the mud, then paused to bend and retrieve the dripping bundle of felt that had once been his hat. As he straightened up to continue on his way, his knee suddenly gave way beneath him, causing him to stumble slightly in an effort to regain his balance.

Carrie, whose shining eyes had never left his retreating form, bit at her lower lip in alarm as she saw his left leg buckle, and she waited until he stood again before impulsively calling out, "Mr. Foster! Please, Mr. Foster, I wish to speak with you!" For a split second she was afraid he would ignore her, but her lips curved upward into a smile of relief as he turned back and approached her with a visible limp, though it was obvious he endeavored to conceal it. The roan mare waited peacefully as the two people talked.

"Yes, Mrs. Rogers?" Gil quietly murmured, meeting her gaze squarely. He was so much taller than Carrie that his head was level with hers, despite the fact that she was elevated by her position in the buggy.

"Please forgive my rudeness," she contritely requested, disturbed by the inexplicable light-headedness she was experiencing as she looked at him. "I . . . I should have realized that you were only trying to help." It didn't seem to matter to either of them that the light rain continued to cost them with a fine sheen of moisture.

"That's quite all right," he responded with a faint smile of his own, his eyes sparkling across at her. "It's just that, from where I stood, it appeared as if you required assistance with the horse."

"I'm sorry you injured your leg on my behalf."

"Injured my leg?" he echoed, then quickly explained, "No, it's . . . it's an old war injury."

"You fought in the war?" she questioned. Then before he could reply, she added somberly, "My late husband was killed in the conflict."

"What regiment?" Gil softly inquired, his heart leaping at the realization that she was a widow.

"He was in the Cavalry with Daniel. The two of them served in the Army of the Potomac," recalled Carrie, hastily averting her gaze.

"I see," said Gil, visibly hesitating before continuing. "I was in the Confederate Army, Mrs. Rogers, the Army of Tennessee." There was neither accusation nor defensiveness in his tone; his words were a simple statement of fact.

Carrie turned to him with an unfathomable, wide-eyed expression on her lovely countenance, but she looked away again before announcing, "I had best be on my way, Mr. Foster." Her slender, gloved fingers tightened on the reins, and, with a barely audible "Good day," she gently snapped the thin leather straps together and drove away without a backward glance, leaving Gil little choice but to step aside and allow the buggy to roll past. He didn't seem to notice that the wheels flung more mud upon his boots and the lower portion of his wool trousers, for he was too preoccupied with thoughts of the petite, spirited widow and her puzzling behavior.

By the time Carrie arrived at the Rolling L, it was mid-morning, and Addie had just returned from an unpleasantly damp ride with Silas to examine another of the early calves Clay and Billy had discovered, which brought the total to half a dozen. Addie considered the calves a good sign, and she had spent the past hour discussing Daniel's plans for a trail drive with an eagerly listening Silas.

They were in the process of settling down in the kitchen for a much-needed cup of hot coffee when Esther, peering out the window, grinned broadly and announced that there was a buggy approaching. Assuming the visitor was Gil, Addie heaved a sigh and slowly headed toward the front entrance hall. Her beautiful face brightened with pleasure when she opened the door to see that it was Carrie who had come.

"Carrie! What on earth are you doing here?" She placed an affectionate arm about the redhead's shoulders and ushered her inside. "Whatever possessed you to travel on a day like this?" she demanded amiably.

"You, of all people, dearest Addie, know how it is when I get my mind set on something!" retorted Carrie, laughing as she drew off her soggy cloak and gloves. "I

325

was planning to drive out to Daniel's, then decided that I would stop and visit with you first. That is, if it's convenient," she hastened to add.

"Of course! I was wondering when the two of us would be able to talk again." They'd had a long, enjoyable conversation together several days earlier when Addie had ridden into town. She had been none too pleased, however, when she discovered that Charity was out "seeing the countryside" with Daniel. It seemed that her jealousy had vastly increased after that day, until disagreeable images of Daniel and Charity together plagued her quite frequently, day and night.

"What's the matter, Addie?" queried her friend, noting the sudden frown on the taller woman's face.

"Nothing," muttered Addie, then forced a bright smile to her lips as she added, "Let's go into the study. I'll have Esther put on a pot of tea for a change and bring us some of that shortbread she made this morning."

"I'm . . . I'm not very hungry right now," said Carrie, strolling closer to the fire as Addie followed behind. "If you don't mind, I think it's time the two of us had a talk—a real talk—about you and my brother." Perching on the very edge of the cushioned bench and arranging her silken skirts about her, she waited for her friend to take a seat beside her.

Reluctant to engage in such a discussion, Addie released a sigh and moved to the fireplace, turning to face her friend with a mutinous expression reflected in her eyes. It was then that her gaze was drawn downward to the mud stains on Carrie's tailored gown of lavender silk.

"What happened to your dress?" she asked with a faint frown.

"It doesn't matter," Carrie evasively murmured, staring toward the fire. It was a moment before she regained her inner composure, however. Finally, she glanced up at the other woman and announced with heartfelt sincerity, "I wish you would tell me what it is that keeps you and Daniel apart!"

"I'm sorry, Carrie, but it isn't something you would understand." A deep sadness replaced the defiance in her hazel eyes as she slowly sank down onto the bench beside her friend.

"You knew I would want some answers sooner or later."

"Yes, I knew. And, as much as I cherish our friendship, I'm afraid that what is between Daniel and myself isn't truly any of your business."

"Of course it is!" protested Carrie, twisting about on the bench and taking a firm grip on Addie's arms. "You are still my dearest friend. Daniel is my brother. The two of you are so obviously perfect for each other, Addie. And if you're still in love, I fail to see how anything else could matter!"

"Carrie," said Addie, her low-voiced words preceding another long sigh, "you couldn't possibly understand what has happened between us. We're from two different worlds, and four years have gone by, years in which we had no contact with one another, years in which your brother fought against what my father and everyone else around here held sacred. Ours was simply a marriage that should never have been!" She rose abruptly to her feet and moved to the window, her gaze fixed unseeingly upon the gray-tinged landscape. "I'm

327

sorry he told you about it. It was something I had hoped would remain a secret."

"Then why haven't you sought a divorce?" challenged Carrie, standing and following after her friend. "If you no longer love my brother, why haven't you filed for a legal dissolution of the marriage you consider such a regrettable error?"

"I was afraid to have it become public knowledge," she wearily replied. "The last thing in the world I wanted was for my father or our friends to find out." As she took a slightly ragged breath, Carrie closely studied her troubled features.

"You know, Addie, my brother never told anyone else about your marriage. He only revealed it to me because he hoped I would hear from you. Not even Charity knows."

"I doubt very seriously if it would make any difference if she did!" Addie retorted in disgust, whirling away from the window now and returning to the fire. "I'm quite sure her vanity—her supreme confidence in her own *charms*—would extend far beyond a moral restriction such as marriage!"

"Why do you say that? You sound as if you are actually jealous of her!" exclaimed Carrie, her skirts gently rustling as she stepped back to Addie's side. Her green eyes were dancing with a purposeful light. "Surely you cannot blame her for wanting to ensnare my brother? After all, he is an extremely handsome, undeniably fine man, isn't he? I suppose you could accuse me of sisterly prejudice, and rightly so, but I think he would make an excellent catch for any woman clever enough to lure him into another attempt at matrimony!"

"Then perhaps, since you are his sister," Addie countered, her temper rising dangerously, "you should remind him that he is not yet free to be lured by the likes of Charity Bransom, or anyone else!" Her eyes were flashing, and a fiery color rose to stain her cheeks as she snatched up the iron poker leaning against the stones of the fireplace and stabbed at the blazing logs with a vengeance.

"But that is quite unfair, my dear! You say you do not want him, and yet it is obvious you want no other woman to have him either. Don't you think it is time you made up your mind?" Carrie impishly prompted, her dimpled smile only widening as her friend rounded on her in barely controlled ire.

"You go too far, Carrie!" she feelingly cautioned.

"If the mere mention of Charity's pursuit of my brother produces a veritable rage of jealousy within your breast, then perhaps you do still love him," the petite redhead calmly pointed out.

"Of course I do, damn it!" Addie vehemently parried, the words bursting from her lips without warning. Her hand flew to her mouth in astonishment, and her eyes grew round as saucers as the truth dawned on her. She had finally given voice to the words which had been forming in her mind for weeks now, words which expressed the innermost emotions she had so desperately attempted to keep buried forever in her heart. She loved Daniel. She had never stopped loving him. She numbly realized that her love for him burned brighter than ever. Their love had not been destroyed by the ravages of either time or war, had not been vanquished by the evil forces which had sought to crush it. No, it was very much alive.

"Oh, Addie," whispered Carrie, throwing her arms about the young woman whose countenance suddenly appeared drained of all color. "I knew it. I could see it in your eyes whenever you looked at him." Tears stung against her own eyelids, and she clasped Addie tighter as the fire softly crackled beside them.

Addie felt too dazed to speak again just yet. She was grateful for Carrie's comforting embrace, for she had experienced a wave of dizziness that had left her body weak and her head spinning alarmingly. The last vestiges of the pride and sense of honor that had bordered on the obsessive melted away, freeing her heart at last.

"Addie," said Carrie, drawing back so that she could face her friend squarely, "you must go to Daniel and tell him of your love. I know that you have suffered much, but so has he."

"It . . . it isn't as simple as that," insisted Addie, her legs not quite steady as she resumed her seat on the bench. "There are so many differences to be resolved between us, so many circumstances—"

"Then the two of you will have to work through these 'differences' together!" her friend staunchly interrupted. "Why don't you come along with me now? Perhaps it will give you courage to have me at your side."

"No, not now," Addie murmured. "I . . . I must have more time to think."

"Very well. Daniel is coming to call upon me and Charity in town this evening. We are planning to share supper together in the hotel's dining room. Perhaps you would consider joining us?" she suggested, then paused expectantly. "I could easily arrange for the two of you to have a few moments alone."

"This is all happening so fast!" declared Addie in bewilderment. But it hadn't been fast at all, she silently mused as another realization struck her. Just as Daniel had once promised, her life had been gradually changed by his presence. It had started with the first time she had seen him standing on the boardwalk in Fort Worth all those weeks ago . . .

"I'll expect you before six o'clock. I know the weather is quite dreadful, but I think the outcome of the evening will provide more than adequate compensation!" pronounced Carrie. Then she hastily brushed Addie's cheek with her lips before moving toward the doorway. "I can't wait to see Charity's face when she discovers that you and Daniel are actually married!"

Addie was only vaguely aware of the front door opening and closing a few seconds later. She lost all track of time as she sat before the fire, and though she was oblivious to the fact that the flames soon dwindled into nothing more than a smoldering pile of ashes, the startling knowledge of her newly awakened love warmed her against the subsequent chill.

Eighteen

Addie braved the damp twilight with mixed emotions as she sat beside Silas in the buckboard. He had been quite adamant about accompanying her into town, and she could not summon enough of her customary stubbornness after Carrie's illuminating visit to be able to refuse.

There were so many questions floating about in her mind, so many things she desperately wanted to ask Daniel, to ask herself. But she knew that none of the answers truly mattered, for nothing could change the simple fact that she still loved her husband. It had taken only a small dose of Carrie's persistence to finally uncover the truth, the truth which had always been present and refused to be denied any longer.

"How late you aimin' to stay, Miss Addie?" questioned Silas, guiding the buckboard down the muddy street toward the row of businesses at the other end of town. The rain had stopped earlier that afternoon, but the cold air was still heavy with a lingering veil of moisture.

"Not more than a couple of hours," she murmured in response, her anxiety increasing as they neared the whitewashed exterior of the hotel. Why had she ever agreed to come? she asked herself with an inward sigh, recalling that she hadn't exactly agreed, but hadn't exactly disagreed either. Although she had no intention of announcing her love for Daniel in so public a place, she longed to be near him that very night, even if it meant being forced to endure Charity Bransom's presence. Another wave of agonizing jealousy washed over her.

"Well, I'll be over at the livery stable till then. If you need me any sooner, just send someone over from the hotel to fetch me."

"I will, Silas," she replied softly, her eyes wide and full of trepidation as the man beside her pulled the horse to a halt. She didn't wait for his assistance before climbing down, carefully lifting her full skirts away from the partially dried mud which coated the boardwalk. She returned Silas's smile as he drove away, then slowly faced the entrance to the hotel.

She had taken great pains earlier with her appearance, and she told herself that she could face the evening with confidence in that particular area, anyway. Her thick hair was massed at the nape of her neck in a becoming chignon, the lustrous chestnut curls enclosed in a chenille-dotted net. Beneath her cloak, she wore a bordered silk gown of emerald green with puffed, elbow-length sleeves, its lace-trimmed neckline dipping toward the shadowed valley between her firm breasts. While she was fully aware of the fact that her years-old finery couldn't possibly compare with what Charity would be wearing, she lifted her chin in an unconscious gesture of pride as she sailed through the doorway and into the lobby.

Carrie was waiting for her, and her lightly freckled face beamed with pleasure when she saw her friend. She linked her arm through Addie's and said, "Daniel hasn't arrived yet. Charity is putting the finishing touches on her toilette. And oh, Addie, I'm so glad you came!"

"I don't think I'll be able to eat a thing," whispered Addie. "And I'm not at all sure I should have come!"

"Nonsense. You didn't want to leave an open field for Charity tonight, did you? I know we're supposed to be quite adult and mature about this whole thing, my dear—" she remarked, drawing Addie down onto the edge of a brocade chaise with her.

"Precisely!" Addie interjected. "And here I find myself behaving like some jealous, lovestruck schoolgirl who feels she must battle a rival for the affections of her beloved," she finished in self-disgust. What reason had she to be jealous of Charity? Why couldn't she simply believe that Daniel Jordan loved his wife, and set aside all the terrible doubts assailing her? But that was just it, she reflected. She was sure of her love for Daniel, but not of his love for her. In spite of what he had said, in spite of all that had passed between them, she felt a certain insecurity.

"There's Daniel," announced Carrie, nodding toward the tall man who had just entered the hotel and was striding in their direction. Addie inhaled sharply, whirling about in alarm as her sparkling eyes flew across the lobby to encounter Daniel's surprised gaze. His lips were already curving upward into a heart-melting smile, and his black leather boots trod softly upon the polished oak floor as he approached.

His movements bespoke a masculine self-confidence, an easy, virile grace which she had always found intriguing. His handsome face appeared the same above the snowy whiteness of his collar, his eyes were the same steely gray they had always been, and yet he seemed vastly altered to Addie. But then, she dazedly mused, she hadn't been the same herself since acknowledging, at long last, her love for him. Nothing would ever be the same again.

"Good evening, ladies," he proclaimed with mocking gallantry as he paused before them. "I didn't know you were coming tonight," he murmured to Addie, his glowing eyes for her alone as he turned away from his impishly smiling younger sister.

"I hadn't planned to come, but . . . but Carrie persuaded me," Addie explained uneasily, her stomach doing a strange flip-flop as she met her beloved's gaze. *How could I have been so foolish?* she belatedly lamented. *Whatever possessed me to believe I could stop loving a man such as this?* He was so firmly entrenched in her heart, her mind, her very soul. *Why had it taken her so long to reach this inevitable conclusion?* she wondered. All of a sudden, she longed to fling herself upon his broad chest, to have him hold her and tell her once again that he still loved her. She longed to tell him of her fateful discovery, to declare her love for him and confess to having been the worst kind of idiot about their relationship, both past and present.

"You look beautiful tonight, Addie," observed Daniel, his voice deep and mellow, his gaze moving over her imperceptibly trembling form with tender possessiveness.

"I happen to think your sister looks quite well, too," Carrie piped up, dimpling outrageously as she raised her chin.

Her attire, consisting of an embroidered white blouse and cocoa brown skirt and jacket trimmed with black braid, was undeniably flattering, and Daniel grinned down at her in brotherly amusement as he sardonically admonished, "Providing your own compliments isn't at all seemly, little one."

"I wouldn't have to provide them if you'd at least make a show of noticing someone other than your wife!" she merrily retorted. Addie colored at her words, while Daniel merely chuckled quietly. None of the trio happened to notice the dark-haired woman who abruptly paused at the foot of the staircase a short distance away, her ears having easily detected Carrie's shocking remark. She quickly recovered her composure, however, and swept regally across the lobby, the flowing skirts of her elegant, cobalt blue silk dress rustling softly as she forced a cool smile to her perfectly formed lips.

"Good evening, Daniel," Charity Bransom proclaimed in a low, melodious tone. She gracefully extended a gloved hand to him when he turned to welcome her with a smile, and her oddly glistening eyes narrowed slightly as he raised her hand briefly to his warm lips. "You neglected to mention that Miss Caton was to be in attendance tonight, dearest Carrie," she said to her watchful young friend, her cultured voice holding more than a touch of annoyance. She spared Addie only a passing, decidedly lofty glance.

"Did I?" responded Carrie with a look of wide-eyed innocence.

"It was a pleasant surprise to me as well," Daniel

337

noted wryly, bestowing another beguiling smile upon a suddenly pale Addie. She had immediately recognized the light in Charity's eyes as that of fierce determination, and she unhappily realized that the evening was going to be every bit as much of an ordeal as she had feared. More than ever convinced that she shouldn't have surrendered to the temptation to come, she compressed her lips into a thin line of displeasure as she watched Charity place a hand upon Daniel's arm and start leading him toward the brightly lit dining room adjoining the lobby.

"Courage, Adelaide," Carrie whispered hearteningly, tightly grasping Addie's hand as they followed after the other two.

"I have little patience for such battles," she asserted in a low voice, her eyes kindling, "but courage is not something I lack!" Carrie squeezed her hand again in response, prompting Addie to smile ruefully at the petite redhead. "I thought Charity was your friend, and yet you seem bent on seeing her toppled from her self-erected pedestal." Her gaze moved to where Charity was favoring Daniel with an openly seductive look from beneath her slightly lowered eyelashes. Addie's hazel eyes blazed in renewed anger.

"We have never been particularly close," confided Carrie, "and it was my aunt's idea to invite Charity to accompany us to Texas." The two of them fell silent as they reached the small round table where Daniel was pulling out a chair for his self-appointed companion. Addie wasted no time in seating herself opposite Charity, but Carrie waited impatiently for her brother to offer her the same chivalrous service he had given the haughty brunette.

Talk soon turned to what each of the foursome was

going to order for supper, and it was some time later before Charity inclined her head in Addie's direction. A faint smile rose to the woman's lips, a smile which did not quite reach her coldly glistening eyes as she said, "Daniel finally agreed to enlighten me a trifle more about the cattle drive the two of you are planning. Will you be going along as well, Miss Caton?" Her words, though smooth as silk, were laced with malicious intent.

"Yes," answered Addie.

"No," Daniel interjected at the same time.

"I most certainly am!" Addie vehemently insisted.

"We've already settled the matter," contended Daniel.

"I suppose most women would be quite unwelcome on such a journey," opined Charity, noting with smug satisfaction the way Addie was glaring at a solemn-faced Daniel. "But then, you are rather more like . . ." she began, leaving the sentence unfinished as she pretended to be searching for words. "Well, like the other . . . *cowhands,* I believe you call them," she concluded, her movements bespeaking a fluid feminine grace as she took a sip of water from the goblet before her on the table.

"I'm proud to be like them, Miss Bransom, and since I am so much like them," Addie meaningfully declared, her eyes darting back to Daniel, "I have every intention of going along on the drive!"

"This is neither the time nor the place to discuss it," he authoritatively decreed, his tanned features visibly tightening.

"From what I understand, your annual roundup should take place soon, shouldn't it?" Carrie broke in, resolutely attempting to change the subject.

"We should be able to start within the next week or two, if all goes well," supplied Daniel, his faint scowl relaxing into a smile as he glanced toward his sister. "Are you and Charity still planning to stay that long?"

"Are you hinting that you would like to get rid of us even sooner?" quipped Carrie, her green eyes sparkling in mock affront.

"Of course not. My partner and I are looking forward to displaying our skills at roping and branding, aren't we, partner?" he asked his wife, a teasing note in his voice.

"I didn't know you were skillful at roping and branding," Addie countered with a frown, meeting his searching gaze with a lingering defiance in hers.

"There are still a great many things you don't know about me," he softly murmured, staring deeply into her suddenly widening eyes.

Charity chose this particular moment to lightly clear her throat and arrogantly observe, "What a pity you could not tear yourself away from your *duties* long enough to accompany Daniel and myself on one of our many rides about the countryside, Miss Caton. I have learned so much, and dearest Daniel has provided absolutely fascinating details about the various sights."

"Has he?" Addie responded disinterestedly, though she cursed silently as she experienced another sharp pang of jealousy.

"Yes. And there was one place that was especially poignant—" began Charity, only to be interrupted as the waiter finally arrived with a large wooden tray of food and set the steaming dishes of roast beef, potatoes, biscuits, and apple preserves before them. The unpleasant conversation resumed a few short moments later, however, following another remark by

Charity concerning the disgustingly heavy meals people in Texas consumed.

"What was that you were saying about some place being poignant?" Carrie prompted the brunette as she raised a forkful of potatoes to her mouth.

"What?" responded Charity, then smiled faintly as she said, "Oh yes. The abandoned homestead Daniel showed me." She wrinkled her nose in distaste before forcing herself to sample some of the thinly sliced beef.

"Abandoned homestead?" echoed Addie, an awful feeling of dread suddenly gripping her. Don't be ridiculous! she silently berated herself. There are many abandoned homesteads in the area. Daniel wouldn't have taken Charity to the same place they . . . or would he? She felt a sense of betrayal at the thought.

"It appeared to have been a relatively charming place at one time," mused Charity, "though it is now in a regrettable state of disrepair. The roof of the barn appeared quite hazardous, and the cabin was filthy. It looked as if some poor injured soul had spent the night in the cabin recently, judging from the bloodstains on the floor. But Daniel and I didn't mind, did we?" She laughed softly as she leaned closer to the man beside her. "As a matter of fact, we spent a shocking amount of time alone together in the cabin," she added with another coquettish laugh.

"Where is this abandoned homestead you're talking about?" Addie quietly demanded, her gaze riveted upon the scarcely touched plate of food before her.

"Oh, I have no sense of direction, Miss Caton, so you'd best ask Daniel," replied Charity with a dismissing wave of her hand. "I should like to visit it again soon, however," she pronounced, casting a knowing, eminently enticing smile at a strangely pensive Daniel. His unfathomable gaze was fastened unwaveringly upon an increasingly flushed Addie. "Our little jaunts about the countryside here have only served to remind me of the similar outings we shared back home. Did you know that Daniel and I were once engaged to be married, Miss Caton? Of course, it wasn't precisely official, but it had always been understood between ourselves and our families." She smirked in triumph as her rival caught her breath at the news, and Addie's eyes flew to glare accusingly into Daniel's.

"That was a long time ago," he reminded Charity in a low voice, glancing only briefly at the woman beside him.

"Perhaps. But not so long ago that I cannot remember . . . well, so many things we shared," she countered in a voice heavy with meaning, gently placing her hand atop Daniel's.

Addie furiously told herself that she'd had enough. Tossing her napkin to the table with a vengeance, she rose to her feet and announced in a voice filled with barely concealed rage. "Your point is well taken, Miss Bransom! In fact, all of your blasted points are well taken!" She gazed intently at Daniel for a moment, her eyes bright with unshed tears, their fiery, anguished depths mirroring the pain she was feeling. Then, without another word, she spun about and made her escape, her hurried strides soon taking her out of the hotel and toward the livery stable. She hadn't gone far when she heard Daniel's voice calling out behind her.

"Addie! Damn it, Addie, wait!" His command did not have the desired effect, however, for she merely quickened her steps along the deserted boardwalk. Her arm was seized in an iron grip an instant later, and she was unceremoniously jerked to a halt. "Listen to me." Daniel spoke in a more pleading tone. She refused to meet his gaze as he forced her around to face him. "We need to talk."

"There's nothing to be said!" she angrily insisted, dashing impatiently at the tears which escaped from her eyes.

"My dearest Addie," he told her in a vibrant tone, "we've got more to talk about than ever before." Finally forcing herself to look up at him, she drew in her breath sharply at the tender, loving expression upon his face. Hardly aware of what she was doing, she nodded mutely in acquiescence, allowing him to lead her along with him toward the livery stable.

"But, Silas . . . he's waiting to drive me home," she weakly protested.

"Then we'll just inform him that I'll be taking you home," asserted Daniel. Neither of them spoke another word until they reached the building where Silas and a handful of other men were passing the time with a game of checkers. Silas, Addie was later to recall, didn't seem more than mildly surprised when Daniel declared he would drive Miss Addie home later in the evening. The older man simply accepted the fact and returned to his game, while Addie found herself being lifted up onto Daniel's horse. Her husband swung agilely up into the saddle behind her and issued a soft command to the animal before they rode out of the stable and away from town.

Addie pulled her cloak more closely about her body as she leaned against the comforting warmth of Daniel, oblivious to the fact that her silken skirts were now spattered with mud. She waited anxiously for Daniel to offer some sort of explanation of his intentions, but he remained strangely silent. The moon had at last broken through the thinning clouds, and its soft light cast a silvery glow over them as it illuminated their way. They rode within sight of Addie's house, but Daniel urged the horse onward toward the west, his powerful arm clamped securely about his wife's slender waist.

When they arrived at Daniel's home, he dismounted and reached up to lift Addie down, and she was startled when he unexpectedly maneuvered her so that he could carry her within his arms like a mere babe as he strode inside the darkened confines of the cabin. She was set upon her feet an instant later, while Daniel moved to light one of the lamps and place more wood upon the glowing embers that had once been a roaring fire.

"Would you like some coffee?" he quietly asked as he rose from the fireplace and faced her. Shrugging out of his coat, he tossed it and his hat onto a chair, then stepped slowly toward Addie. Her eyes were wide and full of breathless expectation, but he merely unfastened her cloak and drew it off, relegating it to the chair as well.

"No, thank you," she managed to say, desperately trying to still the sudden trembling of her body. She approached the fireplace and sank gratefully onto a bench in front of the newly awakened flames.

"All right. Then we might as well begin," he announced evenly. Addie was stunned when he came to take a seat on the floor beside her, masterfully pulling her down into his embrace and cradling her upon his lap.

"What are you doing?" she tremulously demanded, experiencing a bewildering combination of both joy and sorrow. She couldn't forget the way Charity had spoken of her times alone with Daniel, of what they had once meant to each other. The memory still served to bring an ache to Addie's heart.

"I want you where you can't turn away from me, you beautiful wildcat. I have something very important to say to you, and I want to make damned sure you listen!" His arms tightened about her, and she was vividly aware of his powerfully muscled thighs beneath her silk-covered hips.

"If it's about Charity Bransom, I have no desire to hear any further tales of your 'little jaunts' with her!" She pushed against him in an effort to escape, but he would not relinquish his firm hold.

"Jealousy becomes you, Adelaide," he murmured with a devilish grin, hugging her tighter. "But enough is enough. You have absolutely no reason to be jealous of Charity."

"Did you bring me all the way out here just to tell me that?" she snapped, despising herself for the tears which returned to her flashing eyes. She renewed her futile struggles briefly before surrendering.

"That, and much more. But let's get Charity out of the way first."

"Can we accomplish that with mere talk?" Addie retorted sarcastically.

"As far as I'm concerned we can. Charity means nothing to me, Addie. She never has," Daniel earnestly declared.

"Then what was all that about your *unofficial* engagement?"

"It was something our families wanted, not what I wanted. Charity has known for years now that there can never be anything more than friendship between us. I'll grant you, however, that she seems determined

345

to do her best to goad you, to try to pretend my attentions have stemmed from more than just loyalty to an old friendship. Her behavior is most probably due to the fact that she senses how I feel about you. Why she's trying to cause trouble between you and me is beyond my comprehension," he ruefully admitted. The dancing flames created a myriad of shadows behind them, and the golden firelight played over them with a confident disregard for the diminishing chill which had at first enveloped the room.

"Why have you spent so much time alone with her?" demanded Addie, a renewed surge of hope springing to life within her. He didn't care for Charity Bransom at all, and there had never been an engagement between them, she silently repeated.

"Charity exaggerated about the amount of time we've spent together," he revealed in a low chuckle. "I took her out riding a couple of times, that's all. And I only did so at Carrie's request."

"Carrie's request?" echoed Addie in confused surprise.

"Lord, save us from interfering sisters," he mockingly quipped. "I think she knew exactly what she was doing. She once told me that she intended to do all she could to get the two of us back together."

"But you went along, didn't you? And why the devil did you take Charity to the very cabin where you and I—"

"It honestly wasn't my idea. Before I realized what I was doing, I had taken us close to that place. And when Charity saw it, she insisted that we do some exploring. I tried to dissuade her, but she was adamant, and I suppose I wanted to get another glimpse of it myself. That rainy afternoon you and I spent there is still very fresh in my mind, Addie," he told her, a slow smile rising to his lips as he glanced down at the young woman in his arms. "I'd even brave another attempt upon my life in order for the two of us to share a similar—"

"Oh Daniel!" Addie sighed, her eyes clouding. "I've never felt so utterly helpless as I did when I saw that you had been shot." A moment of highly charged silence followed, during which the only sounds heard were the faint popping and crackling of the fire.

"Do you believe I love you, Addie?" Daniel unexpectedly asked, his hand gently cupping her chin so that she met his burning gaze squarely.

"I . . . I want to," she admitted, her voice barely above a whisper, her eyes soft and luminous.

"Do you believe me when I say that you've no reason to be jealous of any woman?" She didn't answer, but instead stared deeply into the glowing, steely depths of his eyes in an effort to read the truth. "There's never been anyone but you, Addie. I'd never loved anyone before you, and I've never loved anyone since."

"How could we have allowed so much time to pass before this moment?" she whispered, her fingers lightly, lovingly tracing the strong line of his jaw as she blinked back the tears.

"Say it, Addie," he huskily commanded.

Both of them knew what he meant, and it took only a moment's hesitation before Addie looked directly up at him and steadily declared, "I love you, Daniel Jordan." Another silence followed, and Addie could scarcely breathe while she waited anxiously for his reaction.

"Say it again," he insisted, displaying one of the special, heart-melting smiles he reserved only for her.

"I love you. I've always loved you. I will never stop

loving you, nor will I even try to do so ever again," she feelingly vowed. "I love you, Daniel, and I want you to be my husband in every way again. I want to be your wife again."

"Lord, thank you for interfering sisters," he jubilantly declared, his strong arms enveloping Addie in an almost painful, decidedly possessive embrace as her soft, slightly parted lips invited his kiss and he joyfully obliged. The kiss rapidly deepened, and it wasn't long before Daniel rose to his feet, pulling his wife up with him, the two of them fairly trembling with the force of their mutually inflamed desire.

"Make love to me, Daniel," she whispered, smiling up at him with innocent seductiveness as her arms entwined about his neck.

"With pleasure," he responded with a lovingly wicked grin, scooping her up in his powerful arms and moving purposefully toward the bedroom, which was aglow with silvery moonlight streaming in from the single window. Time lost all meaning soon thereafter as they gave themselves completely to each other. Addie met her husband's passion with an unrestrained passion of her own, and Daniel gloried in the priceless gift of his wife's love, so freely and wholeheartedly expressed.

Their clothes were scattered in careless piles on the wooden floor. Nearly every inch of their warm, naked bodies was touching as they lay together in the bed, the quilt covering them as protection against the cold in the semi-darkened room. They had discussed many things throughout the past half hour, many things which neither of them had ever revealed to the other, things about the present as well as the past.

"I've nearly gone crazy these past few weeks, wanting

you so much and yet determined that I wouldn't allow myself to touch you!" Daniel finally admitted with a low, contented chuckle. Although the first storm of their passion had abated, he was already experiencing the stirrings of yet another swiftly increasing desire, a desire he knew would never be totally quenched as long as he and Addie lived.

"It serves you right!" retorted Addie, pressing a soft kiss upon his shoulder. "It was no easier for me, Daniel Jordan," she insisted, frowning up at him as her fingers traced a provocative, repetitive path amongst the soft golden hair on his chest.

"What made you finally face the truth about us, Addie?" he wanted to know, his hand moving smoothly across the silken planes of her firmly rounded hips.

"So many things," she answered with a tiny sigh. "I didn't want to love you, Daniel. Just like you, I attempted to forget all about what we'd once had together. And, I must admit, I felt a great deal of bitterness and pain all these years. But when you entered my life again . . . well, nothing has been the same since. While your coming here brought all the painful memories to the surface again, it also brought other, undeniably cherished recollections to light. I suppose one of the first major turning points was when I discovered your letters."

"You never told me how you happened to find them after all this time."

"Quite by accident. They were hidden away in a secret compartment in my father's desk. He . . . he apparently intercepted them and concealed them from me." It still hurt to think that her father had done such a thing, and yet who was to say that things would have worked out any differently had she known about the letters? she philosophically reflected.

"What was the next major turning point?"

"There were so many! But everything came together at last during your sister's visit to me earlier today."

"Carrie again?" he responded with humorous disbelief.

"The inevitable subject of Charity Bransom entered the conversation," Addie recalled with an ironic smile, "and before I knew what was happening, I had told Carrie that I still loved her brother."

"Remind me to express my undying gratitude to her," Daniel instructed, hugging her close.

"To whom?" his wife teasingly questioned. "Charity or Carrie?" She was rewarded for her impertinence by a playful slap upon her bare bottom.

"So much time has been wasted, Addie, time we should have spent together," he said, growing serious. "Let's not waste any more. I want to let everyone know right away that we are husband and wife."

"We . . . we can't do that just yet," she disagreed, raising herself up so that she could look into his eyes. "I want everyone to know just as much as you do, but we'll have to wait a little bit longer."

"Why?" he demanded, obviously puzzled.

"Because of the roundup. I believe the men will do a better job if they think they're working for two separate bosses. I know you're more readily accepted here than ever before, but it still wouldn't be the same."

"Why should it be any different after the roundup?" Daniel then asked. Addie could easily see that her insistence upon continued secrecy, even for such a brief period of time, was a source of displeasure to him.

"I'm not sure I can explain it to you. It's just that you're still somewhat of an outsider, whereas I've been here nearly all my life. I don't want to be known only as Daniel Jordan's wife, which is how I'm afraid the men would treat me if they knew about our marriage!"

"You're right. I don't think you can explain it to me," he replied in a rather tight voice, his eyes gleaming dully now. "What's so wrong with being known and treated as my wife?"

"It would undermine my hard-earned authority!" Addie declared in growing exasperation, sensing that he wasn't even attempting to be reasonable about the matter. "I'd be just another woman to them then, don't you see?"

"And what the hell are you to them now?" Daniel countered with a deepening frown.

"I'm Miss Addie Caton, that's what! I'm nobody's daughter, nobody's wife, nobody's mindless possession!" she dramatically exclaimed. Drawing herself into a sitting position, she draped the quilt about her as she once again endeavored to explain. "While it's true that I'm a woman, it just isn't the same. The men around here respect me as a fellow rancher. They will, in time, respect me as your wife, Daniel. But I want to get the financial affairs of the Rolling L settled before we make an announcement, and that means we'll have to wait until after the roundup, and possibly until after the cattle drive."

"Do you have any idea of how much time you're talking about?" he ground out, his temper flaring to a dangerous level. She was his wife, damn it, he silently fumed, and he wanted her to be known as such, wanted the two of them to live together like a normal hus-

351

band and wife! He had been patient long enough.

"A month or two, I suppose. But most of that time will be passed on the drive. We won't have much opportunity for marital intimacy anyway, surrounded by all those other men," she pointed out, tossing her head so that her long, shining hair tumbled wildly about her creamy shoulders. "Although," she thoughtfully added, an unholy light of amusement in her eyes, "I suppose we can manage a few times—"

"You're not going on the drive, Addie," Daniel briskly interrupted, abruptly sitting up and placing a pillow behind his back as he leaned against the iron headboard of the bed.

"Yes I am," she blithely retorted.

"No, my love, you are not," he sternly insisted, his intense gaze catching and holding hers. "But I will attempt a compromise," he said in a more reasonable manner. "I'll agree to keep our marriage a secret until after the roundup. In return, you'll make no further mention of going along on the drive. Is that understood?"

"That's blackmail!" she vehemently protested, her face flushing slightly.

"Call it whatever you like. Those are my terms."

"Why, you . . . you . . ." she indignantly sputtered, gasping loudly as she was suddenly yanked against the unyielding hardness of her husband's body.

"Don't be so mule-headed!" Daniel complacently ordered, inching downward beneath the quilt and drawing her along with him. "Save us both a lot of trouble and simply agree for a change." When she opened her mouth to offer a suitably defiant retort, she discovered that the words would not come. Instead, she

352

inhaled sharply, and an involuntary shiver ran the length of her spine as his long fingers began persuasively caressing her soft curves.

"You ... you can't expect to solve all of our problems in such a manner!" she managed to gasp out, stifling the moan which rose to her lips as his mouth fastened greedily about the delightfully sensitive tip of her breast.

"Can you think of a better way?" he parried with a low chuckle, his warm tongue lazily encircling the rosy peak as Addie instinctively strained upward against him, her fingers tightening within his wheat-gold hair. All else was once again forgotten as they became lost in their own special world of sensual pleasures.

His lips teased enticingly at her other breast, but it was soon his turn to gasp as Addie's hands boldly stroked and explored the secret places of his masculine form. Her warm mouth and nimble fingers played amorously over his bronzed flesh, so that it was all he could do to refrain from taking her then and there. It was his intent, however, to prolong the exquisite torture they inflicted upon each other, so he muttered a mockingly ferocious oath and set about returning the favor as his lips trailed a fiery path downward from her breasts to the smooth skin of her abdomen, and lower still.

Addie was driven nearly mindless by Daniel's seemingly magical expertise, and her head tossed restlessly to and fro upon the pillow as she felt her pulse racing and her passions spiraling heavenward. Finally, she was gently turned upon her stomach, and she cried out softly as her husband's moist caresses continued across the silken curve of her back, following an imaginary line along her spine, then pausing at the delectable roundness of her undeniably feminine derriere. She blushed rosily as the creamy flesh of her buttocks was gently nipped, and her cheeks flamed even more crimson a moment later when Daniel knelt behind her and lifted her hips slightly, pulling her back into his vibrant embrace, his manhood pressing insistently at the entrance to her femininity.

"Daniel, what—" she breathlessly questioned, her unfinished query answered in an undeniably satisfying manner as he plunged within her velvety warmth and began a slow, infinitely erotic rotation of his hips. Her movements instinctively matched the rhythm of his, and she could scarcely breathe as a wondrous mixture of sensations assailed her and hurled her toward the ultimate peak of satisfaction.

One of his hands moved to tenderly clasp her breast, and his other hand reached beneath her as his fingers sought the secret, womanly place between her trembling thighs. A soft moan of sheer pleasure escaped Addie's lips, her eyelids swept closed, and the tempo of their rapturous union increased as she leaned farther back into her husband's dizzying thrusts. The shattering fulfillment which soon followed was more powerful than any either of them had previously known, and it was with a sense of wonderment that they clung together in the languid aftermath of their frenzied passion.

It was quite late before a thoroughly contented Addie was returned to her home by an equally sated Daniel, the two of them parting with tender words of love and assurances of a bright tomorrow.

Nineteen

The roundup began less than two weeks later, and Addie mused that she had never before experienced such anticipation for the event. The days had passed in a whirl of preparation, the nights in dreaming of the times she and Daniel had secretly been together since the evening of the disastrous supper at the hotel. She had never felt more gloriously alive, and she knew that it was because of Daniel. The security of their mutual love filled her entire being with an inner glow, a glow that manifested itself on the outside by a tendency to smile at life in general.

Even Charity Bransom failed to dampen her soaring spirits. Carrie and Charity were still in town, though Carrie had revealed to Addie that they were planning to return to San Antonio within a day or two after the beginning of the long-awaited roundup. It seemed that Charity had become quite frustrated in her pursuit of Daniel, for the two of them were never allowed a moment alone together due to the clever planning of both Carrie and Addie. Although the elegant Miss

Bransom had discovered the truth about Daniel's relationship with his "business partner," she had remained undeterred. At last, however, she had begun to realize that she was facing a humiliating defeat, and she had reluctantly acceded to Carrie's insistence that the two of them leave Fort Worth.

Finally, all the preparations for the early spring gathering of the stock were completed. A number of mustangs had been broken and trained to become the reliable cow ponies which were so essential, several extra men had been hired to assist in the branding, and all the necessary equipment had been purchased and assembled.

"Well, this is it, Miss Addie," stated Silas, his lined face alight with pleasure as he and Addie downed their last cup of coffee just after sunrise on what promised to be a cloudless March day. They began drawing on their outer garments, their mutual excitement visibly increasing.

"You take care of yourselves, you hear?" admonished Esther, handing Addie an extra bundle of supplies for the day. "The Lord have mercy," she declared, then added by way of comment as her critical gaze swept briefly over the younger woman's masculine attire, "your mama would've had a fit if she'd seen you lookin' like that!"

"This is the first true roundup we've been able to have in over four years," Addie reminded her, smiling unconcernedly as she glanced down at her clothing, "and I'll be damned if I'm going to be hampered by skirts that will only get in the way!" Her long hair was braided on either side of her head and pinned securely up beneath her broad-brimmed hat. The ubiquitous

356

bandanna—a square piece of bright red cloth used not only to keep out dust but for a variety of other reasons as well—was knotted loosely about her neck. Her shirt was of a thick, typically colorless cotton, and her heavy denim trousers fitted snugly at the waist. A pair of flat-heeled, round-toed boots with filed down rowels on the spurs and a jacket made of a canvaslike fabric completed the uniform, except for the seatless leather coverings known as chaps which would be drawn on and buckled at the waist as soon as she reached the barn.

"It just ain't decent," grumbled Esther, eyeing the way the trousers displayed the obviously feminine shape of Addie's lower body.

"Leave her be, old woman," Silas chastised good-naturedly, giving his wife an indulgent kiss before following Addie out of the house. They found that Trent, Clay, and Billy were already waiting for them just inside the barn, as were the other young men, hardly more than boys in actuality, whom they had recently employed. After a few brief words from Addie regarding the plans for the day, they each mounted up and rode toward Daniel's ranch.

Daniel had hired several of his own hands for the event, and it wasn't long before he and his men had joined Addie's group and were headed out across the sun-drenched range. None of them would even attempt to estimate exactly how many head of cattle they would find, for there were vast herds of longhorns—many without brands—wandering across the unfenced lands of Texas at that time, and the unmarked stock would become the property of whoever could round them up and brand them.

"I hope you slept well last night, my love," Daniel murmured as he reined his horse close beside an eagerly prancing Twister, his voice low and for her ears alone. He grinned at the blush which rose to her cheeks.

"Shhh! Do you want someone to hear you?" Addie halfheartedly scolded, the pale color deepening as she recalled the wonderfully abandoned ecstasy they had shared the day before. Glancing hastily about and noting that they were a safe distance away from the other riders, she returned her gaze to Daniel as she said in a voice barely above a whisper, "It's a shame we're going to be too exhausted during the next several days to even think of such things!" Her eyes sparkled with loving mischief.

"The hell we will!" he retorted, his own gaze alight with a silent promise. He chuckled softly to himself as Addie was unable to suppress an answering smile. Urging her horse away from his, she easily caught up with Silas, who favored her with an inscrutable grin as the two of them began discussing their impending tasks.

By the time the sun had moved directly overhead in the brilliantly blue sky, an impressive number of cattle had been located, and Addie was satisfied to see that the Rolling L brand marked several of the lean, rawboned animals. Next came the branding of the heretofore unclaimed members of the small herd. It was no easy chore for the cowboys, who roped and hauled the wildly plunging, fiercely battling cattle toward the branding fire. Two ranch hands held the longhorn while a third quickly branded its side, after

358

which the furious, indignant animal was released to rejoin its loudly bellowing companions.

Esther arrived at the roundup grounds just after noon, driving a buckboard loaded with a generous supply of beef stew, beans with salt pork, sourdough biscuits, and good, strong coffee. The men, whose appetites had grown to near epic proportions as a result of the morning's hard work, pounced on the food with a vengeance. Addie discovered that her own appetite was quite healthy, and, after the others had filled their plates and cups and moved away, she strode to the buckboard with Daniel falling in beside her.

"Where did you learn to rope like that?" she demanded, referring to his surprisingly expert handling of the lariat which she had witnessed that morning. Schooling her features to remain outwardly cool and a bit aloof, she was nevertheless unable to keep the telltale sparkle from her hazel eyes whenever she looked at him.

"Just natural talent, I guess," he mockingly quipped, flashing her a disarming grin. "Actually, my father taught me. We didn't have many head of stock, but there was ample opportunity for me to practice." He nodded politely toward Esther, who was perched on the rear of the buckboard. "Good day, Mrs. Fremont," he cheerfully proclaimed, accepting the plate and fork she handed him.

"Looks like your roundup's goin' mighty well, Mr. Jordan," she responded with a broad smile. Glancing at the young woman beside him, she teasingly added, "Yes sir, it must be the smell of those mangy beasts that's bringin' such a glow to Miss Addie's cheeks." She laughed softly as Addie's startled gaze flew to meet hers.

A pair of dark, piercing eyes darted toward the companionable group at the buckboard with watchful frequency. The eyes narrowed in silent fury as they took note of the way the Yankee seemed to hover possessively about Miss Addie, and the way her eyes shone so brightly whenever they rested upon the tall outsider. Trent Evans forced himself to conceal the jealous rage which held him in its deadly grip, his fingers clenching the plate so tightly his knuckles turned white. The next time he fired a shot at Daniel Jordan, he vowed malevolently to himself, it wouldn't be in warning—it would be to kill.

It was mid-afternoon when Addie sighted the buggy rolling unevenly along the deeply rutted path which only faintly resembled a road but was used as such. Leaving her work at the branding fire, she tugged off her hat and crossed the short distance to the path. A welcoming smile curved her lips as she watched Carrie pull the horse to a halt and climb down from the small, open-sided conveyance. Her smile faded slightly when she glimpsed the haughty features of Charity Bransom's face as the dark-haired young woman carefully gathered up her skirts and made a great show of alighting from the buggy.

"I know you're terribly busy, dearest Addie, but since we've only two days left, I thought perhaps you wouldn't mind if we came to have a look at what you and Daniel are doing," explained Carrie as she quickly scanned the sea of activity in an effort to locate her brother. Glancing back to Addie, she grinned impishly

360

before exclaiming with a laugh, "You do look a sight!"

Addie merely smiled in response, while Carrie's companion approached and said, "If I didn't know better, Miss Caton, I would mistake you for one of the men."

"Would you? Then I suppose I should count myself fortunate that you are indeed aware of my true sex, Miss Bransom!" Addie declared enigmatically, turning back to Carrie with another smile. "Daniel should be returning soon. I'm afraid there isn't really any place for the two of you to sit, but you're welcome to stay and watch."

"Thank you. And don't worry, we'll manage," the redhead answered before Charity could raise her voice in protest. Addie returned to her work, leaving the two daintily clad young women to make their way across the rocky ground. Carrie resourcefully discovered two logs for them to sit on, though her friend complained quite vocally about the primitive conditions she was being forced to endure. To make matters worse, Charity was very much aware of a decidedly unpleasant aroma carried on the gently blowing wind, the smell of a red-hot poker burning its mark into the tough hides of the longhorns. Not even Daniel's charming presence could provide enough consolation for her suffering and Charity breathed a great sigh of relief when Carrie finally agreed to return to town nearly an hour later.

The sun was already beginning to sink slowly below the western horizon when the first day of roundup was called to a halt. It was judged a tremendous success by all, and Addie's optimism had grown considerably. Although she and Daniel were weary and desirous of warm baths and hot meals, the two of them were eagerly looking forward to the next day as they made their separate ways home, having parted with nothing more than a look full of tender meaning passing between them.

Carrie's thoughts were centered on her brother and sister-in-law as she stepped out of the hotel and strolled leisurely down the boardwalk. She had been anxious to escape the stifling confines of the hotel, as well as the disagreeably moody behavior of Charity. In some ways, she reflected with an inward sigh, she would be glad to rejoin her aunt in San Antonio, for she would then be free of her responsibility as Charity's companion. But it had been worth it, she silently concluded, her green eyes literally dancing with a mixture of amusement and satisfaction. Addie and Daniel were together again at last, and they would soon be sharing a new life as true husband and wife.

Bewildered by the sharp pang of loneliness and the inexplicable sense of emptiness she suddenly experienced, Carrie's steps slowed to a halt. She seemed not to notice the men and women forced to detour around her as she stood in the middle of the boardwalk, and it took a number of seconds before she emerged from her melancholy reverie and became aware of her surroundings again.

The sky was ablaze with pale color as dusk approached, and the cool evening air was a refreshing balm to her suddenly feverish skin. The streets cleared as the town's inhabitants returned to their homes for supper and a welcome rest from the day's worries and activities.

Carrie gasped softly when she realized that she was standing all alone in front of Turner's Mercantile. Her hand abruptly tightened within the folds of her velvet skirts, and, as she slowly turned to peer through the window, her widening eyes immediately focused upon Gil Foster. Apparently in the process of closing the store for the night, he moved about the interior and blew out all but one of the lanterns, then retrieved his hat and coat from the hall tree in the corner beside the doorway.

It was obvious to Carrie that he hadn't seen her yet, and she felt strangely numb as she watched him. Gil extinguished the last source of light and swung open the door, which prompted his lovely observer to come to life again. She whirled about and hurried away, back toward the hotel and the sanctuary of her lonely room.

"Carrie!" Gil's voice rang out behind her, bringing about a momentary pause in her flight. It was the first time he had ever addressed her as anything other than "Mrs. Rogers," and she turned to face him with a look of stunned amazement on her face. He wasted no time in striding forward to confront her, his hands instinctively reaching out to her before he forced them back to his sides. "Why did you run away like that?" he quietly demanded.

"I . . . I wasn't running away!" she falsely denied, a telltale blush coloring her lightly freckled countenance. She had yet to meet his steady blue gaze, but she knew that his eyes were full of kindness, and something more . . .

"For two weeks now, I've tried to talk to you," Gil stated, his voice low and resonant. He held his hat between his hands, his coat over one arm. The faint evening breeze which swept across them tousled his light brown hair, while his attractive features remained immobile, reflecting little of his inner turmoil.

"It makes . . . it makes no difference now," Carrie stammered in confusion, her gaze still fixed upon the buttons of his white linen shirt. "Miss Bransom and I will be leaving Fort Worth the day after tomorrow." She had avoided him since that day in the rain and had refrained from all but the barest civilities whenever the two of them had chanced to meet. He had called upon her at the hotel twice within the past week, but she had left instructions with the desk clerk that she would receive no male visitors other than her brother.

"You're leaving?" he echoed, his voice deepening with intense disappointment at the news. Carrie finally forced herself to raise her eyes to his, and she was startled by the fierce light shining within his usually gentle gaze.

"Yes," she murmured, her breathing oddly irregular as she turned about and attempted to leave again. A faint cry of alarm escaped her lips as Gil's arm shot out and seized her about the corseted waist, pulling her almost roughly back against the slender hardness of his tall frame. Her eyes were round as saucers as they flew upward to encounter his. "What in heaven's name are you—" she breathlessly started to demand, only to be firmly cut off by a voice that was raw with mingled pain and suppressed longing.

"You can't leave, Carrie. I can't allow you to simply disappear from my life after you've made such a shambles of it!" His eyes, which now contained a savage gleam, bored into hers, and she gasped loudly.

"Let go of me!" she cried. Looking wildly about for assistance, she was like a small, trapped animal, pushing helplessly against him. Yet she was painfully aware of the fact that she was fighting against her own feelings as well as his. She hadn't wanted to care about him, hadn't wanted to care about anyone ever again the way she had cared about Alan. It had happened entirely against her will and with lightning-quick speed, she desperately realized. And, to make matters worse, he had been Alan's enemy, which made her feel like a traitor to her beloved husband's memory. She could not, would not allow herself to love him!

"We both know it's no use," decreed her captor in a gentler voice, as if reading her hopelessly rebellious thoughts. Then, to prove his point, he tugged her closer and lowered his head as his lips claimed hers in their first, wondrously fateful kiss. Fully cognizant of the fact that he had never felt such a dizzying combination of love and desire for any other woman, not even Miss Addie, Gil poured his whole heart into that kiss, not caring that his hat and coat slipped heedlessly to the dusty boardwalk as his other arm tightened about Carrie's shoulders.

Carrie, too, lost herself in the searing embrace, vaguely recalling an old saying about desperate times requiring desperate measures just before her brain became incapable of forming rational thought. There was only Gil, only the magical reawakening of her long-buried desires. She met his passion with an equal fervor, her arms moving of their own volition to wrap about his tautly muscled body, her lips willingly parting beneath the stimulating onslaught of his.

Kyle Townsend whistled a lively tune as he ambled

out of his father's livery stable down the street, enjoying his hard-earned freedom after a day spent "imprisoned" in the simple frame schoolhouse located at the opposite end of town. Withdrawing a hand-rolled cigarette from his coat pocket, he confidently struck a match and raised the flame to the tobacco, puffing contentedly as he headed down the boardwalk on his way to the rear of the courthouse to meet a group of his friends. As soon as his meandering gaze beheld the startling sight just ahead, his steps were momentarily arrested, for it wasn't every day that Gil Foster could be seen kissing the Yankee's sister in such a public display of passion.

"Damn silly females!" the boy muttered to himself, laying the blame entirely at Carrie's feet. His expression was one of youthful disdain for such disgustingly sentimental behavior, and he scowled deeply as he slowly shook his head and took himself off to engage in more worthwhile pursuits, scornfully musing that news of Gil Foster's ridiculous impropriety would be all over town by morning.

The second day of the roundup had dawned as clear and pleasantly cool as the first, and it was all Addie could do to force down more than a forkful each of Esther's ham and eggs before snatching up her hat and coat and flying outside to join the men. There were a number of plans spinning about in her head, plans for making several much-needed improvements around the Rolling L, plans for the wonderful life she and Daniel were going to have together once the roundup and trail drive had been successfully completed. There was no longer any doubt in her mind that the drive was the best solution to the problem of selling their cattle, and dreams of a future with Daniel at her side filled her heart with song.

However, the fact that Carrie was leaving the next day cast a slight shadow upon Addie's happiness. She had grown to love her friend even more dearly, and she felt that she owed the vivacious redhead a debt of gratitude that could never be repaid. Carrie and Daniel would be joining her at the Rolling L for a farewell supper that night—Miss Charity Bransom having pleaded an "indisposition"—and Addie now determined to push any thoughts of sadness from her mind as she greeted the hands with a smile and swung lithely up into the saddle to begin the day's work.

And work it was. In addition to the usual tasks of rounding up, roping, and branding, there were calves to be castrated, horns to be trimmed, injuries to be doctored, as well as the particularly difficult job of pulling a number of longhorns from bog holes. This was accomplished by roping the trapped animals and tugging them out with the lines snubbed around the men's saddlehorns. It took a great deal of physical strength and endurance, and the young steers nearly always emerged fighting and bellowing furiously, ungratefully turning their horns against their rescuers as they charged. Billy Kendrick received his first taste of such belligerence later that same day.

"You're sure you're all right, Billy?" questioned Addie, her lovely face reflecting genuine concern as she swabbed the purplish wound on his leg with a bandage soaked in alcohol.

"Yes, ma'am. I reckon I'll be able to sit astride my

horse all right, but it's a good thing I'm not aimin' to be kickin' up my heels on a dance floor any time soon!" he observed with a rueful grin, an irrepressible twinkle in his light blue eyes. Counting himself fortunate, he glanced down at the wound, eyeing the neat round hole in his trousers, made when the tip of the animal's sharp horn pierced the heavy denim. He had managed to rein about and escape before the horn did anything more than break the skin and leave a painful bruise.

Fortunately, Billy's injury was the only one of the day, and by the time dusk approached, the number of cattle had grown to nearly two hundred. Addie hurried home to bathe and dress, though she knew Daniel would have to do the same and then fetch Carrie before presenting himself for supper. She looked forward to the evening, not just as a last visit with her friend; Daniel had exacted a promise from her that she would accompany him when he delivered Carrie back to the hotel, then spend some time alone with him at his cabin before returning home.

Wondering—not for the first time of late—what it was going to be like to live under the same roof with her devilishly irresistible husband at last, Addie began to hum a soft tune as she climbed from the tub and quickly toweled herself dry. She could just imagine the shocked reactions of both Esther and Silas when she broke the news of her marriage to them. Daniel had tried to persuade her at least to reveal the truth to the couple who had looked after her for so long, but she had remained obstinate about waiting until after the roundup, wanting that knowledge shared only by herself and Daniel for a little while longer.

"You'd best get a move on, Miss Addie, honey!"

exhorted Esther from her position at the foot of the stairs. "Mr. Jordan's buckboard ought to be rollin' this way pretty soon!"

"I'll be down in a few more minutes!" Addie called in response, Esther's words prompting her to hastily draw on her undergarments and set about choosing a dress. She smiled to herself and her face colored a bit when she settled upon the lavender silk she had worn to the Christmas dance. Daniel had told her that she looked beautiful in it, and she wanted to look beautiful for him again, especially given the fact that he now usually saw her wearing dusty trousers and shapeless cotton shirts. But it doesn't matter, that tiny voice at the back of her mind asserted, for he knows better than anyone what the woman underneath the clothing looks like!

Supper proved to be every bit as enjoyable as Addie had expected. Later, while the trio strolled from the dining room into the warmly lit, seldom-used parlor, Daniel surprised Addie by announcing that he wanted to have a few words with Silas, and Carrie seemed visibly relieved when he left her alone with her friend.

"What's troubling you?" Addie immediately demanded, drawing Carrie down beside her as she took a seat on the printed cotton sofa. Recalling that her sister-in-law had been unusually preoccupied all evening, Addie was anxious to know what was causing such obvious disquiet.

"I suppose it's merely the disagreeable prospect of leaving tomorrow," Carrie murmured with a sigh, her eyes shining with sudden tears. "No, that isn't true," she amended an instant later, turning to Addie with a slight catch in her voice. "Oh, Addie, I don't know what to do!"

369

"Why don't you tell me what you're talking about? Perhaps I can help."

"No one can help. It's just that . . . that I've got a decision to make, and I shouldn't have even allowed myself to be in this position!"

"What position?" queried Addie with rapidly increasing curiosity.

"The position of finding myself in love with a man I've known scarcely any time at all, a man who possesses the unexplainable capacity to make Alan's memory little more than a hazy blur in my mind! And, to make matters worse, Gil was an enemy of my late husband's," finished Carrie with another long sigh, her troubled, tear-filled gaze meeting Addie's startled one.

"Gil? Are you talking about Gil Foster?" Quickly reflecting that she hadn't noticed anything unusual taking place between her two friends or glimpsed any sign of a budding romance, she frowned in bafflement over Carrie's totally unexpected revelation. And when the redhead merely nodded faintly in confirmation, Addie gently questioned, "Why didn't you tell me what was happening?"

"For the simple reason that I didn't want to admit that anything was happening! It wasn't until yesterday evening that I finally faced the truth. I didn't want to fall in love like this again, Addie," confided her friend, her green eyes clouding with remembered pain. "Though I believed I should someday marry again, I didn't intend to feel such . . . such anxiousness, such inflammatory tenderness, which is precisely what I experience whenever I am with Gil!"

"Why should falling in love with Gil cause you such distress? He's a very fine man, Carrie. I consider myself quite fortunate to have him as a friend." Gil Foster and Carrie! she mentally repeated in wonderment. Not so very long ago Gil had believed himself in love with her! But then, concluded Addie, a secretive smile tugging at the corners of her mouth, that was before an irresistible little whirlwind with sparkling green eyes and flaming red hair entered his life . . .

"Because I don't think I'm ready to make the sort of commitment he's asked me to make. I know it's been two years now since I lost Alan, and I know I've voiced my determination to get on with my life and all that," Carrie sought to explain, her words making little sense even to her, "but it just seems too soon!"

"You mentioned a commitment. Has Gil asked you to marry him?" Addie quietly inquired, studying the myriad of emotions playing across her friend's lovely countenance as the firelight cast a soft, golden glow over Carrie's smooth skin.

"Yes," affirmed Carrie in a low, tremulous voice. She stared unseeingly toward the flames, grateful for Addie's comforting presence beside her. "And to tell the truth, I'm tempted to accept. He's insisting that I not return to San Antonio with Charity, that I remain here instead and marry him right away. But I just don't think I can do that, Addie. Not yet. And Gil won't listen to reason."

"You mean he isn't willing to wait?"

"I suppose he would be, but I haven't asked him to. We had a terrible quarrel earlier this afternoon, and I'm afraid both of us said some regrettably harsh things. And I'm leaving on the morning stage tomorrow," she noted despondently. "What am I to do?" she demanded once more, a look of desperation evident on her face as she turned to Addie again.

"I'm afraid, dearest Carrie, that I have not always been wise when it comes to matters of the heart," Addie ruefully observed, smiling briefly. She quickly sobered before adding, "But I do know this—if you and Gil truly love each other, then you should be together. Don't ever allow anything or anyone to stand in your way once you're sure. If Gil loves you, he should be willing to grant you more time to make your decision. And if you love him, then your decision won't require much time!"

"You make it sound so simple," her friend murmured, rising to her feet and crossing her arms beneath her bosom. She took her seat again a moment later, obviously still quite confused. Addie lovingly endeavored to help set her mind at ease, but to no avail.

"Have you said anything to Daniel about this?" Addie finally asked, vaguely wondering when her husband would join them in the parlor.

"Not yet. I . . . I don't want Daniel to know anything until I've made a decision. Please, Addie," implored Carrie, "please don't tell him! I love my brother dearly, but I don't think he would approve of his baby sister's falling in love with a perfect stranger!"

"And I think you are underestimating your brother's powers of understanding," retorted Addie. Carrie, however, remained adamant, and her brother's wife had little choice but to agree. When Daniel strolled into the room a short time later, Carrie bravely attempted to conceal all evidence of her perplexity, and the remainder of the evening passed all too quickly.

Though Addie was sorely tempted to mention Carrie's dilemma to Daniel as the two of them drove away from town a short time later, she successfully quelled the temptation. And once she and her husband arrived at his ranch, thoughts of Carrie were temporarily relegated to the back of Addie's mind as she was transported to another world, a world inhabited only by Daniel and herself.

The last of the passengers boarded the stagecoach just after nine o'clock the following morning. Carrie had spoken briefly with Gil the night before, but things had been left unsettled between them. As she now took a seat inside the cramped, stuffy coach, with Charity on her right and the window on her left, she raised her faintly reddened eyes. She inhaled sharply as her gaze fell upon Gil, whose deep blue eyes seemed to burn into her very soul. He was standing merely inches away from where she sat tense and unmoving, the expression on his face inscrutable as he, too, remained silent and strangely immobile.

Finally, he took a step forward. Carrie's eyes, bright with a new surge of unshed tears, were full of expectation as he approached. Her heart ached terribly, and she choked back a sob when Gil, after visibly hesitating while his fingers tightened upon the bottom edge of the uncovered opening which served as a window, evenly declared, "I love you, Carrie. And I think you should know that I'll be coming to San Antonio before too much longer. You're mine. Nothing else matters."

"What?" Charity gasped out from her place beside a stunned and joyful Carrie. "Carrie Rogers, surely you don't intend to allow this . . . this *shopkeeper* to get away with such degrading impertinence!" Her proud features were suffused with a dull color, and she sharply nudged the younger woman's arm to emphasize her words.

"Oh, Gil!" breathed Carrie, totally ignoring her companion's indignant outrage. "I love you, too. And I'll be waiting."

"Carrie!" admonished Charity, her shocked disapproval reaching even greater proportions as she watched the way her young friend leaned forward and allowed herself to be thoroughly and most satisfyingly kissed by Gil Foster. The driver cracked his whip above the heads of the matched team a few seconds later, and the stagecoach rolled southward with a cloud of dust in its wake.

The parting left both Gil and Carrie with an undeniable sense of inevitability, each of them dazedly marveling at the clarifying power of true love. The knowledge of the truth did indeed set Carrie's heart free, and she knew that she would be anxiously counting the days until the fulfillment of her destiny arrived in the person of Gil Foster.

Twenty

"You can't do it, Miss Addie! A cattle drive ain't no place for a young lady and you know it! Livin' with them men for days on end, beddin' down alongside them at night—it just ain't decent!" Esther vigorously protested.

"Half of those cattle are mine. There's no way on God's green earth I'm going to stay behind while they're driven to market hundreds of miles away!" countered Addie, her hazel eyes glistening with anticipation and an ever-growing sense of adventure. Stuffing the last of her things into already-bulging saddlebags, she flashed the fiercely scowling older woman a conciliatory smile. "I'll be fine, Esther. And I know I can rely upon you and Silas to look after things until I return."

"Don't do it, honey," Esther now pleaded, bustling forward and placing her plump hands on Addie's shoulders. "I know you got it into your head that you're just as tough as any man, but you ain't. There's no tellin' what might happen to you on a long drive!"

"The two of you raised every possible objection last night," Addie pointed out, her glance darting to include the man seated at the kitchen table. Dawn was breaking, and a subdued, yellow-orange glow illuminated his countenance as he faced the window and idly sipped his coffee, his ears not missing a single word.

"You just gonna sit there and let her go gallivantin' off like this?" Esther challenged her husband, growing more and more distraught.

Silas finally spoke, his gaze moving lazily toward the two women as he slowly lowered his cup. "Well, I guess if Miss Addie's so bound and determined to go, there ain't no way we're gonna stop her. She ain't a child now, Esther. I think even Mr. Will Caton would have agreed that we got to let her go her own way sooner or later," he quietly ventured, only to find himself the recipient of a sternly quelling look from his wife. Addie, however, sent him a warmly grateful smile.

"What does Mr. Jordan say about you goin' along?" Esther sharply demanded, trying another tactic. "From what I heard, he was thinkin' you were gonna stay behind!"

"Mr. Jordan will . . . well, he'll be pleased that I've decided to go along!" Addie defiantly asserted, knowing full well that she was placing herself in the unenviable position of facing Daniel's considerable wrath as a result of her disobedience. They had said their farewells only the night before, with her husband fully believing it would be several weeks until they saw each other again. She had wanted to reveal her intentions to him, had wanted at least to prepare him for what she knew would be a disagreeable surprise.

But, she mutinously reminded herself, she hadn't ever actually agreed to remain behind!

"That man ain't gonna be pleased," disagreed Esther, shaking her head emphatically. "Like as not, he's gonna be mighty upset that you was so mule-headed you wouldn't listen to reason! I think he's gonna be the first one to agree that a trail drive ain't no place for a woman!"

"Damn it, a woman's place is wherever she wants it to be!" Addie cried in exasperation, impatient to end the discussion and be off. She took a deep, steadying breath, then calmly revealed, "I'm sure you, dearest Esther, would be the first one to agree that a wife's place is with her husband. Well, you and Silas might as well know that my place is with Daniel Jordan. The two of us are husband and wife and have been for five years!" And they had celebrated their recent anniversary in the best possible way, she mused with an inward smile.

"The Lord have mercy!" gasped Esther, clutching at the back of Silas's chair for support. Her brown eyes were very round and her mouth slightly agape. "I . . . I knew the two of you was courtin'—"

"Yes, sir, it all makes sense to me now!" Silas unexpectedly interrupted, slowly rising to his feet and grinning broadly at Addie. "I knew there was somethin' between the two of you. Seems like I knew it from the first time that tall Yankee set foot on the Rollin' L!"

"Five years?" his wife numbly murmured. "You been married five years and never told us. You never told your papa, either." It was obvious that Addie's startling news had begun to sink in, and the realization of her young mistress's secretiveness brought a sudden pain to Esther's heart.

"I'm sorry, Esther," Addie sincerely apologized, wrapping her arms about the other woman and giving her a brief, affectionate hug. "I don't have time to explain all my reasons now, but I promise to explain everything to your satisfaction as soon as I return. I simply wanted to set your mind at ease, and this was the only way I knew how. You see, I'll be with my husband. That's the most important thing, isn't it? You and Silas don't have to worry about me."

"But your husband don't know you're comin'," Silas reminded her, appearing decidedly paternal as he eyed her with obvious disapproval. "Mr. Jordan himself told me you wanted to go along, but that he wouldn't allow it. Said you wasn't likin' it none, but that I was to see to it you didn't fret too much before he got back."

"He . . . he told you that?" stammered Addie, very much surprised. "Well, it makes no difference!" she declared an instant later, marching toward the back door at last, the saddlebags slung over her shoulder. "I'll be as good a drover as any of the others! Daniel will have no reason to regret my presence!"

"Maybe so," stated Silas, placing a comforting arm about Esther's shoulders as she began to weep softly, "but are you gonna have reason to regret it yourself, honey? I know you think you got everything all thought through, but I don't think you know what you're lettin' yourself in for."

"And this will more than likely be my only opportunity to find out!" she retorted. She could easily see how unhappy they were with her decision, and their disapproval prompted a moment's hesitation on her part. But, staunchly telling herself that she did not want

378

to face another separation from Daniel and that the exciting challenge of a cattle drive was something she could not miss, she determinedly squared her shoulders and swung open the door. She relented long enough to hurry back across the kitchen and embrace the two people who had cared for her throughout the entirety of her young life, then left without another word.

After saddling her horse and buckling on her chaps, Addie mounted up and rode toward the spot just north of the Rolling L where the herd awaited the beginning of the drive. It was still a source of deep pride and satisfaction to her that the past two weeks' work had produced nearly two thousand head of cattle. It was the first week of April now—normally the time when a roundup would just be starting instead of drawing to a close, she reflected, attempting to keep her mind on anything other than the one subject which persistently continued to demand her attention. Releasing a heavy, resigned sigh, she finally allowed herself to speculate on Daniel's possible reactions to her unexpected appearance that morning.

That he would be angry, she was certain. Exactly what course of action his anger would take, however, she did not know, and she dreaded the discovery. He was already quite annoyed with her for not yet announcing their marriage, though she had assured him she would do so within a few days' time. But she knew that his displeasure regarding that point of disagreement would seem insignificant when weighed against his anger over this latest disobedience.

She loved him with all her heart, but she had convinced herself that she was doing the right thing in going against his wishes. After all, she certainly didn't want to face the prospect of enduring the next two months without him. And how content would she have been to sit at home and wait and wonder about what was taking place hundreds of miles away? Damnation! she swore in silence. She'd already had more than her share of waiting!

Slowing Twister to a halt, she glimpsed the sea of cattle in the near distance, just beyond the gentle rise of the greening landscape as she faced northward. It didn't take long for her rapidly scanning eyes to find Daniel, who was apparently in the process of issuing some last-minute orders in his capacity as trail boss. He and the other men, numbering eleven in all, were taking their assigned positions as the huge mass of longhorns milled restlessly about, bellowing noisily and pushing against one another in confusion.

Clay and Billy had been granted the honor of riding point, which placed each of them on either side of the herd in the lead position behind Daniel. Trent and a young man known only as Fletcher took the middle position of swing, with two former Confederates named Lee Burnett and Joe Rourke riding flank, toward the rear of the herd. Jesse Abbot and Dave Pryor, two young men who couldn't have been more than sixteen or seventeen, were given the least-favored job of riding drag, bringing up the very rear of the line. In this position they would be forced to breathe the dust of the herd through their brightly colored bandannas as they made certain the weaker cattle, newborn calves, and orphaned yearlings kept up with the rest.

The all-important job of cook fell to an older man by the name of Slim Cooper, his name a complete contradiction to the considerable size of his girth. Slim would drive the chuck wagon just to the north of the trail boss, whose duties included riding ahead to scout for water and a place to pasture the herd for the night. The wrangler, a lanky, experienced cowboy by the name of Graham, was responsible for the remuda, a sizable herd of extra horses that was a necessary part of the drive, for the drovers required a change of mount as much as two or three times a day.

Addie shifted in her saddle, watching in breathless excitement as Daniel raised his arm and signaled for the drive to begin. Deciding to wait until they were well under way before making her presence known—which wouldn't be at all difficult, she mused, given the fact that the herd could only travel ten to twelve miles a day—her eyes sparkled as they fell upon the lead man. He rode tall and self-assured as he easily took control, making it appear as if he had filled the position of trail boss many times before. Her heart swelled with pride at his instinctive powers of leadership, and his willingness to accept such responsibility prompted her to view him with increased respect.

"Daniel Jordan, you're one of a kind," she observed aloud, a soft smile curving her lips. Twister snorted quietly and tossed his head. Addie soothed the restless animal with a gentle hand on his smooth neck, then peered overhead at the lightening sky, realizing that she both feared and eagerly anticipated the moment when she rode up to Daniel and informed him of her decision to become part of the drive.

Even her worst fears, however, had not prepared her for Daniel's uncharacteristically violent reaction. Shortly before the hour-long break for the noon meal, a lone rider traveled past the long, narrow column of cattle, in which a select number of steers led the cows and calves in a line of five or six abreast. The drovers were too occupied with their work to notice the extra rider, who pulled her hat low over her head and gently spurred her horse to quicken his pace as she approached the trail boss some distance ahead.

Addie's face wore an unusually tentative smile as she drew up alongside Daniel, and she gazed expectantly across at him as he turned back from motioning an order in Slim's direction and became aware of the new arrival riding beside him.

"What the—" he muttered in astonishment, breaking off as his handsome features became suffused with a dull, angry color. Addie felt the knot in her stomach tighten as she viewed the savage gleam in his steely eyes, eyes that narrowed dangerously as they raked furiously over her suddenly trembling body.

"Oh Daniel," she hastened to explain, "I . . . I had to come!" Her tone grew increasingly defensive as he merely glared intently at her, his mouth compressed into a tight, thin line of near-explosive displeasure. "I have every bit as much right to go along as anyone else!"

"Damn it, Addie!" he ruthlessly ground out, striving to maintain control of his temper. He had never experienced such all-encompassing fury toward her as he now felt, and he was afraid of what might happen if he allowed himself to say or do anything at that particular moment.

Addie swallowed hard and fell silent as she watched him signal curtly toward the chuck wagon, indicating to Slim that he could begin his preparations for the "nooning." The burly cook nodded his head in response and pulled the horses to a halt, sparing only a brief, curious glance for Addie as he jumped down from the wagon and hurried to start a fire.

"Well? Aren't you going to say anything?" she tersely demanded, whipping the hat from her head and feeling grateful for the warm sunshine which beamed down upon her glistening chestnut braids. "Why don't you just go ahead and rant and rave at me and get it the hell over with!" Raising her chin in defiance, she inwardly blanched at the fierce light in the gaze he turned upon her. Again, however, he said nothing, and she felt her apprehension rapidly growing as he merely reined about and headed back toward the herd, offering her the choice of either following after him or dismounting and awaiting his return. Muttering a wrathful oath, she chose the latter.

His behavior had taken her completely by surprise, reflected Addie, and the terrible anxiety she now experienced caused her head to ache as she dismounted and approached the chuck wagon. Nevertheless, she forced a smile to her lips as she casually ventured, "Hello, Slim. Is there anything I can do to help?" Her smile temporarily faded as she received a decidedly hostile look from the large, irascible fellow who was certainly not noted for his diplomacy.

"You can head on back home where you belong!" he growled, snatching an iron pot from the chuck box perched at the rear of the broad-beamed, sturdily built vehicle that was in actuality a rebuilt army wagon. The fire was already blazing nearby, and he wasted little time as he scurried about to set the presoaked beans and salt pork to cooking. "In all my years, we ain't

383

never had no woman on a drive!" he sourly noted a few moments later, spooning a generous supply of freshly ground coffee into the coffeepot.

"Then I suppose it's high time you were granted the experience," Addie mischievously retorted, not the least bit intimidated by his display of blunt unfriendliness. She had known Slim less than a week, but the two of them already understood each other quite well.

"If you really want to make yourself useful, just stay out of the way!" Slim suggested. Reaching inside the chuck box once more, he withdrew several other items and didn't speak again while he hurried to have everything ready before the hungry drovers arrived. Addie's gaze moved frequently to the industrious gray-bearded man as she stood beside the chuck wagon and watched for signs of the herd.

Finally, she glimpsed the unmistakable cloud of dust and heard the faint sounds of bawling and moaning which the calves and their mothers made as they struggled to keep from being separated amidst the steady thudding of hooves and clatter of horns. More than half of the men came riding toward the wagon, while the others kept watch over the cattle and impatiently awaited their shift for dinner.

Daniel was the first to arrive, and Addie took a step in his direction, peering steadily up into his unfathomable eyes as they immediately searched her out. Clay and Billy happened to be among the first group at the noon meal, and they reined up close behind Daniel, their boyish faces registering almost comical astonishment as their eyes fell upon Addie.

"Miss Addie!" Clay blurted out, swinging down from the saddle and quickly striding toward her.

"What the hell . . . what are you doing here?" he asked, coloring slightly beneath her indulgent stare as she turned away from a leisurely dismounting, deceptively composed Daniel and faced the sandy-haired youngster. Billy soon joined them, his own eyes clouding in obvious bewilderment at finding her there.

"I'll be going with you after all," she informed them, refusing to so much as glance at Daniel as she uttered the defiant words.

"You mean you're goin' on the drive? All the way to Missouri?" Billy questioned in disbelief.

"All the way to Missouri," confirmed Addie, now stealing a hasty look at her husband and noting the disturbingly inscrutable expression on his face. Dave, Fletcher, and Jesse rode up and dismounted nearby, hesitating to do anything more than stand and wait in confusion as they took note of the beautiful young woman's presence. They had been introduced to Miss Addie a few days earlier, but they suddenly found themselves overcome by unaccountable shyness at seeing her in such unexpected surroundings. Like Slim, they hadn't ever considered the notion of a woman going along on a drive, and they glanced expectantly toward the trail boss as he finally began moving purposefully in Miss Addie's direction.

"Come on," Daniel commanded evenly in a low, vibrant tone as he took a firm grip on Addie's arm and began pulling her effortlessly along with him toward a thick cluster of oak and cottonwood trees lining a small creek a short distance away.

"Why?" she demanded, blushing faintly as she noticed the half a dozen pairs of avidly watching eyes fastened upon the two of them.

"To talk," was all he would say. Though tempted to resist, Addie allowed herself to be led along, realizing that she more than likely would be forced to endure a humiliating scene if she refused to accompany him willingly. Unconsciously squaring her shoulders, she raised her head proudly and walked beside Daniel with a show of outward unconcern. Inwardly, however, she was intimidated by the fact that she could literally feel the simmering rage emanating from him, and she knew a moment's cowardice as they disappeared into the cool shade of the concealing grove of trees a few moments later.

"All right, Addie," began Daniel, releasing her arm and lifting a booted foot to rest upon the smooth surface of a large rock jutting from the ground near the softly gurgling waters of the creek, "let's get this settled." Leaning forward a bit, he removed his hat and rested a forearm upon his knee, his fingers tightening imperceptibly about the brim of the felt as he raised dully glowing eyes to hers.

"There's really nothing to settle," she contended, forcing a note of lightness into her voice as she turned away and negligently stripped a leaf from a low-lying branch. "I never promised I wouldn't come, you know. And I simply couldn't allow you to go off without me." Both of her thick braids had come unpinned and now tumbled unceremoniously about her shoulders, making her look more than ever like a girl playing at being a cowboy in an older brother's cast-off clothing. But she was certainly no girl, Daniel angrily mused, realizing that she was deadly serious about becoming an active participant in the drive.

"I thought we had agreed that you would stay put

while I trailed the cattle to Missouri." His own voice was cold and clear, and his lean muscles remained tense beneath the heavy cotton shirt and fitted denim trousers.

"Perhaps you agreed, Daniel Jordan, but I did not!" She faced him squarely now, her bright gaze unflinching as it met the molten steel of his.

"Then let's just say you deceived me well, dearest Adelaide."

"I didn't want to deceive you!" she declared in earnest, stepping closer to him with a silent plea for understanding in her eyes. "I love you more than anything, Daniel, and I truly didn't want to make you so unhappy with me. But I couldn't face the prospect of remaining idle at home while you went off for God knows how long and—"

"And you couldn't bear the thought of missing out on all this excitement and adventure," he quietly finished for her.

"Then you do understand!" she said in obvious relief, smiling engagingly up at him now. "I knew that you wouldn't remain angry with me for long."

"You were planning this all along, weren't you?" he drawled lazily, the faint warning light in his eyes unnoticed by Addie. "That's why you kept procrastinating about announcing our marriage, wasn't it?"

"I told Esther and Silas before I left. As for the others, well . . . yes, I suppose that's why I didn't want the men to know just yet. I thought they might treat me differently on the drive if they viewed me only as your wife."

"Whether they treat you 'differently' or not remains

to be seen, doesn't it?"

"What do you mean?" she asked, frowning in puzzlement.

"I mean that I'm going to reveal the true nature of our relationship to them, my love."

"But you can't do that!"

"I can, and will."

"Why? Are you going to do it as some sort of punishment for my *wifely disobedience?"* she accused with biting sarcasm, her eyes flashing.

"No," he honestly denied as his bronzed countenance grew darker and his eyes narrowed. "I'm going to tell them because I want them to know that you're my woman, that you belong to me. If I allow you to go along on the drive, and I fully realize that it wouldn't do me much good to try to send you back, I want them to know from the very beginning that you're my responsibility and no one else's."

"Your responsibility?" repeated Addie, visibly bristling. "I can damn well take care of myself!"

"That, also, remains to be seen. Nevertheless, the men are going to be apprised of the true facts without further delay. Which brings me to the next point left to be settled between us."

"Which is?" she resentfully demanded, her beautiful face appearing quite stormy as she abruptly wheeled away from him again and fixed her turbulent gaze upon the leaf she still clutched in one hand.

"Turn around and look at me, Addie," Daniel commanded in a low voice. When she rebelliously defied his simple direction, she was forcibly spun about and found herself staring wide-eyed at her husband's dangerously calm features as he towered ominously above her. In the highly charged moment of silence that followed, a lone mockingbird in the near distance seemed to be taunting them with his indiscriminately trilled melody.

When Daniel spoke again, it was in a tone that indicated he would brook no further resistance. "I suggest we come to an understanding, my dearest, headstrong little wife! As much as I love you, as much as I admire your spirit and your courage, I'll be damned if I'm going to allow you to run roughshod over me the rest of our lives! Starting here and now, you might as well get it into that adorable but exasperating head of yours that there can only be one trail boss in an outfit, and it sure as hell isn't going to be you!"

"You know very well that I never intended to act as trail boss on this drive!" Addie indignantly countered, jerking away from him with a wounded look in her blazing eyes.

"This constant battle for supremacy between us has got to end. I've been an idiot to allow you so much freedom. You have a husband now, Adelaide, a husband who wants a wife and not just a secret lover. From now on, you're going to do as I tell you, is that understood?"

"Do you truly expect me to become like all the other domesticated, mindless, gutless feminine creatures you're evidently used to?" she retorted bitterly, her hands on her hips as she confronted him again.

"Though you could undoubtedly use a bit of taming," Daniel asserted, his lips curving into a faintly mocking smile, "I can't imagine you becoming either mindless or gutless!"

"A bit of taming?" Addie echoed, so infuriated she

could scarcely breathe. Before she had paused to consider the wisdom of her fairly smoldering words, she evenly proclaimed, "As I said once before, Daniel Jordan, it would take a better man than you to do it!" To Daniel, whose own inflamed temper had not yet cooled, her angry words offered an irresistible challenge.

"Why not finally admit, my love, that you have already met the man who will be your master?" he complacently responded, his soft, mellow voice in direct contrast to the ire boiling within. In the next instant, Addie found herself yanked toward him as his hand shot out and closed about her wrist. Before she quite knew what was happening, he had returned to the water's edge and lifted his booted foot to rest upon the rock again, then tugged his breathless captive forward and sent her flying facedown across his bended knee.

"Daniel!" gasped Addie, pushing frantically against his powerfully muscled leg, her own trousered limbs flailing helplessly above the ground. Her long braids dangled just above the muddy creek bank. "What do you think you're doing?" she hotly demanded, her cheeks blushing fierily at the humiliating position in which she found herself. She twisted and squirmed wildly, but to no avail. He easily held her imprisoned, his arm clamped like a band of iron across her back. "Damn you, let me go!" The response to her demands came in the form of his large hand connecting forcefully with the well-placed roundness of her denim-clad buttocks. Addie inhaled sharply, her face burning, her futile struggles intensifying.

"If you're going to insist upon behaving like a wayward child, then I'm sure as hell going to treat you like one!" Daniel ground out, his palm already poised to administer another punishing blow.

"You blasted brute!" she feelingly raged, her venomous words ending in a shriek as his hand found its ingloriously wriggling target once more.

"Are you going to obey me, Addie?" he harshly questioned, his eyes darkening, his unmistakably angry features tightening.

"Go to hell!" she replied. The satisfaction afforded her by such defiant bravado was short-lived, however, and after he had spanked her several more times, her vehement protests and blistering curses finally gave way to tears of defeat. "All right! All right, you bastard! I'll do as you say!" she furiously acquiesced.

"Good," Daniel grimly muttered, his hands closing upon her waist and hauling her upright before him. Her narrowed, tear-filled eyes sent invisible daggers hurtling toward his head, and her lovely face was flushed a deep, rosy color.

"I'll make you pay for that, you—" she started to threaten dramatically.

Daniel effectively cut her off with, "I'd strongly advise against any further resistance on your part." There was only the hint of a smile lurking about the corners of his mouth, but Addie glimpsed the way his eyes kindled with a glow of returning humor. "We'd best be getting back. The others are more than likely wondering if I succumbed to the temptation to wring your neck."

Still trembling with the force of her outrage, her backside tingling painfully, Addie shot him a withering glare before once again jerking from his grasp. As she abruptly wheeled about to stalk from the shelter of the trees, her stiff, hurried strides were momentarily arrested when she heard Daniel issuing one last warning behind her.

"You're going to keep your promise to obey me, my dearest wildcat, or we'll have a repeat of this unpleasant little episode. Next time, however, I'll bare that delightful white bottom of yours and paddle it till it's as red as your beautiful face happens to be at this moment."

An involuntary shiver ran the length of Addie's spine, and her lips compressed into a thin, sullen line as she wisely bit back a scathing retort and strode rapidly out of the grove of trees. Her husband followed at a more leisurely pace in her furious wake, watching somberly as she approached the group of men gathered near the chuck wagon and wasted no time in striking up a lively conversation with them.

Daniel's gray eyes became clouded with intense displeasure and more than a touch of jealousy as he noted the way the young men eagerly responded to his wife's purposefully companionable behavior. Deciding that now would be the perfect time to make an announcement of their marriage, he smiled faintly to himself and replaced the hat atop his head as he sauntered forward.

Twenty-One

A flood of embarrassment continued to wash over Addie whenever her thoughts returned to the volatile confrontation between herself and Daniel, which had occurred more than a week ago now. Her relationship with her husband was still more than a trifle strained and full of tension, and she knew that matters weren't helped any by the fact that the two of them were always surrounded by others. Reflecting that the journey was proving to be even more of a test of endurance than she had imagined, she released a long, disparate sigh, as her gaze scanned the gently rolling hills of the sunlit countryside.

She was bone weary at the end of each day, exhausted and aching from endless hours spent in the saddle. Thus far, the drive had been extremely monotonous though fortunately devoid of any major disasters, she mused, glancing up restlessly toward a lone hawk circling high amidst the air currents of the cloudless afternoon sky.

The routine had already been established—a full

morning spent driving the herd, an all-too-brief respite at noon, then back in the saddle until dusk. After a surprisingly delectable supper eaten in almost total silence, Addie would stretch out on her bedroll and peer overhead at the breathtaking panorama of the star-filled Texas sky, listening with only half an ear to the men as they sat around the campfire and exchanged stories and humorous anecdotes about their work, the war, and life in general. Several men rolled cigarettes and Jesse occasionally played his harmonica, but there were also numerous periods of silence, during which the fire could be heard popping and hissing softly and the herd rustling beneath the eyes of the men assigned to the night watch.

Even though Daniel was the only one among them who had fought for the North, there was a curious lack of animosity in the attitudes of the drovers he had employed. It was as if the only world which truly existed for them at this time was the world of the prairie.

Addie had frequently noted, however, that Trent Evans was an exception. He had become even more withdrawn and aloof, speaking only when necessary and holding himself apart from the comradeship which had formed among the others. And although he hadn't openly questioned Daniel's authority, he nevertheless exhibited a subtle but apparent lack of respect toward the trail boss. Whenever Daniel spoke to him, which was seldom, Trent's hawkish features would become a cold, impassive mask, his dark eyes narrowing in silent rancor. He had rarely acknowledged Addie's presence since hearing the news of her marriage, at which time his face had registered obvious shock and displeasure.

But she had wasted little time in worrying over his strange behavior, for she had had enough problems of her own to contend with.

The considerable lack of privacy was only one of the many inconveniences plaguing her. She had managed well enough so far, however, by disappearing into the trees surrounding the nearby streams and creeks along the trail to answer the unavoidable call of nature. Bathing had been done in the chilling air just after sunrise each morning, when she had vigorously soaped and scrubbed, and, shiveringly, rinsed herself afterward beside the plentiful bodies of water.

Just as she had feared, the men had treated her quite differently upon learning that she was the wife of their trail boss. Indeed, she thought with a deep, pensive frown knitting her features, there had been highly noticeable alterations in the attitudes of all the men, but most especially in Clay and Billy. Like the others, they rarely spoke to the woman they now deferentially referred to as "Miz Jordan," which prompted Addie's resentment toward Daniel to increase.

Daniel. Why, oh why did she have to be in love with such an overbearing, impossibly muleheaded man? she silently fumed, her gaze traveling sharply to her husband, who was riding only a short distance ahead of her. Despite the fact that they had managed a few moments alone together during the past week and a half, the rift between them was far from healed.

If only he didn't persist in making her appear little more than a fool in the eyes of the others! she lamented irritably, sighing again in continued annoyance. It wasn't that he treated her so very differently from her fellow drovers; quite the contrary was true. During the day, she was just another one of the hands—neither asking for nor receiving any special favors. But once they made camp, it was almost as if she had ceased to exist for him! And that was precisely the reason she still experienced such discomfiting vexation. Daniel was ignoring her, and she knew damn well it was by design!

Oh, not that he didn't spare her a few crumbs of conversation during the evening meal and just prior to retiring for the night, she mentally scoffed, her countenance displaying an expressive grimace. But she fully believed he was making an effort to force her surrender in the battle of wills which was still taking place between them. Though she was keeping her promise to obey him, she knew that she was doing so with ill grace. But, she reflected with yet another sigh, she simply wasn't accustomed to having a man run her life and order her about! Even her father—strong-willed and outwardly domineering as he was—had allowed her the freedom to do as she pleased most of the time.

"The river's just ahead," remarked Daniel, reining in beside her and inclining his head northward. "We'll make camp early today." He smiled briefly across at her, his irrepressibly twinkling eyes making it seem he was aware of her turbulent thoughts. The day was unseasonably cool, but Daniel had rejected the comfort of his coat, and the light blue of his fitted cotton shirt only accentuated the sparkling flecks of blue in his gray eyes.

"Is it still your intention to cross in the morning?" she idly questioned, inwardly wishing that they could somehow clear the air between them once and for all. She longed to destroy the invisible barriers which separated them, and yet she was bound and determined to show him that, wife or no wife, she still had a perfectly good mind of her own!

The cattle had already begun to increase their pace, bellowing softly as they smelled the water in the near distance, and Daniel curtly nodded in Addie's direction before turning his mount and heading back toward the herd. The orders he issued to the drovers concerned the difficult task of preventing a stampede of the thirsty longhorns into the often treacherous waters of the river, underlaid with patches of quicksand and tangles of driftwood.

Addie knew well that the Red River was an obstacle of critical significance. She'd heard stories about the earlier cattle drives and the problems encountered in taking a herd across. The water was sometimes perilously deep, and both cattle and men had perished within its muddy, red-brown depths.

Gently spurring her horse forward, she soon topped the tall, tree-dotted bank and sat gazing down upon the wide, swirling waterway that presented the last barrier between Texas and Indian Territory. Thankful that they had been provided with plenty of good grass and quiet weather on the first hundred miles of the drive, she realized that the conditions facing them after tomorrow were completely unpredictable. Nevertheless, she felt a slight tremor of excitement when she thought of the adventures which awaited her and the others.

After supper, Addie wandered off a short distance from camp, having suddenly felt the need to be alone.

Taking a seat on the hard ground of the riverbank, she stared outward over the river, the debris-laden waters of which mirrored the pinkish glow of the setting sun. She sighed, and a strange sense of detachment took hold of her as she became lost in a silent reverie, only vaguely aware of the sounds of the cattle milling in the distance and the swiftly coursing river below her.

"They call this place Rock Bluff Crossing," said Daniel, startling her as he quietly approached and eased his tall frame into a sitting position beside her.

"I know," she murmured, favoring him with a seemingly disinterested glance. In truth, her pulses were racing because of his nearness, and she battled the overwhelming urge to throw herself into his arms and admit to the fact that she was lonely and miserable without his much-needed companionship and affection. She yearned to tell him that she missed the closeness they had shared just prior to the beginning of the drive, but she said nothing.

"I forget that you native Texans seem to know *everything* . . ."—he paused dramatically with a low chuckle, grinning unperturbably at her as she sent him a scorching look—"about this state of yours."

"Don't you have things to attend to?" Addie crossly demanded, inching away from him and settling herself on a rocky patch of earth. As she tossed her head in irritation, the unbraided chestnut locks cascaded freely about her shoulders, and she impatiently swept them away from her face, which was now tanned to an even more golden hue.

"I'll be relieving Dave on night watch in a few minutes. Thought I'd have a little talk with my wife until then." He pushed his hat farther back upon his head as he, too, peered outward over the river. His eyes glistened with unspoken tenderness as he turned his gaze on Addie again. "When is this war between us going to end, my love?" he softly asked, his deep voice tinged with a faint huskiness.

"I've done every single thing you've ordered me to do!"

"That you have. And then some. But you're still defying me, Adelaide. I can see it in your eyes, can read it in the way you turn away from me each time I start to talk to you."

"And just when in blazes do you do that?" she angrily cried, rounding on him with flashing, tear-filled eyes. "You haven't even noticed me since that first day!"

"That isn't true," he grimly denied, his own eyes glowing dully. "I'm painfully aware of your presence. As a matter of fact, you're driving me to distraction, woman!"

"Oh?" she caustically parried, cocking an eyebrow at him in mocking disbelief.

"Damn it, Addie, when are you finally going to realize that only one of us can hold a position of authority on this drive, and that the one who does must have the complete trust and obedience of everyone else? I've tried to give you time to adjust to the inevitable way of things, but my patience is wearing thin!"

"Your patience is wearing thin?" she echoed, her low, seething tone giving evidence to her pent-up fury. "Why, you and the others have been treating me as if . . . as if I had suddenly contracted leprosy!"

"I warned you some time ago that this was no place for a woman, but you refused to listen. If I didn't love you so much, I swear I'd—"

"You'd what?" Addie scornfully challenged, her chin lifting proudly, her body stiffening.

"I'd tie you on your horse and have Billy take you back home where you belong!" She failed to notice the teasing light in his slightly narrowed, unwavering gaze.

"The devil you would! Even if you tried it, Daniel Jordan, you know I'd only come back!" Angrily getting to her feet, she confronted him with a decidedly militant expression on her face. "Why don't you just forget that I'm a *mere woman* and—" she coldly started to suggest, only to break off as Daniel came off the ground like a shot and gripped the soft flesh of her shoulders with less-than-gentle hands.

"How the blazes can I forget you're a woman when I'm reminded of it a million times a day? Do you have any idea what it's doing to me to have you so close and yet so inaccessible at the same time?" he harshly demanded, administering a brief shake for emphasis. Addie's eyes were wide and startled as they stared up into the cold steel of his. His hands fell slowly to his sides again as he said more calmly, "That was one of the very reasons I didn't want you along. You're putting me through absolute hell!"

"Well, you've certainly been creating the opposite impression!" she indignantly charged.

"That's exactly what I wanted to do!" he readily admitted.

"Then I really must congratulate you on your success," she declared with biting sarcasm, wheeling away from him and rigidly marching back to camp, her eyes filling with hot tears.

"Addie!" called Daniel, clenching his teeth when she

400

did not stop. Breathing a savage oath, he fought the powerful impulse to go after her. The last thing he wanted to do was treat the curious onlookers around the fire a short distance away to an explosive display of "marital bliss"! Instead, he headed off to take his turn at the watch, though he knew his thoughts that night would be on an entirely different type of female than the four-legged kind which required his attention.

Addie's hurried steps slowed to a halt a moment later, and she turned back to face Daniel, only to see that he was already striding toward the spot just outside the camp where the remuda was situated. Musing that he would be a minute or two choosing and saddling a fresh mount, she was tempted to pursue him, but she stubbornly fought the temptation.

Dashing impatiently at her tears, she returned to the camp and flung herself down upon the sparse comfort of her bedroll, oblivious to the sudden hush which had fallen over the previously murmuring group at the fire. She turned hastily upon her side with one arm pillowing her head, and she bit at her lower lip as she continued to battle the growing urge to unleash a storm of weeping.

To Addie and Daniel, it seemed an eternity before dawn. The night had been long and sleepless for both, and only the exciting prospect of taking the herd across the river made them forget their troubles, at least for a time.

Once again, it appeared the weather was going to cooperate, and the crossing finally began just after eight o'clock in the morning. Everyone knew that it would be hours before the entire herd could be driven across, and they also knew that such crossings rarely went smoothly. They planned to swim the cattle across in the same formation they had used on the trail, hoping that the deep waters weren't too heavily laden with brush and broken trees, and praying that the longhorns wouldn't panic or mill, which could turn the event into a turbulent confusion of horns and heads and bodies thrashing about in the dangerous current.

"All right. Let's head them on into the river!" commanded Daniel, waving his hat in the air as a signal to those drovers out of earshot. Addie was at his side, for he had insisted that she cross last with him. They sat astride their horses and watched anxiously as Lee and Joe, riding point, started driving the first line of animals down the bank and into the water. Earlier, the two men had volunteered to cross alone in order to test the waters, after which they had reported encountering no significant difficulties.

At first there appeared to be some hesitation on the part of the herd, but it wasn't long before the lead steers reached the first point of consequence without incident, immersed in the muddy water up to their lean-muscled necks, the instinct for survival prompting them to swim as they lost their footing on the sandy river bottom. The cow ponies beneath Joe and Lee were strong swimmers, capable of carrying their riders across the deep spots while the men remained astride in the saddle and made certain the cattle continued to move in the correct formation.

"I'd always heard that the quicksand here was pretty treacherous," murmured Addie, pulling her hat lower so that the wide brim shaded her face from the sun. Her horse pawed impatiently as she kept a tight grip on the reins.

"So had I," remarked Daniel, his eyes never leaving the activity below as he and Addie looked down from their position on the rocky bluff. He was prepared to intervene the instant something went wrong, and his whole body was tensed in readiness. "But we've just begun," he somberly reminded her, "and anything could still happen."

Addie said nothing in response. A strange uneasiness settled over her, and she suddenly found herself desperately wanting to make Daniel understand her point of view in the struggle which had been taking place between them. Though she had yet to formulate the words in her mind, she nevertheless opened her mouth and spoke falteringly, "Daniel, I . . . I . . ."

It was then that the first sign of trouble occurred. Slim, who had moved out in the chuck wagon alongside one of the first groups of cattle, cursed loudly and thundered a warning that the whole rig was sinking to its axles in quicksand.

"Damn!" muttered Daniel, wasting no time as he jerked on the reins and urged his mount down the steep embankment to the river's edge. Addie wasn't far behind, despite the fact that Daniel had previously ordered her to stay put no matter what happened. Hearing Slim's yell, Clay and Billy left their swing positions at the middle of the herd and came galloping forward to offer assistance.

Daniel and Billy hurried to unhitch the straining and twisting team of horses from the wagon, while Addie quickly snatched the coiled rope from her saddle and tossed one end of it to Clay, who had dismounted and

403

waited to tie his and Addie's lines around the tongue of the wagon. That done, Addie secured the other end around her saddle horn and watched as Clay swung back up and did the same. Then the two of them spurred their horses in unison in an attempt to pull the wagon to more solid ground. Slim jumped down and splashed around to the rear of the mired wagon, applying his brawny strength as he battled against the tug of the sand.

While Billy took control of the loosened team a safe distance away, Daniel returned to the wagon and quickly looped his own rope around the tongue, then cast a brief, fiercely disapproving glance in Addie's direction before spurring his own mount straight ahead. Fortunately, the cattle were maintaining their orderly crossing under the skillful efforts of the other drovers, and it took only a few minutes for the wheels of the chuck wagon to be freed from the relatively shallow quicksand and pulled to a firmer spot.

"That's it!" called Daniel in satisfaction, after which he instructed Clay and Billy to resume their positions with the herd while he hitched the horses to the wagon once more. That done, he said to Slim, who had climbed up to the wagon seat and had taken control of the reins again, "Just take it slow and easy now. You ought to be able to float it across from here on out."

"I got a good team in front of me. This old rig'll make it," the gruff, bearded fellow asserted with unflagging confidence. Nodding curtly toward Daniel, he snapped the reins and raised his voice in a firm command to the horses.

After pausing to watch until the wagon had reached deeper waters and appeared to be out of danger, Addie reined about and rode from the river, frowning in displeasure as she glanced down and noticed that her trousers were soaked all the way up to her waist.

"I thought I told you to stay put!" snapped Daniel, his tone harsh and whipcord sharp. He drew up beside her, his face mere inches from hers as he abruptly seized her horse's bridle and forced it to a halt. "Aren't you ever going to learn how to obey a simple order?" he furiously scolded, his eyes blazing. Nearly every inch of his own clothing was dripping wet, and it was obvious that he was in no mood to be reasonable about his wife's disobedience.

"I couldn't stand by and do nothing when my help might have been needed!" she lashed back, flushing hotly but meeting his censuring look squarely.

"I'll deal with you later," he ground out, suddenly releasing her bridle as if it had burned him. "Get back up there and ride drag with Dave and Jesse!" He jerked his head toward the bluff. "At least maybe I won't have to worry about your doing something foolhardy if you're at the end of the herd!"

"Foolhardy?" Addie gasped indignantly. Biting back the scorching rejoinder on the tip of her tongue, she briskly reined away and rode back up the steep embankment, her pride smarting and her cheeks flaming as she pondered the injustice of what she considered Daniel's condescending attitude.

What had happened to the man who had once told her he admired her courage and spirit? she wondered resentfully. He was treating her like an insubordinate child again, and she damned sure wasn't going to stand for it! Sooner or later, she told herself, her stormy eyes narrowing, Daniel Jordan would have to realize that

405

she would never embrace the role of a weak-willed, mousy little female who would be content to sit at home with her knitting and wait while her husband took care of all the so-called "men's jobs"!

Pressing the back of her hand to her forehead and negligently sweeping a few stray tendrils of hair from her temples, she headed back toward the rear of the herd, bitterly musing that Dave and Jesse probably wouldn't welcome her "intrusion" either. Nevertheless, she staunchly pulled up her red bandanna to cover her nose and mouth, squared her shoulders, and held her head high as she fell into line between the two men.

Some time later the drag riders finally neared the river. The sunlight was filtering through a thickening cover of clouds by then, and the longhorns bringing up the rear were behaving in a disturbingly restless manner. Addie frowned thoughtfully, noting the way the steers at the very end were beginning to push against one another with increasing fervor as they approached the swirling waters. There had been a few minor incidents with the rest of the herd, as well as one particularly tense moment when several of the cattle had become trapped amidst a heavy tangle of brush near the midway point in the crossing. It had required some hasty, strategic maneuvering by Daniel and a couple of the others to prevent a full-scale panic of the numerous animals swimming frantically toward the opposite shore. But they had succeeded in freeing the tangled cattle and herding them quickly to the other side of the river, and no more than a few bruises and scratches had been sustained by either men or beasts.

Daniel rode forward to meet Addie and the two men flanking her as they approached the water's edge. Trent was helping Graham take the remuda across, and it was obvious to Addie that the trail boss was much relieved that they had not lost any drovers or cattle in the crossing.

"Dave, Jesse, the two of you close in on either side of the herd now and keep them moving. Addie, you come with me," instructed Daniel. She raised her eyes to his and glimpsed in their steely depths what seemed to be a silent apology. Quickly averting her gaze, she visibly stiffened and waited for him to lead the way, which he proceeded to do in the next moment.

The two of them urged their mounts into the river, Daniel riding just ahead of Addie as she murmured soothing words to the animal beneath her and concentrated on unerringly following her husband's trail through the swift current.

They hadn't traveled far from the rocky bank when a jagged piece of driftwood suddenly spooked the well-trained but inexperienced horse Addie had chosen to use in the crossing. The startled animal whinnied loudly and lurched sideways in the river, momentarily losing its footing and then stumbling into a sinkhole, a patch of dangerously soft sand on the river bottom.

Daniel heard his wife's strangled cry of alarm as she struggled in vain to keep from being unseated. But the current finally tore her from the horse's back as the animal thrashed about wildly in a frantic effort to regain its balance. Though Addie's fingers still clutched the reins, she was having difficulty keeping her head above water as she was carried farther out into the river.

"Addie!" yelled Daniel, yanking his own mount to a halt and swinging down from the saddle to make his way toward her. "Let go of the reins and swim!" he commanded loudly, lowering himself into the muddy water and rapidly stroking through its chilling depths with his powerful arms.

"I . . . I can't!" she gasped out, her head bobbing up and down as she desperately tried to use the reins to pull herself back to the animal, which was now striking out for the opposite bank and leading her into even deeper waters. Dave and Jesse were several yards upstream from where Addie flailed and splashed helplessly, the two of them working feverishly to prevent the skittish longhorns from panicking at all the commotion and thereby sweeping both Addie and Daniel down river with them.

"Let go!" Daniel shouted again, only a few short feet away from her now. But just when he reached out to grab hold of her, the reins were abruptly jerked from her grasp as the horse surged forward, and Addie found herself sinking beneath the surface of the river. Her lungs felt as if they would burst, and a deadly panic overtook her as she frantically battled against the undertow of the river.

When she was on the very brink of surrendering to blissful unconsciousness, Addie felt a painful tug upon her thick braids. In the next instant, she was hauled to the surface by Daniel, who lost no time in swimming back to more shallow waters with a coughing, choking Addie clamped securely against the hard, straining muscles of his body.

"Addie! Dear God, Addie, can you hear me?" her rescuer demanded, cradling her in his arms as he waded from the river, then lowering her carefully to the muddy, red-brown bank. His handsome features had taken on an ashen color, and his eyes were clouded with a terrible, heart-stopping dread.

Addie clearly heard him, but when she opened her mouth to answer, she was suddenly seized by a violent paroxysm of coughing, and her eyes filled with tears of pain as her violated lungs sought to dispel the offending water. Daniel lifted her slightly and held her tenderly until the awful fit had passed.

Finally she was able to choke out, "I . . . I . . . can't . . . swim!" Then she collapsed weakly against him. The numerous tendrils of chestnut hair which had escaped from the previously tidy braids were plastered across the smooth skin of her forehead and cheeks, her wet shirt and trousers clung to her trembling body like a second skin, and she shivered uncontrollably as a gust of wind swept across her drenched form.

"You can't swim?" he repeated in stunned disbelief before his handsome features became suffused with a dull, angry color. His eyes blazed down at her reproachfully as he thundered, "Why the hell didn't you tell me?"

"I didn't see any need to," she weakly offered, pulling herself to a sitting position as she fought against the sudden chattering of her teeth.

"Damn it, woman, you could have drowned out there!" It appeared for a moment that he would have dearly loved to have struck her, but instead he yanked her to him and held her tightly against his equally soaked chest. "Oh, Addie, Addie," he murmured in a low, resonant tone, "what am I going to do with you?"

"I like what you're doing right now," she breathlessly quipped, smiling faintly through her tears as she snuggled gratefully against the comfort of his lean muscular body. They remained like that for quite some time, oblivious to the curious stares they were receiving from the drovers on the other side of the river. Jesse and Dave had succeeded in moving the last of the herd across the river by the time Daniel finally rose and pulled Addie to her feet along with him.

"Come on. We'd better be getting ourselves across before it gets any later," he remarked, gently grasping her arm as he began approaching the nearby spot where his obedient horse stood waiting, having followed its master from the river.

"But, my mount—" protested Addie, glancing toward the opposite bank, which the exhausted animal had successfully reached.

"You're riding with me," he interrupted, effortlessly lifting her up to his horse's back. Swinging up lithely behind her, he paused to add encouragingly, "You'll be fine this time. Just hold on to the saddle horn and do as I say."

"Just don't tell me to let go and swim!" she retorted, only half teasing. Although she knew a moment's anxiety when they first rode into the river, she forced herself to remain calm. Her fingers were clenched so tightly about the saddle horn that they became numb, but she told herself that she could place all her trust in Daniel to get them safely across.

And he did get them safely across, without incident and in a surprisingly short period of time. As he dismounted on the opposite bank and reached up for his wife, she smiled softly and declared in a voice barely above a whisper, "Remind me to thank you properly for saving my life, Mr. Jordan."

"I'll see that you have the opportunity later today," he promised meaningfully, his gaze catching and holding hers as he placed his hands at her slender waist and pulled her down with almost seductive slowness. They were surrounded by some of the others a moment later, all expressing concern for Addie's well-being and offering congratulations to the trail boss for a job well done.

Dusk had fallen by the time everyone had finished a supper of fried bacon, called "overland trout" by a few of the drovers, pinto beans, boiled potatoes, and sourdough biscuits. While some of the men followed the usual custom of gathering around the crackling fire with tin cups full of strong coffee in hand, Daniel snatched up several blankets, grabbed Addie's hand, and drifted away with a deceptively casual air, moving slowly but purposefully toward an inviting shelter of trees and shrubs several hundred feet away from camp.

"What in heaven's name will the men think?" Addie questioned in a hushed tone, her face flushing in mild embarrassment as she nonetheless eagerly accompanied her husband.

"It doesn't matter any longer," asserted Daniel, grinning down at her indulgently as he led her along. "For much too long now, I've told myself that I couldn't allow them to think of you being with me in such a way. It was driving me crazy—wanting you so badly and yet not wanting the others on the drive lusting after you!"

"What changed your mind?" she asked in a tremulous voice as they reached the thick cover of trees. She watched Daniel unfold one of the blankets and float it to the ground.

His expression sobered before he answered, "It

scared the hell out of me today when I saw you go under. I love you more than life itself, Addie, and I can't bear being apart from you any longer. You're my wife, and there's simply no use in pretending I don't want to make love to you. I can't prevent wicked thoughts about you from entering the minds of those men back there, but I can make damn sure they realize you're mine and mine alone!"

"Let them think whatever they wish," she bravely proclaimed, stepping into his waiting arms and sighing contentedly as they wrapped about her, "for I care only about being with the man I love." Raising her face to his, she entwined her arms about his neck and pressed her soft curves enticingly against him, whispering an endearment before his warm lips claimed hers in a deeply passionate kiss.

The twilight soon cloaked the two lovers in semidarkness as they lay together upon one blanket and covered themselves with the other, their hastily discarded clothing tossed heedlessly to land in a tangle upon the low-lying branches swaying gently in the faint evening breeze. Naked flesh gloried in meeting naked flesh, and Addie inhaled sharply as Daniel's knowing hands began seeking out all the secret places of her womanly form.

Her eyes popped wide open when he mischievously observed, "Good thing the weather's too cool for snakes." He chuckled softly at the sudden look of trepidation crossing her beautiful countenance, and he instantly sought to make amends for his teasing remark as his lips trailed a fiery path downward from her kiss-reddened mouth to the full, rose-tipped breasts which seemed to be silently pleading for his caress.

His tongue flicked tantalizingly across the silken

globes, and his lips scorched her quivering softness before his mouth fastened about one of the exquisitely sensitive nipples. Addie's graceful fingers curled within the thickness of his golden hair, and she felt her passions spiraling as Daniel drove her to near madness when he drew the rosy bud within his warm mouth and began tenderly yet hungrily suckling, his tongue moving erotically across the delicate peak.

The leaves rustled overhead, and the darkening, cloud-filled sky allowed only a faint glimmer of silvery moonlight to touch the earth. The drovers traded yarns at the campfire, their eyes occasionally darting in the direction of the nearby trees. With the darkness the cattle quieted, and only an infrequent moaning broke the silence as the two men keeping night guard over the animals rode their opposite circles around the bedded herd of two thousand longhorns.

Addie and Daniel were happily oblivious to all these things in their mutual determination to please each other. Once Daniel's lips had practiced their dizzying, arousing techniques at Addie's breasts, they caressed and teased the rest of her wondrously feminine curves, until she suddenly decided that it was her turn to take the initative. With a boldness born of love, she pleasured her husband as never before, her lips and hands playing together across his splendid male flesh until he clenched his teeth to keep from crying out with the intensity of the passion she created in him.

"No more, you little wildcat!" he growled with mock sternness, swiftly rolling so that she was beneath him once again. His hands parted her slender thighs as his lips returned to hers, and she moaned into his mouth as his fingers danced lightly, provocatively across the very essence of her womanhood. Instinctively arching upward, she drew in her breath upon a gasp as his hand settled gently upon the triangle of chestnut curls between her thighs. The skillfulness of his long fingers soon prompted several more gasps and moans, and her yearning increased to a near painful ecstasy that caused her hands to glide demandingly over the hard muscles of his back.

When neither of them could endure any more of the rapturous anticipation, Daniel positioned himself above Addie and plunged into her welcoming softness, sheathing his maleness fully within her honeyed warmth. Matching the age-old rhythm of his movements, she clung feverishly to him as their bodies and souls blended and soared in perfect unison, her soft cries urging him onward until she was seized by such a forceful, all-consuming sensation of fulfillment that she was left breathless and weak and stunned.

Daniel, too, had experienced an unbelievably satisfying completeness, and he fought to regain his breath as he rolled to his back and pulled her pliant form against him. Both of them were coated with a thin sheen of perspiration, and he solicitously tugged the blanket over Addie's bare shoulders as he lovingly pillowed her head upon his gold-matted chest. They were content to remain still in the immediate aftermath of their awe-inspiring intimacy, and several minutes passed before Daniel finally broke the silence.

"Addie?" he murmured, his voice holding more than a trace of huskiness, his gray eyes glowing with tenderness. "Tell me what you're thinking, my love." A soft sigh escaped her lips as she snuggled even closer, delighting in the feel of his hard-muscled body against her.

"I was wishing that it could always be this way

between us," she replied, smiling as he swept a wayward curl from her face.

"It will be," he confidently asserted, "and even better."

"Oh, Daniel. Why can't we always get along so well? Must it only be when we're together like this that we're not at cross-purposes?" she wondered aloud, an unmistakably plaintive note in her low voice.

"It shouldn't be," he stated with a sigh of his own. "And I think it's high time the two of us came to some sort of agreement."

"You know, you haven't exactly been charming to me these past several days!" Addie teasingly accused.

"And you, dearest Adelaide, have been a real pain in the—"

"Daniel!" A quiet rumble of laughter shook his broad chest, and Addie smiled despite herself. Growing serious again, she asked, "You don't really want a wife who sits at home with her knitting, do you? I mean, wouldn't you much rather have a woman who will work beside you, who will be a helpmate and a companion and a lover and—"

"That's quite some woman you're describing," he interrupted with another low chuckle. Pressing a soft kiss upon the top of her head, he hugged her before admitting, "Yes, my love, I want you to be all those things. Actually, I think I've realized that our life together won't be the way I want it to be unless you're happy, and I know good and well you'll never be the type of wife who's content to confine herself to household chores."

"I'll cook and clean and sew for you, Daniel, but I also want to play an active role in the running of the ranch, just as I always have. Even before my father's death, I was more at home out on the range than in the kitchen. I . . . I promise to try to be whatever you want me to be, but I just want you to understand that I can't change entirely."

"Nor would I want you to." He rose up slightly so that he could face her in the semidarkness of the April night, his fingers tracing the smooth contours of her jaw. "I love you just the way you are, Addie Caton Jordan, and I'll always love you. Even if you remain the most hardheaded, disobedient, temperamental—"

"Then you're not still angry with me for coming along on the drive?" she broke in, her hazel eyes widening as they met his adoring gaze.

"I suppose I should be," he answered with a sudden frown. Then his brow cleared in the next second as he added, "But I'm not. How can I remain angry with a woman who offers to cook and clean and sew for me, and who is such a delectable tigress when she's in my arms?"

"If you play your cards right, my darling husband, I might even consent to bearing children as well!"

"And shall we teach all our daughters the wide variety of skills their beautiful mother possesses?"

"Of course. And our sons as well." She gasped in delight as he sank back down and masterfully pulled her atop him.

"Let's just make certain they learn some of their father's skills as well," he murmured, his fingers entwining within her gleaming mass of chestnut hair as he pulled her head lower before adding, "such as swimming." His lips silenced the defiant retort on the tip of her tongue, and soon there was no further need for words between them.

Twenty-Two

As they left the protection of the law of the state of Texas and trailed the herd deeper into Indian Territory—the vast stretch of prairie and mountain land settled by the Cherokee, Comanche, Creeks, Chickasaw, and others—the drovers became increasingly watchful. The Indians raised crops and cattle of their own, and there was no way of knowing how they would react to the trail drive's crossing the untamed countryside.

The good weather finally came to an end a week beyond the Red River. The heavens turned gray and dismal, and the air became laden with moisture. The cattle seemed to plod along with excruciating slowness, which prompted Addie to consider wishing that something would happen to break the awful monotony. Little did she know that such a wish would become reality that very day.

"At least we haven't had any trouble finding water so far," Daniel commented absently, his gaze moving speculatively across the broad expanse of fertile grasslands before traveling briefly upward to the darkening afternoon sky. "We'll be lucky if we're not caught in a downpour before sunset."

"It certainly smells like rain, doesn't it?" agreed Addie, tugging the hat from her head and reveling in the feel of the strengthening wind whipping through the mass of hair tumbling to her shoulders.

"Don't do that," her husband sternly admonished, his fingers tightening imperceptibly upon the reins as he guided his mount a trifle closer to hers.

"Why not?" she impulsively challenged.

"Two reasons. First off, I don't want the men to see you looking so blatantly feminine and desirable! And secondly, it's quite possible we're being watched. I don't want to issue such an irresistible invitation to some young brave who'll decide he'd like to add you to his collection of wives."

"Quite a few tribes are monogamous," she pointed out with a mocking smile, nevertheless twisting her hair back up and securing it beneath her hat.

"Perhaps, but seeing you just might encourage one of those hot-blooded warriors to change his whole way of thinking!" quipped Daniel, amusement flickering briefly over his face. "In any case, stay close to me. It's wisest to anticipate trouble before it occurs."

"Do you really believe we'll encounter trouble then? I thought this was supposed to be a time of peace," responded Addie with a pensive frown. Although she and Daniel were well ahead of the herd, she was vaguely aware of the muffled thudding of hooves and clatter of horns behind them. She pulled the edges of her long coat closer together in an attempt to ward off the dampness which threatened to chill her.

"Peace or not, most Indians are entirely unpredictable—especially the Comanches," he grimly replied.

It was as if his words had been a subtle foreshadowing of things to come, for less than an hour later they spotted a large group of riders bearing down on them, having materialized, it seemed, out of thin air. Daniel and Addie simultaneously reined about and headed back toward the herd, with Daniel issuing the signal for the men to decrease the rather sluggish pace of the longhorns even further.

Addie's eyes widened as the horsemen neared and she was afforded a glimpse of their half-naked, smooth-skinned, masculine forms. Clad only in laced buckskin trousers and moccasins, their bronzed faces—all but one unpainted—wore particularly unsettling expressions of purposefulness. As they drew closer, she could see the harsh, intense light in their brown eyes, and she suddenly felt a tremor of fear coursing through her body.

There were nearly two dozen of them, and each young Comanche brave brandished a rifle in his hand. Their raven hair was unbraided and flowed wildly about their hard-muscled shoulders, and a thin strap of leather encircled each of their foreheads, from which hung a single feather. While it was immediately apparent that they had not come to engage the drovers in battle, it soon also became clear that they had not come with totally peaceful intentions, either.

Daniel motioned for Addie to stay put beside Clay and Billy, then he rode forward to meet the group with an outward air of unconcern. The young Comanches slowed to a halt as the white man approached, their leader—the only one wearing a streak of bright red paint along each high cheekbone—raising his hand in a gesture of peace as Daniel drew up opposite him.

"You speak the white man's tongue?" asked Daniel, his voice steady and sure, his steely gaze unwavering as he faced the young brave, who could not have been more than eighteen or nineteen years of age. The Comanche nodded curtly in response. The others were in a single line behind him, their guns held in obvious readiness. "We are here in peace. We seek nothing more than to take our cattle across your land," asserted Daniel. His own gun remained holstered, though he knew he could withdraw it with lightning-quick speed if the situation demanded it.

"Your cattle ruin our crops and leave our land barren," the young man charged in a low, guttural tone. "You must pay."

"What is it you want in payment?" He had expected this, having heard rumors to the effect that some tribes were demanding as much as ten cents a head for the drives seeking to cross the Territory. They couldn't afford to pay in cash, Daniel told himself, but there was a good chance the Indians would accept a few head of stock instead. It was worth a try.

"Gold. You must pay for each animal in your herd."

"We have no gold. But we could part with some of our cattle."

"How many?" came the expected question.

"Oh, say half a dozen," suggested Daniel. He knew there was no benefit in fighting against the toll, for it was entirely lawful. The land was theirs.

"And what else will you give in payment?" the Comanche demanded scornfully, his fingers tightening upon the rifle as he stiffened on his horse. The eyes of each Indian were fastened expectantly on Daniel. In the near distance, Addie waited in breathless anticipation, desperately wishing she could hear what was being said.

"We have nothing else to give," he insisted, his gaze unflinching as the young brave's countenance grew even more savage. The Comanche nodded to the spot behind Daniel where Addie waited.

"You have a woman! We will take her as well."

"No. She is my wife, my woman," Daniel firmly countered, shaking his head. "She cannot be included in the payment. Take the cattle I have offered you and let us go in peace." Damn! he swore inwardly. He had known that Addie's presence was going to cause trouble sooner or later. And though he realized that she could not be faulted for being such a beautiful young female, he suddenly wished nevertheless that she weren't so distractingly well formed!

"I will buy her from you," decreed the Comanche.

"She is not for sale."

"I could kill you and take her!" the young brave fiercely asserted.

"Maybe you could," Daniel lazily drawled, the merest hint of a smile on his face, "but I don't think you'll try. I've always heard that the Comanches are people of honor. What honor can there be in murdering a man and stealing his wife?"

The other man appeared to hesitate at that, his brown eyes glowing as he waged a silent battle with himself. Daniel waited, his whole body tensing imperceptibly as he stared across at his youthful adversary. Several moments passed before the Comanche unexpectedly raised his arm and shouted a command. Then he abruptly guided his horse about and galloped swiftly away, the other Indians following in his wake. Daniel watched them go, a deepening frown forming on his face.

When he finally returned to Addie's side, he was met with an anxious look from his wife as she asked, "What did they want?"

"Payment for crossing their land," he replied in a preoccupied manner. Momentarily turning to Clay and Billy, he instructed them to resume their positions and quicken the pace of the herd as much as possible. Once they had gone, he urged his mount into an easy canter and resumed his own position ahead of the herd.

"What sort of payment?" Addie persisted, riding close beside him once more.

"They asked for gold, but I offered them some of our stock."

"And did they accept your offer?"

"No." He paused briefly, another frown on his face as he contemplated the disquieting situation. "But they left before making any further demands. Except for one."

"What was it?" she insisted, growing impatient at his obvious reluctance to enlighten her about the episode.

"Their leader wanted you as part of the payment. And when I refused, he offered to buy you from me."

"He . . . he did?" she stammered in shocked amazement. Her eyes mirrored the horror which was slowly dawning on her. "What . . . what did you tell him?"

"What the devil do you think I told him?" Daniel sardonically retorted, still engrossed in thoughts of what he viewed as the Comanche's dangerously puzzling behavior. However, he forced a smile to his lips as he glanced at her and wickedly teased, "Come to think of it, maybe I was a bit rash in my decision. After all, I might have been able to bargain for three or four damned good horses—"

"Is that so?" Addie interrupted in mock outrage. "Well, I might have been tempted to go with him had I known of his offer! Perhaps he would truly appreciate a woman of my caliber!" Her husband chuckled softly in response, but the playful humor between them soon evaporated. Addie could tell that Daniel was still quite concerned about the incident, and she felt her own apprehension mounting as afternoon drifted into evening.

It was just after dusk when the rain came, the bulging gray clouds releasing a veritable torrent upon the grateful earth. But the trail drivers felt no gratitude, for their tasks were made much more difficult by the soaking downpour. The cattle milled restlessly, and a cursing, complaining Slim did his best to prepare a semblance of a meal for the several men and one woman whose hunger still waited to be appeased. An extra man had been assigned to the night watch, leaving the others to make camp underneath the sparse shelter of a canvas tarpaulin stretched outward from the chuck wagon and held aloft by two rough-hewn poles.

"We been lucky not to get any rain before now," Jesse idly observed, squatting closer to the fire that he and three others were attempting to shield from the wind and rain. Even though everyone wore long, waterproof jackets, it was impossible to remain totally dry in the sheeting wetness that filled the air.

"You think them Comanches are gonna try anythin' in weather like this?" Fletcher quietly asked Daniel. The two of them were standing beside the chuck wagon, their hands clutching steaming tin cups of the strong, bitter brew that Slim called coffee. Slim had actually accepted Addie's offer of assistance, and she was doing her best to mix up a batch of corn bread near the rear of the wagon.

"Hell, man, you think rain will stop any damned Indian from takin' what he wants?" Trent startled the group by rasping out in a low voice edged with scorn. He met Addie's wide-eyed gaze as she looked at him in surprise. Trent stood just within the shelter of the tarpaulin, and Addie was struck by the unfathomable warning his dark, piercing eyes seemed to flash before he turned back around and stared outward over the drenched, puddle-ridden landscape.

"There's no use in trying to second-guess them," opined Daniel, casting only a brief, dismissing glance in Trent's direction. "But, particularly until we reach the Canadian River, we'll have to post an extra man on the night watch. It's my intent to prevent the loss of even one head of stock, though I'll be the first one to admit such a thing is next to impossible."

"You ever had any dealin's with Indians before, Jordan?" Fletcher mildly questioned, draining the last bit of coffee in his cup and stepping to the fire to fetch more.

"Yes. I was stationed at Fort Laramie before the war. But that certainly doesn't make me an expert," he ruefully admitted, meeting Addie's eyes and flashing her a quick, albeit tender smile. "To be on the safe side, we'll post a guard here at the camp as well. I'll take the

424

first watch."

A short time later Slim gruffly announced that supper, such as it was, was ready and that if he heard so much as one remark about the rather soggy food he'd toss the entire meal out in the rain. His threats were met with mumbled, almost unintelligible comments and accompanying snickers, and Addie couldn't help but smile at the burly cook as he favored the men with a ferocious scowl.

By morning, not a single trace of such playful humor remained. It had been a long and miserable night, and none of the drovers had rested well during the endless hours of the storm. Those bearing the most obvious ill effects were the members of the night watch, who were exhausted and soaked to the skin by the time the first light of dawn appeared. The rain had dissipated, having tapered off into nothing more than a faint drizzle, but there was an even sharper reminder of the night's downpour than the telltale mud and swollen creeks.

There were more than a dozen longhorns missing. And none of the men who had maintained the nighttime vigil over the herd could explain the animals' disappearance.

"You're sure you didn't see or hear anything out of the ordinary?" Daniel reiterated, his expression thoughtful and concerned as he shifted a bit in the saddle.

"No, sir," Clay unhesitatingly responded. "Me and Billy took the opposite positions, while Dave here stood guard a short ways away. It was rainin' so hard, we couldn't hardly see one another, but we still didn't see nothin' or no one that could've gotten hold of them cattle."

"It was rainin' mighty hard," affirmed Dave, his own features looking quite troubled. "But I still don't see how that many head could disappear right from under our noses!"

"I can't understand how those Comanches were able to steal away before either me or Clay caught sight of them," observed Billy, shaking his head. Glancing up to meet Daniel's steely gaze, he asked, "You do think they were the ones who did it, don't you?"

"I'd say it was a fairly safe assumption," he replied. Replacing his hat atop his head, he tightened his slack hold upon the reins and said, "It appears that they were perfectly willing to take advantage of last night's storm—which is just as well for us, since their usual methods involve creating a stampede. We'll take the herd as far as we can today, then set up an extra guard tonight. It could be that they've taken what they wanted and won't bother us again," he finished, but his last remark was uttered with a noticeable lack of conviction. He fully anticipated further trouble, and he was well aware of the fact that the Comanches had apparently embarked upon some sort of game, since they easily could have inflicted a lot more damage upon the drive. It was best to be prepared for another visitation, he mentally concluded as he reined about and moved to take his place ahead of the herd.

The men remained warily attentive during their watches for the next two nights, but nothing happened. Addie couldn't help noticing that there was a certain unrest in the air, and she voiced her own increasing

426

apprehensions to Daniel on the third night following the rustling episode.

"You don't truly believe we're out of danger yet, do you?" she asked him. The two of them were enjoying a quiet moment together as they walked about the perimeter of the camp. The gathering twilight surrounded them with a welcome coolness, and the cloudless sky was aglow with the last rays of the setting sun.

"I'm not sure," he confided honestly. Reaching for her hand, he squeezed it in a gesture of encouragement. "You know, Addie, we've been pretty fortunate so far. And I must admit," he added with a teasing grin, his eyes sparkling down at her with loving devilment apparent in their gray depths, "you've made one hell of a drover!"

"Did you expect anything less of me?" she countered with an expression of mock hauteur. Her lovely countenance grew serious then as she sighed and remarked, "I wish we could be alone tonight. I . . . I can't seem to shake this feeling that something's going to happen. As you said, we've been fortunate so far. But good fortune can't last forever."

"Maybe not. That's why we're going to try to be prepared for anything. I know the extra duty is hard on the men, but it will pay off." They had reached the spot where the horses were staked, and Addie stepped forward to deliver soothing pats along Twister's neck. Daniel's face wore a faint smile and his eyes softened lovingly as he watched her. "You know, I've heard there's a hotel of sorts at Fort Gibson. I thought you might be looking forward to a hot bath and a real bed for a change."

"I'd even be grateful for the opportunity to bathe in a muddy pond at this point!" she insisted, heaving another sigh. "I'll certainly be glad when you think it's safe enough for me to do more than take a sponge bath behind the chuck wagon. I'm as willing to accept hardship and inconvenience as the men, but I must confess to a feminine proclivity for cleanliness!" He chuckled quietly at that, and Addie impulsively launched herself at his broad chest and stood on tiptoe to entwine her arms about his neck.

"What's all this about?" he demanded, at the same time happy to oblige by enfolding her within his warm embrace.

"You have an eminently seductive laugh, Mr. Jordan. Far be it for me to try to resist!" she huskily declared, punctuating her words with tiny kisses along his chiseled jawline.

"Blast it, woman, you have the worst sense of timing," he groaned, valiantly fighting against his rising desire.

"What do you mean?" she innocently queried, her even, white teeth nipping provocatively at his lips.

"I'm on watch with the herd tonight!" he gruffly reminded her, his handsome features tightening as he gently but firmly set her away from him. His hands remained upon her shoulders as he peered down into her visibly disappointed countenance. "Even if I weren't, it's simply too dangerous for the two of us to try to be alone right now. Until those Comanches make another move—"

"So you do believe they're going to try something else," Addie murmured, her eyes wide and clouded with returning anxiety.

"I do. And I want you to stay close to camp, understand? No matter what happens, you stay put," Daniel sternly decreed.

"I have a gun and I know how to use it, probably better than any of the others!" she stubbornly declared.

"I have very little doubt that you're a dead shot, my darling wildcat, but just remember that those Indians weren't attempting to buy any of the other drovers!" He released her shoulders, and took hold of her arm as he began striding back to camp, oblivious of the fact that Addie moved somewhat stiffly beside him. After leaning down to quickly brush her cheek with his lips, he was gone, leaving her to stand staring after him, a decidedly exasperated look on her face.

Joe Rourke had been assigned to stand guard over the camp that night, and he diligently took his place alongside the chuck wagon as the others sought what little rest the hard ground had to offer. The scant light of the quarter moon was obscured by a new covering of billowy white clouds moving in from the west, and the countryside was thrown into almost total darkness as the campfire burned down into a pile of softly glowing embers.

It was well after midnight when Addie awoke with a start. Lying still upon her bedroll, she listened carefully, hearing Twister's unmistakable whinny a moment later. Her gaze immediately flew toward Joe, who sat slumped upon the ground, his rifle still clasped in his hands, his youthful features relaxed in a dreamless slumber.

Addie eased herself upright, and her eyes quickly adjusted to the darkness as they scanned the surrounding area. The men were apparently still asleep, and she hesitated about her next course of action. Endeavoring to convince herself that the mere whinnying of a horse was not a cause for concern, she nevertheless felt a certain uneasiness, an uneasiness that increased when she detected the animal's seemingly frightened snorting.

It was then that she heard the plaintive howl of a lone coyote in the near distance. Breathing an inward sigh of relief, she smiled to herself, musing that the coyote must have made Twister nervous. Climbing stealthily to her feet, she bent down to tug on her boots, then she snatched up her gun and headed toward the remuda, intent upon reassuring her horse and making certain that the coyote didn't move in too close.

"It's all right, boy," she whispered, stepping closer to where Twister pawed anxiously at the ground. As she reached out to touch him, her arm was suddenly grabbed and twisted behind her back and the gun wrenched from her hand before a bronzed, lean-muscled arm seized her about the waist. Instinctively opening her mouth to scream, she felt her breath cut off as a hand clamped itself securely across the lower half of her face and pressed against her parted lips with bruising force.

Addie struggled wildly against the man who held her captive, but her struggles abruptly ceased when she heard his guttural voice muttering close to her ear, "I will kill you if you scream!" There was no doubt in her mind that the Indian would carry out his cold-blooded threat if she chose to defy him. Her mind was racing, her heart pounding, but she forced herself to remain calm. Rapidly deciding that it was best to cooperate for the moment, she nodded against his hand to indicate her surrender. She was aware of her captor's identity even before he spun her about to face him and menacingly pressed the sharp point of his knife against the vulnerable pulse at the base of her throat.

"Wha . . . what do you want?" she hoarsely whispered, raising her chin in an unconscious gesture of bravado in spite of the sheer terror which threatened to paralyze her. Her gaze met his squarely, though she inwardly blanched at the malevolent gleam in his eyes.

"You will come with me," the Comanche leader commanded, his own voice scarcely audible, but his meaning quite clear. Withdrawing a long, thick piece of leather from the top edge of his buckskin trousers, he jerked Addie closer and tied the leather strip across her mouth, effectively silencing any screams of warning she might have been courageous, or foolhardy, enough to emit. That done, he spun her back around and knotted a piece of the rawhide about her wrists, then forced her about to face him again. "You are my woman now!" he fiercely proclaimed, bending lithely downward to lift her high and toss her over his shoulder like a sack of meal.

Addie closed her eyes in a silent prayer, fighting against the panic starting to overtake her. She was carried to the Comanche's horse and tossed unceremoniously across the animal's bare back. Although she found herself lying face-down, she had caught a brief glimpse of the Comanche's numerous companions, who had been in the process of stealing the remuda before she had arrived on the scene. Now, however, it appeared that their leader felt they had captured a much better prize, and he gave the signal for them to leave the horses and follow him as he urged his mount forward and took flight, riding swiftly away from the camp with his prisoner bouncing uncomfortably before him.

Addie now prayed fervently that someone had seen or heard the Indians, that Joe had perhaps awakened and discovered her empty bedroll, that something, anything would make Daniel aware of what was happening. Dear God, she desperately pleaded, her eyes filling with hot, anguished tears, please help me! Please help me know what to do! Please help Daniel find me before it's too late!

Later recalling that the Lord does indeed work in mysterious ways, Addie could hardly believe what happened next. Her captor suddenly kicked his horse into a gallop and headed directly toward the spot where the herd was settled for the night. He seemed to be totally unconcerned with the danger awaiting him and his companions as he raised his voice to a blood-curdling yell and brandished his rifle above his head. The others did the same, which succeeded in prompting the sea of frightened cattle to rise in one quick, graceful motion and rumble to life.

Daniel was the first to catch sight of the Indians as the stampede began. He drew his pistol and roared, "All hands and the cook!"

The longhorns moved with surprising speed, their hooves pounding and their horns clashing as they thundered across the darkened land, but the trail boss was more concerned with the Comanche leader and his captive, for he now realized that it was Addie whom the Indian held.

Daniel's heart seemed to stop for a split second. As the drovers stumbled through the dark to mount their horses and make a blind dash toward the running herd, he turned his own mount to give chase to the fleeing Comanches. While his men spurred hard to catch up with the steers leading the stampede, Daniel closed the gap between himself and the Indians, oblivious to the danger of his chase as he sought to rescue Addie.

Addie, meanwhile, could see her husband drawing nearer and nearer, and any fear for herself gave way to fear for Daniel's safety, for she knew he would stand little chance against so many. The drovers were totally occupied with trying to stop the pounding charge of the cattle, and there was no way of knowing if any of them were even aware of what was taking place a short distance away.

Without pausing to reconsider, Addie resolutely decided to make what she knew was a desperate, extremely risky bid for freedom. If it worked, and if she wasn't killed, then perhaps the Comanches would abandon all thought of taking her captive, and perhaps Daniel wouldn't be faced with the deadly prospect of single-handedly battling nearly two dozen Indians. She could see no other way out of this predicament.

Silently uttering one last prayer, she jerked her entire body backward. It all happened so quickly that the startled Comanche could only watch in astonishment as she threw herself toward the grassy earth. The horse was traveling at a full gallop, and Addie felt a sickening moment of panic as she slipped from the animal's back and her legs made forceful contact with the hard ground. The landing jolted her more than she had believed possible, and the breath was knocked from her body as she rolled and rolled, the rocks and dirt tearing into her exposed skin.

Finally, she lay stunned and only half-conscious. She was dimly aware of Daniel bending over her a few moments later and his anxiously examining her for any broken bones. The strip of leather about her mouth had been removed and her hands untied.

"Addie? Addie, answer me!" he was urgently demanding.

"Are they . . . are they gone?" she gasped out, wincing with the pain of a thousand bruises.

"For now," he answered with a curt nod. Helping her into a sitting position, he scowled and muttered a savage oath. "Damn it, Addie, you could have killed yourself!" He didn't give her time to answer, however, before he tenderly lifted her in his strong arms and carried her to his horse. Carefully placing her in the saddle, he mounted behind her and drew her back against his comforting hardness.

"Do you think they'll come back?" she questioned, unable to fight back the tears stinging against her eyelids.

"We can't wait to find out." He was filled with a murderous rage as he viewed the myriad of scratches and reddening bruises on her beautiful, dirt-streaked face, but he forced himself to think only of getting her safely back to camp. Quite shaken at the realization that the Comanches had very nearly succeeded in abducting her, Daniel tightened his hold upon her as he reined about and headed back toward the deserted campsite.

The drovers had finally managed to turn the longhorns after a chase of three terrifying miles. The cattle had begun to circle and mill, but there had been a particularly anxious moment when young Lee Burnett had become trapped amongst the jammed animals. The men knew well that there had been times when a horseman had been jostled from his mount to fall beneath the crush of hooves, leaving his comrades to find nothing afterward but the unfortunate man's gun. Lee, however, was lucky, emerging from the dangerous situation with only a severe case of strained nerves. But nearly half a dozen calves had been trampled to death during the melee, and the exhausted men returned to camp to recount the details to their trail boss.

Addie found herself surrounded by solicitous well-wishers as she lay near the rekindled fire. She was really quite touched by the men's display of concern for her welfare, and she was tempted to laugh aloud at their expressions of almost ludicrous amazement when Daniel related the tale of her capture and daring escape.

Most of all, however, she had been touched by Daniel's love and kindness during the short time the two of them had been alone. He had tenderly bathed her cuts and scratches, and he had cradled her soothingly in his lap and rocked her as the aftereffects of her terrifying ordeal took hold and she sobbed as helplessly as any babe. Though, too, he had chastised her repeatedly for endangering her life by throwing herself from the Indian's horse, his tone had been contrarily gentle.

They received another visit from the Comanches the following morning. It appeared that the Indians had come in peace, since they did not make a point of displaying their guns and their leader rode alone to meet with Daniel, who instructed his own men to remain watchful as he kept a tight rein on his explosive temper and rode forward to speak with the man he held responsible for Addie's injuries.

"You may go in peace now," the young Comanche unexpectedly announced, his gaze meeting Daniel's squarely.

"Why have you changed your mind?" Daniel demanded, eyeing the adversary with visible distrust. It was all he could do to control the vengeful impulse to issue a challenge to the man, though he was well aware of the fact that if he surrendered to the temptation he would only be placing Addie in further danger.

"Your woman is brave. She was unafraid. She valued her freedom above her life. Because of this, we will allow you to go in peace." Daniel initially wondered if this was some new trick, but he quickly decided that the Comanche was in earnest. After all, he reflected, they'd had every opportunity to start a war before now. It seemed that they were no more eager for bloodshed than the trail drivers.

He said nothing in response, merely nodding once to indicate that he had heard and understood the Indian's words. The young Comanche paused for a moment, and his gaze wandered briefly toward the spot where Addie stood beside Slim before he turned his mount and rode away, his back straight and rigid, his shoulders squared in a manner which bespoke an inherent dignity.

"What did they want?" Addie was the first to ask when Daniel returned to the group, whose breakfast had been interrupted by the Comanches' appearance.

"We can fight if need be, Mr. Jordan!" avowed Dave as several of the others nodded in agreement.

"There'll be no need for that," Daniel revealed, turning back to Addie with a slow smile curving his lips. "It seems they were impressed with your courage, my love. Because of that, they've decided not to bother us again."

"You mean simply because I—" Addie started to remark in disbelief, only to have Slim interrupt.

"Yes sir. Next time any of us has trouble with them bastards, we got to remember the best thing to do is just what Miz Jordan here done—fall off the damned horse!" There was an explosion of raucous laughter from the men, and Addie could feel her face coloring rosily.

"I didn't fall off!" she protested indignantly. Her flashing gaze flew to Daniel, who had now traitorously joined in the laughter. She could no longer suppress a grudging smile, for she realized that they were treating her as an equal. She had read the admiration in their eyes, and it was with an inward sigh of mingled gratitude and relief that she willingly accepted the dubious honor of their comradeship.

Twenty-Three

Fort Gibson represented the approximate halfway point for the eleven men and one woman driving the herd of longhorns from Fort Worth to Sedalia. Having already crossed the Canadian and Arkansas Rivers, they were now within a week of the Missouri border. As the weather had grown warmer, their troubles with the herd had increased. There had been too many nights of lightning and rain, which had filled the air with tension and had intensified the ever-present danger of a stampede. Hailstorms, which presented quite an alarming hazard to the men and beasts out on the virtually treeless prairie, had become even more of a possibility. Water, once in plentiful supply, had now become harder to find, but at least this situation had provided Daniel with the opportunity to make shrewd use of the cattle's thirst, since the animals moved along at an even brisker pace whenever they sensed water ahead.

Just as Daniel had heard, there was indeed "a hotel of sorts" awaiting Addie at Fort Gibson. It was a decidedly ramshackle edifice, but it offered a great deal more comfort than she had known in the past several weeks, and so it was with rapidly growing anticipation that she allowed the proprietor's wife to lead her up the stairs to her room. The first thing Addie did was to order up a hot bath, and her eyes feasted upon the rough wooden tub as if it were a thing of absolute beauty.

"Your husband gonna be joinin' you later?" the proprietor's wife inquired conversationally as she filled the tub with buckets of water she had fetched from downstairs. She was a slender woman, perhaps ten years older than Addie.

"I hope so." Daniel had escorted her into Fort Gibson to make sure she was settled at the hotel, then he had returned to the location just outside of town where the herd would remain quartered for a day or two. It was the first time either Addie or the men had been allowed a respite from their trail-driving chores, and it was a very welcome break for all. She felt a tremor of excitement when she recalled the way Daniel had announced that, barring any unforeseen trouble, he would join her at the hotel before nightfall.

"You a newlywed?" the other woman asked, closely scrutinizing Addie's noticeably joyful features.

"In a way," Addie responded with a rather secretive smile.

As the proprietor's wife left the younger woman to her bath and trudged back downstairs with the last of the buckets, she shook her head, asking herself how anyone could be newly married *in a way*. Either she was or she wasn't, the woman mentally determined, which meant that, in all likelihood, the girl upstairs wasn't yet wed to the man who had brought her to the hotel that afternoon. But, she concluded with a sigh, it wasn't any of her business. All that truly mattered was that the girl's man had been willing to pay good money for the room!

Addie was happily ignorant of the other woman's assumption as she took up the cake of lye soap and scrubbed every inch of her skin until it was pink and glowing. It took her some time to wash her long hair, but she considered the result well worth the effort when the chestnut tresses were finally clean and damply curling about her face and shoulders. She lay back against the tub, luxuriating in the feel of the warm, soothing liquid as she closed her eyes and floated blissfully in the soapy water.

The water had turned cold by the time she stood up and briskly toweled herself dry. Hurrying over to the saddlebags she had tossed near the iron bedstead, she unbuckled one of them and withdrew the single dress she had impulsively packed. It was a simple blue calico, but she knew that it was a far sight prettier than her attire of the past several weeks. She vigorously shook out a few of the wrinkles before tugging the gown over her head and settling it into place on her womanly curves. Then she brushed the tangles from her sun-streaked locks and coiled them into a chignon, securing the becoming hairstyle with a handful of pins she had also thought to include with the dress. After donning a pair of soft, kidskin slippers, she took a seat on the bed to wait, hoping that Daniel wouldn't be delayed much longer.

Less than half an hour later a knock sounded at the door. Addie leapt from the bed and raced to answer it, but her face took on a crestfallen appearance when she found that it was the proprietor's wife who stood in the narrow, dimly lit hallway.

"I was wonderin' if you'd be wantin' any supper," the woman said, only the ghost of a smile on her rather severe countenance as her eyes took note of Addie's vastly altered appearance.

"No, thank you. I . . . I think I'll wait until my husband comes."

"The night's approachin'. It's not real safe to travel after dark," she pointed out. "If you should change your mind about supper, I'll be happy to set somethin' aside for you."

"No, thank you," Addie repeated, forcing a smile of gratitude to her lips. She slowly closed the door as the woman turned and left. Wandering aimlessly toward the single window, she stared down upon the dusty street below, her fingers distractedly fidgeting with the faded gingham curtains hanging on either side of the streaked glass.

A sudden motion caught her eye. She glimpsed several men moving about in the semidarkness below, but there was one man in particular who drew her attention. He was standing across the street near one of the brightly lit saloons, and his hat rested low over his face as he lifted a cigarette to his lips and leisurely struck a match. Addie was certain he was familiar to her, though she wasn't afforded a clear view of his features before he turned and sauntered back inside the noisy, crowded saloon.

An instant later another knock sounded at the door, and her lovely countenance radiated a smile of deep pleasure when her eyes beheld the identity of her tall visitor. "Daniel! I was beginning to wonder if you were going to make it at all!" she happily declared, tugging him firmly inside as he merely laughed softly at her impatience.

"I'm sorry to be so late, but we had a little trouble with the herd," he offered by way of explanation, then lost no time in removing his hat and tossing it negligently upon the bed. As he turned back to his wife, his appreciative gaze swept rapidly up and down her undeniably feminine form. Flashing her a teasing grin, he said, "I thought I was to meet my wife here. But, on closer inspection, I think you'll do just as well!"

"It hasn't been all that long since you saw me in a dress!" she saucily retorted, her eyes shining with the promise of passion as he moved closer and closer. "Oh Daniel, it seems like ages since we've been together like this!" Her slender arms wrapped themselves about his neck as he pulled her tightly against him, and his lips claimed hers in a tender kiss that swiftly grew in intensity. His hands traveled downward to her rounded hips, and he lifted her higher into his inflamed embrace as his mouth virtually ravished the willing softness of hers.

"I'm looking forward to making love to you in a real bed again," he commented rather huskily, freeing her lips just long enough for him to lift her in his arms and carry her purposefully toward the iron bedstead. Their desire-filled gazes met and locked as he lowered her to the quilt and gently placed his own body atop hers.

"You might at least take off your boots, Mr. Jordan," Addie lovingly taunted, her slippered feet making contact with his leather-clad ones.

"Later," retorted Daniel with a low chuckle, his knowing hands already working their sensuous magic upon her trembling curves. Addie moaned quietly, and liquid fire coursed through her veins as Daniel's lips descended upon hers once more while his long fingers stroked and explored her softness through the thin layer of calico.

Suddenly, she was aware of a sensation of breathlessness that had nothing to do with their lovemaking, and her eyes widened in horror as they fluttered open and saw that the room was rapidly filling with dense, blinding smoke. Daniel abruptly released her and rose to his feet beside the bed, his hands reaching downward to quickly haul her up before him. She was already beginning to cough with the choking thickness of the air, and she raised eyes full of terror to her husband's face.

"Daniel! Dear God, the . . . the hotel's on fire!"

"Stand back!" he ordered, hastily pushing her away from the window near the bed. The smoke continued to pour into the room with deadly speed, until it became increasingly difficult for them to see each other. Daniel attempted to open the single window but cursed when he discovered the lock jammed. Following an instinct for survival that had replaced all other thoughts, he took up the only chair in the room and sent it crashing through the glass, then used his booted foot to kick away the slivers of glass remaining about the weathered frame. Addie had just enough time to snatch up her saddlebags before he grasped her shoulder and yanked her toward him, lifting her in his strong arms. His own breathing was ragged and punctuated with coughs as he gasped out, "We'll have to jump!" She nodded to indicate that she had understood, for her coughs had become so violent now that she could not speak.

Daniel placed Addie upon the window sill, lowering her as far as he could with one arm before instructing her to let go and jump. She hesitated only the fraction of a second before relaxing her grip upon his arm, landing with a jolt upon the dusty street, her legs buckling beneath her, her skirts flying up about her knees as she lay sprawled on the ground. Immediately turning her tear-filled gaze upward, she breathed an audible sigh of relief when she saw Daniel agilely jump from the window and land in the street a few feet away.

"Addie! Are you all right?" he hoarsely demanded, getting to his feet and hurrying to her side.

"Yes," she managed to rasp out, still fighting back the violent coughing which plagued her. Daniel bent down and lifted her up beside him, holding her against him thankfully as he peered upward at the heavy smoke streaming through the broken window. A crowd was now beginning to gather in the street in front of the hotel. The proprietor and his wife, sleeping downstairs, had finally become aware of what was happening above them and now hurried to make sure the hotel was evacuated.

Daniel pressed a quick kiss upon Addie's forehead, then headed back inside the narrow wooden building to aid a group of men who were trying to extinguish the fire. When they emerged a relatively short time later, they brought with them the astonishing report that the fire had apparently, and quite mysteriously, started right outside Addie's room, and that they had managed to control it before it had done any major damage to the other rooms. The hallway and the room where

Addie and Daniel had been, however, bore the damaging effects of the fire. The door had been burned clean through, and the flames had been spreading across the wooden floor to the bed when the men had successfully conquered the blaze. Everyone agreed that the young couple had been very lucky to have escaped unharmed.

"You and Miz Jordan all right?" asked Fletcher, striding toward them just as Daniel rejoined Addie in the street. Several of the drovers had been allowed to accompany the trail boss into town that evening, while those left on duty with the herd would have their chance for relaxation the following night. The first thing the men had done was head for the saloons, where they had been shocked a few minutes ago to hear the startling news that the only hotel in town, where they knew Addie was staying, was on fire.

Daniel merely nodded in response, hugging Addie close. Fletcher, Dave, Jesse, and Lee expressed relief for the Jordans' safety, then made their way back to the saloons to continue with what they considered their well-earned drinking, gambling, and the like. After the proprietor and his wife had profusely apologized for what had happened to their guests, they anxiously returned inside the building to examine the damage for themselves.

"I . . . I still can't believe it! The one night, after all these weeks, that we get to spend in a real hotel . . ." Addie observed with bitter irony, her voice trailing away as Daniel looked down at her with a faint smile on his smoke-blackened face. "Oh, well," she concluded with a resigned sigh, "at least I did get to take a bath." But what good did it do? she mused unhappily, glancing down at her dust-covered form.

"It does stretch the realm of belief, doesn't it?" he wryly noted, his arm still draped about her shoulders as he paused to retrieve her saddlebags before beginning to lead her away from the hotel. There was a thoughtful silence between them as they moved across the dusty street to the horse Daniel had left tied beside several others at the hitching post in front of one of the saloons. Addie was the first to speak again, her own smudged and tear-ravaged countenance visibly troubled.

"I wonder how the fire got started. Don't you think it's a bit odd that it started just outside our room? I mean, someone must have been in the upstairs hallway and tossed either a match or a cigarette . . . but I still don't understand how it could have spread so quickly."

"They used lamp oil, Addie," Daniel grimly informed her. When she turned to stare up at him with a wide-eyed look of surprise, he explained, "I found evidence of the oil near the doorway. The fire might have been deliberately set, and your room might even have been the intended target." He put his hands at her waist and lifted her up to the horse's back, tossed the saddlebags in front of her, then swung up behind her and leaned forward to grasp the reins.

"But why?" she wondered aloud, a mounting horror leaving her numb as she pondered her husband's words. "Why would anyone want to—"

"I don't know," Daniel broke in, reining the horse away from the saloon. There was just enough light remaining in the warm evening sky for them to be able to clearly view their surroundings as they rode back toward camp. "It could have been anyone, though I sure as hell can't think of who might be wanting to do you harm." He released a long sigh and pulled her closer. "It's still possible that your being there had nothing whatsoever to do with the fire. And since there's no way of knowing for certain, I suggest we try to forget about it." He knew good and well that he wouldn't forget about it. He had already decided to return to town in the morning to further investigate the mysterious events.

"You . . . you don't think there's cause for alarm then?" Addie questioned, her uneasiness refusing to dissipate entirely in spite of Daniel's reassurance.

"I think there's nothing to be gained by worrying about it. It could well turn out to be nothing more than an unfortunate accident."

As they neared the place where the herd was settled for the night, on a broad, grassy patch of earth beside a stream, Addie realized that she suddenly felt very tired. Although she and Daniel had managed to escape the fire without injury, she had been left with a certain nagging apprehension. And, in addition to the danger the two of them had faced, she ruefully thought as they reached the boundaries of the camp and Daniel reached up to lift her down from the horse, her time alone with her husband had been cruelly interrupted. She silently cursed the fact that it seemed they were destined to remain apart for another interminable length of time.

Although Addie insisted upon accompanying Daniel into town the following morning, he firmly refused to allow it. He instructed her to remain close to camp and spend the day resting, reminding her that they would be back on the trail at dawn the next day and wouldn't have another such opportunity for leisure until they reached Sedalia. In the end, she was forced to capitulate but made no secret of the fact that she would rather spend the day at his side.

The morning sun was blazing high in the cloud-dotted sky when she decided to venture to a nearby pond for another bath. Except for Slim, all the men were either in town or out keeping an easy watch over the herd, so she decided to take advantage of the momentary privacy and wash the dirt and lingering smell of smoke from her calico dress as well as from herself. Musing that her long, tangled hair seemed heavy with the dust collected from Fort Gibson's main street, she took a seat on a rock and began drawing off her slippers.

Glancing about to see that she was surrounded only by a thin covering of tall, rather scraggly bushes, she decided it would be more prudent to wade into the pond wearing the white cotton chemise she had donned the evening before. She stood and divested herself of the rest of her clothing, then cautiously stepped into the cool, only slightly clouded water, her gaze frequently scanning the area to make certain she was unobserved.

She paused as soon as the water lapped at her slender thighs, then knelt down upon the sandy bottom and bent forward so that her thick mass of hair was submerged in the cleansing liquid. Raising her head a few moments later, she twisted the water from her dripping locks and smiled to herself as she reflected that Daniel would be pleasantly surprised when he returned and saw that she appeared almost as neat and clean as she had the previous evening. The smile on her face froze when she perceived a flash of movement in the bushes lining the rocky bank.

Her eyes remained fastened upon the spot where she was almost certain she had glimpsed a man's boot. She waited for the space of a full minute, then breathed a sigh of relief when a cottontail rabbit hopped from the cover of the bushes, realized that he was being watched, then hastily returned to the shrubbery to seek his hiding place once more.

Addie laughed softly and chided herself for her skittishness. Reaching downward, she seized a handful of the wet sand and scrubbed lightly at her skin, recalling that her father had always maintained that "good ole sand" was nature's soap. Indeed, she mused when she had finished, her entire body felt quite refreshed. Rising to her feet again, she headed back toward the spot where she had left her clothing, only to draw herself up short and gasp in alarm before she realized that it was Daniel who sauntered forward to nonchalantly perch upon the rock.

"Why in heaven's name didn't you let me know you were there?" she breathlessly demanded. "You nearly scared the life out of me!"

"You shouldn't be here all alone like this," he mildly admonished, his steely gaze sweeping up and down her body with bold intimacy, for her exquisite curves were well displayed by the wet, near-transparent chemise which clung to her womanly form like a second skin.

"How long have you been here?" Addie asked rather weakly, all too aware of the warmth stealing over her body as she watched the way his eyes seemed to devour her near-nakedness.

"I just got back from town," he replied. Smiling faintly, he added, "I was able to retrieve your boots. They're a little smoky but still intact." He suddenly leaned down to begin tugging off his own boots.

"Were you able to discover anything about the fire?"

"I'm afraid not. Seems that no one either saw or heard anything. The best thing for us to do is to forget about it," he reiterated as he stood up and unbuttoned his shirt. "All the same, however, I don't want you traipsing about alone," he added, his handsome face growing stern.

"What do you think you're doing?" she queried, her expression one of mingled puzzlement and expectation as he drew off his shirt, baring the broad, golden expanse of his chest.

"What does it look like I'm doing?" he mockingly retorted, a strange half-smile curving his lips as his hands moved to his trousers. "I've decided to give you your first swimming lesson, my love."

"Swimming lesson?" she echoed in astonishment. "But I . . . I don't want a swimming lesson." Her eyes widened as he drew off his trousers and stood naked and unashamed before her. She could feel her cheeks flaming and knew with certainty that her blushes had nothing whatsoever to do with outraged modesty. Her beloved husband was a splendid specimen of virile maleness, she boldly reflected, and she found herself wishing he had other things on his mind than teaching her to swim!

"I promise you that you will find my teaching methods quite enjoyable," he proclaimed with a deep chuckle, wading slowly toward her.

"But what about the men?" she feebly protested,

gazing up into his amused countenance as he towered above her. She was painfully aware of the way her entire body trembled at his nearness. "Slim will be serving dinner soon and—"

"I've already informed him that you and I may be detained. I've also left orders that our privacy is to remain undisturbed." The expression in his gaze was strangely unfathomable as he smiled down at her. Then his hands closed upon her shoulders, and he began gently but firmly urging her back toward the deeper waters in the middle of the pond. She knew a moment's panic when the cool water reached her slender waist.

"This is far enough!" she vigorously asserted, her hands pushing against his bare chest. "Truly, Daniel, I have absolutely no desire for a swimming lesson today!" There was a deepening frown of displeasure on her lovely face as he refused to heed her objections. Instead, he wrapped one of his powerful arms about her and leaned forward to submerge himself in the pond as he tumbled her relentlessly backward. She gasped, clutching at his broad shoulders for support as she found herself losing her footing.

"Relax," he instructed with another soft laugh.

"Is it your intention to drown me?" she countered heatedly, striving to escape him and return to the safety of more shallow waters.

"It isn't more than chest deep here, Addie," he calmly pointed out, holding her securely against him as he took them both gliding through the water. Her struggles were futile against his superior strength, and she finally accepted the inevitable and allowed him to support her weight as he agilely kicked and swam with his relaxed burden for what Addie deemed a mercifully short time. Finally, Daniel cradled her in his arms and stood up again, the water concealing the lower half of his magnificent body.

"That wasn't so bad, was it?" he complacently demanded, hugging her close. He felt a surge of desire as he once more became aware of the way the wet cotton of her chemise clung so revealingly to the delectable roundness of her rose-tipped breasts.

"Perhaps not, but I still don't know how to swim!" she retorted with a slight edge to her voice. "And I'm starting to get cold, so will you kindly release me and allow me to get dressed?" She was pleasantly surprised when he denied her request and lowered his head, positioning his lips to capture hers in a heart-stopping kiss that effectively conquered the chill that had begun to touch her. Her arms tightened about his neck as she pressed her barely covered softness more snugly against his hard nakedness, and she drew in her breath sharply an instant later when she found herself abruptly released, her feet making contact with the sand on the bottom of the pond as she splashed downward. "What are you—" she started to question, only to break off as he grasped her about the waist and lifted her up into another ardent embrace, his hands curling about her firmly rounded hips and his lips claiming hers once more.

Addie moaned and strained upward against him, her arms locked about his neck, her toes sinking into the soft sand as she sought to bring their bodies even closer together. Her breasts tingled as they pressed against the bronzed skin of his chest, and she was scarcely conscious of the moment when Daniel sank to his knees in the pond and gently seized her legs to place

453

them on either side of his lean hips.

The chemise floated up about her midsection, leaving her completely bare below the waist. She released her breath upon another gasp as she felt Daniel's aroused manhood sliding insistently back and forth across the sensitive place between her parted thighs. His fingers tightened upon the silken flesh of her buttocks, and he skillfully tutored her into a slow, undulating motion that sent her senses soaring and caused her to moan low in her throat.

Her passions increased to a fever pitch when he impatiently tore at the neckline of her chemise, freeing the beautiful globes of her breasts from the confining fabric, so that his lips could proceed downward to feast hungrily upon the quivering peaks. Her fingers threaded in his thick golden hair as his tongue demandingly flicked across one of her rosy nipples, and his hands returned to her hips to continue with the deliciously erotic torture he was so masterfully inflicting upon her.

Soon, however, Daniel could no longer contain his own raging desire, and he lifted Addie slightly before bringing her back down upon his maleness, sheathing himself expertly within her in one swift motion. Neither one of them seemed to be aware of the water swirling about them as they surrendered to the overpowering rapture of their mutual passion.

Addie's legs tightened about Daniel's waist as she breathlessly matched his rapidly escalating movements, her long tresses cascading wildly about her face and shoulders, her arms clinging feverishly to him as if she were indeed drowning. The bursting fulfillment soon held them both in its grip, and their soft cries of ultimate release mingled joyously in the sun-warmed air.

"I told you you'd find my methods to your liking," quipped Daniel, a teasing light in his loving gaze as he carried Addie from the pond and lowered her to her feet beside the rock where she had left her clothing.

"You were supposedly referring to a swimming lesson, remember?" she parried saucily, her features becomingly flushed in the afterglow of their rapturous union. Quickly drawing off her torn chemise and pulling on her shirt, she bent over to retrieve her trousers, then squealed softly in mock protest as Daniel suddenly wrapped an arm about her waist and tugged her playfully against him.

"I suggest we have another 'lesson' at the earliest opportunity," he huskily proposed, spinning her about and pressing a warm kiss to the inviting spot at the base of her throat where her pulse was once again beating at an alarming rate of speed.

"You're insatiable!" she remarked with an indulgent smile, inhaling sharply as his lips followed an imaginary path downward, and his fingers impatiently swept aside the unbuttoned edges of her shirt. "Daniel! If we don't get back to camp soon, the others will begin to—" she started to object, her voice obviously lacking conviction.

"To think that the trail boss and his wife have found better things to do than partake of Slim's cooking," he wickedly supplied, already smoothing the light blue cotton from her shoulders.

"But, isn't it too soon—"

"Love provides the most powerful stimulation in the world, dearest Adelaide," he assured her with a disarming grin. There was a look of such warmth and tenderness in his glowing eyes that Addie found herself happily surrendering as he slowly pulled the length of her naked body toward his.

The noon sky was aglow with sunlight. The only sounds drifting on the gentle breeze were the lowing and milling of the cattle in the distance, the screeching of two hawks soaring above, and the voices of the men raised in jovial talk and laughter as they ate their dinner of stew and biscuits in the camp just over the hill from where the two lovers lay entwined and totally oblivious to the rest of the world.

Twenty-Four

Addie was later to wonder how they had managed to escape any real disaster for so long. She had sensed that their long run of good fortune would come to an end sooner or later, that some sort of major trouble was inevitable. Indeed, Daniel had cautioned his drovers to expect resistance once they reached the Missouri border, saying that there was a distinct possibility that they would be met by angry farmers who would claim that the longhorns trampled their croplands and, what was worse, carried Texas fever.

There had been a widespread outbreak of the fever several years earlier, in 1858 and 1859, which had prompted more than one state to impose quarantines against the longhorns. The tick-conveyed disease had killed thousands of other cattle, but the Texas stock had been found to be mysteriously immune to the devastating illness. The trail drivers, though certainly aware of the quarantines ordered before the war, were convinced that they could successfully run what they considered an outdated blockade. To be on the safe side, however, Daniel had announced his intention to keep the herd well isolated from other cattle along the way. He was confident that by doing so they could avoid the bulk of opposition which might be awaiting them as they left Baxter Springs, Kansas, and crossed into Missouri.

They were now within two days of reaching their destination of Sedalia, where the Missouri-Pacific railway would provide transportation for the herd to St. Louis and then on to the newly opened Union Stockyards in Chicago. And, although they had encountered some opposition in the past few weeks, fortunately there had been nothing more worrisome than having to appease a handful of farmers, whom Daniel had skillfully handled by diplomatically offering to make certain that the animals in his herd were never closer than a mile from the farmers' stock. The farmers, most of whom had been wielding shotguns, had agreed to leave in peace only after Daniel had also paid something in the way of financial retribution for any anxiety facing them.

The sun had disappeared below the western horizon a short time earlier. Slim was busy wrestling with his pots and pans, while the drovers who had just completed their duties for the late spring day sank wearily onto the hard ground about the fire. Addie accepted a cup of coffee from her husband, flashing him a warm, grateful smile as he took a seat before her, the two of them several feet away from the others.

"You look pretty beat," he told her with a low chuckle, carefully sipping the hot, aromatic brew in his cup.

"You look none too perky yourself," she retorted

with a playfully haughty expression. Releasing a sigh a moment later, she smiled across at him again, and, as she reached up to remove her hat, the long, escaping braids tumbled down about her shoulders. "Oh Daniel, it's difficult to believe we're almost there, isn't it?"

"In some ways. I must admit, however, that I'm looking forward to the day we drive these mangy beasts into town and relinquish them. No more cattle drives for us, my love," he decreed, tossing his own hat to the grassy path beside them.

"Why not? You've done an admirable job as trail boss. And I think it would be exciting to make this a yearly tradition!"

"That's just it. I've had more than enough excitement and roaming about to last me a lifetime! Through all those years of the war, the one thing that kept me going when times were the roughest was the dream of settling down with you, Addie. I want us to have a real home, our own enchanted little kingdom," Daniel confided with a rather boyish grin, his gray eyes twinkling. "We're going to stay put in one place from here on out, Mrs. Jordan."

"But how are we going to spend all the money we make on this drive? I was hoping you'd be agreeable to a second honeymoon in St. Louis, and then possibly a trip abroad—" teased Addie, her own eyes kindling.

"I'll agree to the second honeymoon and nothing else," he quietly interrupted, sending her a look of such undisguised passion that it caused a delicious shiver to run the length of her spine.

Darkness began to close in, and it wasn't long before Addie and Daniel lay side by side upon their separate bedrolls. The fire had died down to nothing more than a smoldering pile of ashes, but the myriad of stars and a nearly full moon ablaze in the night sky illuminated the landscape with a silvery glow. The herd was quiet and still, and the two men on night duty maintained their leisurely, though watchful guard.

Suddenly a shot rang out, abruptly shattering the peaceful stillness of the cool air and rousing the slumbering drovers to instinctive readiness. They were aware of the unmistakable rumbling in the near distance and could feel the telltale trembling of the ground beneath them as the cattle began thundering across the countryside in a frenzied panic brought on by the gunshot.

There was no warning shout from either of the drovers on night watch, prompting Daniel to order, "Fletcher, you and Joe take a look and see what's happened to Billy and Clay. The rest of you come with me!" Turning hastily to Addie, he added, "You stay here at the camp with Slim!" She was already twisting up her unbound hair and pulling on her hat when she was met by his unexpected command.

"Stay here?" she echoed in disbelief.

"I haven't got time to argue! Now stay here, damn it!" he roared, his eyes blazing down into hers in the semidarkness before he spun away and started toward the horses with the other men following close behind. They hadn't traveled more than a few yards when another shot rang out, prompting them to jerk about in defensive alarm, their hands immediately moving to the revolvers they each carried.

"Hold it right there!" a man's harsh voice barked out, sounding undeniably sinister and deadly. Addie, standing as if frozen to the spot near the chuck wagon,

460

watched wide-eyed and breathless as the voice's owner rode forward, his long-barreled shotgun pointed threateningly toward the group of drovers. Within seconds, at least a dozen more horsemen appeared, surrounding the camp and also leveling guns at the startled assembly.

"Who the hell are you and what do you want?" Daniel tersely demanded.

"I'll do the talking here!" growled the leader of the intruders, his bearded face appearing evil and menacing in the moonlit darkness. "You and the others toss your guns over there!" he brusquely instructed, jerking his head in the direction of the dying fire. When Daniel and the men around him visibly hesitated, the bearded fellow issued a grim warning. "I'd just as soon kill each and every one of you bastards! Now do as I say or I'll give the order for my men to cut you down where you stand!"

Daniel muttered something to his own men and negligently tossed his pistol to the ground near the fire. The others followed suit, their slightly narrowing gazes never leaving the faces of the armed band who surrounded them. Addie's eyes flew to meet her husband's, and she was certain she could read a silent command in their steely depths. Exactly what it was, however, she could not discern. Dear God, she frantically wondered, her mind growing numb with dawning horror, what could these men want? And what had happened to Clay and Billy?

"We've taken over your herd," the man declared with a malevolent grin and a deep rumble of triumphant laughter. "Thought you might like to know that we call ourselves Jayhawkers. We don't hold with your kind

461

dirtying our land. And this here's a warning in case you got the fool-brained notion to try and follow us," he proclaimed, twisting about in the saddle and firing his gun directly into the chuck wagon. His men did the same, and the shotgun blasts rang out with deafening force in rapid succession. Slim and Addie flew toward Daniel and the others as the outlaws merely laughed at the destruction they created. Addie pressed close to her husband's side, but he firmly pushed her behind him.

"We're gonna be generous and leave you your mounts, but only so you can get the hell out of Missouri and head on back to Texas where you belong! Oh, and just in case the little display we just treated you to doesn't convince you to leave, then just take a look at another 'method of persuasion'," the bearded ruffian instructed with another malicious chortle, his gaze darting to the spot where the surrounding outlaws made way for yet another Jayhawker, who rode leisurely forward and unceremoniously dumped a moaning, bleeding Clay upon the ground.

"Why, them damned—" Slim ground out, biting off his words as Daniel, whose own features visibly tightened, shot him a warning look. Addie felt hot tears stinging her eyes as she stared across at the sandy-haired drover, scarcely more than a boy, who lay half-dead with a bullet hole in his back.

"Count yourselves lucky you didn't get more of the same," the outlaw leader sneered, abruptly reining about and raising his voice in an order for his men to follow. They were gone as quickly as they had come, disappearing into the shadowy night, the sound of the thundering hoofbeats of their horses growing dimmer and dimmer until all was quiet once more.

Daniel and the others wasted no time in racing forward to retrieve their guns. Addie and Slim hurried to Clay's side, relieved to find that the young man was still alive.

"He's probably lost a lot of blood," she dazedly remarked to the burly cook, fighting back the tears as she cradled the injured drover's head in her lap. Slim muttered a blistering oath as he stripped off Clay's shirt and examined the wound as best he could.

"Somebody build up the fire, damn it!" he snapped. Daniel moved to kneel upon one knee beside Addie, while several of the men took themselves off to try to discover what had happened to Billy, who had been with Clay on the night watch.

"Why did they shoot him? There was no reason to shoot him in the back as if he were nothing more than an animal," Addie tremulously murmured as her gaze met Daniel's.

"Men like that don't have to have a reason, Addie," he said, his own voice low and laced with smoldering fury. "What do you think, Slim?" he then asked the grim-faced cook as the fire blazed to life again a few feet away and provided much-needed light. "Will he make it?"

"Can't say as yet. I'll have to get the bullet out of him before I can tell." Dave and Jesse moved forward then, offering to help Slim move the unconscious man nearer to the fire. Daniel gently pulled a pale, faintly trembling Addie to her feet as they moved away.

"It . . . it seems like a nightmare, and yet it's all too real, isn't it?" She faltered then and was grateful when his arms closed about her and his lips brushed against her forehead as her hat fell unheeded to the ground.

463

"Clay will make it. He's young and strong," he confidently asserted. Releasing her for an instant, he cupped her face in his hand as he peered intently down into her swimming gaze. "Thank God they didn't notice you, my love."

"What do you mean?" she questioned in puzzlement.

"They didn't suspect you were a woman." He drew her tight against the comforting warmth of his body once more, and Addie closed her eyes against the awful realization of her narrow escape.

"Oh, Daniel, what are we going to do now?"

"We're going to wait until morning, then go after them."

"What?" she breathed in disbelief, drawing away to face him again. "You heard what they said! And you know they'll not think twice about killing you—" she feelingly protested.

"I don't intend to give them the opportunity to kill me," Daniel broke in, the ghost of a smile curving his lips. "We're going to get the herd back, Addie. Threats or no threats, we're going to take back what is ours."

"But how?"

"We'll use the same methods they used, though hopefully without any bloodshed. However, I'll feel no remorse whatsoever if we have to kill every blasted one of them," he quietly asserted, a dangerous, savage light in his eyes.

"When do we leave?" she asked, heaving a resigned sigh.

"You and Slim will remain here with Clay," he decreed, anticipating her demand to accompany him. "The rest of us will follow their trail tomorrow, then make our move after nightfall. They won't be able to get far with the herd."

"I think it would be better if Clay were taken into Sedalia to see a doctor at once. Slim won't need my help for that," Addie determinedly ventured.

"No, Addie."

"You're out of your mind if you think I'm going to sit and wait while you—"

"No, Addie."

"In case you've forgotten, Daniel Jordan, half of those cattle belong to me!" Daniel's hands gripped her shoulders as he opened his mouth to issue one last command, only to find himself interrupted at this point by Fletcher.

"We found young Billy," he announced. "He was just comin' to. Seems he was the luckier of the two—got nothin' more than a bump the size of a goose egg on the back of his skull." Addie's gaze traveled to where Billy was being helped into camp by Joe and Lee. She shot her husband one last speaking glance before hurrying forward to the side of an unsteadily walking Billy, and the boy smiled somewhat sheepishly as she expressed genuine concern for his injuries. For most of the other drovers, the remainder of the disastrous night was passed in sleepless anticipation, while Slim and Addie did their best to tend to a restless, softly moaning Clay.

It seemed to Addie to take an unusually long time for the sun to set the following evening. She waited in a densely wooded area atop a gentle rise, and her fingers tightened upon the reins as a look of mingled impatience and apprehension crossed her lovely features.

"There ain't no use in gettin' all worked up just yet, Miz Jordan," whispered Billy, a faint smile lurking about his lips as he leaned a bit closer. "That husband of yours knows what he's doin'."

"Yes, but that's beside the point! Anything could go wrong, and you know it. Damnation!" she muttered, her eyes flashing in the darkening twilight. "Why the devil didn't he relent and let the two of us go along?" she lamented for what seemed to Billy to be the hundredth time.

"Good enough reasons, I guess," her companion responded with a noncommittal shrug.

Good reasons when it came to Billy, she silently allowed, well aware of the fact that the young man beside her was still suffering somewhat from dizziness after the blow to his head the night before. As for herself, however, she was convinced that Daniel was unjustly treating her like a child again!

But, a tiny voice at the back of her mind reasoned, at least he hadn't carried out his threat to make her travel into town with Slim and Clay. And he *had* granted her permission to wait a safe distance away with Billy, having instructed the two of them to head for Sedalia at the first sign that things weren't going the way they hoped.

"I can't see a blasted thing, can you?" she whispered, an unmistakable edge to her voice.

"Only that campfire down there, and about a dozen men sitting around it, and maybe a dozen more walking about—" Billy enumerated, glancing at her in bemusement when she cut him off with a muffled curse. Daniel and the others, they knew, would be making their move soon, since the two men drawing night duty had already taken their positions with the herd.

They'd had no difficulty whatsoever in tracking the men who had stolen their cattle, recalled Addie, thinking back to the way they had bided their time all afternoon after discovering the unmistakable signs left by the herd of two thousand Texas longhorns. And, if all went as planned, they'd be driving the animals into Sedalia the very next morning. If all went as planned, she repeated silently with an inward sigh, her anxiety mounting with each passing moment.

"I'm going in closer for a better look!" she suddenly declared, already tugging on Twister's reins.

"You can't do that!" insisted Billy, a look of consternation swiftly crossing his boyish countenance. "Mr. Jordan said we were to wait here—"

"I know what he said, but I'm only going to move in a trifle closer. You'll no doubt be able to see me quite well," Addie noted wryly, flashing him a quick smile. "Don't worry. I'll be back before you know it!" With that, she guided Twister out of the trees and down the hill, heading for another concealing shelter of thick undergrowth and trees several hundred yards away. Billy's mouth compressed into a tight, thin line of displeasure, but he knew there was no way he could stop her. He could only wait and pray she didn't get into trouble, for he was certain that Daniel Jordan would have his hide if anything happened to the beautiful, headstrong woman who had captured the hearts of them all.

Although she was indeed afforded a better view of the outlaw camp from her new vantage point, Addie still was not satisfied. The truth was, she admitted to herself, she wouldn't be satisfied until she was close enough to the camp to take part in the maneuver Daniel had planned!

Reining about once again, she guided her cooperative mount toward yet another grove of trees even farther down the hill, grateful for the cover of darkness as the dusky twilight edged into a cloudy night in which the moonlight was nothing more than a dim glow. She could hear the outlaws who were gathered about the roaring fire, their voices rising in boisterous laughter as they reveled in their good fortune. Several bottles of whiskey were passed about the group, and one of the outlaws began playing a lively tune on his harmonica. Addie's eyes scanned the raucous scene for any sign of Daniel or his men as she swung down from the saddle and looped the reins about a branch.

"Well, well, what've we got here?" an unfamiliar voice asked behind her, prompting her to gasp audibly and whirl about in alarm. She found herself face to face with one of the Jayhawkers, a tall, wiry man with a full head of shaggy blond hair and a piercing gaze that seemed to be stripping her naked. It was then that she remembered, belatedly, that she had removed her hat when she had felt the pins slipping from her chignon, and she realized that her gleaming mass of hair was now cascading riotously about her face and shoulders.

"Who . . . who are you?" demanded Addie, momentarily faltering beneath the amused, unmistakably lustful gleam in his eyes before gathering her courage once more. "And just what the Sam Hill do you think you're doing, sneaking up on me like that?" she accusingly reproached, tossing her head as her flashing, indignant gaze unflinchingly met his. Realizing that she was faced with the choice of withdrawing her pistol in her own defense and alerting the entire camp to her presence, or attempting to bluff her way out of her difficulty, she chose the latter. "I asked you for your name, mister!" Her tone was coolly imperious, and she hoped she sounded a good deal more courageous than she felt.

"Come on," he said, lunging forward and seizing her arm in a bruising grip before she could escape.

"Let go of me!" she wrathfully directed, struggling frantically against him as he merely laughed and jerked her hard against his coarse, unkempt form. Feeling that she no longer had any choice, Addie reached for the pistol hidden in her coat pocket, but the man easily wrested it from her hand before she could take aim.

"We'll just see what Tanner has to say when I show him the pretty little spy I caught me!" her captor remarked with a decidedly evil laugh. Twisting futilely in his grasp, Addie found herself dragged out of the trees and down the hill toward the camp, the outlaw obviously enjoying her struggles and curses as he yanked her along.

Within minutes, she was being pushed forward into the very midst of the boisterous group, and a sudden hush fell over the assembly of rustlers as their startled gazes beheld the beautiful, fiery-eyed young woman with the cascading mass of chestnut hair. Their eyes raked her body insolently, and she found herself wishing—perhaps for the first time in her life—that she was wearing skirts instead of the revealing denim trousers.

"Where'd you find her?" the leader demanded, slowly rising to his feet beside the fire. Addie recognized him at once, and she held her head proudly erect, her entire demeanor bespeaking undaunted dignity. Inwardly, however, she blanched at the pure lust she glimpsed shining forth from so many pairs of predatory eyes, and she began feverishly praying that the ordeal facing her would be mercifully short. Daniel and the others should be making their move any second now, she told herself, thinking that perhaps her husband could see her at that very moment. Oh, my love, where are you? she silently wondered.

"Caught her up there, Mr. Tanner," explained Addie's captor, jerking his head in the direction of the wooded spot a short distance away. He grinned, displaying teeth that were crooked and stained with tobacco. "Yes sir, she was up there all by her lonesome."

"And he had no right whatsoever to drag me down here!" Addie stormed, rounding on the unsmiling, bearded man called Tanner. "I insist that you allow me to retrieve my horse and be on my way at once!"

"You're in no position to make any demands at all, missy," replied Tanner, a contemptuous sneer marking his dark features. "Suppose you tell me what you were doing up there this time of night? No decent woman would be out riding alone so many miles from town!"

"Why not?" she shot back, her eyes blazing. "Even a *decent* woman has places to go and business to tend to, doesn't she?" She was still acutely aware of the way everyone was staring at her, and she felt a tremor of fear deep inside as Tanner took a step closer to stand large and menacing before her, his malevolent features appearing even more ominous with the firelight playing across them.

"What sort of business would you have this time of

night?" he tersely challenged, his eyes narrowing and emitting a savage gleam as his suspicions became even more aroused. "Who sent you to spy on us?" he demanded.

"I am not a spy!" she adamantly denied.

"Hey, Tanner!" called out one of his outlaws. "I say we make certain she ain't carryin' any *concealed weapons!*"

His suggestion was met with a loudly enthusiastic response, and another man, already well on his way to being quite intoxicated, added, "Strip her naked! Strip her and let's have a look at what she's got hidden underneath them men's clothes she's wearin'!"

Addie inhaled sharply, her cheeks burning. It required great strength of will for her to remain calm, to keep from displaying the sheer terror the man's words had struck in her heart. Daniel! her mind cried in rapidly escalating desperation. Daniel, where are you?

"Now, hold on!" Tanner roared above the din of derisive laughter and lewd, humiliating comments directed toward Addie. "Maybe we ought to give the little lady a chance to explain what she's doing out here." The crowd gradually quieted, and Tanner turned to a pale, wide-eyed Addie. "Well?" he asked, his eyes glowing in anticipation of the stripping he believed to be a certainty.

A slow, almost wolfish smile rose to his lips as Addie hesitated. Her mind raced as she sought to think of something, and she finally opened her mouth to declare in a voice that was not quite steady, "I . . . I was on an errand for my . . . for my sister. Her child is ill and in need of a doctor."

"If you were in such an all-fired hurry for a doctor,

then why was it Carson found you up there?" questioned Tanner, disbelief written on his face. "The road to Sedalia's a good ways to the north."

Addie swallowed a sudden lump in her throat before meeting the man's gaze squarely and saying, "I've been riding all day. My horse needed the rest."

"Aw, come on, Tanner! Let's put a stop to all this damned foolishness and get on with the strippin'!" interjected one of the youngest of the group, his loins tightening as he thought of what lay ahead. Addie watched in horror as Tanner laughed softly and nodded to indicate that the stripping was to commence without further delay.

"No!" gasped Addie, her eyes wide and full of disbelief at what was happening. Dear God, please let Daniel come now! her mind cried in dizzying panic. She sent Tanner one last defiant glare. "You have no right to do this! I've done nothing to—" she attempted to vehemently protest, only to find her words cut off as the same young man who had just expressed impatience strode forward and grabbed her, clamping a filthy hand across her mouth to stifle the screams which rose in her throat. She fought like a wildcat as a handful of eager volunteers swarmed about her and several pairs of hands clutched frenziedly at her shirt. It would easily have been torn from her violently twisting and squirming body if not for the shot which rang out so clearly and unexpectedly in the night air.

"Daniel!" breathed Addie as she stumbled in an effort to regain her balance after the clawing hands abruptly released her. The ruffians abandoned their lustful activity as they scurried about drunkenly to fetch their weapons and discover the source of the

472

gunshot. Addie's gaze flew to encounter Tanner's look of furious surprise, and the outlaw caught the expression of mingled relief and triumph reflected in her eyes just before she spun hastily about and darted toward the group of riders now encircling the camp.

Tanner snatched up his gun and took aim at the young woman's fleeing back, then roared in pain an instant later when Daniel unhesitatingly fired his pistol directly at the man's upper body. The impact of the bullet knocked Tanner to the ground. His shotgun clattered harmlessly downward to land beside him, and the leader of the Jayhawkers could only sit mutely by, blood streaming from the wound in his shoulder, as Daniel and the trail drivers effectively surrounded the band of outlaws and held their guns in visible readiness as they ordered the rustlers to drop their weapons.

"We're taking back what belongs to us," proclaimed Daniel, reaching down to lift Addie effortlessly up before him, his eyes never leaving Tanner's pain-reddened, bearded features. "Count yourselves fortunate I don't kill you here and now for what my wife has suffered!" he ground out. The firelight seemed to play tauntingly over the faces of the Jayhawkers as they reluctantly tossed their weapons to the ground.

"You won't get away with this, you damned Texas son of a bitch!" snarled Tanner, an evil, malevolent light in his piercing gaze. "We'll find you and hang you by your—" he started to threaten, only to be cut off by a derisive chuckle from Daniel.

"We'll leave the issue of hanging to the law," he retorted. Then Daniel nodded a silent command to Dave and Fletcher, who dismounted and hurried forward to gather up the weapons on the ground about

473

the fire. "You've got a long walk ahead of you, so get moving," Daniel instructed the band of outlaws, his own pistol still leveled at their leader.

"It won't do you no good to hand us over to the sheriff in Sedalia," Tanner asserted with a mocking snort of laughter. "Folks in these parts know better than to interfere with us!"

"Then I'd say it's about time they learned differently," Daniel nonchalantly rseponded, signaling to the drovers to begin herding the outlaws toward town. He paused briefly before reining about. "As for the sheriff in Sedalia," he informed Tanner with only the ghost of a smile on his face, "I think he'll prove quite cooperative. You see, it so happens he served under me during the war." With that, he issued one last order to his men, then tugged firmly on the reins and rode away from camp with his wife, heading toward the spot just over the next hill where Trent, Lee, and Billy waited with the herd.

"I was beginning to think you wouldn't come in time!" Addie dazedly remarked, gratefully leaning back against him as she took a deep, shuddering breath. Her hair streamed about her like a disheveled curtain, and she seemed unaware of the fact that her heavy cotton shirt was torn in several places.

"Adelaide, I ought to—" he feelingly muttered, his handsome features suffused with a dull, angry color as he broke off and fought for control over his raging temper. Finally, he released a long sigh and said, "I don't suppose there's anything I can do to you that's any worse than what you just went through back there. I just hope you've finally learned your lesson," he grimly concluded, his strong arm tightening possessively about her slender waist. "Damn it, woman, how the hell do you think I felt when I arrived and found you in such danger? I nearly went out of my head when Billy intercepted us and said you had been captured! Do you realize what might have happened if—"

"I know it was wrong of me to disobey," she interrupted, releasing a ragged sigh of her own, her beautiful eyes sparkling in the dim moonlight. "Oh Daniel, I . . . I'm sorry. I realize now that I could have jeopardized your entire plan because of . . . because of my foolishness." She valiantly endeavored to fight back the tears but failed miserably as the shock of her recent ordeal took its toll upon her emotions.

"Actually, my love," he consolingly admitted, a returning glimmer of amusement in his steely gaze as he hugged her closer, "you created a very timely diversion. Those bastards were so busy with you, it was easy for us to overcome the few men carelessly watching the herd and then surround the camp." Addie was perfectly content to relax against him for the space of several moments, but suddenly she sat bolt upright again.

"Twister! I left him—"

"Billy's got him. You and I are going to head on into town. I'm going to leave half the crew with the herd, while the others see to it our prisoners get to Sedalia safe and sound. We'll ride back out at first light and take the herd in."

"Were you telling the truth when you said the sheriff served under you during the war?" she asked, frowning slightly as she twisted about to face him in the darkness.

"As a matter of fact," he replied with a grin, "I was."

"Why didn't you tell me?"

"There's a great deal I haven't told you, dearest Addie," he quipped as they finally reached the small valley where the longhorns rested peacefully. "And I estimate that it will take you at least fifty or sixty more years to discover all there is to know about me—providing I don't decide to trade you for a younger, more sedate woman before then," he added with a low chuckle, guiding his horse to where Billy waited with Twister.

"You just try it, Daniel Jordan," retorted Addie, lowering her voice so that Billy couldn't hear as they drew closer, "and I'll make damned sure she doesn't enjoy the benefit of all that I've taught you!" She narrowed her eyes meaningfully at him, and he laughed softly once more as he dismounted and reached up to lift her down.

"Sure glad to see you didn't come to no harm, Miz Jordan," said Billy, tipping his hat in her direction. It was obvious that he was anxious to hear all about the successful retaking of the herd, and Daniel quickly recounted the details before he and Addie set off toward Sedalia, which lay only a few miles to the north.

Twenty-Five

Addie hummed softly to herself as she drew on her fresh white undergarments, then took a seat before the mirrored dressing table and began carefully brushing the tangles from her damp chestnut locks. The hotel room in which she sat alone was filled with a blaze of afternoon sunlight, and the pleasantness of the early June day was a perfect match for her soaring spirits. Less than forty-eight hours had passed since she had ridden into Sedalia beside her husband, and it seemed unbelievable, she reflected as a faint sigh escaped her lips, that so much had happened in so short a space of time.

The first thing they had done upon reaching town was to contact Daniel's former comrade, a man by the name of Floyd Vinson, who had served as Sedalia's sheriff ever since the end of the war. It had been obvious to Addie that Floyd bore great affection and respect for the man he still called "Colonel," and it had taken no persuasion whatsoever to convince the sheriff to arrest and incarcerate every one of the thieving

Jayhawkers who had been delivered to him under armed escort just after midnight.

Next, Addie had accompanied her husband to the residence of the only doctor in town, where they had been greatly relieved to learn that Clay was much improved. After locating Slim and stopping to send a message to William McDougall, Daniel's friend in St. Louis who had contracted to purchase their cattle, Addie and the men had eagerly headed back out of town to bring in the herd. Dawn had just started breaking by then, the clear blue sky was tinged with brilliant golden hues, and the morning air was crisp and faintly scented with the aroma of vast carpets of wildflowers that bloomed across the fertile country-side.

She knew that she would never forget the feeling of excitement, the sense of accomplishment she had experienced when she took her position beside Daniel. And once they had reached the outskirts of Sedalia again, time seemed to pass even more quickly. Soon the cattle had been driven into the waiting corrals, which signified the end of the trail drive at long last. Then the full day of rest and celebration for the weary yet satisfied drovers had begun.

"Daniel, Daniel," Addie whispered to her reflection, her hazel eyes kindling with a spark of remembrance of the way she and her husband had spent the previous night. Musing that they had finally been afforded the comfort of a real bed, a slow smile touched her lips. Several seconds passed before she mentally shook herself and rose from the dressing taable, and she suddenly realized that Daniel and Mr. McDougall were awaiting her in the lobby downstairs.

She frowned as she drew the creased calico gown over her head, almost wishing she had taken the time to purchase something more elegant but recalling with satisfaction that she had postponed any shopping in order to take her place beside Daniel and the others as they watched the cattle being loaded aboard the train a short time earlier.

Feeling greatly refreshed from her bath, Addie hastily twisted up her hair and secured it with a few well-placed pins. Then she checked her appearance in the mirror one last time before hurrying out of the room and down the stairs. As she remembered that the train would be pulling out soon, she also dazedly realized that she and Daniel would now be several thousand dollars richer, for the two men had been settling accounts while she bathed.

"I was hoping I'd have the pleasure of seeing you again before I left, Mrs. Jordan," remarked William McDougall with a broad smile on his face as he caught sight of her. He and Daniel rose to their feet as she approached, and her husband reached out to grasp her hand and pull her to his side.

"Well, my love, how does it feel to be married to a wealthy man?" teased Daniel, lightly patting his coat pocket to indicate the money the older man had just given him.

"As I've been forced to remind you several times, my dearest husband," retorted Addie, flashing a playful smile up at him, "half of those cattle belonged to me!" Turning back to William, who was watching the two lovers with an indulgent grin tugging at the corners of his mouth, she spoke with complete sincerity. "Thank you again, Mr. McDougall. Your generosity has ensured the salvation of my . . . of *our* ranch," she quickly amended, glancing briefly up at Daniel once more.

"Generosity has nothing to do with it, my dear," the kindly, gray-haired man assured her. "Believe me, I stand to make a substantial profit for myself once I get these longhorns to Chicago. They're desperate for beef up there, and I hope your drive is just the first of many heading our way."

"Come on, William," interjected Daniel at this point, "we'd better see about getting you to your train. It wouldn't do for those cattle to get to St. Louis without you!" Drawing Addie's arm through his, he donned his hat and waited while his friend gathered up his belongings. Then the three of them stepped from the hotel and out into the warm sunshine that was beating down upon the main street and its bustling activity.

"Well, when can I expect you to bring up another herd?" William McDougall asked as he climbed the steps of his private railroad car a few minutes later. The longhorns, milling restlessly about in the numerous cattle cars behind them, moaned and bellowed as the steam engine puffed and smoked in readiness. The relatively few passengers bound for St. Louis had already boarded, leaving the station and the surrounding area virtually deserted.

"I'm afraid this was the first and last from us," replied Daniel, smiling warmly as he took the other man's proferred hand and shook it. "Addie and I are going to concentrate on making the Rolling L the best damned cattle ranch in Texas from here on out."

"See if you can get him to change his mind, Mrs. Jordan," William laughingly requested.

"I have a strong suspicion that any efforts on my part would prove entirely futile," she answered with a soft laugh of her own. Daniel hugged her close, murmuring so quietly that William could not hear.

"Not entirely, my love." She could feel the color rising to her cheeks, but she resolutely turned her attention back to the man who was bidding them a hearty farewell. Once he had disappeared inside the car, Daniel and Addie stepped back from the railroad tracks and paused to take one last look at the train which would carry their herd east.

"It's . . . well, it's a bit sad now that it's finally happening, isn't it?" remarked Addie, her eyes shining with sudden tears as she listened to the sounds of the animals.

"A bit, maybe. But I'm glad it's finished." Another burst of steam accompanied the shrill noise of the train whistle as the engineer warned of the train's imminent departure. Addie slowly turned away, her eyes momentarily downcast. When she raised them an instant later, she drew in her breath upon an audible gasp, which prompted Daniel to wheel about, his fingers closing protectively upon her shoulder.

"What is—" he started to demand, only to break off abruptly as his gaze fell upon the man who was just emerging from his hiding place near one corner of the station building. The man held a cocked revolver in one hand, and his finger twitched imperceptibly upon the trigger as he pointed the gun directly at Daniel.

"Don't make a move for your gun, you Yankee bastard, or it'll be your last!" threatened Trent, his dark eyes glistening with unmistakable hatred.

"Trent!" Addie's eyes were wide and full of bewildered astonishment. "Trent, what are you doing?" Before Daniel could draw his own gun and take aim, Trent had lunged forward and seized Addie. He held her tightly before him like a shield, his pistol pressed against her head.

"Throw your gun over here," Trent commanded Daniel. "And don't try anythin' or I'll put a bullet through her skull!" The most intense fury Daniel had ever experienced blazed deep within him, but he knew he had no choice but to obey. His heart twisted as he glimpsed the mute terror in Addie's features, the trembling of her body as Trent held her with an arm clamped about her waist. A feeling of deep anguish and helplessness assailed him as he accepted the unavoidable truth of the situation—he couldn't chance firing at Trent. He reluctantly complied with the other man's orders by tossing his gun on the boardwalk lining the tracks.

"Let her go, Evans," Daniel ground out, a fierce light evident in his steely eyes. "Whatever it is you want from me, she's not involved."

"Isn't she?" Trent mocked with a malevolent sneer. "Now, give me the money," he directed. Addie's instincts forced her to remain still and unresisting, but her mind screamed for her to do something, anything, to prevent whatever evil Trent was planning. Her thoughts were a painful whirl in her head as she frantically searched for an avenue of escape. Desperately, her gaze flew to meet Daniel's.

"Take it," Daniel savagely muttered, withdrawing the money from his coat pocket as Trent eyed him warily, "and let her go!" He tossed the packet of bills to land beside the pistol at Trent's feet.

Pressing the revolver even tighter against Addie's head, Trent forced her to bend with him as he instructed her to pick it up. She did as he said, then gasped in growing alarm as he declared, "I'd like nothin' better than to shoot you down like the dog you are, Jordan! But I've thought it over and decided to let you live. I want you to think about your wife bein' with me, want you to spend every minute thinkin' about the fact that she's mine now, mine like she always should've been!"

"No!" breathed Addie in horror. The train jerked forward at that moment as the slowly turning wheels connected noisily with the tracks. Within seconds, Trent had dragged her backward with him, then up the steps of William McDougall's private car. Kicking open the door, Trent tugged her roughly inside.

Daniel had taken only a single step toward the car when William McDougall appeared. His hands were raised as high as his head, and his eyes immediately encountered Daniel's fury-filled gaze. Giving a brief, cautioning shake of his head, he climbed down the steps and jumped to the boardwalk beside Daniel as Trent stood in the doorway with his captive. The engine was picking up speed now, and the train edged away from the station, the wheels turning with ever-increasing regularity. It had all happened so fast that no one else was aware of the fateful drama taking place.

"Don't try to come after us, Jordan!" warned Trent, raising his voice to be heard above the roar of the engine. He yanked Addie back inside the car and slammed the door.

The train had soon traveled a considerable distance from Sedalia, but Daniel wasted no time as he spun about and tersely commanded a visibly stunned William, "Contact the next station and have the train ordered to stop there!"

"What are you planning to do?" demanded William.

"Go after them!"

"You can't go alone!" protested his friend.

"It's the only way!" Daniel impatiently thundered. Without another word or explanation, he raced to the nearby livery stable and retrieved his mount. His movements were sure and purposeful as he swung up into the saddle and reined about to give chase to the train that was taking his beloved wife farther away with each passing second.

Inside William McDougall's private car, Addie numbly sank down onto a chair after Trent finally released her. She stared up at him in breathless suspense, desperately wondering if she would be forced to defend herself against his attack. She was puzzled, however, when he made no move toward her but instead took a position near the doorway and kept his gun pointed menacingly in her direction.

"I've waited a long time for this, Miss Addie," Trent quietly informed her, his piercing gaze raking over her as she bravely lifted her chin and faced him squarely.

"Why are you doing this?" she calmly demanded.

"I'd have taken you before now if it hadn't been for the money," he scornfully revealed. "The drive never would've made it if not for the fact that I wanted the money as well as you. And I'd have killed that damned bluebelly you call your husband a long time ago."

"You still haven't told me why. I hired you on when no one else would, Trent," she pointed out. "You were a good worker. You never caused any trouble."

"That's because, until Jordan came, I was content

484

just to be near you! I figured if I was patient enough, you'd come to care for me as I did for you. I hadn't planned to stay on at the Rolling L all that time, but then I hadn't counted on fallin' in love with you."

"Falling in love with me?" Addie repeated in amazement. She frowned, and with eyes flashing she said in obvious disgust, "You've got a strange way of showing your love, Trent Evans!"

"Don't call me that!" he snarled unexpectantly, his features growing quite ugly. "My name isn't Trent Evans. I just took that name so they wouldn't find me and hang me as a deserter. Does it offend your Southern pride to hear that I ran out on the Confederate cause, Miss Addie?" he taunted cruelly. "I only joined up because I was wanted for murder over in Santa Fe. The army was the only way I could escape the hangman," he told her with a short, humorless laugh. He moved a step closer, his eyes literally blazing into hers. "It was me that shot Jordan that day I saw the two of you at that cabin together! It was me that started that little fire back at the hotel in Fort Gibson! And you want to know why, Miss Addie? You want to know why I didn't just go ahead and kill that son of a bitch you married?"

"Dear God," she whispered, her eyes very wide and full of dawning horror.

"It's a bit ironic, isn't it? You, a proud daughter of the glorious old South, playin' whore for a Yankee! I didn't want to believe it at first. But I watched the two of you together. And I spied on you through the window in the cabin that day." He paused then, and his lips compressed into a thin line of vengeful fury. "You were naked, those beautiful white breasts of yours—"

"Stop it!" cried Addie, abruptly rising to her feet. "I

was never Daniel Jordan's whore. I have been his wife for more than five years now!"

"Which makes it all the worse!" Trent spat out. "You let me believe you were untouched, Miss Addie. I loved you partly because no man had ever made you his own, because I thought you were pure and innocent, different from all the other women I'd known. I was nothin' but a fool for lettin' you deceive me so easily!"

"I didn't set out to deceive you!"

"It doesn't matter now. It wouldn't even have come to this if it hadn't been for the drive. I'd have killed Daniel Jordan at the cabin that day, but I didn't want the law comin' in and maybe figurin' out I wasn't who I claimed to be. And back in Fort Gibson, the simple truth is that I got drunk and got to thinkin' about the two of you over at the hotel. So I arranged for your little meetin' to be interrupted!" he confided with another evil laugh.

"Why are you telling me all of this now?" asked Addie, her hands clenching into fists at her sides. She was vaguely aware of the steady clickety-clack of the train's wheels, of the unceasing sway of the car in which Trent held her at gunpoint. Suddenly she glimpsed something through the uncurtained glass of the small window near her head. She stifled a cry of joy when she saw that it was Daniel urging his horse inexorably onward, past McDougall's car. Her eyes flew back to Trent, and she endeavored to keep her expression impassive as she listened to his revolting words.

"I wanted you to know how long I waited! I wanted you to know how many chances I gave you. Damn you!" Trent muttered belligerently, advancing on her now, the gun still aimed directly at her heart. His brown eyes shone with a maniacal light, and Addie felt

486

a tremor of fear shaking her as he drew closer and closer. "I loved you and you betrayed me! You're no better than any other woman after all, are you? You're no better!"

"You'll never get away with this!" Addie defiantly asserted, refusing to display cowardice as he halted merely inches away from her. In the back of her mind, she feverishly wondered when Daniel would make his move and what he would do. It occurred to her then that she should do her best to distract Trent, so she inched even closer, raising her arms and entwining them about his neck. As she pressed her full breasts boldly against his chest, he momentarily lowered his gun. "There's no reason why we can't come to some sort of *agreement* about this, is there?" she seductively murmured, smiling faintly as she forced herself to touch him.

"Get back!" he harshly commanded, confused by her unexpected willingness. Raising the gun and taking a step backward, his dark gaze bored into hers. "What kind of game are you playin', Miss Addie? It won't do you any good," he curtly insisted. "You've got everythin' I'm gonna do to you comin' to you!"

"I'm not playing any games," Addie maintained, her arms stealing upward about his neck once more as she edged closer in pursuit. "If I had only known that you loved me all this time, things would have been quite different." She was satisfied when the hand clutching the revolver fell slowly to his side, though he continued to eye her with visible suspicion. "But then, we have plenty of time to make up for the past, don't we?" She clasped him to her, suppressing a shudder of revulsion as she pressed her lips upon his. Following only a moment's hesitation, Trent growled out a curse, then his arms tightened painfully about her softness as he savagely ground his mouth down upon hers.

Addie desperately fought against the nausea rising deep within her, against the faintness which threatened to overwhelm her as Trent's lips brutally ravaged hers. She fought against the moan of pain which rose in her throat as his groping fingers relentlessly bruised the soft flesh of her breast, and she felt her entire body trembling at the repulsive caresses it was forced to endure.

Finally, her ears detected a noise up above. Before either she or Trent knew what was happening, Daniel had jerked open the fire door atop the car and was agilely lowering himself downward. Temporarily drugged by the sheer force of his raging desire, Trent opened his eyes slowly, and when he spotted the other man, he raised his arm and prepared to fire the revolver at the easy target Daniel presented. At that instant Addie screamed a warning and instinctively brought both of her arms down upon Trent's. He cursed and flung her aside, but Daniel was already hurtling himself forward by then, his hands closing about Trent's wrist as he forcefully wrested the gun from Addie's abductor.

"Daniel!" Addie stridently whispered, watching as Trent delivered a well-placed blow to her husband's jaw. Daniel appeared almost totally unfazed, and, as his own fist smashed into Trent's face, he seemed like a man possessed. Each time he hit the other man, he thought of all that Trent Evans might have done to Addie, and it was with a savage vengeance that he battled his smaller but heavily muscled opponent.

Trent's features were battered and bloody by the time he managed to deliver a particularly punishing blow to Daniel's midsection, which rendered the taller man temporarily powerless and thereby enabled Trent to fly to the front door of the car and fling it open. Before Daniel could regain his breath, he had disappeared through the doorway and outside.

"Stay here!" Daniel gasped out to Addie, rising to his feet and unsteadily following after Trent. The other man was already in the process of climbing the narrow-runged metal ladder to the top of the passenger car hitched in front of McDougall's when Daniel caught up with him. His hands closed upon Trent's booted ankles, and he yanked him back down to the platform. The sun-drenched landscape flew past as the train's wheels rolled swiftly along. The two men grappled with each other for several long moments, until Trent hoisted himself upward upon the railing around the platform and sent Daniel a vicious kick.

Addie stood just within the car's doorway, her fingers tightening around Trent's gun. She was just about to raise her arm and fire at the man now climbing up the ladder again as his opponent struggled to regain his balance on the platform.

Before Addie could pull the trigger, however, providence intervened. Trent's booted foot slipped upon the ladder, and he fell. Frantically, he grasped at the platform railing, and his legs flailed helplessly as he fought to keep from being crushed between the wheels and the well-worn track.

"Help!" he screamed, his face a mask of sheer terror as his hands began to lose their hold upon the cold metal.

"Daniel!" yelled Addie, but he was already reaching out in an attempt to grab Trent's hand and pull him back up. It was too late. There was a bloodcurdling shriek as Trent, no longer able to bear the agonizing strain, lost his grip and slipped beneath the train's wheels to be killed instantly, his crushed and battered body left lifeless upon the tracks as the train continued on its way.

Daniel's arm wrapped about his wife's body, and he hugged her so tightly she was certain her ribs would crack. But she didn't care. They were safe now. She was in the arms of the man she loved more than life itself, and their love—a love so powerful that it had withstood four years of war and heart-breaking separation—had triumphed over evil once again. They knew it would endure forever.

"Addie, Addie," Daniel whispered into the fragrant mass of chestnut hair as he brushed the top of her head with a gentle kiss. His steely eyes glowed with tenderness, and his heart was filled with gratitude that she was unharmed.

"I was so afraid," she softly admitted, snuggling contentedly against his broad chest, inhaling deeply of his familiar masculine scent.

"It's all over now, my love. It's over and we're going to head back to Texas, back home where we belong." Home, he silently echoed, vaguely aware that the train had begun slowing down as it approached the next station. It was how he had come to think of it, for the simple reason that it was so much a part of the beautiful woman he held in his arms. It would now become his home as well, and the thought gave him a great measure of comfort as he envisioned the bright future he and Addie would share.

"Home," repeated Addie, raising her shining face to his.

Twenty-Six

"It was a beautiful wedding, wasn't it?" remarked Addie, sinking down upon the bed with a contented sigh.

"Yes, it was," Daniel agreed idly, slipping off his black linen coat and reaching up to remove his tie. "And I suppose you and your matchmaking inclinations are mighty pleased with yourselves!" he added with a low chuckle, negligently tossing the discarded coat and tie onto a chair.

"I had nothing whatsoever to do with your sister's romance!" his wife adamantly denied, her fingers curling about the thick wooden post of the bed. The bedroom, once hers alone and now shared with Daniel, was filled with the soft glow given off by the single lantern she had brought upstairs with them.

"But you knew about Carrie and Gil, didn't you?" he good-naturedly challenged, turning to face her with an unfathomable gleam in his eyes.

"Yes, and I would have told you, but Carrie made me promise not to. I'm so glad she and Gil waited to ask your permission," she added with another sigh as she stretched back lazily upon the bed, her arms folding beneath her head. Carrie had confided to her sister-in-law that she had been quite apprehensive about revealing her engagement to her older brother.

Daniel and Addie had been pleasantly surprised to find Carrie, fetched back to Fort Worth by Gil Foster, living at the Rolling L and anxiously awaiting their return. And Daniel, Addie mused, her gaze fixed lovingly upon him as he undressed, hadn't been at all perturbed about the fact that his youngest sister was marrying a former Confederate. He and Gil had willingly and wholeheartedly made their peace, she happily recalled.

A month had passed since she and Daniel had returned home, and it was a constant source of amazement to her that her Yankee husband was encountering no difficulty in filling his role as the new master of the Rolling L. Both Esther and Silas liked and respected him, and even the townspeople, who had once so bitterly resented his presence, had finally begun putting aside their long-held prejudices. Of course, she knew that Daniel's position as the husband of one of their own helped him win acceptance. But he had also gained a great deal of respect and admiration for having led the cattle drive—the first in so many years—with such overwhelming success.

"By the way," said Daniel, interrupting her silent reverie as he stood near the foot of the bed, clad in nothing but his underwear, "Silas told me that Rascal took off after Clay and Billy when they went to make their rounds this morning. It seems he proceeded to have a little run-in with a skunk," he finished with another chuckle, his eyes alight with amusement now. "You know, that mutt is the worst cowdog I ever saw!"

"You have only yourself to blame for that!" retorted Addie, smiling saucily up at him. "I warned you that Kyle Townsend is one of the biggest liars in the county!"

"Speaking of which . . ." murmured Daniel, taking a seat on the bed beside her and leaving his sentence unfinished. An expression of puzzlement crossed her beautiful features as she stared expectantly up at him. His eyes met hers, and she noticed the telltale glimmer of merriment within their steely depths. "I seem to remember someone promising to cook and clean and sew for me. Well, dearest wife," he charged with a look of mock ferocity, "you have yet to fulfill any of those promises!" She laughed softly and drew herself upright, her hands reaching out to glide lightly across the broad, golden expanse of his muscular chest.

"Perhaps not," she readily admitted, her arms tugging him closer, "but I shall most willingly fulfill another promise I made to you at the same time."

"And what promise might that be?" His fingers were skillfully unfastening the buttons of her lavender silk dress, and his warm lips followed a teasing, imaginary path from her ear to the graceful curve of her neck.

"Don't you remember?" she lovingly taunted, inhaling sharply as his nimble fingers bared her full breasts, then reached up to carefully tug the pins from her thick tresses. The sun-streaked locks tumbled riotously about her silken shoulders, and it became increasingly difficult for her to concentrate upon her current line of thought, upon any thought at all. "I believe there was some talk of my bearing your children, Mr. Jordan."

She smiled up into his handsome countenance as he paused in his intoxicating efforts just long enough to ask huskily, "Do you really want to bear my children, Addie? Are you certain—"

"Remember, we're to have both sons and daughters," she interrupted, her eyes shining with all the love in her heart. "And their father will teach them to swim." There was an unspoken promise in her bright gaze, a silent assurance that she was ready to embrace every wondrous opportunity of her womanhood.

"I love you, you beautiful little wildcat," Daniel murmured in his deep, resonant voice, their bodies as one as he hugged her close.

"And I love you, Daniel." Then there was no need for any further talk between them, for they communicated in the oldest and most fulfilling way known to men and women. Their very souls were entwined, and so they would remain for the rest of their lives, lives that would be rich and rewarding . . . and never dull.

RAPTUROUS ROMANCE
by Wanda Owen

ECSTASY'S FANCY (1467, $3.75)

From the moment Fancy met Nicholas Dubois aboard the *Memphis Belle*, his flashing white smile haunted her dreams. She knew his reputation as a devil for breaking hearts, yet when he took her in his arms she gloried in the sweet ecstasy of surrender . . .

THE CAPTAIN'S VIXEN (1257, $3.50)

No one had ever resisted Captain Lance Edward's masculine magnetism—no one but the luscious, jet-haired Elise. He vowed to possess her, for she had bewitched him, forever destining him to be entranced by THE CAPTAIN'S VIXEN!

TEXAS WILDFIRE (1337, $3.75)

When Amanda's innocent blue eyes began haunting Tony's days, and her full, sensuous lips taunting his nights, he knew he had to take her and satisfy his desire. He would show her what happened when she teased a Texas man—never dreaming he'd be caught in the flames of her love!

GOLDEN GYPSY (1188, $3.75)

When Dominique consented to be the hostess for the high stakes poker game she didn't know that her lush, tantalizing body would be the prize—or that the winner would be Jared Barlow, the most dashing man she had ever seen. On first glance at the golden goddess, Jared couldn't wait to claim his fortune!

Available wherever paperbacks are sold, or order direct from the Publisher. Send cover price plus 50¢ per copy for mailing and handling to Zebra Books, Dept. 1622, 475 Park Avenue South, New York, N.Y. 10016. DO NOT SEND CASH.